A Little Bit of Charm

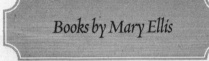
Books by Mary Ellis

The New Beginnings Series
Living in Harmony
▶ http://bit.ly/LivinginHarmony

Love Comes to Paradise
▶ http://bit.ly/LoveComestoParadise

A Little Bit of Charm
▶ http://bit.ly/LittleBitofCharm

The Miller Family Series
A Widow's Hope
Never Far from Home
The Way to a Man's Heart

The Wayne County Series
Abigail's New Hope
A Marriage for Meghan

Standalones
Sarah's Christmas Miracle
An Amish Family Reunion

A Little Bit of Charm

MARY ELLIS

HARVEST HOUSE PUBLISHERS
EUGENE, OREGON

Cover by Garborg Design Works, Savage, Minnesota

Cover photos © Chris Garborg; Bigstock / volgariver, Elenamiv, molodec, IgorKovalchuk

A LITTLE BIT OF CHARM
Copyright © 2013 by Mary Ellis
Published by Harvest House Publishers
Eugene, Oregon 97402
www.harvesthousepublishers.com

Library of Congress Cataloging-in-Publication Data
Ellis, Mary,
A little bit of charm / Mary Ellis.
     pages cm. — (The New Beginnings Series ; Book 3)
ISBN 978-0-7369-3868-6 (pbk.)
ISBN 978-0-7369-4305-5 (eBook)
1. Amish—Fiction. 2. Christian fiction. 3. Love stories. I. Title.
PS3626.E36L56 2013
813'.6—dc23

                                                              2013000684

Printed in the United States of America

     13 14 15 16 17 18 19 20 21 / LB-JH / 10 9 8 7 6 5 4 3 2 1

This book is dedicated to Virgil Bray,
approaching one hundred years on God's earth,
lifelong Kentucky farmer, father of eleven,
grandfather and great-grandfather of dozens.

Virgil's favorite quip:

"Look at that man.
He's acting like he eats chicken for breakfast."

AMAZING GRACE

John Newton, lyrics 1779

Amazing grace! How sweet the sound
That saved a wretch like me!
I once was lost, but now am found;
Was blind, but now I see.

'Twas grace that taught my heart to fear,
And grace my fears relieved;
How precious did that grace appear
The hour I first believed!

Through many dangers, toils and snares,
I have already come;
'Tis grace hath brought me safe thus far,
And grace will lead me home.

The Lord has promised good to me,
His Word my hope secures;
He will my shield and portion be,
As long as life endures.

When we've been there ten thousand years,
Bright shining as the sun,
We've no less days to sing God's praise
Than when we'd first begun.

Amazing grace! How sweet the sound
That saved a wretch like me!
I once was lost, but now am found;
Was blind, but now I see.

ACKNOWLEDGMENTS

Thanks to Pete and Donna Taylor for providing my home away from home during my research, and to my wonderful research assistants, Taylor, Jessie, and Keeley and their mother, Julie Miller. You are all family to me.

Thanks to Linda Hitchcock of Barren County, Kentucky, for her tireless assistance with contacts in the Amish and Mennonite communities and for plenty of storyline ideas.

Thanks to my agent, Mary Sue Seymour; to my lovely proofreader, Joycelyn Sullivan; to my editor, Kim Moore; and the wonderful staff at Harvest House Publishers.

Thanks to Emma of Mount Hermon and Michelle of Hillside Greenhouse and the helpful folks at Sunny Valley Country Store in Liberty, Kentucky, for answering all of my questions.

Finally, thanks to the charming Old Order Mennonites of Barren, Hart, Metcalf, Monroe, and Casey Counties who allowed me to peek into their lives. While they are real, Charm, Kentucky, is a fictional town.

ONE

Amazing grace! How sweet the sound

Paradise, Missouri

Whew, it's already the middle of September and still hotter than blazes."

Rachel looked at her younger sister in horror. "Shush, Beth, before someone hears you. What will the Gingerichs think of us?"

Beth looked up with an innocent expression. "Is 'blazes' a bad word? I've heard *daed* say 'build a blaze in the woodstove' or 'a blazing sunset.'"

Rachel rolled her eyes. "Just shush on general principles. You'll be on your way back to Lancaster County soon, and then you can revert to your normal self. But let's put our best foot forward while we're still visitors here."

Beth's green-eyed focus turned wary. "What do you mean by *I'll* be on my way back to Pennsylvania?"

Rachel ignored a question she wasn't yet ready to answer. "Look, here comes the blushing bride and groom." She grinned with a heart swelling with joy and love for their sister.

"Who would ever guess Nora would get hitched to Lewis Miller? Surely not me." Beth's words were an audible whisper. "I thought she'd end up with that wily fox, Elam Detweiler."

Rachel shifted her weight to her other foot, which she then placed directly atop Beth's. No other admonishment proved necessary.

Nora and Lewis approached with the glowing faces only a wedding day could inspire. "Well, my dear *schwestern*, did you enjoy seeing us get married?" Nora wrapped an arm around each of their shoulders, drawing them close.

The three-way hug brought a rush of moisture to Rachel's eyes. "Truly, I did. I've never seen you looking so pretty…or so happy." Tears cascaded down her cheeks with the realization the four King siblings would not only be in four different districts, but different states as well.

A couple of years ago they were like any other Old Order Amish girls living at home, with their grandparents just next door. They dreamed of a future around the corner, married to boys they had known their entire lives. But a house fire had changed everything. It took their parents to the Lord and their two older sisters to where their hearts led them. Amy, the eldest, settled in Harmony, Maine, where her fiancé's brothers lived. Nora, however, didn't find the ultraconservative district to her liking. So when the handsome, fence-sitting Elam Detweiler, Amy's new brother-in-law, took off with his secret driver's license and his secondhand red Chevy, Nora followed soon after.

But new beginnings are often hard to predict. Not long after moving to Missouri, Nora's independent streak began to fade. For the first time she longed to fit in and be part of a loving, supportive community. If Nora's facial expression today could be trusted, she had found what she was looking for in a town called Paradise.

A frisson of anxiety spiked up Rachel's spine. She thought of her upcoming plans and wondered whether she was making a big mistake. Would she cause her *grossmammi* grief and worry for nothing? Shaking off the notion, she joined Beth in cleaning up after the wedding meal while the happy couple walked guests to their buggies, expressing gratitude for the gifts and good wishes and thanking them for sharing in their most special day.

Later that evening, while fireflies lit up the backyard with a thousand twinkling lights, Rachel sat on the Gingerich porch. Sleep wouldn't come—that much she knew. But she didn't wish to pace the bedroom floor and keep Beth or her gracious hosts awake. She tried to pray, but the only words that came to mind were the rote prayers learned as a child. After several silent "Our Fathers," she clenched her eyes tightly shut. *Please, Lord, grant my sister a long life with many* kinner *and much joy.* Unbidden tears started anew. Her emotions seemed to be a roiling kettle of soup, rattling the lid and threatening to overflow.

"Why are you out here crying?" Nora gently pulled on her sister's *kapp* ribbon before slipping into the rocker next to hers.

"A better question would be what are you doing out here on your wedding night?" Rachel wiped her face and arched an eyebrow. "Don't you and Lewis have some business to attend to?"

A pretty blush rose up Nora's neck. "Don't speak of things you know nothing about." She pinched Rachel's arm. "Besides, I'll join him in a little while. We're both too nervous to sleep much tonight. Tomorrow we move to our new home. It's not much, but it's ours." She rocked with the satisfied assurance of a woman whose life was laid out before her like a well-organized quilt.

Rachel knew no such contentment. Her future looked like an early spring sky—patchy clouds, intermittent rays of sunshine, and the smell of a coming storm. "I wish Beth and I could stay longer to help you pack."

"Worry not. My friend Violet arranged everything for our

move and hers before she and Seth left on their wedding trip to the Gulf of Mexico. Violet might not be able to run, but she still maneuvers at the speed of light. She absolutely refused to use her crutches at her marriage ceremony. Her poor *daed* kept hovering as though she might fall over." *Creak, creak, creak.* For several moments the only sound came from the rolling wooden slats on the porch boards. Then in a hushed tone, Nora asked, "Care to tell me what's troubling you? And don't say 'nothing.' You've been weepy eyed all day. That isn't like you, Rachel. You know we'll take a wedding trip in November after the harvest is in. We'll visit Amy and John in Harmony and then come to Lancaster County to see you, Beth, *grossmammi,* and *grossdawdi.*"

Rachel debated only half a second. There was no point in withholding the truth any longer. "When you get to Pennsylvania, you might only find one sister." She stared into the darkness as the moon slipped behind a cloud. "I've decided to take the bus from St. Louis to Louisville after I put Beth on the train to Chicago."

Nora stopped rocking. "Who on earth do you know in Louisville?"

"Not a soul. Once I'm in Louisville I'll board a bus to Elizabethtown. Then I'll arrange for a hired van to take me to Charm."

"You're planning to visit Cousin Sarah? But you hate chickens."

Rachel laughed. "I do not hate chickens as long as they're in a pot with celery, onions, and dumplings." They shared a chuckle. "The fact that Sarah and her husband operate a free-range chicken farm doesn't deter me. Kentucky is known for only one thing, and it isn't Rhode Island Reds. The Blue Grass state raises the prettiest horses in the world."

"Prettier than Old Smokey after you braided his mane and tail with ribbons?"

A pang of nostalgia filled her heart. Old Smokey was her father's favorite Belgian draft horse, now relegated to light work with *grossdawdi* in his twilight years. "*Jah*, even prettier than him if magazines and library books can be trusted."

"If you've decided on visiting Sarah on your way home, why not take Beth?"

A long minute spun out in the humid evening air while Rachel chose her reply carefully. In the end she decided on a short, honest answer. "Because if I find living on a chicken farm tolerable, I intend to stay permanently."

"Whatever for? I know you love horses and have read more about them than any Amish person in the country, but horses are big business in Kentucky. What would a Plain gal who's never held a paying job in her life do there?"

Somewhere a faraway train blew its whistle. "I haven't the slightest idea. All I know is Lancaster County is a lonely place since *mamm* and *daed* died. I love our grandparents and I'll miss little Beth something fierce, but I can't see myself sticking around any more than Amy or you could. There are too many sad memories." A lump the size of a rock rose up her throat, threatening her composure.

"I of all people cannot find fault with your plan, but I hate the idea of us spread across the eastern United States."

"Missouri is certainly not the East. Have you checked a map lately?"

"Truly, it is not," agreed Nora with a laugh. She flicked away a mosquito.

For several moments they rocked and listened to tree frogs and crickets fill the air with a late summer serenade. Each of their hearts grew heavier as the irrevocable future closed around them like heavy fog. "No matter where I end up, you will always be my *schwester*," murmured Rachel.

"And I, yours." Nora clasped her hand in the shadows as they savored memories of their shared childhood. Impulsively Nora leaned over and kissed her cheek. "*Gut nacht*, Rachel. I believe I've kept my new *ehemann* waiting long enough." After a nervous giggle, the bride went inside the house, leaving her sister alone with her thoughts and fears for the future.

When Rachel fell asleep that night, frolicking colts, majestic stallions, and gentle mares filled her dreams, giving her the best sleep she'd had in weeks.

ⅆⅆ

The next day Rachel and Beth accepted tearful hugs and a packed lunch that would feed far more than two, and then they climbed into the back of a hired car bound for downtown Columbia. After paying their driver, they boarded the bus to St. Louis— a frightening city in terms of the amount of fast-moving traffic. Rachel waited almost until the bus pulled into the terminal to drop her bombshell.

"What do you mean you're only buying one train ticket to Chicago?" demanded Beth. "How do you intend to get home?"

"After I put you on the train, I'll take a cab back to the Greyhound station. I'm traveling by bus to Louisville." She patiently spelled out the sketchy details as she'd done the night before to Nora.

Beth listened to the explanation without interruption and then wailed, "That's fine and dandy, but why can't I go too? I've never been to Kentucky either."

"Because if all goes well, and if Sarah and Isaac allow it, I will stay and work. You're too young to move away from *grossmammi* and Aunt Irene yet."

"Will you court boys there?" Beth turned toward her on the seat.

The unexpected question caught Rachel by surprise. "I'm not thinking about courting now. I just want to find a job."

"But you're already twenty." Beth sounded aghast.

"That's not that old in this day and age. People are waiting longer to marry."

"Why can't I come with you? If you decide to stay longer than a visit, you could put me on a bus home then."

Finally, the question she had dreaded. "Please don't be hurt, Beth, but I truly wish to try this out by myself." With a shaky hand, she pulled a printed sheet from her purse. "I wrote out directions on how to change trains in Chicago to catch the Capitol Limited to Pittsburgh and then the Pennsylvanian on to Harrisburg. There you'll catch the bus to Mount Joy. It's all spelled out very carefully. It's exactly what we did on the way here in reverse."

Beth shrugged. "*Grossmammi* is going to be miffed, even more so than she was about us attending the wedding unchaperoned." She shivered dramatically, as though picturing their grandmother's seldom-displayed temper.

"True enough. That's why I wrote her a long letter to explain as best as I could." Rachel withdrew a sealed envelope from her purse. "Will you give her this when you get home?"

Beth stared at the white envelope and nodded. "*Jah,* I suppose. But maybe I'll just lay it on the kitchen table and hide in the barn until the steam clears. What about Amy?"

Rachel patted her bag. "I wrote her a letter too. I'll post it the first chance I get. I told Nora last night after the wedding. She seemed to understand."

"Then it's all decided."

Her plaintive words of resignation cut Rachel like a blade. She wrapped her arms around her little sister, enfolding her in a hug. "You can come visit me once I'm settled. And I promise to come home to Mount Joy too. We'll always be sisters, Beth. Never forget that." The rocking bus, the chatter from other travelers, the scenery passing at breakneck speed, all faded away. Rachel was only aware of the skinny fourteen-year-old she held in her arms and how much she would miss her.

"St. Louis," the bus driver barked into the loudspeaker.

Everyone jumped up to pull luggage from overhead bins and collect belongings from the seat and floor. Rachel felt Beth shrink by her side. "Don't be frightened. You're a smart girl. You have your directions, plenty of food, and money in your purse. Just remember what *mamm* used to say: 'You're never alone in life. God is always with you. So close your eyes and let Him fill your heart.'"

Whether her words did any good, Rachel would never know. Beth was quiet during their walk to the train station and said little as they sat eating sandwiches and fruit, waiting for the next train to Chicago—the hub of the Midwest.

Feeling as low as a crawfish on a river bottom, Rachel went with her sister to the turnstiles. She handed her the tote bag of sandwiches and snacks. "Don't lose your ticket. And don't be afraid to ask questions of kind-looking ladies."

"Promise me you'll write." Beth's green eyes were round as silver dollars and just as shiny.

"Twice a week, every week. And because Sarah is Old Order Mennonite and not Amish, she has a phone in her house. I wrote her number on your directions. You can always call from the phone shed if you're dying to hear my voice."

Beth laughed. "Most likely twice-a-week letters will fill my need for sisterly companionship. Don't go too sappy on me."

True to the youngest sibling's style, Beth had already adjusted to the change, disappointment rolling off her like water off a duck's back. Rachel was able to watch her board the train for home without melting into a puddle of sorrow and indecision. Home— Mount Joy, Pennsylvania—didn't feel much like home since she'd spotted flames leaping high into the starry sky and smelled the acrid smoke that had filled her lungs and then her soul.

That night she dozed fitfully in the train station's lounge per the advice of Jonas Gingerich. More people would be milling about there than in the bus station, where she returned at first light. She washed her face and hands and brushed her teeth in the restroom. She bought a bagel and cream cheese and pint of cold milk.

By the time Rachel boarded the bus to Louisville, excitement had built in her blood like an herbalist's tonic. She couldn't keep from grinning as they crossed first into Illinois, then Indiana, and finally into Kentucky. She thought even the air smelled different.

She arrived in Elizabethtown by late afternoon and called the number provided by her cousin Sarah. A hired driver, a sweet woman named Michelle, picked her up within two hours and drove through Charm before arriving at the Stolls' farm. A historic courthouse with clock tower soaring into the clouds dominated the town square. Stately elms and oaks spread their limbs far and wide, shading the stone walkways and park benches, where elderly men reminisced and young mothers pushed baby strollers. There was a second, new courthouse, along with the sheriff's department, café, furniture shop, post office, pizza shop, and an ice cream parlor. What more did a body need? Two white church steeples loomed above the housetops. Rachel wished she could take a photograph to send to Beth, but, of course, she'd never used or owned a camera in her life.

Charm—the name said it all. Rachel was so eager for a fresh start that she almost broke into song.

༄

Jake Brady climbed up on his favorite gelding and spent the early morning riding the fence line—his favorite chore. But any time spent in the saddle wasn't work to him. He loved to ride, enjoying solitude away from his three younger siblings while checking the boundaries of their twelve-hundred-acre horse farm. Up and down the hills and valleys he rode, while the sun warmed his back and a sweet breeze cooled his skin. Acre upon acre of thick grass rolled for as far as the eye could see. Green grass, not blue, no matter how he squinted or gazed sideways. He wondered if the large Thoroughbred operations around Lexington and Louisville used certain fertilizers or maybe tourists bought special sunglasses at the mall. Because regardless of the season, the pastures at Twelve Elms Stables were the same green as those in Indiana or Ohio.

No matter. Grass color wouldn't make an ounce of difference considering the yearling his family now owned. That colt showed more spirit and heart than any horse Jake had ever bred and raised. With the right trainer, Twelve Elms could have a contender. In another year, they could race him at Keeneland in a stakes race for two-year-olds. It would begin the grand march leading up to the Kentucky Derby on the first Saturday in May—every May since 1875. Jake felt a jolt of electricity in his belly each time they watched the race on TV. Lately, he'd been going to the Derby and camping out in the infield with his friends. Sitting in lawn chairs, they would study racing forms and stats for hours to pick their personal favorites. His dad, a devout Baptist, frowned on gambling, but every now and then Jake placed a two-dollar bet to win. Always to win—never to place or show. Second or third place wasn't good enough. Folks only remembered the names of winners. With Eager to Please, they would have their chance to make history. And with what they had to pay in stud fees to sire the colt, it would be the only chance they would ever get.

Arriving back at home, Jake stabled his horse and then showered in the bathroom off the utility room before strolling into the kitchen, whistling. Ken Brady sat at the kitchen table, hunched over his ledgers.

"How's it going, Dad?" Jake asked as he made a beeline for the coffeemaker.

"Fine, son. All fencing secure?"

"Right as rain." Jake added sugar and a bit of milk to his mug and then settled across the table. Twelve Elms had miles of fences—split rail along the roadways, which were pleasant to look at but hard to maintain—and solar-powered battery-fed electric wire everywhere else.

"Your mom left sausage gravy and a pan of biscuits before she left for work. Just needs to be heated."

Jake scrambled up to light the burner under the skillet and pull the pan of buttermilk biscuits from the oven. "Aren't you eating?" he asked his father before biting into a flakey piece of heaven.

"Not much appetite today." Ken pushed his reading glasses up the bridge of his nose, but his focus remained on the ledgers.

Jake noticed dark circles beneath his dad's eyes and a neat row of furrows across his forehead. "What's wrong? Has something happened?"

"Business as usual." Ken met Jake's gaze over his coffee cup. "The Harts and the Lanskys won't be boarding their horses here after the first of the month. Mr. Lansky has been transferred to California, so the family will be moving. And Jeff Hart lost his job at the lumberyard. They had already been having trouble paying their bills because his wife took sick. Now they've decided to sell their daughter's Saddlebred and stop her lessons."

"Little Maddy will throw a fit. That child is used to getting her own way."

"Unfortunately, English saddle and dressage are luxuries families can't afford on unemployment compensation. Little Maddy will have to get over it." Ken gazed out the kitchen window to where their employees were cutting a field of oats to be ground into winter horse feed. His blue eyes looked paler than usual, as though worry had bleached the color right out of them. Jake's father was aging before his time.

"People move away and new folks come to take their place. Little girls will always love horses and talk their dads into lessons and then a horse of their own." Jake tipped up his mug to drain the last drop of coffee.

Ken walked to the stove for a refill. "Yeah, but all of that costs money. The trouble is when a factory closes its doors in Casey County and lays off workers with no other business opening up to take its place. Without jobs people don't move here. And without our boarding, riding lessons, and trail ride income, we'll be forced to cut our own staff."

Jake swallowed down a sour taste in his mouth. Why did his dad always have to look on the negative side of everything? You didn't see big-time owners and trainers creeping around the horse auctions with hangdog expressions. They held their head high, walked with confidence, and left the bean counting to the accountants. They had learned a cardinal rule—success breeds success. If you acted like a winner and had faith in what you were doing, you had a chance at the garland of roses, but if you fretted and moaned and dealt with your peers like a scared rabbit, the outcome was a foregone conclusion. "Like the preacher tells you every Sunday morning, you gotta have faith, Dad."

Ken turned his watery blue gaze on his son. "My faith in the Lord never wavers, Jake. I'm just not so sure about our recent business decision." He took one cold biscuit from the pan and slathered on some soft butter. "We paid a king's ransom to have Pretty in Pink bred with Man of His Word. We're lucky the insemination took hold. That kind of money and no guarantees..." Ken clucked his tongue.

"The best things in life seldom come with one." Jake mopped up the last of the sausage gravy with his third biscuit. "But now that we have Eager to Please, it's time to step up to the plate."

"I'm not sure I understand how a baseball analogy applies to our situation."

Jake sucked in a deep breath. "That colt has more spirit than any other horse in the stable. He practically eats his body weight in feed every day and grows stronger by the week, but I'm not a skilled horse trainer, Dad. I know my limits. Bloodlines like his deserve a professional trainer who can take Eager to Please all the way to the top in two years."

"Did you drink some bad apple cider? Big-buck horsemen work out of Louisville and Lexington for a very good reason. Those owners have checkbook balances in the six figures. In case you haven't noticed, we give tours to busloads of senior citizen groups to generate income, and your mom has signed up to work weekends for the extra pay." Ken laughed as though Jake had told a good joke. "You're a fine trainer, son. Don't sell yourself short. Maybe one of those big names has written a book filled with pointers, but you'd better check the book out at the library instead of buying it at Barnes and Noble. Our checkbook balance is barely three figures." Ken rinsed his cup and plate and placed them in the dishwasher. "I'll be at the computer in my office if you need me." He shuffled toward the door.

Jake bit back a reply and rose to his feet. Losing his temper with his mild-mannered father had never gotten him anywhere in the past and wouldn't help now. He grabbed his hat from the rack and went in search of his sister. If he couldn't win Jessie to his side, he didn't stand a chance. And Eager to Please would never win anything better than "best in show" at the Casey County fair.

"Let me get this straight. You want Mom and Dad to take out a second mortgage on our farm to hire somebody to do *your job*?" His twenty-year-old sister, the second oldest sibling, stood in a horse stall in knee-high rubber boots with a shovel in her hand.

Jake thought it wise to grab another shovel and start filling the cart with soiled wood shavings as well. "Let's call it a business loan, not a mortgage. Only a professional trainer will know the ins and outs of the national racing circuit. He'll know which races are mandatory for a two-year-old to enter and how to get our colt ready to compete." Jake kept shoveling while he talked, not daring to meet Jessie's eye. "We don't have to hire a top level trainer, but it takes money to make money. Cinderella didn't go to the ball wearing homespun sackcloth. She was dressed and ready to take her shot at winning the prince." He grinned, pleased he had alluded to his sister's fondness for fairy tales. When he glanced over at her, Jessie was leaning on her shovel, smirking.

"Nice try, but Cinderella had a fairy godmother with one of those handy wands. I leave for college on Sunday. I'll come home on weekends to give tours if the demand remains high, but I really don't want to." Her smile faded. "Competition is tough to get into vet school, and I'll need to maintain my grade point average. I would hate having to leave campus every weekend."

Jake's stomach wrenched with guilt and disappointment. "Am I the only one who wants this? I thought we were in agreement when we had Pretty in Pink bred with a horse with champion bloodlines."

Jessie softened. "We are in agreement, big brother. I would love to go to the Derby as an owner. I would even go out and buy one of those fancy hats, but there's a limit to what this family can do, especially with me in college. Payments would have to be made on that second mortgage. We can't tell the bank to patiently wait to see if the colt finishes in the money. I wish Keeley was old enough to take over the tours, but she still can't remember the details. Who wants to listen to a guide who says 'and stuff like that' every other sentence?" Jessie swiped at her forehead with the back of her hand.

"If I have to take a night job away from the farm to help pay training expenses, I will. This is our only shot." Jake resumed mucking out the stall with renewed energy. "Please take my side during the next family business meeting. Otherwise I'll be outvoted."

Jessie sighed. "All right, Jake. I'll vote with you, but you'd better come up with a plan that doesn't involve finding a magic wand in the oat bin."

"I plan to say plenty of prayers between now and the meeting."

"Down on your knees in prayer?" She raised a skeptical brow.

"As you can see, I'm desperate."

She smiled with tenderness. "He hears the pleas of the desperate. I hope He'll also like our motives as well." Jessie picked up the handles of the garden cart and wheeled it toward the door.

Jake was left wondering if God cared one iota about the outcome of a horse race.

TWO

That saved a wretch like me

It was dark by the time Rachel arrived at Stolls' Free-to-Roam Chicken Farm. The hired driver dropped her off in the drive-way turnaround, accepted payment, and lifted her bag from the trunk. A mercury vapor light burned in the barn's eave, casting a yellow circle of light on the yard.

"What if they're not here?" asked Michelle. "Maybe I'd better wait to make sure." She stepped into her van but rolled down the window.

"I'm certain they are home. I wrote that I was coming. Maybe they already went to bed." Rachel waved goodbye to her before climbing the steps to the porch, dragging her heavy suitcase. Just as she opened the screen door, lights snapped on inside the kitchen.

The sweet face of her cousin Sarah appeared in the doorway. "There you are at long last. I'd given up hope for tonight. I'm sure you're exhausted. Are you also hungry?"

Rachel felt her stiff muscles relax with the warm welcome. "I am tired but not hungry, and I'm very glad to be here. When I saw no light on in the house, I thought *grossmammi* was wrong about your using electricity."

Sarah released her and tugged the suitcase from her grip. "No, our grandmother was right. I'm Old Order Mennonite now since my marriage to Isaac Stoll. We have electricity to our homes, besides our business, but we don't like running up the bill for no good reason. I had dozed off in the chair. Don't need lights to do that. I have a phone too." She pointed to a cordless phone sitting in the charger on the countertop. "And Isaac and I both have cell phones."

"Do you have a car too?" Rachel's tone revealed her excitement at the prospect of coming and going more easily and quickly, and without having to pay a driver.

"No, we have a horse and buggy, same as you. Our district farms with draft horses too. No tractors or combines. Each conservative Mennonite district decides how much technology to use. If you drive over to Barren and Hart Counties, you'll see their members using every sort of conveyance except for motorcycles."

Rachel blinked, stifling a yawn. "What county is this?"

"Casey, but there will be time enough to learn the ins and outs once you're rested. Let me show you to your room. Isaac is already sawing logs. He gets up before dawn and needs his beauty sleep." Sarah flicked on a low-wattage bulb at the top of the narrow staircase. She left her kitchen pitch dark—no night-light for midnight refrigerator raids.

Rachel climbed the wooden steps as quietly as possible, pondering Sarah's expression. "Oh, you mean your husband snores. I've never heard it put that way, but I'm familiar with snoring, having shared a room with Beth my entire life."

"If you happen to hear it through the walls, a chainsaw will definitely come to mind." Sarah swept open a bedroom door. "This room will be yours for as long as you like." She set Rachel's suitcase on the blanket chest at the foot of the bed. "How old is your baby sister now—twelve, thirteen? I'll bet she didn't want to go back to Pennsylvania alone."

Rachel hesitated before answering as she assessed the small, tidy room. It contained more furniture than an Amish bedroom, and used a closet instead of wall pegs for clothes, but it was still austere by English standards. "Though Beth is fourteen now, she seems younger. I think she needs more time with our grandmother and aunt, but I told her she could visit someday." Rachel bit the inside of her cheek and swallowed hard. *Maybe Sarah expects this to be only a short visit.*

Sarah nodded in apparent agreement. Then she said, "Everything in here is self-explanatory. The bathroom is down the hall, and another one is downstairs off the kitchen. Breakfast is at eight after the first round of chores, but feel free to sleep late tomorrow. I know how tiring travel can be." With a final smile at her young cousin, she marched from the room, pulling the door shut behind her.

Rachel lowered herself to the bed, barely able to contain her excitement. She was in Blue Grass country. And she had no one to take care of but herself.

❧

The next morning Rachel was unpacked and waiting in the kitchen when Sarah and Isaac returned from the barn. Sarah made introductions, even though Rachel had met Isaac Stoll twice before. He was a man of few words. He grunted a *welcum*, ate his toast and cinnamon oatmeal, drank two cups of coffee, and then headed out the door.

"Don't worry about him. He doesn't say much even to folks he's known his whole life. After we finish I'll give you a tour. Free of charge," Sarah added with a wink. She then divided the remaining oatmeal between two bowls as though leftovers were unheard of.

After consuming as much as she could of her second portion, Rachel discreetly scraped the remaining cereal into the trash while Sarah filled a sink with suds for dishes. The tour of the chicken farm lasted longer and smelled worse than Rachel had expected. However, the size of the humane operation, with birds free to scratch around in grass and dirt and coming and going by ramps to their nesting boxes, was quite impressive. The Stolls had several barns with huge, fenced outdoor pens.

"Our eggs and hens are finally fetching a decent price now that we're certified organic. We grow our own feed with no pesticide or herbicide residue on our crops. No tight cages where a poor bird spends its whole life unable to turn around or get any sunshine. Who would want to stand on wire mesh all day? Our way creates a challenge to keep the farm clean, but that's why we move the flocks around between pens. We can clean up properly and let the grass recover in certain areas." Pausing, she crossed her arms and gazed over a particularly active flock of chickens. "Have you ever seen prettier or happier birds?"

Rachel laughed. "No, cousin, I have not." She decided not to mention that her favorite view of a chicken involved celery, onions, and dumplings.

"Isaac and I have built quite a business for ourselves. I'm not saying that to brag, but merely to express sheer surprise over our good fortune." Sarah went to a chicken pen, opened the gate, and motioned for Rachel to follow her. "Step lively now, before they stage the great escape. You must come with me if you want to see inside. And don't worry. We use highly efficient fans. It's not hot at all in our barns."

Heat wasn't high on Rachel's list of fears. It seemed that half the hens were eyeing her slyly from one of their tiny eyes, as though she were a fox come to steal their eggs or babies. But because she knew of Sarah's vocation before arriving in Charm, Rachel bravely marched into the pen and closed the gate behind her.

"That's better. At first we concentrated on selling cage-free eggs." Sarah resumed her narrative. "We built up a customer base at local stores. Many people who truly like eggs are willing to pay extra for the superior taste of organic. Plus our browns are higher in omega-3 and folic acid, and they have less saturated fat. Nothing bad is hidden in our yolks, ready to do a person bodily harm in old age, except maybe a little cholesterol."

Rachel gingerly moved through the flock, careful where she stepped to avoid scat. Midway to the barn she noticed the birds opening a path for Sarah, like the Red Sea parting for the Israelites, but then they closed ranks behind her. Again, several pairs of eyes contained an evil glint. Rachel hurried to stay on Sarah's heels to prevent separation from her source of safety. "I love omelets and fried egg sandwiches," she said, eager to make conversation. "And I've been known to take deviled eggs to potluck socials many a time."

Sarah turned on her heel, causing Rachel to smack into her. "Do you mix sweet pickle relish and horseradish in with your egg yolks?"

"Of course," she said, grateful their grandmother had taught their *mamms* the same recipe.

Sarah slid back the steel barn door. "In that case, we'll get along just fine." She gestured inside. "Welcome to my world."

Because Rachel wanted nothing better than to stay in Charm, she stepped inside a noisy barn that, despite an odd odor, was surprisingly clean and orderly. Hens clucked contentedly atop nests, keeping eggs warm until they could be collected and refrigerated. "Where's the rooster?" she asked, surveying the area.

"Not with this flock. I'm not interested in fertilized eggs. In another barn, where we have brooding hens, it's a different story. Don't worry; we're not that high-tech. You'll still be awakened at dawn by the crow of roosters, in case you miss home." Sarah giggled and then explained about their egg sorting machine in detail.

Rachel's sinuses began to run, but she listened attentively and tried to ask appropriate questions. "When did you expand the business from organic eggs to free-to-roam chickens?"

"A few years ago, when horror stories hit the newspapers and television about antibiotics, growth hormones, and whatnot in the food industry, a lot of folks became interested in natural meat, especially for their children. Louisville, Lexington, Bowling Green, and even Somerset grocery stores started selling free-range meat. We took out a farm loan, enlarged our facilities, and never once regretted the decision."

Rachel sneezed.

"*Gott segne dich.* Let's walk outside." Outdoors, Sarah continued her saga. "Now restaurants are jumping on the bandwagon. I suppose if those upscale places dare to charge twenty bucks for a chicken breast with a few roasted spuds, they had better have something special to say on the menu. We can't keep up with the demand from Louisville." Sarah rested her hands on her hips. "I'm sorry if I sound prideful. I'll return to my humble self tomorrow."

Already Rachel loved her chatty, forthright cousin. "Folks are permitted to boast during a tour. It's expected." However, a sharp pecking on her tennis shoe was not. She glared down at an irate hen who apparently had an intense dislike for white leather footwear. Rachel moved back, giving the creature plenty of room to maneuver. But the chicken didn't wish to scratch the dirt for fallen corn. Instead, she strutted forward with a mean glint and resumed pecking at Rachel's foot. She even caught Rachel's ankle bone and broke the skin.

"*Ouch!*"

"Mabel, stop that!" scolded Sarah. She swept the fat bird into her arms. "Mabel has never done that before."

"Have you named every single one of these chickens?"

"Of course not. Just my favorites." Sarah smiled fondly at the bird in her arms.

"Watch those talons." Rachel feared for her cousin's eyesight.

But the chicken immediately calmed and settled her feathers, mild as a lamb. She began to cluck softly. Sarah petted the tyrant like a cat. "Horses and dogs can sense when a person doesn't like them. Apparently, that works for chickens too." With one final stroke, Sarah gently set the bird down.

"Hard to imagine with so small a brain." Rachel watched her waddle back to her cronies.

"Let's wash that scratch and apply some antibiotic cream."

Once safely back in the Stoll kitchen, properly salved and bandaged, Rachel calmed her nerves with a cup of tea. "I want to thank you and Isaac for letting me visit, Sarah, but I must confess I would like to live here for a while if you'll have me." She held her breath.

"I figured as much. Nobody comes this far to say how-do to a cousin. Lancaster County is not the same since your parents died, *jah?*" Stretching out her arm, Sarah dropped her voice to a soft whisper.

"No, not the same." Rachel clutched her cousin's warm hand. "Living next door to where our house once stood is a sorrowful reminder. We hauled away the rubble but still need more clean dirt to fill the basement. Some mornings I can still smell smoke in the air."

Sarah patted her arm. "A change will do you a world of good. I must admit I got excited reading your letter and thought of offering you a job here. Isaac and I could sure use your help." She pointed at Rachel's bandaged ankle. "But you might not relish the idea of working around wild animals."

"It's not that. I hold nothing against Mabel. And I certainly plan to do my fair share of chores, but I came because I want to work with horses." Rachel released a sigh. "It's been my dream forever."

Sarah's smile filled her face. "I should have suspected as much. What exactly do you have in mind? You're too tall to be a jockey." She threw her head back and laughed.

"Who knows? I would love to work around Thoroughbreds, even if it's mucking out stalls to start."

"I have an idea. To celebrate day one of your new life, let's take the buggy into Charm for lunch, just like the fancy English ladies do in their convertibles. We can even put the top down if you like." Sarah rubbed her hands together. "Don't think this is business as usual for the Stolls, but one of the restaurants in town has a bulletin board for customers. Folks thumbtack things for sale, houses or farms for rent, and available jobs in the area."

Rachel's heart swelled inside her chest. "We can go today?"

"Why not? It will be my treat. You can buy lunch the next time we go."

Rachel sprang from her chair. "If I do find a job, I'll turn over my whole paycheck for room and board. Maybe it'll be enough to hire someone part-time to help you out here...a chicken lover."

"Don't get too ahead of yourself, cousin. Jobs are hard to come by in Casey County, even for those with experience. You might end up buying metal shin guards and working for us after all. Now, let's get our housework done. I can taste the fried chicken and cheese pierogis already."

Pierogis? But later Rachel had a little time to contemplate an unusual item on the delicious buffet of traditional country food and huge salad bar. After she and Sarah finished soft-serve sundaes, Rachel pored over the bulletin board at the Bread of Life Café. As Sarah had predicted, she wasn't remotely qualified for any job offered in the area. Then one colorful flyer caught her eye: *Twelve*

Elms Stables—boarding, trail rides, lessons in Western, English, and dressage riding. Tours of a working Thoroughbred operation. Adults— six dollars, children—one dollar, every Wednesday, Friday, and Saturday, in season.

"Look at this." Rachel pointed at the photo of a handsome stallion with her finger.

Sarah peered over her shoulder. "That farm isn't far from us. Would you like to take a tour tomorrow?"

Rachel's vision clouded with moisture. She nodded, not trusting her voice to speak.

"What are you crying about? It's just a tour." Sarah pulled her away from the bulletin board. "Or are you still worried about Mabel lurking in the rosebushes, ready to attack when we get home?"

Rachel couldn't explain what she was crying about. It was just like her *grossmammi* always said: *"Sometimes the soul knows when something really special is about to happen."*

༄

"Hey, Donna, don't you live in Casey County?" A voice floated over the partition wall of her cubicle at the county Board of Health.

Donna Cline pushed her glasses up her nose and sighed. You would think her boss would know where she lived after all these years. "No, I live in Russell Springs, Russell County." She returned to her computer monitor.

"But you're close to the Amish settlement, right? Within twenty miles?" His voice again broke her concentration.

Swiveling around, she pushed herself back from her desk. "I'm sure I wouldn't want to walk, but *you* could probably spit that far." Because Phil didn't seem inclined to come to her, Donna walked around the partition and into his office. Once she approached his desk, she understood why. A box with a six-slice deluxe pizza was open next to his monitor. Five pieces were already gone, greasy out-lines marking their former locations.

"I thought your wife put you on a diet. Aren't you supposed to be counting points or something? How many points did you just eat? Fifteen thousand?" Donna perched on the plastic chair in front of him.

"You're right. I meant to order a plain salad." Phil offered a sheepish grin. "You gonna tattle on me the next time you talk to Julie?"

Donna rolled her eyes. "Not unless she asks a direct question about your lunch habits."

"In that case, why don't you finish the last piece?" He wiped his fingers on a paper napkin.

"No, thanks. I had a salad. Why were you curious about where I live?" She tucked a lock of hair behind her ear.

Phil tapped his mouse a few times to bring up a certain e-mail. "I just heard from the Department for Public Health, Division of Epidemiology in Frankfort, who heard from the hospital admin-istrator here in Charm. A case of polio has turned up in Casey County."

"Polio in the United States? How rare." Donna walked around to read over his shoulder.

"According to the report, the new case is a child who's Amish or Mennonite or something like that."

"Don't they vaccinate their children?"

Phil pulled off his glasses to massage the bridge of his nose. "Doesn't sound like it to me. What I've read about them on the Internet didn't address the subject of inoculations, but the arti-cle said they don't put lightning rods on their houses or barns or install smoke detectors. They believe those things interfere with God's will."

Donna studied his face to see if any disparagement would

follow. It did not. A long time ago he once called her a Bible-thumper. He'd asked why she went to church twice a week instead of only once. *Do so many people fall asleep during the sermon that the preacher has to repeat his song and dance twice?* She had promptly told him off. Afterward, they circled around like junkyard dogs for days until Phil apologized. Since then they had more or less been friends, but they avoided the twin topics of politics and religion like a plague.

Like the plague that could be headed toward Casey County?

"Do you think the Amish would feel the same about vaccinating children as they do about lightning rods and smoke detectors?" With the scents of pepperoni, sausage, and cheese calling to her, she closed the pizza box.

"Don't know. That's why I'm sending you to find out."

"I thought all US schools required shots before students can start kindergarten."

"These kids go to one-room Amish schoolhouses. According to a Supreme Court decision years ago, their schools are exempt from our laws based on religious freedom."

Donna reflected for a moment. She often passed their black buggies on the road, charmed by towheaded youngsters waving from the back window. She loved to buy their fruits and vegetables because most had been grown without using chemicals. And she respected the Amish commitment to God and family. However, her contemplation had gone no deeper than that. "Sounds as though there's not much we can do."

Phil rubbed his stubbly chin. "According to the Commissioner and the CDC in Atlanta, we have to try." He grinned mischievously. "Didn't you put yourself through college selling Avon door-to-door? I believe your fine husband once mentioned that to me."

Donna rose to her feet. "Remind me to issue a gag order for

Pete before your next cookout. What specifically do you want me to do?" With the work she already had dancing through her mind, a headache began to build.

"Go from farm to farm. Talk to the women of the household. Explain the horrors of polio. Show them file photos of crippled children from the nineteen forties if you must. Appeal to their maternal side. I know you can be mighty persuasive when you want to be." He reached for the pizza box.

Donna's hand moved faster. She yanked it from his slippery fingers. "I'm staging an intervention for the sake of your arteries. If I must drive around on unpaved roads in Casey County, tracking down women in their cabbage patches, this piece is mine." She grabbed the last slice and tossed the box toward his trash. Ignoring the fact that she missed the can, Donna smiled all the way back to her cubicle. The pizza tasted delicious. And any time away from the Board of Health offices would be time well spent.

❧

Jake tried to pray while cleaning water troughs and refilling hay bins. He tried praying while raking the indoor riding arena with the tractor. But his mind refused to stop wandering. When he thought about what he planned to ask his family—to go out on a limb in a still-weak economy—his anxiety ratcheted up a notch. His mother already worked long hours at a big chain drugstore as a pharmacist. She always looked dog tired whenever she had a day off. Soon Jessie would return to the University of Kentucky in Lexington, unable to help with the cooking, cleaning, shopping, or laundry. Keeley weeded their quarter-acre garden and picked ripe produce, but after the second deerfly bite, she retreated to the sofa to watch TV in air-conditioning. Twelve years old was twelve years old.

Jessie had worked all summer giving tours. She had even agreed to come home weekends throughout the fall. But what if the vet school refused her application due to less than perfect grades? Jake could never live with himself if his sister was denied her dream. Virgil helped their dad with chores, but at fourteen he still had four more years of high school.

That left him. Jake needed to generate more income. Plenty of stables already gave lessons and arranged overnight trail rides into Daniel Boone National Forest. Competition for boarders was fierce. A prize-winning colt in their stable would generate publicity. And a win all but guaranteed a rosy future from stud fees. Eager to Please was their best and only shot. The more Jake weighed the risks and rewards, the better that yearling looked.

Unfortunately, his nightly prayers for divine intervention only numbered one before his father called a meeting for the next day. When he arrived at breakfast, he found his parents and Virgil waiting at the kitchen table. "Got the day off, Ma?" Jake asked, pouring coffee.

"I traded with someone to work on Saturday." Taylor Brady smiled over her bowl of Special K with sliced strawberries. The constant bombardment of medical and dietary information in her life usually made her meal choices healthy.

Jake heated some pastry strudel in the toaster. His metabolism and long hours of physical labor would prevent weight problems for years to come.

"Because your mom is home," said Ken, "we'll hold our family meeting as soon as your sisters come downstairs." He poured a bowl of cereal to pacify his wife.

"Today?" squawked Jake.

"Is something wrong with today?" Ken leveled a cool blue gaze on him. "I thought you wanted to put this matter to rest."

"I do." What could he say? *I wanted time for God to take my side? Me, Jake Brady, a man who's used every excuse in the book to avoid going to church on Sundays?* By the time he finished a second raspberry pastry, Jessie and Keeley sauntered into the kitchen, sleepy eyed.

"Hi, Mom. Will you be home all day?" Jessie pulled a carton of orange juice from the refrigerator.

"All day and night. Catch me while you can." Taylor Brady opened her arms to her youngest child as Keeley ran toward her at full speed.

Once both girls sat down with bowls of cornflakes and berries, Ken called the monthly meeting of Twelve Elms Stables to order. He explained the recent cancellations of two of their boarding clients, stated Jake's proposal to hire a professional trainer for Eager to Please, and reminded everyone that Jessie would leave for college over the weekend.

His mother, who usually kept a low profile during stable business, murmured four deadly words regarding her husband's sole possible solution to their financial situation: "Good grief, another mortgage?"

Jake stated his argument succinctly. After all, he was a former member of the Charm high school debate team. While he made his case, his mother nibbled her cereal and his dad stoically remained quiet. Afterward, Virgil and Keeley shrugged their shoulders in typical teen fashion. They seldom formed opinions except for which video games to purchase or what movies to watch on family movie night. Jake waited, barely able to draw breath.

Finally, Jessie set down the spoon and cleared her throat. "Well, since we paid all that money to sire the colt, we might as well go the distance. It's too bad Jake feels unable to train the horse by himself."

He might have hoped for a bit more confidence in his plan and diplomacy from his sister, but at least she had voiced her support. "Thanks, Jess."

"I'll come home weekends to keep giving tours. That will bring in some income until winter." She shot a smile in his direction.

Virgil poured more cornflakes into his bowl. "I don't know what I can do other than my chores."

Keeley propped her head on her hand, fighting off sleep. "You can have my babysitting money to help pay this guy."

Taylor looked at her husband, meeting his gaze without speaking.

Ken opened his palms. "Just to make sure everyone understands the consequences involved, to pay this second mortgage we'll have to cut our budget down to basics. It could work to our advantage in the end, but there are no guarantees a pro can take the colt all the way to the winner's circle. If Eager to Please fails to measure up, we might lose the farm to the bank and have to rent a house somewhere."

"That would be the worst-case scenario," said Jake, grinding down on his back teeth.

No one spoke. No one moved except for Virgil and Keeley, who continued to eat as though it were any other weekday breakfast. "If there is no more discussion," said Ken, "may I see the hands of those who wish this family to go deeper into debt to improve Eager to Please's chances as a three-year-old?"

Jake's hand shot up first, followed by Jessie's, and, after a moment, Virgil's. Keeley peered from one of her siblings to the next, a little surprised. But because she seldom disagreed with her brothers and sister, she lifted her arm.

"Those opposed?" asked Ken. Taylor joined her husband in opposition. "As your parents, we could override this vote because we bear the financial responsibility for the family, but we won't." He met Jake's eye. "There comes a time when a man needs to follow his gut instinct and his dreams. You have your chance, son. Use it wisely. Start checking the availability of good trainers who are willing to move to Charm."

"Thanks, Mom and Dad," he croaked, oddly choked up.

There was no need for more speeches. A much paler Ken Brady

reached for his Cincinnati Reds ball cap and strode out the back door. His mother scraped the rest of her breakfast into the garbage disposal and left for her morning run. Taking a few deep breaths, Jake headed to the computer in their office on legs wobbly with excitement.

THREE

I once was lost, but now am found

People didn't get any nicer than Sarah and Isaac Stoll. Especially Sarah. Rachel had been a guest at their farm for two days, and she had yet to do farm chores around the place. Now she was on her way to take the tour of Twelve Elms Stables in Sarah's buggy, but at least she'd washed the dishes and swept the kitchen before leaving.

"You won't know if Twelve Elms would be a good place to work unless you see it for yourself," declared Sarah that morning.

Rachel hugged Sarah so hard she yelped like a dog. "Goodness, you Lancaster folk are a hugging sort, *jah*?" Sarah squirmed to escape.

"It's me, not the whole county. I like to show my gratitude."

"A simple *danki* will suffice. I pity the poor man or woman who offers you a job if that's how you react to the loan of a horse and buggy." She laughed good-naturedly.

"I try to control myself with strangers," Rachel said, smoothing her palms down her skirt.

"See that you do. If you like the looks of this stable, why not ask if they're hiring? Here are two bottles of water and a ham sandwich for your lunch. Be on your way before you miss the tour." Sarah practically pushed her out the door.

In case I like the place? What was not to like? A beautiful split rail fence enclosed rolling pastures for half a mile before Rachel reached the entrance of Twelve Elms. The driveway was wide enough for two cars to pass side by side or, in her case, one tour bus and one horse-drawn buggy.

Avoiding the main parking lot for obvious reasons, Rachel tied her horse to a tree in a grassy area, hung a feed bag around his neck, and gave him a bucket of water—all supplied by Isaac Stoll. She hurried to join a group of people with name tags clustered in the shade. "Are you folks waiting for the tour?" she asked.

"We are," answered a gray-haired woman who stared at her attire. "Are you Amish?"

"I am. Is this where we buy the tickets?"

"It is," said the woman. "Are you interested in horses?"

"I am." Rachel blushed to her earlobes, embarrassed by her string of two-word answers, but she couldn't think of anything else to say. Fortunately, a pretty woman and a young girl walked down the steps of a building marked "Office." They approached the group with very white smiles.

"Good afternoon," greeted the older of the two. "I'm Jessie Brady. Welcome to Twelve Elms. If you're here for the tour, please pay my assistant—also known as my sister, Keeley—six dollars and then climb aboard the red wagon." She pointed at a conveyance that contained at least twenty benches. With open sides and twin Belgians harnessed to the slats, the wagon had a charming Conestoga cover to keep the hot sun off passengers' heads.

After paying the little girl her money, Rachel climbed up with forty other eager tourists. While they rode up and down lanes separating fenced pastures from fields of oats, barley, hay, and alfalfa, the guide relayed plenty of information. According to Jessie, Twelve Elms had a deep artesian well, two springs, two creeks, and a grist mill from a bygone era. When they arrived at a historic waterwheel, Jessie stopped the wagon. Just about everyone other than Rachel pulled out cameras to take photos.

Jessie turned to the group and explained each crop they had passed, including how each type of grain was planted, harvested, and stored until needed. "Everything fed to our livestock or animals boarded here has been grown on this farm. We use a minimum of pesticides and fertilize only with composted horse manure. It's a natural form of recycling. Are there any questions so far?" She scanned the benches where people were listening politely. The mostly senior citizen crowd smiled but no one raised a hand.

Rachel bravely raised hers for the third time during Jessie's narration. "How do you determine which grain mixture to use for a particular breed of horse?"

"That is a good question." Jessie set the brake just as they stopped in front of the office. "We use a manual that's published by the U of K Department of Equine Sciences. Basically, the formula takes into account the age of the animal, their level of physical activity, the breed, and several other factors. Let's disembark our luxury train and head inside the indoor arena. If anyone would like to feed Buster or Bess here a treat, a basket of apples is under that tree." She tied the horses' reins to a fence post.

"Goodness," muttered a woman. "I'm not putting my hands close to that horse's mouth. Did you see the size of those big yellow teeth?" Her companions chuckled as they filed toward the barn.

Only Rachel chose to reward the hardworking Belgians for their efforts. "Your teeth aren't yellow," she murmured close to one ear. "They are the color they're supposed to be." She held out a red apple in her palm. The mare named Bess sucked it up with her tongue.

"I'm not surprised you're unafraid of draft horses," Jessie said behind her.

Rachel startled, but she kept her hand steady while offering Buster a treat. "What's to be afraid of?" She selected two more apples from the bucket.

"But I *am* surprised you know so much about Thoroughbreds. They are too high-strung to be used for buggy horses. They would bolt the first time a car blew its horn. And they surely wouldn't pull a plow if their lives depended on it."

Rachel stepped back before she turned to face the tour guide. The young woman seemed in no hurry to rejoin her group. "I love horses and read everything I can get my hands on about Thorough-breds. I hope I didn't annoy you with my questions." She absently fiddled with her *kapp* ribbon.

"Are you joking?" Jessie tipped up her cap to wipe her forehead. "It's wonderful to talk equine with someone instead of fielding the usual questions from a group. 'Do you offer pony rides for chil-dren's birthday parties?' or 'Where are the restrooms?'" Her dim-ples deepened with a smile.

"Although Bess is a beauty, I would love to see your Thorough-breds up close. High-strung or not, there are no prettier horses in the world."

"You are singing my song." The young woman tugged off her gloves. "Jessie Brady. I'm pleased to meet you," she said, reintro-ducing herself.

Rachel hesitated, thrown off by her expression for a moment. "Rachel King. And the pleasure is mine."

"Let's join the others in the arena, where my younger brother and sister are putting on a demonstration. Then when the group heads to our ice cream and gift shop, I'll take you into the barn to show off my favorites. We don't allow large groups near the stalls. It's too crowded, plus some ladies prefer horses at a distance or on postcards." She pinched her nostrils to illustrate her point.

Feeling like a trained pony herself, Rachel smiled and nodded her head for the hundredth time that afternoon. "I would appreciate that."

When the performance ended, Keeley led the group out of the arena, and Jessie took Rachel into a huge gambrel-roofed barn, the size of which she had never seen before. With wide aisles and oak plank floors, the stable contained stalls made of polished wood with porcelain water troughs that were large enough for six horses. Everything was clean, orderly, and well ventilated. "Wow," she murmured, letting her gaze travel skyward. Without an overhead hayloft, no barn swallows nested in the eaves as in Amish barns. No cats prowled the hay bales, searching out mice for lunch.

"Yeah, our *guests* definitely have nice accommodations. Look around all you like." Jessie leaned against a post.

Rachel peered into one stall after another at mares, stallions, geldings, and foals—each more magnificent than the next. "Does your family own all of these?"

"Goodness, no. Most are boarded here in between horse shows or for some type of training or because we're keeping a close eye on a pregnancy. Another one of our barns has horses for trail rides, barrel racing, and that sort of thing." She straightened and looked at her watch. "We'd better get back to the group. I need to pass out brochures about our services before folks start to leave."

"Why are there no cats in the barn?" Rachel couldn't resist one last question.

"I have two cats in the house, Luke and Leia. But some owners don't like cats around skittish horses. You use a Standardbred with your buggy, right?"

"Yes. I have my cousin's gelding today."

"That breed, as well as draft horses, don't spook nearly as easily as Thoroughbreds."

Rachel and Jessie rejoined the crowd exiting the gift shop. Everyone carried dripping ice-cream cones or bags of souvenirs. A few grandchildren marched out with stuffed pink ponies. While Jessie passed out flyers, Rachel entered the shop and wandered the aisles, in no hurry to leave the farm. She purchased a scoop of butter pecan in a cup to eat on her way home. Intent on not making a mess from the ice cream, Rachel didn't notice Jessie leaning against an elm along the walkway.

"Let me ask *you* a question." The English woman pushed off the tree trunk. "Would you like to stay for supper with me and my family? I think Mom is making chili and corn bread tonight."

Rachel blinked while ice cream dripped from her spoon onto her dress. "No, thank you. I'm expected for supper at my cousin's farm. Besides, I need to return her rig in case she needs it." She dabbed at the stain with a paper napkin.

"Of course. Nobody would sit down for dinner with a pack of strangers, no matter how much they like horses." Jessie laughed easily while she kept pace at Rachel's side.

"It's not that." Rachel felt her face grow warm. "I'm sure your family is nice, but I'm already a guest in someone's home. I don't want to...press my luck. I believe that's how you *Englischers* say it."

"I understand, so I'll stop beating about the bush and ask the real question on my mind." Jessie forged ahead without drawing breath. "You aren't looking for a part-time job, are you? Because I sure could use someone to take my place when I return to college this Sunday."

A second glob of butter pecan hit Rachel's skirt. This one would remain ignored until laundry day. "A job? Here at Twelve Elms?"

"Yep, giving tours three days a week. I think you know almost as much about horses as I do. I can teach you the stable history stuff and what kind of services we offer. What do you say?"

"I say yes! When can I start?"

"Hold on. Before you get too excited, we only pay minimum wage." Jessie shrugged. "That's all I make."

"Minimum wage will be enough."

"We give fall tours on Wednesdays, Fridays, and Saturdays. Would that schedule work for you?"

"It's perfect. The other days I can help my cousin on her chicken farm. I need to earn my keep."

"Oh, wait a minute. Maybe you'll only want to do the Wednesday and Friday tours." Her blue-eyed gaze scanned down Rachel's dress and full-length apron. "Our Saturday tour takes place on horseback instead of using the farm wagon. I doubt you'll want to climb on a trail horse wearing your long pretty dress."

In a fraction of a second, two ideas shot through Rachel's brain: *I would be able to ride the lush hills and valleys of Twelve Elms mounted on one of their fine horses. And I can spend workdays doing what I love best—talking about horses.* She answered without hesitation. "That won't be a problem because I'm still on *rumschpringe*. That means I haven't officially joined the Amish church yet. I have a pair of blue jeans and a couple T-shirts. I also have tennis shoes but no leather riding boots with a heel." She lifted one foot for display.

"You're allowed to do that? Wear jeans and shirts that advertise Twelve Elms Stables?"

"For now I can, until I am baptized." Rachel lowered her foot to the ground while her palms began to sweat.

Jessie stared at her feet. "Say, what size do you wear?"

"Seven and a half."

She grinned. "Then riding boots won't be a problem either. I have tons. I buy every pair I find at the Goodwill Store. Folks purchase them on a lark and then end up donating them to charity without ever wearing them out."

"Maybe you could sell me one of your spare pairs? I'll pay you from my first check."

"Done deal. Wait here and then I'll walk you to your buggy. I put together a notebook for Keeley to use. You can take it home to study. Could you be here by nine o'clock tomorrow to start training?"

"You bet." Rachel swallowed hard. "Thanks, Jessie. I'll work hard and do the best job I can."

"I know you will." Jessie stuck out her hand.

Shyly, Rachel shook for the second time that day. Shaking hands wasn't common among Amish women.

She was sure it was the first of many new experiences to come.

❧

Jake leaned back in his father's chair and rubbed his neck. He'd been at the computer so long, his back was stiff and his neck had developed a painful crick.

"How's it going, son?" Ken spoke from the office doorway, sipping his fourth cup of decaf.

Jake almost fell over backward in surprise. "Good, real good." He waited until his feet hit the carpet before replying. "Come take a look at what I've set up."

Ken pulled up a chair and made himself comfortable.

"I updated our website with the services we provide along with our price schedule. I posted recent photos of events we've held. Most of the information on our site was pathetically out of date." He tapped on each photo to enlarge it.

"Great job. That looks very professional. Your night classes at the community college were well worth the money."

"I know I need to get out of the barn every now and then and help build a client base." Jake leaned back judiciously this time. "I started a blog that I'll update once a week with new photos and scheduled events. That way we won't have to wait for a website redo. Twelve Elms will have a calendar page for upcoming barrel races, dressage shows, children's rodeos, and charity events like that polo club competition we held here. Horse lovers who subscribe to our blog can leave comments and ask questions. Groups can even make reservations to take a tour. There's a link to the blog from the website." Jake clicked on the link and then turned the monitor toward his father.

"Very impressive." His dad nodded with approval. "A couple of old fashioned horsemen have joined the twenty first century."

"I'm just getting started. I set up a Facebook page for the business and a Twitter account too. The blog will feed updates to both to save time."

"I'll take your word that that's a good thing." Ken's eyes crinkled into a web of deep lines.

"It's the way companies advertise these days, Dad. Folks use Google instead of paging through the phone book. I'll have a tech buddy of mine optimize our search engine placement." Jake tapped the link to their Facebook page.

"You've lost me, but I'll bet Jessie and Virgil will be impressed."

"Customers surfing the web for services we happen to offer will find us on the map, so to speak. People with horses to board or those wishing to take lessons might even choose Charm if they're planning to move."

Rising to his feet, Ken slapped him on the back. "Good work, son. I'll report to your mother that Twelve Elms is about to enjoy a renaissance."

Jake closed down the web pages with a rare feeling of pride and accomplishment. "I'd better hit my barn chores, but I'll check out more professional trainer ads later." As he shut the laptop, a curious sight out the window captured his attention. Jessie was talking to a woman in the side yard. The two were huddled over some type of binder. Jake tapped on the windowpane and waved. Both women looked up. His sister waved, but the other merely shielded her eyes from the sun. Jake squinted to better focus on the stranger. In jeans and a peach-colored top, she was the loveliest woman he'd seen in a long time.

"Who…is…that?" he asked, drawing out the three words for emphasis.

His father crossed the floor and pulled back the curtain. "Pretty, isn't she? That's our new tour guide, hired yesterday by your sister. Jessie said that if you could hire a replacement, so could she. Her name is Rachel something or other. She'll take over tours while Jessie's in school so we don't lose the bus group income. I guess you're not the only one implementing changes around here. Your mom will be pleased we're keeping the evil bank repossessor at bay." Ken chuckled as he left the room.

"You're not kidding she's pretty," murmured Jake to no one in particular. He continued to stare like a besotted teenager instead of a grown man until the two women moved out of view. Sprinting down the hallway into the kitchen, he peeked at their newest employee from the back window. For a brief moment he considered dashing out to join them once they disappeared inside the barn, but then he thought better of the idea. His past performance with women his own age was nothing to brag about.

"Who are you spying on?" A voice spoke from behind him. Virgil pulled open the refrigerator door.

"Nobody." Jake let the curtain drop in place and leaned against the windowsill.

True to the curious nature of a fourteen-year-old, Virgil opened his can of soda at the other window and scanned the empty backyard. "I'll bet it was the new girl, Rachel. She's really nice."

"You've already met her?" Jake's face screwed up into a scowl.

"Of course. You need to get away from horses more often, big brother. I ate lunch with her and Jessie." Virgil headed out the door with his cold drink.

Jake popped open a soda and spent the next ten minutes formulating a plan of introduction that wouldn't involve stuttering, stammering, or asking stupid questions such as: "So, you're new around here, aren't you?" His track record for dating girls was abysmal. He never went to bars and seldom attended church socials or anyplace else people his age might meet. From his experience, horse auctions and used tack sales weren't great places to meet women.

By the time he drank the entire can, no particular intuition had arrived on how best to handle meeting her. He strode outside in time to see Jessie and the new hire enter the Brady family barn, so Jake headed to the indoor arena to exercise Eager to Please. He'd accustomed the yearling to the bridle and was working him in half-hour increments on a twenty-foot lunge line. The colt stepped lively and put up no fuss, proof of his assertion they owned a future champion. After checking his watch, Jake took the colt back to his stall for a good rubdown. Training at his tender age took place in baby steps, not in leaps and bounds. Just as he released Eager to Please from the cross ties, Jessie wandered up the main aisle.

"He's growing bigger day by day." She chewed on a long green weed.

Jake added a few cups of feed to the colt's bucket and closed the gate behind him. "You're exactly the person I want to talk to." He bobbed his head left and right to see if anyone was with her.

"Bet I know what you want to talk about." Jessie lifted one of her boot heels to a tack trunk.

"Who's the new girl?" They both spoke simultaneously.

Jake busied himself scrubbing the water trough to hide his embarrassment. "I know her name is Rachel and that she'll give tours while you're in college. Virgil told me that much."

"Yeah, he ate lunch with us at the picnic table. I believe that boy is smitten with Rachel. He kept watching her from the corner of his eye, subtle-like, at least in his own mind."

"Is that so?" Jake refilled the newly cleaned trough with the hose.

"Well, she sure is attractive. Don't you think so?"

Jake shook his head and faced her. Never in his life could he keep a single secret from his sister. Jessie had been born with the intuition allotment meant for a dozen people. "I suppose she is, but what I want to know is where did she go?" He turned one of the plastic chairs backward to straddle.

"She's taking Buster and Bess around the tour circuit a few times to get used to handling them and so they can get familiar with her. If she keeps giving them apples, they'll be putty in her hands." She plopped down on the trunk lid.

"By herself?" Jake felt oddly protective of a stranger. "Why didn't you go with her?"

"Yes, by herself. We already rode around twice together. Now she needs to relax and practice without someone watching over her shoulder." Jessie glanced up at him. "She'll have to do it alone soon enough."

"How will she know what to say?"

"I gave her the notebook I made for Keeley as a training manual. It has everything in it you're supposed to say on a tour, including the history and background on Twelve Elms in case people ask questions." Her lips pulled into a smile. "She's caught your eye as well as Virgil's."

Jake checked the open doorway. "Few women under forty show up here, so why wouldn't she catch my attention?"

"Rachel is a dream come true for me, Jake. She knows a lot about horses and is willing to memorize everything in the manual. She should be ready to give the tour next Wednesday." Jessie crossed and uncrossed her feet at the ankles, unable to sit still for long. "And if she runs into trouble, one of my Sir Galahad brothers will ride to her rescue. Be sure to saddle up a *white* horse."

Jake ignored the wisecrack. "What else do you know about her?"

"Let's see...her name is Rachel King. She lives on Route 738 with a cousin and her husband—"

"Rachel's husband or the cousin's?"

"The cousin's. They own an organic chicken farm." Jessie propped her chin on her index finger. "She doesn't much like free-roaming chickens except for supper, so that's why she needs a job. Oh, and she's from Pennsylvania." She jumped to her feet. "That's about all I know. I don't demand official résumés with references for part-time, temporary jobs."

"I'll have to find out more details when I sweep her off her feet with my wit and charm," he said with false bravado. He stood and pushed away from the stall wall, ducking his head.

Suddenly, Jessie's eyebrows arched as though remembering another detail. "Hold up there, big brother. Before you go all dewy eyed, I just thought of something that's a deal-breaker for both of you. You had better advertise for business from younger clientele if you want to expand your dating pool."

The little hairs rose on the back of his neck. "What do you mean? I just want to get to know her. Don't let your imagination run away with you." His tone betrayed his irritation.

"All right, don't get sore. Forget I said anything." She headed toward the doorway.

But Jake followed at her heels. "Why do you have a bug up your nose about her? What's wrong? Doesn't she like the same music videos as you? You women can be so—"

Jessie pivoted and slapped both palms on his chest. "Stop. I really like Rachel. I think she and I could become friends if I wasn't leaving Charm this weekend."

He stepped back. "Then what is it?"

Jessie rolled her eyes. "Rachel leaves here around four. Why don't you lurk along the path to the parking lot? Then you can *nonchalantly* run into her and introduce yourself. There's one little personality trait you need to see for yourself." Turning on her heel, she sprinted away.

Jake slapped his hat against his pant leg. Women were so confoundedly cryptic. Despite the fact he had no hope of saying the right thing with Miss King, he sure planned to give it a try.

At four o'clock, Jake Brady, a relatively mature man for twenty-three years old, hid in their lilac bushes, waiting for his prey like a red-tailed hawk. He had showered, donned a fresh shirt and jeans, and shaved...again. He had even splashed on cologne Keeley had bought him for Christmas. But when he inhaled a whiff, he washed the stuff off.

Five minutes after the appointed hour, Rachel walked from the horse barns with her nose buried in the training manual. She'd slung her tote bag across her back and perched her sunglasses atop her head, nestled in the shiniest blond hair in Kentucky. She moved with a feminine, delicate stride, not shuffling her boots through the dust the way some girls did. Sunlight added a burnished glow to her peaches-and-cream complexion. Even from his vantage point, hidden behind thick waxy foliage, he recognized flawless skin.

He was about to step from his refuge and make his presence known when she abruptly diverged from the path into the ladies' room. His dad had built modern outdoor restrooms for their visitors several years ago before they began offering tours.

Jake used the time to his advantage. He sprinted down the walkway into the parking lot and turned around. He would plod along, pacing himself, and then run into her as she exited the facilities. A more perfect scheme had never been hatched.

Almost on cue, the lovely Rachel King walked outdoors and

slung her bag over her shoulder, the training manual nowhere in sight. Jake, with timing to match his perfect plan, halted a few feet in front of her. "You're...you're Amish," he stammered.

Rachel pulled her sunglasses down to the bridge of her nose. "That I am," she replied, stepping around him.

"Wait," he demanded as he repositioned himself in her path. "I saw you earlier today and you weren't Amish."

One corner of her mouth lifted. "I assure you I've been Amish for a while now. Ever since birth, actually. But if you saw me earlier, why are you still here?" Her half smile faded as she glanced at the empty parking lot.

For a moment he thought she might bolt like a white-tailed deer at the sound of gunfire. "Please, let me explain. I saw you with my sister from inside the house. My name is Jake Brady." He stretched out his hand. "I'm Jessie's brother."

She stared at his hand briefly before shaking. "Rachel King, the new tour guide. If you'll excuse me, Mr. Brady, I need to start for home. I'm already late."

"Mr. Brady is my father. Call me Jake. And please give me another chance to start off on the right foot. I'm usually only this big of a jerk during first introductions."

Halting twenty feet away, Rachel glanced back. "Because I wear English clothes while working here, not realizing I'm Amish was an honest mistake. So you must not be *the* biggest jerk...Jake." Her smile returned. "And because your sister is so nice, it's hard to believe you're a jerk at all. I'll see you next Wednesday." She straightened her bonnet and marched down the path at double time.

He stared until her cornflower blue dress disappeared from sight. Such a pretty shade of blue—almost as pretty as the color of her eyes.

Amish or not, Jake Brady had just met the woman of his dreams.

FOUR

Was blind, but now I see

Wednesday

"You're not running off to your new job with an empty belly." Sarah stood at the bottom of the stairs, yelling in a fashion atypical of most Amish people.

"I'll be right down," hollered Rachel, equally boisterous. She looked once more into her hand mirror before sticking it into the dresser drawer. She'd braided her long hair, coiled it atop her head and fastened it with pins, and then pulled on her *kapp*. Once at work, she would remove her head covering and the pins, allowing the braid to trail down her back. She tucked her English clothes into a tote bag and applied the tiniest bit of blush to her cheeks. Because she was never outdoors without a bonnet, she was pale compared to Jessie. She'd bought the makeup at the Dollar Store back in Lancaster while feeling particularly bold one Saturday afternoon.

"Rachel, anyone with your God-given beauty has no need for cosmetics." Her sister's declaration ran through her brain, bringing along a fresh wave of homesickness. Amy—content raising organic celery and other vegetables in upstate Maine. And Nora—preparing to leave on a trip home to Pennsylvania with her new husband. Both of her older sisters were married and settled. Rachel sent up a silent prayer for them without the slightest shred of jealousy. The only thing she wanted was to give her first solo tour without forgetting everything she'd been memorizing for days.

Please, Lord, stay close so I don't make a complete fool of myself or get fired on my first day. With her prayer on its way, Rachel grabbed her bag and bolted down the steps.

"There you are," huffed Sarah. "Sit. Isaac is hitching up the gelding. I made bacon, blueberry pancakes, buttermilk biscuits, and fried eggs. We have orange juice and coffee too."

Rachel poured a mug and sat down at the table. "Is that all? That's barely enough to keep a sparrow alive." She winked at her cousin.

"That's why I packed you two sandwiches plus fruit and chips for your lunch." Sarah sat across from her and they bowed their heads in silent prayer.

Afterward Rachel bit into a biscuit dripping with butter. "*Danki.* I am in your debt."

"Nonsense. With all the housecleaning you did yesterday, I'm in yours. I should have invited you to Kentucky long ago. Oh, I almost forgot—I have a gift to celebrate your new job. I bought it at our English neighbor's garage sale last summer." She handed Rachel an insulated travel mug that read: I love Fridays. "It will keep drinks either hot or cold."

"This will come in handy. Thank you." Rachel concentrated on her plate to avoid becoming too emotional. After all, she was starting her first job, not leading the Israelites out of Egypt.

With her new mug in hand, she drove the three miles to Twelve Elms Stables. As instructed by Jessie, she turned Isaac's gelding into a paddock near the family barn and left the buggy in the shade.

After changing into jeans and a T-shirt that advertised the stable in bright red letters, she walked into the employee break room.

Everyone turned to look at her. One woman smiled and pointed to a box sitting on the table. "I believe that's for you if your name is Rachel."

"Thanks," she said, picking up the box wrapped in blue tissue paper with a big white bow. Inside she found a pair of almost-new riding boots. Jessie had enclosed a card that read, "Good luck and (don't) break a leg." Oddly, the word "don't" had been enclosed in parentheses. Then an entire line of *x*'s and *o*'s followed Jessie's signature. Rachel slipped the card into her pocket and the boots onto her feet. She wondered if she would ever understand all of the English expressions, but at least the boots fit perfectly. No sore feet by the end of the day.

She grinned at the grooms, stable hands, and farm workers who wandered in and out of the room. People nodded and smiled while filling coffee mugs or heating up breakfast pastries. Someone had left a box of donuts on the table, while two huge dispensers provided chilled water. Rachel went over to one and filled her travel mug before stashing it with her tote bag in her new locker. Someone had placed a label identifying "Rachel King" in the little metal window. A wall sign reminded employees to "Clean up after yourself because your mother doesn't work here."

Rachel headed from the break room to the barn of Buster and Bess, grabbing some apples from the basket along the way. She greeted her new equine best friends with gentle strokes and tasty treats. After leading them into the sunshine, she easily hitched the pair to the red tour wagon as Jessie had taught her. Next she wiped down the wagon seats and handrails with sanitizer and paper towels, and then she swept the floor to make sure not a speck of dust remained. Once she had parked the wagon in the designated loading zone, she entered the stable office. Keeley sat alone in the room, spinning around in the swivel chair.

"Hi, Rachel," she sang out.

"Good morning." Rachel greeted the girl fondly.

"Jessie said I should ask you if you wanted me to tag along during your first tour or if you would prefer I just collected money and let you take the bull by the horns solo." Keeley gave the chair a final spin.

The child's multipart question took Rachel a moment to decipher. But once she did, she answered with traditional Amish succinctness: "Solo, thank you."

"Good to hear. I would hate to miss my game shows on TV."

An abstract thought occurred. "Why aren't you in school today? It's Wednesday."

"Dad let me stay home because it's your first day." Keeley handed over a plastic contraption. "This is a walkie-talkie. I have one inside the house. If anything goes wrong, just press this red button and speak normally into it. Dad or Jake or I will come running."

"What kind of things do you mean?" asked Rachel, inspecting the gadget.

Keeley gave her chair another spin. "Oh, old people having heart attacks, or if one of the horses breaks a leg in a gopher hole, or if a wheel falls off the wagon." She glanced at the wall clock, grabbed the cash box, and headed out the door.

Sarah's heavy breakfast churned in Rachel's stomach. "Do those sorts of events happen often?" She followed Keeley down the steps into the late summer sunshine. The cool breeze felt wonderful on her skin.

"Not so far, thank goodness. But Jessie told me to explain the walkie-talkie and what it's for." Keeley looked up at her. "Jessie really likes you and hopes you will like giving tours."

"And I, her. I'm sure I'll enjoy working here."

"I like you too." The girl grinned with the exuberance of a twelve-year-old.

The English directness again stymied Rachel. "Thank you. I appreciate the walkie-talkie in case of an emergency, but don't worry. I will be fine." She had followed Keeley without paying much attention to the surroundings. They stopped in front of a group of no less than thirty-five senior citizens. Everyone wore name tags directly over their hearts. Rachel's earlier confidence evaporated like dew on the lawn.

"Good morning. I'm Keeley Brady. Welcome to Twelve Elms. If you're here for the tour, you're standing in the right place. This is Rachel King, your guide. Please cut her some slack because this is her first day." Keeley's grin stretched from ear to ear. "If you still want to go, line up in front of me and pay six dollars. I'm her assistant."

Rachel dared not breathe waiting to see what decision the crowd would make, but everyone lined up to pay their admission. With anxiety building in her veins, she untied Bess and Buster from the post. She held their leather reins in her sweating palm as one by one people climbed up under the white Conestoga cover. Many nodded, a few wished her "Good luck," and not one looked as if they feared for their life.

Shaking the reins over the horses' broad backs, Rachel tried to relax as the wagon began to roll. Then, as though a strange virus attacked her brain, she couldn't remember a single thing she had memorized from Jessie's training manual. Her head was as empty as a wallet before payday. She cleared her throat as the horses stopped at the first photo-taking location. Bess and Buster knew more than she did at the moment. "Welcome to Twelve Oaks Stables," she croaked after an uncomfortable silence.

"Ain't it called Twelve Elms?" asked a male voice from the back.

Everyone laughed except for Rachel, who reached for the walkie-talkie. With her finger hovering over the bright red button, three options swam through her mind.

Should I demand Keeley meet me at the next stop to take over the tour?

Should I ask Mr. Brady to hitch my gelding to the buggy because I've suddenly become ill?

Should I buy nose plugs and learn to appreciate chickens? After all, baby chicks truly are adorable.

Then the image of Jessie popped into her head. Rachel had given her word she would try her best. No way could she head for her buggy without working at least one full day. She set the gadget on the seat, shoved her hand in her pocket to keep it away from the red panic button, and faced her audience. "It *is* Twelve Elms, but I'm so nervous I can't remember a single bit of the information I've studied for days. To jog my memory, could somebody please ask a question?" Her voice had dropped to a mere whisper.

The tour group stared. A few chuckled, a few rolled their eyes, and a few looked downright embarrassed for her sake. Then one or two slowly raised their hands.

"Yes, woman in pink?" Rachel forced herself to smile.

"How long has this farm been in Casey County?" The question came from a sweet-faced grandmother.

Rachel released her breath and cleared her throat. "Twelve Elms has been in the Brady family for four generations, beginning with Jeremiah Brady back in eighteen seventy-eight. Thoroughbreds have always been here, besides a variety of other breeds, including Arabians, American Saddlebreds, Morgans, Tennessee Walkers, and working stock such as Belgians, Percherons, and Haflingers." Rachel scanned the crowd. "Lady in the blue dress?"

"Are there only horses, or do other animals live here?" She spoke in a singsong voice as though addressing a toddler.

"Throughout the years, this has been a sheep farm, cattle ranch, and dairy cow operation. One year the family tried tending goats because Mrs. Brady loves goats' milk cheese, but that didn't work out too well. Descendants of those original goats still live wild up in the forest. Every winter they wander close enough to the house to be spotted." Rachel exhaled with relief. "Now let's move to our second stop. Along the way I'll explain about the crops we grow here and why they make the best horse feed in the state." Rachel sat and released the brake. The wagon began to roll as Buster and Bess pulled them down a lane between two pastures. Behind her, the group broke into a round of applause. Voices called out: "We knew you could do it," and "Everybody has had a first day sometime or another." She had to concentrate to keep from crying tears of joy.

At the end of the tour, Rachel could have hugged each and every one of the guests. As the facts she had memorized returned, she ended up saying everything she had planned, just in a different order. When the crowd wandered into the gift shop, she fed apple after apple to the draft horses. Then, when her tour group left the shop with souvenirs and ice cream, Rachel passed out the Twelve Elms brochures, thanking them for being so patient.

The grandmotherly-type in the pink dress lingered to peruse the services. "Say, Rachel, I don't see a price for pony rides. Doesn't this stable have ponies for children's birthday parties?"

"No, ma'am, but if you drop by our website, there's a link on the home page to pony ride vendors in the area. Mr. Brady speaks highly of every one of them."

The woman gave her a quick hug and then boarded the bus. Rachel stood in the parking lot waving her hand vigorously. She'd done it. She hadn't made a fool of herself after all. And she'd enjoyed every minute of it...at least, every minute after tour stop number one.

❧

Donna tapped on her GPS mechanism for the third time since leaving her office in Charm. For some reason it couldn't lock onto a satellite signal and kept reverting back to the licensing agreement page. She had spent the entire day yesterday studying the information provided by the Division of Epidemiology and Health

Planning, along with reports about the first case of polio in the area. Last night she pored over Internet websites devoted to the Amish lifestyle. She read the fascinating history of how the Amish fled Europe due to religious persecution and settled in Lancaster County, Pennsylvania, where many still resided. During the past thirty years, some had moved north and west in search of more plentiful and cheaper farmland.

After pulling into a driveway to consult her county map, Donna knew she was in the right area but that was about all. Electric lines running to the home indicated that Old Order Mennonites probably lived here. Somewhere to the west were farms of the Old Order Amish. Here in Casey County, each district decided how much technology to embrace…or how little. Blanket generalities didn't work. Most *Englischers,* of which she was one, referred to all Plain people as Amish. The information provided by the state's Department of Health described the family of the polio victim as Amish, yet that might not be the case. When she gave the black box another tap, the GPS simply shut itself off.

Gazing out the car window at the tidy three-story house, Donna copied the address from the mailbox onto her clipboard and drove slowly up the rutted lane. Laundry flapped on long clotheslines, and brown-and-white cows chewed their cud behind an electric wire fence. In the distance a large herd of cattle wandered the hillside in search of the proverbial greener grass. She felt peace in the barnyard as she parked her car in the shade. Peace and a sense of tranquility. Carrying her briefcase, she approached the house with the sensation of being watched. As she suspected, three sets of eyes stared from between the white porch rails. They were owned by blond-haired little girls wearing blue dresses with black pinafores. Their hair had been braided and coiled atop their heads. Unlike the older girls Donna had seen, these wore no bonnets.

"Hello," she called.

No one spoke. The oldest, a girl of around seven, smiled shyly.

The siblings watched with wide-eyed fascination as Donna climbed the steps. "Is your mom home?" Her second query received the identical reaction as the first. Donna rapped on the front door, keeping an eye on the threesome.

Within a few minutes a thin boy appeared behind the screen door. "You've come to buy eggs? We're already sold out. I took the sign down by the road." He looked guilty as though personally responsible for a disappointed customer.

"No, I'm not here for eggs. I need to speak to your parents—to your mother and father." She wasn't sure why she'd explained the word "parents" because the youth spoke perfect English.

The boy considered for a moment and then mumbled, "Wait here." He disappeared into the dark, mysterious interior of the house and remained gone for at least five minutes. Donna half expected the parents to go rattling down the driveway in a beat-up pickup truck, scooping up the three girls on the run like some TV comedy from the nineteen sixties.

Instead, a woman of around thirty stepped onto the porch. She carried an infant, while a two-year-old boy clung to her skirt with both fists. Running a quick tally, that meant a minimum of six at-risk children in this one family. "May I help you?" asked the woman, hefting the baby higher up her hip.

"I hope so. I'm Donna Cline from the Casey County Department of Health. Is there someplace we can talk comfortably?"

"Here is good." She pointed toward a porch swing. The three little girls sprang up and raced down the steps into the yard.

"Thank you." Donna walked to the swing. "Is your husband available? This might interest him as well, Mrs...."

The woman didn't supply her last name. "No, he'll be in the hayfields until six o'clock. I doubt you would want to wait till then." There was no hostility in her voice, just a simple statement of fact.

Donna sat, as did the woman, and the swing began to move. "You have a fine family," she said. "Beautiful children."

"Thank you." A hint of suspicion clouded the woman's eyes.

"They are the reason I am here…to keep them healthy. A case of polio has turned up recently in Casey County in the Plain community—a little girl either Amish or Old Order Mennonite."

"Polio?" The woman's eyes rounded. "I've heard of it, but I'm not sure what it is."

"It's an infectious disease, very rare these days, thank goodness, but unfortunately not completely eradicated." Donna gulped, regretting her choice of words. She'd been advised by Phil to use only basic terms. "It's a virus that hits primarily children and young adults. It can cause weakness and paralysis in the limbs, especially the legs. The effects often last a lifetime."

The Mennonite mother blinked and shifted the sleeping infant to her other shoulder. "Who is this child?"

Donna softened her expression. "I'm sorry, but federal law prohibits me from disclosing the child's name."

"What's the family name?" Her expression of mistrust heightened.

"The law protects the privacy of the family too. I can't say more about the patient, only that the child is receiving the best medical care available."

She frowned. "Will they get better?"

"That depends on the individual. If it's a full-blown paralytic infection, they might regain some mobility, but not necessarily. There is no cure. That's why prevention is so important."

The woman's complexion paled.

"But the reason I'm here is to protect your children from contracting the disease. A vaccine is available, a shot, that would take just a few minutes to administer and within weeks full immunity would be reached. I'm a registered nurse besides being a licensed social worker. I'm equipped and qualified to administer vaccines, but I would need your written consent. Then you would have no worries about your children ending up in the same circumstance."

The young woman rocked the swing and stared across the yard, where cows grazed and corn stood dry and tall, waiting to be cut and ground into livestock feed. Her pale blue eyes seemed focused on sights only she could see. "God will protect my *kinner*. He shall keep them safe. And if it be His will that we be tested by illness, we shall accept His plan for our lives."

"I am a devout Christian myself, ma'am, but I don't believe that immunizing against viruses interferes with God's plan."

Cocking her head, she raised one eyebrow. "You can speak for the Lord? Your heart knows God's plan for people you met five minutes ago?" Again her inquiry contained no condemnation.

Donna drew in a deep breath. She'd been warned not to get involved in theological debates and to just state scientific facts and medical probabilities, but what if those weren't enough to convince people whose faith lay at the very center of their lives? "No, ma'am, certainly not. Perhaps you can read this brochure about the long-term effects and expense of the disease and talk the matter over with your husband." She pulled a pamphlet from her briefcase—one that the woman made no attempt to accept. "I wrote my phone number on the back. Call me if you wish more information. I would be happy to return. There would be no cost to your family for the shots," she added.

The mother lifted her chin. "Money isn't the issue here." As though on cue, her baby began to cry. She rose, patting the child's back. "Thank you for stopping by, Mrs. Cline, and for your concern." Without another word she walked into the house for a feeding or a diaper change—either way the meeting was over. The older boy, who had stood like a sentinel on the other side of the porch, strode inside after her. Donna left the brochure on the rail, to be blown away with the next gust of wind.

She had underestimated the farmer's wife and mother of six, eight, or who knew how many. She assumed she could appeal to a maternal instinct or take some authoritative position—a person who knew what was best for the county residents. But she had been no match for a devout person's unflappable faith. She witnessed it personally when her mother had received a terminal cancer diagnosis. The oncologist insisted on a grueling regimen of chemo and radiation that might extend life by six months. Her mother refused, turning instead to intensive prayer. Without subjecting her body to chemical bombardment, she placed her future in God's hands. Mom had lived another three years—a gift of spontaneous remission—and those years had been relatively pain-free. Donna wouldn't have believed in the power of faith if she hadn't seen it with her own eyes.

But she was no preacher or faith healer. She was trained to share medical information and explain available services to area residents. Without stopping for lunch, she visited farm after farm on that road and then the next. Each response was different but the outcome remained the same.

"All my children feel fine. We have no need for your shots."

"Our district doesn't follow English ways."

"I heard those vaccines contain bits of the virus. I won't chance my children getting sick from the shots."

"I shall pray on the matter. Why don't you come back next summer?"

In two cases the homeowner listened politely and said, "No, thank you." Then the door was shut in Donna's face as if she were selling door-to-door candy. Hot and tired, she walked back to her car feeling as though she'd accomplished nothing. But as she drove back to Russell Springs she knew she couldn't give up. She would return to Casey County tomorrow and every day thereafter until she had knocked on every door. Too much was at stake—the healthy future of every Amish and Mennonite child in the area.

༒

Jake watched the new tour guide lift her hand and wave at the departing bus. Seeing her smile allowed him to relax for the first time that day. He'd been waiting for Rachel to finish the tour with a mixture of anxiety and anticipation.

"Hi, Rachel," he called as the bus pulled from the parking lot with a blast of diesel exhaust.

She turned slowly and smiled upon recognition. "Hi, Jake. I did it! I gave my first tour and it went pretty well. That is, after a rocky start." A blush darkened her cheeks.

When he reached her side they walked up the gravel path toward the stable office. "What kind of a rocky start? Did someone give you a hard time?"

"Oh, no. Everyone was very sweet, but when I got to the first stop, I drew a total blank. I completely forgot everything I learned from the manual." Her blue eyes widened. "Please don't think I didn't study. I practically memorized the entire notebook."

"I believe you." He nodded agreement with more energy than necessary. "The first time I announced events at a horse show, I forgot half the stuff I was supposed to say. And I pronounced everyone's name wrong—even folks I'd known most of my life."

"Thanks for telling me that." Rachel's braid danced across her shoulders as she moved. "I was tempted to push the panic button."

Jake scratched his jawline. "What panic button?"

"The red button on the walkie-talkie that sends messages." She held her balled fist up to her lips. "Help, come get me! I'm surrounded by tourists and don't know what to say!"

Laughing louder than he should, Jake kicked a stone down the path. "One of us would have come running. We don't allow guests to maul employees on their first day at Twelve Elms." He glanced at her from the corner of his eye.

"What a great place to work!" She threw her arms out, palms skyward.

"I take it the information in the manual finally came back to you?"

"Nope. I had to beg people to ask questions to trigger my memory, but by the second stop I had caught my stride, and by the last I was able to relax and enjoy myself." She kicked the same stone another dozen feet. "How has your day gone so far?"

He shrugged and sighed. "I've not been astride a horse all morning. I've been holed up in the office on the computer doing e-mails, posting to our blog, and updating our Facebook status, while the horses under my care grow fat and lazy."

"I don't know what all that means, but I presume it's a waste of time compared to your equestrian work?"

She mispronounced the word "equestrian," but he thought it sounded so charming he wouldn't correct her in a million years. "It's time-consuming but too soon to tell if it's a time waste. Businesses need a strong presence on the Internet if they want new customers to find them. We can't grow our business if we stay locked in the twentieth century." Jake bit his tongue. Would his comments offend a woman who wore bonnets and drove a buggy?

"I get it. If they write to you electronically, you need to make time to write back. And writing letters whether on paper or a computer takes time." Her braid swung so invitingly he yearned to catch it between his fingers. Unfortunately, they had reached the entrance to the stable office.

"I'm starved. Want to grab some lunch with me in the break room?" He flourished a hand toward the door as though beckoning her to a banquet.

Rachel skipped up the steps. "Sure, as long as you help me eat what I brought. My cousin packed enough food for a small village. I'll wash up, get my lunch bag, and meet you at the table." She disappeared into the ladies' room.

Jake bolted into the lounge to make sure no one had left half-eaten donuts or dirty coffee cups lying about. He spritzed the table by the window with spray cleaner and wiped it until the surface gleamed. When she returned, he was leaning back in his chair, relaxed and at ease. At least, that's how he hoped he appeared.

She opened her insulated lunch bag. "I like having a locker here—a place to stick my stuff." While talking, she pulled out two sandwiches and two apples and placed half in front of him.

Jake unwrapped the waxed paper and bit into the thick ham and cheese. Before he could swallow, Rachel bowed her head in silent prayer. He felt like a heel. Sometimes his family remembered to say grace, but often his younger sister started expounding on some schoolyard drama first. "Sorry," he whispered when she lifted her head. "My manners are a little rusty."

"It's all right." Rachel took small, dainty bites of her sandwich.

He slowed his pace so he wouldn't resemble a ravenous stray dog. "What does your schedule look like for the afternoon?"

"One more tour, but it's not until two thirty. Then I'll be finished for the day. Your sister explained that bookings are lighter in the fall than during the summer." She sipped from her water bottle.

"Would you like to see the old maple sugar shack? My granddaddy used to boil down sap from our trees and make the best pancake syrup around."

"I would if I can get back before my bus group arrives."

"No problem. It's not far."

He cleaned up their trash while Rachel stowed her bag. Jake noticed every head in the room turn when she walked by. He wasn't the only male to notice how pretty she was.

On the way to the sugaring cabin in the bright afternoon sunshine, Rachel didn't seem to mind their temporary lull in conversation, but the silence was killing him. How could he appear witty, charming, and intelligent if he couldn't think of a single thing to say? What should he talk about with an Amish woman? She probably didn't follow sports or popular music or go to movies on weekends. Fortunately, Skinny Joe sauntered out of the tall weeds at that moment.

"Goodness, a one-eyed cat." Rachel bent down to scoop the orange kitty into her arms. "You are beautiful despite your disability." She held the cat nose-to-nose before settling him in the crook of her arm. "I suspect there's a story here."

"His name is Skinny Joe. I found him hiding in the bushes by our mailbox. He'd been thrown out of a car and was in pretty bad shape. I rushed him to the vet for treatment, but his eye couldn't be saved." He scratched Joe behind the ear. "Our vet is an animal lover, same as me, so she made me a deal. She spays or neuters any feral cats I bring in and provides shots for twenty-five dollars. Afterward, she notches an ear so the animal warden knows to leave these cats alone. As long as strays are healthy and don't add to the cat overpopulation problem, they can run wild and keep down the number of mice and other rodents."

"How many have you taken to her so far?" Rachel stroked his fur continually while Joe purred as loud as a lawnmower.

"Twenty-eight and counting. Everybody thinks the countryside is a great place to dump pets." He shook his head. "Jessie already has two house cats, and my dad doesn't want too many around the horse barns. I've found homes for most of them, but nobody fell in love with Skinny Joe."

Rachel clucked her tongue. "Nobody until now. I would take him home in a heartbeat if I wasn't a guest at my cousin's. People must be blind to his inner beauty." She bent down and kissed Joe's fuzzy head.

"I'd bet he feels the same about you." They had reached the cabin, and a moment later Jake swept open the door to a bygone era.

Setting the animal down, Rachel stepped inside. Joe scampered up the narrow steps to the loft in search of tasty critters. "I love this place." She ran her hand along the rim of a huge evaporation kettle. "I can still smell the scent of maple sugar. Doesn't anybody tap your trees anymore?"

"No. Dad and Mom are too busy. My mother is a pharmacist, and Dad has the stable to run. Every year we talk about tapping trees in January, but there's always so much to do. Maybe we will someday once my little brother gets old enough to be serious help around the place. I would love to bottle a batch labeled 'Grandpa Jeremiah's Secret Recipe.' The tour groups would snap it up in the gift shop. Profits would soar."

"You can count on me for your first sale. I drown my pancakes in syrup." Rachel smiled at him almost as warmly as she had at Skinny Joe.

Suddenly the shack felt uncomfortably warm and airless. Jake loosened his collar and crossed his arms. Beads of sweat began forming across his forehead. Like Rachel at her first tour stop, he couldn't think of a single thing to say—not about maple sugar or one-eyed cats or anything else. He was alone with the prettiest girl in Kentucky in his favorite spot on the farm, and he could barely breathe.

As though she sensed his discomfort, Rachel walked around the cabin conducting an inspection. "I would say all this place needs is a good cleaning, and then it will be ready to fire up the woodstove next January. But now I must go back to the office and prepare for my next group. I want to review the manual to make sure I don't panic this afternoon." She took a step toward the door. "Thanks, Jake, for the tour of the sugar cabin and helping me eat lunch. I'll see you later." Without waiting for his response, she bolted out the door and down the path without a backward glance.

And that was a good thing. Because Jake stood in the center of the room with his mouth agape and his mind spinning in ten different directions at once.

FIVE

'Twas grace that taught my heart to fear

Friday morning

And did you know that *grossdawdi* Brady used to tap their maple trees and boil down the sap into pancake syrup?" asked Rachel, buttering her second piece of toast. "Just like our *grossdawdi* did back in Mount Joy."

Sarah rolled her eyes. "How could I have known that? I don't keep up with what *Englischers* do around here." She placed three strips of bacon beside a hearty mound of scrambled eggs and set the plate before her quiet husband. After she scooped up more modest portions for Rachel and herself, she sat down at the table. "All I know is you haven't stopped talking about Twelve Elms since you got home Wednesday evening. You have much to say even though you've only given two tours so far."

"Enough, *fraa*," murmured Isaac. "Let's bow our heads so we can eat." When they finished, he glanced at Rachel and then his wife. "Everything is exciting when you're new. Remember the summer you worked at Bread of Life? You went on and on about their desserts. One would have thought they invented sweet potato pie." He ate a piece of bacon in two bites.

Sarah laughed. "*Jah,* I remember. I earned such good tips serving lunch. But by the end of the week I was too tired to do my work around the house. When the tourist season ended, I was glad to return to my lovely chickens…and to you, *ehemann."* She laid her small hand atop his large, calloused one. Isaac blushed liked a teenager on his first date.

Rachel ate her breakfast faster than usual. "*Mir leid,*" she apologized. "I don't mean to sound prideful or overly concerned with the English. But I do like giving tours, and the Bradys have been very nice to me."

"Isaac is right. The bloom will soon fade from the rose. Enjoy yourself while you can. You will quickly learn that work is just that…work." Sarah sipped her coffee. "You were such a big help yesterday that I have nothing to complain about. Thank you, cousin."

Rachel carried her plate and cup to the sink. "There's nothing to thank me for, Sarah. I live and eat here, so I should help with chores. Moving to Kentucky doesn't change how we both were raised." She filled her travel mug and snapped on the lid. "I'm leaving now so I won't have to hurry." She tucked the lunch packed last night into her tote bag while guilt lay beneath her bacon and eggs. Even though she had chatted endlessly about her new job, she failed to mention she wore English clothes while at Twelve Elms.

Officially, she was still on *rumschpringe*—a period of testing the waters before baptism and joining the Amish or Old Order Mennonite church. During this time, she was permitted to court young men and work outside the home. Many of her friends took trips to Walt Disney World or learned to drive cars or bought English clothes to wear away from home. Rachel had never been so inclined…until now. Wearing Amish garb during tours would trigger too many questions about her instead of the stable.

"I'll see you tonight, cousins. Watch out for angry hens," she teased on her way out the door.

Soon she was on her way to Twelve Elms on a perfect autumn day. She thought about the chores she helped Sarah with and decided she must never be late or forget to pass out brochures or do anything else that could get her fired. They had scrubbed out nesting boxes, swept floors, and raked the areas that enclosed specific flocks. After a long hot shower, she had fallen into bed exhausted, sick of hearing *cluck-cluck-cluck* as the chickens scratched around for corn. Those silly birds would continue to eat until they exploded. But with her current tour schedule, she only had to help Sarah three days a week, leaving three days of pure pleasure, and one day for rest. "Life was good in Charm," to quote Keeley.

After two back-to-back tours that morning, Rachel headed into the break room for lunch. She was starving. When she spotted Jake across the room, her spirits soared even higher. If they ate together, she could ask him questions about the yearling she kept hearing about.

"Hi, Jake." She dropped her lunch bag on the table.

"You're just the person I wanted to see." He pulled a grocery store bag from the refrigerator and sauntered across the room. "Because you were kind enough to share your lunch on Wednesday, I packed us a picnic." He opened the sack to reveal several plastic containers. "Fried chicken, potato salad, sliced peaches, and iced tea." His brown eyes sparkled with warmth. Instead of his usual T-shirt, he wore a pressed cotton shirt tucked into his jeans.

"You fried up chicken?" Rachel lowered her voice to a whisper, aware that several other employees were listening while they ate.

"Nah. Mom made plenty last night for supper so we would have leftovers for today." He tucked a stack of napkins into the bag. "What do you say?"

It took little time to decide. "Sure. I'll save my sandwich for tomorrow. Should I look for Keeley so she can join us?"

But Jake had already headed out the door instead of sitting at a table. Rachel glanced around the room. With him gone, six pairs of eyes fastened on her. Suddenly shy and embarrassed, she threw her lunch in the refrigerator and hurried after him.

He was waiting for her outside. "No, Keeley always eats in front of the TV in the air-conditioning. There are shows she hates to miss. I left enough for her, Virgil, and my dad in the house."

"Good to hear your family won't starve." Rachel lifted an eyebrow.

He strolled down the steps, slinging the bag over his shoulder. "I thought we could take our picnic to the old waterwheel on such a nice day."

Rachel felt a mixed bag of emotions with his suggestion. On the one hand, she was thrilled at the prospect of eating lunch with one of the owners of Twelve Elms. Jake knew everything about Thoroughbreds. But on the other hand, the thought of slipping away with an *Englischer* made her feel sneaky…sort of like the jeans and T-shirt hidden in the bottom of her tote bag when she left the Stolls' house. "Okay, as long as we're not gone too long. Jessie explained I get a thirty-minute paid lunch break. If I need more time than that, it's off the clock."

"We'll head back in exactly twenty-five minutes." Looking at his watch, Jake handed her the large bag. "You carry our lunch and start down the path toward the river. I'll catch up after I get something from the porch." He sprinted off the moment her fingers grasped the handles.

She was being silly. If she worked in the English world, she needed to think like an *Englischer* for six hours a day. Men and women probably shared meals all the time in modern society without anyone thinking it strange or starting rumors. She relaxed as she hiked downhill toward the old mill, the sun warming her back and shoulders. Crickets and grasshoppers leaped before each footfall, while their friends and relatives created a din in the nearby shrubbery. Overhead hawks and eagles wheeled on warm air currents, pestered by darting smaller birds in their wake. Everywhere life seemed intent on frenetic activity as though aware the cold winds of winter were only weeks away.

Jake caught up just as she ducked through the mill's low doorway. "You beat me, Rachel. You're a fast walker. Here, I picked these for you early this morning." He produced a huge bunch of flowers from behind his back. "I wanted to give you them before they wilted."

Rachel stared at the bouquet as though unfamiliar with mums, asters, roses, and Queen Anne's lace. "I don't know what to say, Jake. This was so…unnecessary."

"Since when do gifts have to be necessary?" He stared at the outstretched bouquet. "What's wrong? Don't you like flowers? Are you allergic or something?"

Setting down their lunch, she accepted the bouquet. "No, I'm not allergic." Rachel walked to the ancient wall that separated them from the cascading river far below. Ivy climbed the stones, covering the mossy wall with greenery. "It's just that with my people, those who work together don't give each other presents." She let a few moments pass so that her meaning was clear. "That's only for courting couples."

Jake set out chicken and potato salad in between them on the wall, and then he handed her a cloth napkin for her lap. "That's pretty much how it is with English people too." He focused on the salad he was spooning onto their plates. "That's why I did it. I thought maybe we could go out to dinner or to the movies sometime." He glanced up but then looked away quickly.

"That would not be a good idea." She took a bite of the chicken leg for something to do.

Jake held his piece aloft, inches from his mouth. "Why not? I assume you're old enough to date. I'm twenty-three—that's plenty old enough."

The plaintiveness in his voice broke her heart. "I'm twenty, well into the courting years. And I like you just fine. That's not the problem." She gulped down some iced tea.

"Then what is it? Do you have a boyfriend back home?"

"I have no…boyfriend back home." Two blackbirds took flight far overhead, drawing her attention. "You know I'm Amish. We talked about that the day we met." She ate some potato salad, suddenly eager for the picnic to be over.

"What difference does that make? Amish folks are Christians, same as my family. And I don't care what kind of clothes you wear when you're not working. I like you, Rachel. So why can't we go out a few times to see if you could like me?"

She dropped the chicken onto her plate. "I like you just fine, Jake, but I won't court anyone who isn't Amish or at least Mennonite. I'll only date my own kind."

When the birds exited through a high open window, not a sound could be heard in the old mill. "All right," he said after a few uncomfortable moments. "But there's no reason we can't be friends." He resumed eating his lunch.

"No reason at all. But please, no more flowers or private picnics for two. We don't want folks getting the wrong idea."

"Certainly can't have that." The sarcasm shading his words changed the atmosphere inside the mill.

Rachel spent a most uncomfortable ten minutes eating everything on her plate, as she'd been taught, while neither of them said another word until they were halfway back to the office.

❧

"Would you like me to put those in a coffee can of water?" Jake pointed at the flowers once they reached the house. "That way they won't wilt before it's time to go home."

"That's a good idea. Thank you. I was wondering what to do with them for the rest of the day. I have another tour at two."

"They'll be on the back porch. Don't bother returning the coffee can. We have lots of them." He pulled the bouquet from her hands.

The sound of a diesel engine caught her attention. "Goodness, a bus is already at the drop-off. If that's my tour, they're a full hour early. What should I do?" She peered up at him.

Jake shielded his eyes to read the inscription on the side. "Nope. That group is for me." As they talked, occupants of the bus began to clamber down the steps. They wore dark glasses and held onto a long knotted rope as they disembarked.

"Are those children blind?" asked Rachel in a soft voice. "What's the rope for?"

"The rope keeps them together so no one wanders off. Every Friday I give free riding lessons to the local school for the blind. Most of them have developed acute senses of hearing, smell, and touch so they can learn to control a horse using sounds and their knees and thighs." He looked down at her with a small smile. "If you'll excuse me, Rachel, I need to put these in water and greet my group."

But Rachel didn't head toward the office as he expected. Instead she trailed after him. "Some of those kids don't look older than seven or eight. Aren't they afraid to mount so large a beast?" She marched up the porch steps practically on his heels.

Jake felt a pang of disappointment as he stuck the flowers into the makeshift vase. His endeavor this morning in his mom's garden hadn't generated the intended response. "They can't see how big the horses are. They won't be able to form an accurate perspective of size until they've ridden a few times and dismounted on their own. By that time, they will have figured out there's nothing to fear." He swept off his cap and ran a hand though his hair. With Rachel standing so close, his scalp was sweating.

She laughed with that wonderful, musical sound. "Of course. I wasn't thinking. How old must they be to take lessons? Have any of them had eyesight at one time and seen a horse, even in pictures? How long do their lessons take?"

Jake stared at her. At the mill she'd barely said ten words to him. After he'd given her the flowers, she clammed up as though she had instantaneous laryngitis. Now she was shooting question after question at him. "Let's see...the kids must be at least seven to participate with their parents' signed authorization. The lessons take an hour, and then we lead them around the arena to practice for another thirty minutes. After that we serve juice and cookies before sending them home." He sidestepped around her.

Rachel jogged by his side as he approached the group. "What about my other question?"

He shook his head, trying to remember. "Yeah, one little girl lost her eyesight only two years ago due to—" He stopped himself, unsure if the medical privacy act applied to horse trainers. "You'll have to excuse me, Rachel, but I need to greet Mrs. Ingraham and get to work."

She halted on the path. "Would you mind if I watched until my tour group arrives? I promise to stay out of your way."

Would he mind? Just minutes ago he had confessed his desire to date her, wearing his heart on his sleeve like a catsup stain. "Watch all you want. If you notice a child needing help, jump in. The stable liability insurance covers all our employees." He didn't look at her. He didn't want his disappointment about her decision not to date him to spoil his favorite time of the week.

Fortunately, Keeley bolted from the house at that moment. "What's the holdup, Jake? The kids are almost to the barn." She ran past him without slowing down. Keeley loved to spend time with the youngsters almost as much as he did.

"Good afternoon, Mrs. Ingraham," he greeted, once he reached the teacher's side. "I see everybody showed up today. Nobody played hooky?"

Small heads turned in the direction of his voice "Hi, Jake!" they sang out in unison.

"Howdy, pardners. Are we ready to mount up and ride off into the sunset like cowboys?"

Shouts of agreement and plenty of giggles provided his answer. "All right, let's get started. Hang on to the rope so you don't get trampled in any cattle stampedes."

More laughter—the six boys and four girls appreciated his sense of humor. "Robert, you listen for rattlesnakes and sound the alarm."

"Are there rattlers in Casey County?" asked a little girl. "My dad said we only have copperheads and cottonmouths in Kentucky."

"Don't worry about snakes, Bethany." Keeley grasped the child's hand. "We chased them back to the desert where they belong. Brady land is rattler-free."

"Keeley!" Bethany turned up her face. "I want to ride with you."

"Your wish is my command. You'll be first." Keeley buckled a helmet over the little girl's dark hair.

Jake and Mrs. Ingraham fastened helmets on every rider and then Jake lifted Bethany onto a small Morgan. Twelve Elms kept six of these gentle, unintimidating horses specifically for this purpose. Keeley climbed up behind her, wedging the child firmly between her and the saddle horn. They rode around the indoor arena a few times and then left the barn by the back door, heading up the farm lane. Nothing beat free-riding, as the kids called it. Each one would get their turn in the fresh air with the breeze blowing through their hair. In the meantime, Jake and the teacher adjusted saddles and stirrups and helped the remaining girls onto their mounts. Mrs. Ingraham climbed up on her own Haflinger, tethered the horses together, and led her group around the arena at an easy pace. The girls would gain confidence and a sense of accomplishment as they controlled their horses using knees and thighs.

The boys were Jake's domain. He lined up the six children and reviewed everything they learned last week. Then he adjusted the saddle and stirrups for each boy and let them mount full-sized trail horses. If his father wasn't busy, he would lend a hand. Today was no exception as Ken assisted two of the young equestrians.

As soon as everyone was ready, Jake swung up onto his Saddlebred gelding. "Men, we'll start in the ring today. The horses will be tied to long leads but it's up to you to control your mount. We'll practice starting and stopping, then left and right turns. Remember to press hard with your right thigh to turn left and vice versa. Remember, you control the horse. Don't let him control you. What do we say to get moving?"

"Giddyup and shake the reins." Six voices hollered in unison.

"And to slow him down?"

"Whoa. Pull easy on the reins to slow down and pull hard to stop." Several boys chanted the memorized words like a beloved catechism.

Jake grinned at his young protégés, even though they couldn't see his pleasure. "Sounds like this posse is ready to ride." He clicked his teeth and Pretty Boy took up a gentle, even pace. The boys rode around the arena to regain comfort and familiarity as he reviewed last week's lesson.

From the corner of his eye, he spotted Rachel sitting on the bottom row of bleachers. If her expression was any indicator, she enjoyed the progress his young riders were making.

At least something around Twelve Elms pleased her, even if it didn't happen to be him.

I will only date my own kind.

What did that make him—a two-headed alien from Mars? Jake

tried to force thoughts of her from his mind, but with Rachel only yards away it was impossible. This hadn't been the first time he'd been turned down for a date. He'd been refused on several occasions when he'd asked girls to school dances or a church outing. Then there had been the prom fiasco when he asked one of the cheerleaders. *Sure, Jake, as long as I haven't patched things up with Nathan Grimes. I'm still hoping the two of us get back together before prom.* But the cheerleader's thoughtless words hadn't stung as much as today's rejection over lunch. Never had he spent a more uncomfortable fifteen minutes as those in the old mill.

He couldn't relax until Rachel noticed the clock on the wall and left the arena for her tour. Then he settled into the most enjoyable two and half hours of the week.

Afterward, Jake walked his group back to their bus. Every child kept a tight hold on the rope held by Mrs. Ingraham. "Next week we'll practice mounting and dismounting and then try some balance exercises. You'll also learn how to safely approach the horse to put on a halter. Sighted or not, everyone needs to learn the basics."

"But how will we reach their heads?" asked Bethany. "I'm not tall enough."

Jake patted the child's back. "I'll let you think about that between now and next week." He shook each small hand as they climbed the bus steps for the ride back to school. On his way to the office, he passed Rachel as she finished her last tour for the day.

"Remember, Twelve Elms offers lessons in western pleasure, western showmanship, hunt seat, English riding, jumping, and barrel racing for ages seven and up." She passed out stable brochures as the tourists headed toward the parking lot. "As you can see, we have something here for everyone."

Jake clenched hard on his back molars. "Everyone but me," he muttered, letting the screen door slam behind him with a bang.

❦

Saturday morning

Rachel left the chicken farm while Sarah still slept and Isaac was busy with early morning chores. She grabbed an apple with plain bread and cheese to eat on the way because she was too excited to cook breakfast. Today would be her first mounted tour, not as instructor but as a participant. Jessie had promised to come home for the next two Saturdays to allow Rachel time to get accustomed to her new horse. She had been assigned Calamity Jane, an aging Thoroughbred mare. Her name must be some kind of English joke because the horse was as gentle and even-tempered as any Thoroughbred ever born.

Rachel absolutely loved her. In between tours on Wednesday and Friday, she groomed and exercised Jane on the lunge rope. She talked to her constantly so the mare would get used to her voice, usually telling her how beautiful she was. Before heading home yesterday, Rachel saddled up and rode Jane around the paddock. Everything came back to her despite not having ridden in several years. Some skills a dedicated horsewoman never forgot.

Because she'd driven the buggy faster than normal, she turned Isaac's gelding into the pasture and arrived early at the Brady residence.

"Hi, Rachel." Jessie stepped onto the porch. "You're here bright eyed and bushy tailed. How about some coffee?" She held open the screen door. "We have an hour before the ride."

"Sure." Rachel ran the rest of the way to the house. Slipping into the tidy kitchen, she silently prayed she wouldn't run into Jake. Not that she didn't like him, because she truly did. And not because she didn't find him attractive. She thought he was the handsomest man she ever met. But every time an Amish person courted an *Englischer* back home, the results had been disastrous. Her job at the stable was too important to jeopardize with foolish romantic nonsense.

Jessie handed her a mug laced with cream and sugar. "We have six reservations for this morning. That's a perfect number to give everyone a bit of personal attention. Don't try to take notes during the ride. If you fall off Calamity Jane, it'll reflect badly on my teaching ability." She threw her head back and laughed.

Rachel grinned, although the idea of note taking had never occurred to her.

"We'll start in the barn. Each rider saddles and tacks his or her own horse. This week and next you'll just act like a student and simply observe. I'll do all the talking. First, we'll ride into the pasture in a single file line to practice diagonals. When each rider reaches a flag in the center, the rider must head toward a different corner of the pasture on the diagonal. Horses love to follow one another and will do so like circus elephants if you let them. Mastering quick, immediate responses is paramount for intermediary riders."

Rachel nodded, sipping her coffee, but the excitement building in her veins was better than any jolt of caffeine.

"Next, we'll head to the trails. Twelve Elms has miles of groomed trails between the pastures, through the woods, and along the river. We'll ride for at least an hour in whatever direction the spirit takes us before we turn around and come back."

"What do you mean by 'groomed?'"

"Either Jake or Keeley drives around the entire property in one of our quads—up into the hills, everywhere. They'll move any long branches that fall down across the path. We don't want horses confusing them with snakes and throwing their riders. Horses don't like snakes. Jake takes along a chainsaw in case a tree blocks the way. Keeley calls on the walkie-talkie if she needs help because she can't run a saw. They'll make note of any break in the fence or a rock slide. You have no idea how much maintenance a riding stable demands, including the woodlands and pastures."

Rachel washed her mug out in the sink. "I understood everything except for what a 'quad' is."

"It's a vehicle with four big tires you ride off-road. It's easier to show you than to explain. They're so much fun. Just ask Keeley."

"Ask me what?" The youngest Brady strolled into the room.

"Goodness, you're already awake and dressed for the day?" Jessie stared at her sister. "I've never seen you up this early on a Saturday. I'd better call nine-one-one."

"Very funny." Keeley stuck her tongue out at Jessie, but she hugged Rachel around the waist. "Hi, Rachel. Is it okay if I tag along? I haven't taken a trail ride in a while."

Jessie snapped open her cell phone. "Hurry! We have an emergency here at Twelve Elms!" Her tone feigned distress.

Keeley rolled her eyes. "Don't pay any attention to her. She thinks she's funny."

Rachel patted the girl's back. "It's fine with me if you come, but I'm not the one in charge." Both turned their attention to Jessie as she snapped her phone shut.

"Anybody who tacks and saddles their own horse *and* rubs them down afterward may join us. I won't even charge you the thirty dollars, but don't even think of leaving your chores for a stable hand to do."

Keeley ran out the door while Jessie threaded her ponytail through her ball cap. "Wow, there's a first time for everything. You're a good influence on that girl."

Rachel wasn't sure if it was her influence or not, but Keeley fell in step with the instruction without the slightest complaint. The six riders paid attention during the lesson and enjoyed an absolutely perfect morning. Calamity Jane responded to Rachel's commands, allowing her to appear competent and prepared to take over in two weeks. None of their customers were beginners, but many were unfamiliar with Twelve Elms. Before heading to the hills, Jessie followed the same path taken by the farm wagon, explaining many of the facts Rachel had already memorized.

Jessie dropped back to where Rachel rode. "Because some of

our riders are new here, this will be a combination mounted tour and intermediate lesson. Saturday mornings we give customers what they want, whether it's some sort of lesson or farm tour or just a trail ride for relaxation."

"I'm not sure I could teach anything yet." Rachel said under her breath.

"Then we'll only schedule mounted tours for you and no lessons. Keeley said you're already great on the wagon. Before you know it you'll be ready to teach. But until you say the word, Jake can provide Saturday lessons while I'm at school." With a light kick of her heels, Jessie galloped to the head of the line.

Jake. There was no way to avoid him even if she wanted to. And part of her didn't want to avoid him. She had few friends in the English world—few friends in Kentucky of any type. After watching Jake's enthusiasm and patience with the blind kids, Rachel knew he could teach her a lot.

Once their group reached the midway point, Jessie ordered everyone to dismount and tie their reins to small trees in the shady glen. Then she lifted saddlebags from her horse and headed up a narrow path. "This way, everyone." The students quickly fell in step behind her.

"Where are we going?" asked Rachel of Keeley. They would follow the last paid guest in line.

"Wait till you see." Keeley's young face glowed with joy. "It'll be a surprise."

After an uphill hike of ten minutes, they reached a shimmering pool bathed in sunlight and surrounded by tall pines. At one end, the crystal clear water dropped over a ledge, cascading down rocks and outcroppings below. Everyone exclaimed over the beauty of this hidden retreat.

"We have this natural spring regularly tested," announced Jessie. "The water is pure, so feel free to fill your bottles. Then please find a seat and I'll serve lunch." Everyone plopped down in the long grass to enjoy ham-and-cheese sandwiches and pretzels. Jessie passed around tiny packets that turned their water into lemonade.

Leaning back on her elbows, Rachel studied the patch of blue sky overhead while the sun warmed her face and a cool breeze refreshed her skin. Even Jessie's packed lunch tasted like gourmet fare. Throughout the break, Rachel couldn't stop silently thanking God for bringing her to Twelve Elms. Never before in her life had she felt this happy.

SIX

And grace my fears relieved

Rachel's near euphoria lasted all the way back to the Stoll farm. Isaac offered to rub down the gelding, so she had nothing to do but stroll up the mum-lined path to the back door. When she entered the house, Sarah was folding laundry in the mudroom and humming a hymn.

"*Guder nachmittag*," Rachel greeted in *Deutsch*.

"Good afternoon to you." Sarah reached for another load of towels from the dryer. "There's a fresh pitcher of iced tea in the fridge if you're thirsty."

"Thanks." Rachel padded across the kitchen but halted halfway. Folded laundry sat in piles on the table, waiting either to be carried upstairs to drawers or to be ironed. She spotted her designated pile immediately. Two freshly washed T-shirts advertising Twelve Elms Stables—Finest Thoroughbreds in Casey County—sat atop the heap. A frisson of anxiety took hold and began to grow in her gut.

"Because my loads were light, I grabbed your clothes hamper from your closet." Sarah set down the basket of towels to stir the soup. "If I'm running the machine, I might as well fill the tub."

Rachel fingered the soft cotton of the top shirt. "You're probably wondering about these," she said, feeling ten years old.

"I figured they are part of some uniform for your job. And if you wished to tell me about them, you would have by now." Sarah didn't turn from her position at the stove.

"I'm sorry I was secretive, Sarah. I change into the shirt when I arrive at work. Otherwise, tourists would ask more questions about *me* than the horses." Rachel poured a glass of tea and took a long swallow.

Her cousin turned, wiping her hands down her apron. "You wear that T-shirt over your dress?"

"*Nein*. I own a pair of pants I bought back in Lancaster." She picked up the tote bag abandoned by the door. "Jessie Brady provided me with a pair of riding boots too. Today's tour was on horseback, which would have been difficult in a long dress and apron."

Her cousin seemed to ponder all of that while she crossed her arms. "What kind of pants—baggy old trousers or those tight jeans I see on English teenagers?"

Rachel's response proved redundant when a red face revealed her shame. "That's the way blue jeans fit."

"Uh-huh. Well, you might as well throw them into the washer. I would assume by now they could use laundering." Sarah's tone was cool and crisp as she began peeling turnips.

Rachel pulled the jeans from her bag. "I'm sorry if I disappointed you, but girls back home sometimes wear English clothes during *rumschpringe*." She slipped an arm around Sarah's waist at the sink.

"I'm not your *mamm*, Rachel. Goodness, I'm not old enough for that. But I think you should write to *grossmammi* and tell her about your uniform. *She* might have something to say. If you would fix a salad and set the table, we'll be ready for supper soon. I'm starving, aren't you?"

"Famished." Rachel dropped the jeans into the washer before scrubbing her hands and arms at the stationary tub.

"There's a social tonight for young people," Sarah called from the kitchen. "A volleyball game just down the road, not too far. Everyone will be from our conservative Mennonite district—only horses and buggies, no cars. You should feel right at home."

"Do Amish folks ever attend your get-togethers?" Rachel dried her hands on a checkered towel.

"Sometimes. It depends on how far they feel like driving their rigs." Sarah studied her curiously. "You're twenty, right? Were you courting someone back in Pennsylvania?"

"Yes, I'm twenty. But no, I hadn't starting riding home from socials with anyone."

"But you had gone to socials, right?" Sarah's left brow arched.

"Of course. I went to singings and volleyball parties and cook-outs. I had been waiting for my older sisters to marry first." Rachel carried in a basket of lettuce and tomatoes from the porch to wash and slice.

"Good to hear you're not planning to jump the fence." Sarah stirred the chopped turnips into her soup. "And now both Amy and Nora have married." She shot Rachel a grin before heading out the door to hang the last load of sheets on the line. Although Sarah owned an electric dryer, she preferred the scent of sunshine in her bed linens.

Rachel focused on making the salad. "Looks like I'm going to a social whether I want to or not," she muttered. Truth was she had been ready to start courting, but her parents' deaths had put a damper on everything. How could she smile and make polite conversation while torn up by grief? But now that two years had passed, she was as ready as she ever would be. She'd planned to fall in love someday, get married, and have a houseful of children. But that *someday* had always been far in the distant future. If Sarah had her way, she would be returned to *grossmammi* with a brand-new *ehemann* in tow. "He just better be a horse lover," she said to the tomatoes.

During supper Rachel ate a bowl of soup and another of salad, and then she walked the two miles to the volleyball party. Surprisingly, Isaac said he needed the rig tonight, even though he usually went to bed at eight thirty. Sarah insisted that Rachel take a pan of fresh-baked walnut brownies. Amish or Mennonite, Plain folk loved their desserts. As she walked up the driveway, she struggled to recall the names of people she'd already met at church. Fortunately, one of her few acquaintances spotted her the moment she arrived.

"Rachel," called Bonnie. "Come join us." She patted the long grass beside her.

"I'm glad you remembered me." Rachel handed her dessert to the hostess and strolled toward the volleyball game. As often happened when games continued for a while, the teams ended up all male while the girls found comfortable spots on the lawn to watch. Most women disdained sweating far more than men.

"Let me introduce you," said Bonnie. "This is Ruby, Rosanna, Abby, Joanna, and Mary." She aimed an index finger at one blue or green dress after another. "Everybody, this is Rachel King from Lancaster County. She's staying a spell with her cousins, the Stolls, on 738."

For the next forty minutes, Rachel found herself an object of curiosity. Once Lancaster County was mentioned, the questions began to fly. Everyone knew people who still lived there and was eager for news. Unfortunately, she didn't know many of their inquiries, and of the few she did, she possessed no current information. But the girls were so friendly that Rachel tried her best to be a good sport. Not until the volleyball landed squarely in the center of their circle did their barrage of questions pause. Unaccustomed to being the center of attention, she welcomed the interruption.

"Are you going to let the new girl come up for air?" A sandy-haired young man approached from the volleyball game. "Or will you scare her off, never to be seen again?" His lips drew up into a smile.

Five women giggled while Bonnie rolled her eyes. "We let her breathe five minutes ago, Reuben Mullet. I think you're just angling for an introduction." Bonnie tossed him the ball with more force than necessary.

"Guilty," he stated without hesitation. "I haven't seen a *friendly* face in this crowd in a very long time."

While the girls made a variety of dismissive noises, Reuben reached a hand down to Rachel. "Reuben Mullet, at your disposal."

Rachel shyly clasped his hand and allowed him to pull her to her feet. "*Danki*. I'm Rachel King."

"The only thing that should be disposed of is you, Reuben," Bonnie teased without a hint of malice of her voice. Everyone laughed, including him. Bonnie scrambled up, dragging another girl with her. "Don't worry, Rachel. He won't bite, and if he does, he's had all his shots."

Reuben tossed the ball back toward the game. "It's true. I have a piece of paper in my wallet in case you need to see it." He crossed his arms over his chest.

"That won't be necessary." To Rachel's horror, the other girls wandered off, leaving her alone with him. It was as though they followed some unwritten code that allowed males equal time to make first impressions. She felt lost without a road map.

"I saw you at church services last week," he said. "I tried everything to get your attention from across the room except stand on my head."

"Back in Pennsylvania, standing on heads during a sermon would be frowned on by the bishop."

"It is here too." Reuben pushed his hat to the back of his head. "That's why I decided against it. Plus my *daed* kept clearing his throat and jabbing me in the ribs each time I looked at you."

"I'm sorry I made your thoughts stray during church." Rachel walked in the direction the women had headed.

"Are you going to the barn for a snack? I would love to try something you brought."

She laughed, glancing at him from the corner of her eye. "Subtlety is not your strong suit, is it?"

"I believe patience and subtlety are highly overrated." His blue eyes twinkled with amusement.

"Goodness, I feel right at home." They had walked into a cavernous barn, where plates of cake, pie, and cookies covered the surface of several long tables. "Old Order Mennonites must be as fond of sweets as the Amish." They joined the line at the end.

"I'd heard that an Amish gal had infiltrated our ranks." He scratched his clean-shaven jaw. "Have you come to steal our soybean secrets?"

"Nope. I'm here to work with Thoroughbred horses."

Reuben's forehead furrowed with creases. "A woman who loves the noblest of beasts? Be still my heart. Tell me which one of these delicacies you brought." He flourished a hand over the buffet.

When Rachel pointed at the pan of walnut brownies dusted with sugar, Reuben loaded his plate with five of them, ignoring all of the other desserts. Rachel took two peanut butter cookies and a glass of lemonade before sitting down to eat.

Reuben devoured the five brownies one after another and then smacked his lips. "Those were the best I've ever tasted," he declared, brushing sugar off his shirt.

"I'll be sure to tell Sarah when I get home because *she* baked them, not me." Rachel hid her grin behind a napkin.

"I stuffed myself with those for nothing?" Mischief danced in his irises.

"I thought they were the best you ever tasted. What did you hope to achieve if I had baked them?"

He leaned against a hay bale. "You would be so flattered you would let me drive you home." His lower lip protruded like a pouting child.

"But we've only known each other for ten minutes."

"It's just a ride home, Rachel, no strings attached. And I promise not to say anything embarrassing."

She studied him over her cup. "Okay. Honestly, I'm not eager to walk another two miles. Bonnie says you're harmless, and I can probably outrun your horse anyway."

"Tonight you would be able to since I plan to take my time." Reuben blushed to a deep shade of scarlet, as though he'd been surprised by her answer.

Surprised, but definitely pleased.

⁂

Jake hadn't meant to eavesdrop on his parents that rainy Thursday night. He was exhausted from teaching students and working with Eager to Please along with his regular chores. He planned to check e-mail to see if any of his employment offers had been accepted. *Somebody* must be willing to move to Charm for a chance to train a colt with impressive bloodlines. But Mom's plaintive voice caught his attention before he reached the door to the home office. Jake stopped dead in his tracks.

"I know I agreed to go along with the family decision," said Taylor, "but as the weeks pass I'm becoming fearful about our future."

Jake could almost see his mother winding a lock of hair around her finger—a habit whenever she was stressed.

"What are you afraid of in particular?" asked Ken. From the squeak of the swivel chair, Dad was leaning back precariously.

"We just paid for Jessie's tuition and books in addition to our homeowner and business insurance for another year. We paid the health insurance for our employees, the property taxes, and the vet bills. Soon winter will be here, and if we get a cold one, heating the indoor arena for lessons and shows will cut deeply into whatever profits we might have made."

"Everything you mentioned sounds like business as usual to me," said Ken. "Nothing out of the ordinary."

"That's true. But we've never had a second mortgage before, especially not with a payment larger than our first mortgage." Her voice had dropped to a whisper, as though even mentioning so much debt might make the situation worse.

"Just send minimum payments wherever you can and we'll cut back on household expenses."

"The family still needs to eat, Ken, and so far no one has acquired a taste for oats or alfalfa."

Jake swallowed hard. He couldn't let his mom put doubts into his dad's head. Only a winning attitude would pull them through, not her defeatist outlook. He popped his head in the door. "Sorry, Mom and Dad. I heard you talking so I stopped to listen."

"To eavesdrop, you mean." Ken sounded disappointed. "You know better than that, son, especially because we keep no secrets from you."

Jake's shirt collar tightened around his throat. "I apologize, but the budget concerns me too." He looked his father in the eye. "I'm trying quite a few things to generate new clients. My ideas seem to be working, but profits won't show up overnight or even in a few weeks."

"We know that. Your mother and I are proud of the way you've stepped up the business side of Twelve Elms a thousand percent. We're getting more customers every day besides plenty of positive feedback."

Taylor perched on the arm of the upholstered chair. "Jake, we're not critical of you in the least." She smiled with effort.

"But your mom deals with the financial reality of life, like paying bills and grocery shopping. The best-laid intentions still need to pay their debts."

"That's why I wanted to go the other route with your banker." Based on his past experience, Jake tried not to sound defensive.

"What other route?" Taylor looked from Jake to her husband and back again without blinking.

"A route I already rejected." Ken glared at his son. "That's why I didn't mention it."

Taylor slid down onto the chair and crossed her legs. "Perhaps you should tell me now."

Jake leaned against the door frame, trying to calm down before explaining. "Mr. Moore presented another option for financing that involved a shorter term with a balloon payment at the end. His rate of interest was a little higher because it's a riskier investment for the bank, but the good part was that no payment would be due during the duration of the loan. We'd have no trouble paying our regular bills because it would be business as usual."

Ken growled low in his throat. "It's not quite as rosy as that." He swiveled to face his wife. "The interest rate is substantially higher. And it can't be forgiven even if we repay the loan the day after signing the contract. At the end of the term the entire principal plus balloon interest is due without the possibility of renegotiation."

Jake slumped into a chair, somewhat deflated. "These loans are written all the time in the business world."

"Yes, because the horse racing industry is full of gamblers and high rollers. You know what the preacher says about gambling."

"It's a *business* loan, Dad. We're not plunking money down at the pari-mutuel window." Jake's tone turned sarcastic despite his good intentions.

"Aren't we risking *everything* based on the outcome of one race?" Ken's voice rose too. "That sounds like a gamble to me!"

"Wait just a minute," demanded his mother. "What would happen if Eager to Please loses the race and finishes out of the money?" She leaned toward them on the edge of her chair.

"Tell her, son."

Jake cleared his throat. "The bank could take the farm because the property would be pledged as assurance."

"Not *could* take, but would take the farm. We would lose our life's work and the legacy from my grandfather, as well as the home we live in." Ken rubbed his eyelids.

"Heaven help us," she murmured with an expression of horror. "All on the outcome of a horse race?"

"We would still have options," said Jake. "We could go to a different bank for a regular loan to pay off the balloon payment."

Taylor stood abruptly. "Are you even listening to yourself, Jake? Because I am, and my head is starting to spin. This tangled ball of yarn keeps getting bigger and bigger."

"He's a great colt, Mom. We opted to give him a chance to prove himself. Nothing has changed since the family vote."

Ken held up a hand—"the raised palm of reason" as Jessie called it. "You're right. Nothing has changed. Things will stay as they are. We'll make the second mortgage payment and manage bills the best we can."

"Because I need to open the pharmacy at six *a.m.*, I'm going to bed," said Taylor. "I think I've heard enough to give me nightmares anyway."

"Okay, but remember that one of my offers for a professional trainer is bound to be accepted eventually. Then we'll have that man or woman's salary on top of everything else. It needs to be factored in. But we won't win unless somebody gets Eager to Please ready to race."

Visibly paler, Taylor shook her head and marched from the room.

Ken sighed as though housing the homeless, feeding the world's hungry, and ending all wars rested on his shoulders. "I understand. That will throw a monkey wrench into our tight budget, but let's not act rashly."

"Dad—"

"No, Jake. You're tired. I'm tired, and I need to pray about this matter. God has never failed me whenever I've turned a problem over to Him, and He won't now. Get some rest. Maybe a little praying on your part wouldn't hurt the situation." Ken shuffled from the room.

Jake sat, speechless and immobile. What could God do? Deliver a giant check to their front door like some magazine publishing outfit? A check large enough to make the Brady family problems disappear overnight? Sometimes Dad acted as though they were the Brady Bunch, that television family from the 1970s. *Everything will be all better after church on Sunday, so let's just put on a happy face.*

Jake shook off his bad temper and opened his computer. He might as well catch up on e-mail because sleep wouldn't come for a long while tonight. Scanning down the ads from tack suppliers and feed co-ops, he answered a few queries about rates and arena availability. Then his gaze landed on a name that rang cowbells in his ears—Alan Hitchcock—one of the many Lexington trainers he'd contacted by mail. With a shaky hand, he clicked on Mr. Hitchcock's message:

> *Dear Mr. Brady,*
>
> *Due to a recent change in circumstances, I might be interested in your offer to train your colt. I'm familiar and impressed with his bloodlines. I'm willing to drive to Charm to meet the horse and to see if agreement can be*

reached regarding terms of employment. Kindly reply to this
e-mail to let me know when we could arrange a mutually
convenient meeting.

Jake dug a handkerchief from his pocket because his eyes had
filled with tears. He hadn't cried in too many years to remember.
But with his life's dream moving one step closer, he couldn't seem
to stem the tide.

ॐ

Friday

Donna was filling bowls with cereal as her daughters came into
the kitchen.

"You have the day off?" asked the older of the two.

"Pretty cool. The same day as the teacher's in-service day." Ten-
year-old Kristen retrieved the gallon of milk and three glasses.

"Don't be a blooming idiot," said fourteen-year-old Amber.
"The fact we're home *is* why Mom took the day off. She doesn't
want us dyeing our hair purple or painting our rooms orange."
Amber pulled out the bowl of sliced strawberries.

"Nobody is an idiot." Donna sipped her second cup of coffee,
which she considered necessary fortification for dealing with teenagers. "Purple hair or orange walls never occurred to me. I just love
spending the day with my sweet girls."

Kristen grinned, while Amber snickered. "Yeah, but you also
probably needed a break from your office. Does that guy still have
you going door-to-door?" She drowned her cornflakes with milk.
"I'd tell him to get lost."

Donna ate her cereal dry. "That *guy* is my boss, and in the real
world a person is not permitted to tell a boss to get lost."

"He would probably find his way home anyway," offered Kristen, eating her berries first.

"That's why I refuse to have a boss. I shall work for myself, painting cityscapes in a loft in Paris or seascapes in a cottage on the Mediterranean." Amber pondered the merits of one location over the other. "Wherever my creative spirit takes me."

"You'd better plan to marry a rich man, then. France is filled with starving artists."

"You're so old-fashioned, Mom. Women don't need to marry in this day and age." Amber rolled her mascaraed eyes. "So where are we going—the mall? I need jeans and sweaters. It's starting to get cold."

"It does every year about this time," said Donna, shaking her head. "But no, we're going to the horse farm that gives tours. It's Kristen's turn to do something she likes."

The younger Cline sibling beamed.

"Fine," said Amber, "but maybe we can swing by the mall on our way home. I don't have anything to wear to Saturday's dance."

"Go naked," suggested Kristen with a bout of uproarious laughter.

"You are such a—"

"—delightful little sister." Donna finished Amber's sentence with a warning glare.

Soon the Cline women had finished breakfast and were on their way to an enjoyable autumn outing. At the horse farm, Donna spotted the pretty blonde while still fifty feet away. Surrounded by senior citizens, she was handing out papers and nodding her head energetically. "That must be the tour over there. Hurry up, girls."

Her daughters complied, but as they joined the group, a round of "thank-you's" and "we had a nice time's" indicated the tour had concluded. They waited patiently to speak with the young woman.

"Hi, we're the Clines from Russell Springs. Can we join the next tour?"

The guide's face fell. "Oh, dear, we just finished. The next one won't be until two o'clock."

"That will be too late to hit the mall," whispered Amber.

Donna ignored her firstborn. "We'll wait. Is it all right if we walk around a while?"

"Of course," said the guide, pulling her gaze from Amber. "But there's no reason to wait. How would you three like a private tour?"

"That would be super! Thanks so much," Amber answered without a second thought.

"Are you sure that won't cut into your lunch hour?" Donna shifted to stand in front of her daughter.

"I'll have time to eat before the next group arrives. I feel guilty doing nothing during downtime anyway."

"Where do we pay our money?" Amber sidled around her mother. "My little sister just loves horses and can't wait to get up close and personal."

"She's my kind of girl. I'm Rachel King. Welcome to Twelve Elms. You can follow me and pay at the end, six dollars a head."

They fell in step behind her with Kristen chattering like a magpie. Autumn leaves swirled along the path, while the sun still provided plenty of warmth. Donna silently rejoiced over today's choice of outings.

Suddenly the guide stopped in front of a huge canopied wagon—a conveyance that could carry several dozen people. "We're riding in that?" asked Kristen. "But there are only four of us."

"Maybe we could walk the tour," offered Donna. "I, for one, could use the exercise."

"Give her time to think, Mom." Amber wasn't one to break a sweat unless absolutely necessary.

Rachel turned her head left and right for half a minute, deep in thought. "It would be ridiculous to ride around in so large a wagon when I have something smaller. Why don't you wait here and I'll be right back." She pointed at an elm and took off running. In a few minutes, she returned driving an open carriage. "Climb aboard, ladies, and we'll start our tour."

Donna climbed into the backseat with Amber, allowing their horse lover the premier spot. Kristen scrambled up without hesitation. Rachel clicked her tongue to the horse and they were off. "Isn't this an…Amish buggy?" asked Donna after a few minutes.

Rachel smiled over her shoulder. "It is conservative Mennonite, to be exact. Not that there's much difference." When she shook the reins, the horse picked up his hooves and went along at a brisk pace.

"Why would you have one?" asked Amber. "This stable isn't owned by Mennonites, is it?"

Donna slanted Amber a warning look. "Feel free to ignore my daughter's nosiness," she said.

"Absolutely. I ignore her all the time," added Kristen.

Rachel laughed. "Questions are no problem. The Bradys, who own Twelve Elms, aren't Plain, but the owners of this buggy are Mennonite. I'm staying with them while I visit from Pennsylvania. I'm Old Order Amish."

"Cool," replied Amber.

"How come you don't look Amish?" Kristen sized up their guide as though she'd missed something.

"I do when I'm not at work. It's just easier to wear your type of clothes here. Now, at our first stop you'll notice fields of alfalfa hay, oats, and barley on our left." She began her tour in earnest to the rapt attention of both Cline daughters. Kristen asked several questions Rachel seemed happy to answer. Even Amber asked a few to prove the tour had captured her imagination too.

But Donna's mind whirred a mile a minute as she sat back and enjoyed the buggy ride—her first in her life. *Our guide is Amish and lives with Mennonites? Could this be the entrée I need for access into a private, closed culture?* Once they climbed down in front of the stable office, Donna followed Rachel to pay their admission. "Thanks so much for the private ride. We enjoyed ourselves immensely."

"It was my pleasure. As you can guess, horses are my hobby. There is our gift shop and ice-cream parlor." Rachel pointed to a white cottage with red-striped awnings. "Here are brochures in case anyone is interested in boarding or riding lessons." She looked directly at Kristen.

"Thanks. I am interested." Kristen accepted the pamphlet and pressed it to her heart.

"Don't get your hopes up," Amber said to her sister. "Dad will never buy you a horse, but I'll buy you an ice-cream cone." She pulled her sibling toward the shop.

Donna remained behind on the shaded lawn. "May I speak to you about something, Miss King?" She waited until her daughters disappeared into the store. "This is a professional matter concerning my job at the county board of health. You might be able to assist me."

"Of course, if I can." Her sweet face couldn't have looked more sincere.

Donna poured out her story about polio and a potential epidemic in their community, and how she'd spent the past week of her life.

Rachel listened wide eyed and then shrugged. "If there's anything I can do to help, it would be my pleasure."

"That takes a load off my mind." Donna felt herself relax for the first time in weeks.

SEVEN

How precious did that grace appear

Saturday's second mounted tour was every bit as exciting for Rachel as the first. Jessie again took charge as promised, so Rachel was able to gain even more confidence on Calamity Jane. She'd exercised the mare twice that week after work, riding around the paddock and down the lane. Jane was smart, responsive, and not overly high-strung. Keeley declined joining the group today because the riders were experienced and uninterested in a lesson or instruction of any kind. These repeat guests were well-acquainted with the history, landmarks, and available services of Twelve Elms. The group rode hard into the hills for hours and then stopped for lunch on the shady bank of a slow-moving creek. When they returned to the barn, everyone spent more than an hour grooming their mounts and cleaning tack. Today's customers had either trailered their horses to the stable or boarded there on a monthly basis.

During her drive back to the Stoll farm, Rachel contemplated her options regarding Calamity Jane. Maybe she could offer the Bradys a fair price because she and the mare seemed of like-minded temperaments. Although she gave Sarah most of her paycheck for room and board, Rachel had inherited one quarter of the farm sale proceeds following her parents' deaths. She could write a check drawn on her Lancaster account. Or if Calamity Jane wasn't for sale, perhaps Jake knew of a suitable mare that was. Never before had she so yearned to own a horse. Not the family's buggy horse or one rented by the hour or an animal loaned by a generous employer. She wanted one that would be hers alone.

But what would happen when I return to Lancaster? Have her shipped back in a crate? Her grandmother would think her batty—Thoroughbred riding horses were unheard of in Mount Joy. Rachel parked the buggy next to the Stoll barn, unhitched the gelding, and rubbed him down, still mulling her conundrum.

"There you are, finally." Sarah marched into the stall and grabbed Rachel by the sleeve. "Come along. I'll send Isaac to tend the horse. You need to take a quick shower and get ready." She dragged Rachel from the barn like a sack of grain.

"Get ready for what? I'm exhausted."

"Nonsense. You'll perk up with a bite to eat and a cup of coffee." As though fearful Rachel might escape, Sarah didn't loosen her grip. "I made a pot of chicken stew."

"*Danki* for making supper without me, but why do I need to perk up?" She climbed the porch steps on Sarah's heels.

"Bonnie, Ruby, and Joanna will pick you up in an hour. Ruby's cousin has a car. There's a singing in the western part of Casey County, so there's a good chance Amish will come."

"Your conservative district isn't much different than mine, so it's not that big of a deal." Rachel dug her soiled English clothes from the bag.

"No, but I'll tell you what is a big deal." Sarah lowered her voice as Isaac passed them on his way out. "Reuben Mullet has been asking about you from everyone he bumps into."

"How do you know that?"

"Because Bonnie called and said so." Sarah furrowed her brow.

"*Jah,* I forgot your district has phones in their homes beside businesses." She pulled out the knob to start the washer. "I wonder why he's been asking about me."

Sarah pressed the back of her hand to Rachel's forehead. "Were you too long in the sun without your bonnet? Surely you know why a man asks about a woman."

"Oh, that." She tried to hide her smile.

"*Oh, that.* Jump into the shower and use plenty of soap. You don't exactly smell like peaches and cream at the moment. I'll have a bowl of chicken stew cooling."

Sixty minutes later a black sedan pulled up the drive and stopped by the porch. A young man yanked opened the back door. "Your carriage for the evening, Miss King." Ruby's cousin, Josh, turned out to be sweet and attentive…to Bonnie, thank goodness. He hung on every word she said and laughed at all her jokes and stories.

Rachel had time to ponder the Calamity Jane question, but all too soon they joined the throng entering their host's barn, where loud singing drowned out her thoughts. She enjoyed raising her voice in hymns of praise, along with a few contemporary songs, even though Beth insisted she sang like a bullfrog. After the singing, Rachel had little chance to meet new people, whether male or female. On the way to the snack table with Bonnie and her friends, Reuben headed her off at the turn.

"Hi, Rachel. I'm so glad you came. Quite a crowd tonight, no? I was afraid there wouldn't be anywhere to sit after the stampede went through the line, so I staked out two lawn chairs around back." He yanked on his suspenders. "Want to have a cup of hot chocolate with me?"

"I hate to just rush off from my friends," she said, turning to Bonnie for support.

"Don't be silly. You run along. I'm looking for Josh and a private place we can talk." Bonnie hurried away as though in some kind of race.

"All right then, but in your haste to leave the barn, I hope you didn't trample anybody into the dirt." Rachel focused on Reuben's crisp new haircut. Someone must have trimmed his hair right before he came.

He paled. "Certainly not! I would never knock a person down. And if I did so accidentally, I would stay to help—"

"I was teasing, Reuben. It was a joke."

He clutched at his chest. "*Jah*, of course. I'm not used to girls with a sense of humor. The women around here are droll as old *grossmammis*." He spoke in a whisper. "Come see what I saved for us."

She followed him around the barn to the grapevine-shrouded entrance to the garden and berry patch. Two folding chairs had been set up under the arch with taped scraps of paper proclaiming "Saved." A paper napkin covered an upturned bucket that held two cups of cocoa and a mounded plate of baked goods.

"Goodness, that's quite an assortment. Which small village will be joining us?"

He hesitated only a moment. "Another joke? I'm getting used to you already." He pulled out one lawn chair as though they were in a fine dining establishment.

"*Danki*." Rachel stifled a laugh. She felt a tad foolish sitting under the arch. Everyone else at the get-together chatted in large clusters, while she was alone with a stranger. She ate two brownies in short order, chewing each bite carefully while Reuben talked about his father's dairy farm, mentioning he was the eldest of three sons and the fact their farm never failed to turn a profit.

"So how was work today at Twelve Elms?" he asked upon exhausting his topic.

She set down her third dessert. "It was wonderful. Jessie Brady and I took the customers on miles of trails. We rode into the wooded hills, through the pastures, and even along a river of sorts. Jessie said some of the property doesn't even belong to the Bradys, but their neighbors don't mind trail rides as long as we remember to close the gates. They appreciate an extra pair of eyes on their fences." Rachel sipped the cooled chocolate. "We ate lunch with our feet dangling in a fast stream. Their land takes my breath away. It's so beautiful."

Reuben cocked his head to one side. "Sounds like you were gone for hours. Are there many English gals who like to ride?" He downed his drink.

"No, only two girls. The rest were men." Rachel stretched out her legs.

His smile faded. "Do you think it's wise to venture hours away from the stable in the company of strange English men?"

"It's perfectly safe. Jessie does it all summer long. Besides, most of the time we're galloping hard, not sitting around chitchatting. When we got back to the barn, my jeans were covered with dust." Rachel realized her error the moment the words left her mouth.

"*Your jeans*? You wear blue jeans like an English man?"

"*Jah*," she answered, drawing out the word. "Or like an English woman. I can't ride in this." She pinched up some fabric of her long blue skirt, not hiding her irritation.

After an uncomfortable minute, Reuben leaned back in his chair. "No, I suppose not. I suppose it's not a problem since you're still on *rumschpringe*. That will all change once you're baptized and get married." He splayed his palms across his knees. "Say, why don't I get us more hot chocolate? Something to warm us up." He left the arbor without waiting for her yea or nay.

Rachel endured a miserable rest of the evening, including an interminable buggy ride home. She had been abandoned by Bonnie, Ruby, Josh, and his car. They had assumed she would happily ride home with Reuben, but she was anything but happy as he droned on about what life would be like in the Mullet household after he married.

Blessed relief finally arrived halfway home. She fell fast asleep and, according to Reuben, snored loudly. He didn't wake her up until they reached the Stoll side door. Rachel apologized profusely for her rudeness, but she could barely contain her giggles. Once inside Sarah's cozy kitchen, she buried her face in her hands and laughed until tears streamed down her face. At least he only bored her to sleep. She wondered if there was any truth to the term "bored to death."

ॐ

Whoever imagined that so many racetracks existed in the United States?

Jake rubbed the bridge of his nose, trying to stem the headache building behind his eyes. He'd checked out a stack of horse racing periodicals from the library in Somerset hoping to learn more about the industry he wished to compete in. Good thing he was young, because the more he read the more he realized he had much to learn.

"Is this seat taken or may I sit down?"

Jake looked up to find Rachel standing behind the opposite chair at his table. She wore one of the new long-sleeved T-shirts Jessie had ordered for everyone.

"I'm alone. Sit." Jake rolled the discarded crusts from his sandwich into the plastic wrap.

Rachel pulled out the chair and opened her lunch cooler. "You're finished already? I brought enough to share." She unwrapped a sandwich on the waxed paper. "Chicken salad." She waved it before his face to tantalize. "With grapes, walnuts, and celery."

"Sounds delightful, but I already ate bologna on white bread. If only I had waited."

She took a dainty bite and set the sandwich down. "I hope we're still friends, Jake. I don't have that many." Her blue eyes looked utterly sincere.

The oxygen vanished from the break room. "Of course we are." He took an apple from his brown bag for something to look at other than her pretty face. "I don't have many friends either. All work and no play has turned Jake into a dull boy." He bit into the apple while she took another bite of her delicious-looking sandwich. He stared as though mesmerized. "Anyway, there's something I'm curious about."

Rachel dabbed her mouth with a napkin. "Ask away. I keep no secrets from folks nice enough to loan me Calamity Jane."

"Most of the Amish people around here use computers and the Internet, but you sounded unfamiliar with blogs and Facebook when I described the stable's new website."

"That's because most of the folks here are Conservative Mennonite, not Amish. Many *Englischers* see Plain clothing and assume we're all Amish. The Mennonites here have electricity in their homes, and some districts use tractors, diesel harvesters, and even drive cars and trucks. But I'm Old Order Amish from Lancaster. We have to ask permission to install a phone line for a business, and most of our electricity is produced by diesel generators, so we use it sparingly."

"Sorry," he murmured, ashamed of his ignorance.

"No apology necessary. Some in our district may use the Internet to conduct business, but they're not supposed to socialize or surf the…web. I almost said 'the ocean.'" She laughed with abandon.

The sound of her laughter filled him with longing he hadn't experienced since childhood. "You don't mind talking about this?"

"Not at all. It's not a deep, dark mystery." She tore open a bag of chips, popped one in her mouth, and passed the bag to him.

He took some despite being already full. "Jessie sent me an e-mail from Lexington. She said you did great last Saturday. Do you feel ready for this week's mounted tour?"

"As much as I ever will be, providing Keeley comes along and I have my walkie-talkie. I can always press the red button and scream for help."

"You won't need it, but I'll jump on a white horse and ride to your rescue if need be." Jake sipped his soda to keep from staring at her. Why was he talking as though they were in junior high?

"Last Saturday night I went to an Amish social. I accidentally let it slip that I wear English clothes at work. I might have shocked some of my new friends." She nibbled another chip.

"Will working here cause problems for you?"

"I don't think so. I haven't officially joined the church, so I'm able to do as I please, within reason of course. If a man doesn't like it, he's free to ask out someone else." She poured chip crumbs into her mouth as Keeley had taught her and then cleaned up her mess.

Her activity gave him a chance to tamp down his jealousy. *A man?* He'd assumed the shocked friends had been women. But she'd said she planned to date Amish, so he'd better start acting like a friend instead of a jerk. "Do you think you might…court this guy?"

Rachel dropped her trash in the can. "I thought so at first, but that looks unlikely now. Hey, when do I see this Eager to Please? Jessie can't stop talking about him."

Jake waited until she had shoved her cooler bag in her locker and they had walked into the hallway. He didn't wish to set a time in front of other employees. "How about today after your last tour?"

"Perfect. I'm staying to exercise Calamity Jane anyway."

"When you're finished with her, come to the lunge ring in the main barn. You are in for a rare treat. I don't show this champion bloodline colt to just anybody." He slipped on his Twelve Elms cap.

"Will there be an admission charge?" She offered a crooked grin—the one that never failed to stop his heart.

"Not this time. Maybe when he's a two-year-old."

"Good, because I'm saving money for a matter we need to discuss later. See you after work." Rachel smiled again before skipping out the door.

Her blond ponytail matched the gentle sway of her hips until she disappeared around the corner. Jake knew where she was heading. She always tied the draft horses on long leads in the shade so they could nibble grass in between tours. She always considered the comfort or feelings of both man and beast in everything she did—except for him. His heart broke each time they were together.

Because no matter what he said or did, she would never be his.

❧

"Miss King, I'd like you to meet Eager to Please. He was sired by Man of His Word, and his dam is Pretty in Pink." Jake held the yearling's halter, drawing him near the fence where Rachel stood. "Young man, be on your best behavior. Miss King is a valued employee."

She stared, motionless. "I doubt he knows any other way to behave. He's gorgeous, Jake." She stretched out a hand to scratch the white star between his eyes.

"You would be surprised what bad habits he's already picked up from the local ruffians, and we have no time for charm school."

"He should need very little with those bloodlines." She ran a palm down the side of his face. "I was about to say something stupid like 'he's so thin' or 'why are his legs so long,' but then I caught myself. I'm used to seeing Standardbred buggy horses and Belgians or Percherons." She withdrew her hand slowly.

"Allowing a yearling to put on too much weight would be a big mistake. His proportions are just about perfect. At least, in my estimation. We've hired a professional trainer who'll know more than me. We'll see what he has to say."

Her brows knitted together. "But aren't you a trainer?" She lifted one boot heel to the bottom rail.

"Yes, but mainly for show horses. We had Pretty in Pink bred to a champion because we have high hopes for a Kentucky Derby winner." He felt his face flush. "I hope that doesn't sound arrogant, but this colt truly has potential."

"Not arrogant at all. Racing is what Thoroughbreds have been bred for." She pulled off her ball cap and wound her long ponytail into a coil. Without using a mirror, she pinned her hair into a bun and shoved her hat into her pocket. "I'm glad you're not planning to use him for children's pony rides."

Jake stared while she fiddled with her hair. He had to shake his head to get his mind back on the conversation. "I assure you, we'll never have pony rides at Twelve Elms."

"Never say never. Can I watch you work him on the lunge line?"

He hated to leave the fence, but he would do just about anything she asked. Jake led Eager to Please to the center of the ring and released the rope slowly. With a click of his tongue, the colt broke into a brisk trot. He allowed six or seven turns around the ring and then slowed him to a walk. "Because I worked him earlier, I don't want to tire him out." Jake pulled out his cell phone to hit a speed-dial button.

"Of course not. Thanks for the display."

"Bob, could you come rub down the colt?" he asked once the other end picked up. "We're finished for the day."

Jake struggled with small talk until the groom led the horse away. Then he tapped Rachel on her arm. "What were you planning to ask me? You mentioned something about saving money."

She laughed with the magical sound that would haunt him for

the rest of the day. "I would like to buy Calamity Jane from your family. I love that mare and hope you'll sell her. Name your price." She arched up on tiptoes so they were almost the same height.

"If that's what you want, sure. But you know you could use her indefinitely."

"Thanks, but I would love to own Jane. I'm so fond of her." Rachel seemed to be holding her breath.

"I'll talk to Dad about a price tonight, but in the meantime, consider her yours."

"Thanks, Jake. You've made my day. No, my month or maybe my year! See you on Friday." Rachel turned and strolled from the barn as though walking on air.

Watching her go, Jake was already counting the hours until then. Little did she know he would give her any horse in the barn. He would give her his right arm. All she had to do was ask.

～

Rachel made sure she beat Sarah downstairs to start breakfast the next morning. She hadn't been keeping up with her share around the farm, so today she aimed to make amends. In short order she cracked eight eggs into a bowl, added milk, and then chopped mushrooms for an omelet. While heating the skillet, she grated some cheddar to melt on top, started a pot of coffee, and laid strips of bacon on the broiler pan. By the time Sarah came down and Isaac finished his early chores, the scent of sizzling bacon whetted everyone's appetite.

"You're an early bird today. Did one of my roosters wake you?" Sarah filled three mugs with coffee.

"*Nein*. I set my alarm. I plan to do the lion's share of chores today."

"*Gut*, because we have our work cut out for us in the poultry barns. I thought we could wash and disinfect the walls and floors."

"Splendid," said Rachel. "Splendid" had been Keeley's word of the week. However, Rachel imbued the word with little enthusiasm. She had hoped Sarah would confine their tasks to inside the house. Couldn't they wash living room walls or wax the kitchen floor or perhaps whip up a quilt for the next bride-to-be? But no. Sarah loved her chickens and spent most of her time with them. She squeezed housework into small increments while cooking meals or baking bread.

Rachel dawdled eating breakfast until guilt got the better of her. "Should I wash these dishes? I could meet you in the barn when I finish."

"No, no," said Sarah, shrugging into her coat. "Let's leave them in the sink to soak and catch them at lunch. I'm eager to gather eggs and show you the new chicks before we get dirty." She slipped on a long rubber apron and her oldest full bonnet.

Rachel hated wearing rubber aprons because they were hot even on cool days. But because she disliked ruining her clothes even more, she tied hers on loosely and stepped into matching knee-high boots. "I'm ready," she said, forcing a smile.

As they stepped into the warm October sun and fresh breeze, Rachel thought about her recent blessings and soon forgot their chores. She worked alongside Sarah for a long while with little conversation other than sweet-talking the hens. Once she started telling the birds how pretty they looked, she received no more vicious pecks on her ankles. After an hour, their silence came to an abrupt halt.

"I noticed that Reuben Mullet brought you home in his courting buggy last Saturday." Sarah couldn't have stretched her grin any wider.

"*Jah*, he did." Rachel continued mopping the floor with bleach, trying not to breathe.

"Quite a long way to go in a buggy. He probably didn't get home until late. I bet he was sleepwalking through his chores the next day. " Sarah sounded amused with the idea of a sleep-deprived young man milking cows.

"I hope he didn't fall asleep and end up in Tennessee." Rachel dunked the mop in the bucket and ran it through the wringer.

"That's a good one." Sarah clapped her on the back with a gloved hand. "He must have a soft spot for you to come all this distance." She wriggled her eyebrows up and down.

"Sarah Stoll, you are no more subtle than he is."

"Subtlety is for *Englischers*. I'm eager for news. You know Reuben's future looks bright. His *daed* owns a profitable dairy operation, and he's the eldest son."

"So I heard, many times. His farm is all he talks about—cows, cows, and cows." Rachel tried to scratch her nose without getting chemicals on her skin.

"What else would a dairy farmer talk about? I'm sure you'll find more in common as time goes on. And he's probably nervous around you."

Rachel shrugged. "He's very nice, but I'm afraid our long-term prospects aren't good."

"What do you mean?" Sarah stopped scrubbing.

"I listened to him politely while we were having snacks and during the first half of the ride home. But he was repeating his stories and I was tired from work. And he bundled me up like a bug in a rug. I was too warm and comfy, if you know what I mean."

"I don't. What happened?" She looked confused.

"I fell asleep. I guess he talked right up until I began to snore. He said I snored louder than his *daed* and *mamm* put together."

Sarah's eyes grew very round. "Didn't he wake you?"

"Not until we got back here. I might have snored for miles. Most likely he won't ask to take me home anytime soon."

"There are plenty more fish in the sea. Or, in Reuben's case, cows lined up for the milk stiles." Sarah winked good-naturedly. "Too bad, though. That young man does have good prospects."

Conversation lulled until lunchtime. Then Rachel volunteered some cheerier news over bowls of thick corn chowder and buttermilk biscuits. "Jessie Brady told Jake that my riding was top-notch. He's confident I'll do fine on Saturday's mounted tour."

"*Gut* to hear. Better than falling off and breaking your neck."

"And Jake showed me their prized colt, Eager to Please."

"*Eager to Please*? That's a dumb name. I like Sparky or Blackie or Sam—something simple."

"They bred their best mare with a fancy sire to increase their chances of a fast horse. They plan to race him in the Kentucky Derby when he's older."

Sarah snorted. "The Derby—rich folks wearing fancy dresses and big hats. I can't really see the point to horse racing. Going round in circles and not getting anyplace at all." She made a circular motion with her index finger. "Some people shell out an enormous amount of money for those racehorses."

Rachel didn't know what to say. The last thing she wanted was to become argumentative. "I spoke to Jake about buying Calamity Jane. She's the mare I always ride. Jake said he would talk to Mr. Brady, but he doesn't think there'll be a problem."

Sarah dropped her spoon into her bowl. "Whatever for? I thought you could ride one of their horses anytime you wished. After all, it's part of your job."

"That's true, but I've grown fond of that mare. Like I told Jake, I've always wanted my own horse."

Angling an impatient glance, Sarah resumed eating. "That makes no sense, Rachel. Then you would have to buy feed and pay board or bring it here tied to the back of the buggy. Leave things as they are. You're not thinking straight."

Rachel sopped up the last of her soup with a biscuit. "Jake said the horse can stay there at no charge as part of my benefits package. Then, when I return to Pennsylvania, I can have her trailered home." She held her breath, anticipating a flurry of arguments against buying a horse. But Sarah selected a different topic altogether.

"Jake, Jake, Jake. Do you know how many times you mentioned his name in the last ten minutes?"

"I have no idea." She carried her bowl to the sink.

"Six. You're as bad as Reuben talking about cows. Who is this Jake?"

Rachel tried not to laugh. "He's the son of the owner and one of my bosses."

"Uh-huh."

She didn't like the sound of Sarah's "uh-huh." Very much like *mamm*'s when she'd been displeased. "He's a nice man and he is my friend."

"*Ach*, you're too young to know better. Men don't make good friends, Rachel. That's what women are for."

"They do if they work together."

Sarah peered at her. "It makes little difference. Men soon start thinking something different. It's just how they were made. They say 'friends' but then change their mind."

With a blush Rachel remembered the uncomfortable scene in the old mill. "I already made it crystal clear that I will only date Amish men."

"You did?" Sarah's lips thinned.

"Yes. I wanted to prevent any misunderstandings down the road."

"*Gut*, but don't be surprised if you need to repeat that more than once to this...Jake."

Rachel nodded, unable to say more. Funny how she'd been thinking exactly that on her way home from work.

EIGHT

The hour I first believed

Monday morning

Donna consulted her map for the third time since leaving the house that morning. Again, her GPS refused to cooperate in this part of Casey County. Technology wasn't infallible, but at least it helped. On her drive from Russell Springs she passed several buggies that seemed to be getting nowhere fast. She waved at the passengers, and everyone waved back, friendly-like. She wondered if any were the same Amish or Mennonite residents she had visited.

Perhaps with two members of the Plain community, she would have more success. Sarah Stoll agreed to accompany Rachel King when they visited the district's bishop. "Rachel is only a visitor here and has no say-so," Sarah had explained when she spoke to Donna last Saturday, but she also made no promises. "You can state your case to the bishop and see what happens. I can only assure you that he will listen." Those had been her parting words. Yet it should be enough once Donna explained the dire prognosis of those afflicted with the virus. That...and the little trump card she had tucked up her sleeve.

Because Rachel worked on Friday and Saturdays, and Sunday afternoon was "out of the question," today was the first day both had been available. When Donna finally found Stolls' Free-to-Roam Chicken Farm, home of organic eggs and cage-free hens, she parked near the house and hurried up the walk. A load of solid-colored laundry was already flapping on the clothesline, proving no grass grew under Sarah's feet. She answered the door after Donna's first knock.

"Hello, Mrs. Stoll?" Donna offered her friendliest smile.

"You must be Mrs. Cline," said a small, thirty-something woman. She opened the screen door but didn't invite her in.

"I'm pleased to meet you and very grateful for your help."

Sarah locked gazes with her. "I don't know how much help I'll be, but I'm pleased to meet you anyway. Rachel," she hollered over her shoulder. "Let's go. I have more wash this afternoon, plus my hens to care for."

"Good morning, Mrs. Cline." Rachel materialized behind Sarah in the doorway. "I'm ready to go." The younger woman wore a soft blue dress, black apron, and white cap. Her ribbons fluttered loosely in the breeze. She was breathtakingly pretty with clear skin, large, luminous blue eyes, and a stunning smile.

"Nice to see you again, but please call me Donna. My daughters are still talking about the special tour you gave us. We had such an enjoyable afternoon. Kristen will keep begging her dad for a horse until she goes to college, even though we live on a postage-stamp-sized lot."

Sarah stepped onto the porch. "Then it's a bad idea." She pulled the door closed behind Rachel. "Your husband should hold his ground. If you don't have your own pasture and fields to grow hay and alfalfa, then a horse is nothing but a money pit." She headed toward the car at a brisk pace, while Rachel stayed at Donna's side.

"They do tend to get into a girl's blood," she whispered. "I understand how Kristen feels."

Sarah climbed into the backseat. "Rachel, you sit up front," she ordered. "You have more jawboning to do than me."

Once they reached the county road, Donna glanced into the rearview mirror and then at Rachel. "We'll make one stop before we drive to the home of your bishop. There's someone I think both of you should meet."

Rachel looked eager, but Sarah leaned over the seat. "Who's that? I hadn't planned to gad about all over the county. When you run a chicken farm, you don't get any paid vacation days."

"Truly, I understand," Donna said. "But the distance isn't far, and I think this visit will help you understand how important immunizations are, especially the polio vaccine."

Sarah shrugged and settled back to watch the scenery. Rachel asked question after question about Kristen and Amber, unconcerned about the destination of their side trip. A few minutes later they pulled into the yard of a modest farm on the other side of Charm. The house needed a coat of paint, but otherwise everything looked neat and tidy. Crimson and gold mums still bloomed in the flower beds, awaiting the first heavy frost that was soon to come.

"Who lives here? Are they Amish or Mennonite?" Rachel pointed to a man harvesting corn for silage in the distance. He and his team were small dots against a faraway hill.

"They are an elderly couple who lease their land to Old Order members like you. They have lived here for years. The husband has retired from farming." Donna drew in a deep breath. "I spoke with the woman on the phone. She agreed to talk to you ladies today, although she doesn't spend much time thinking about polio anymore." Turning off the ignition, Donna looked from one to the other.

"What is this about?" Sarah leaned forward over the seat.

"This woman contracted polio as a child, before the vaccines became readily available. She has spent her entire life in a wheelchair, never regaining use of her legs. She eventually married and has enjoyed a good life, so she doesn't want our pity or anyone else's. I explained what the board of health is trying to accomplish in the Plain community. She said we could visit, but we can't stay long."

Rachel and Sarah exchanged a glance and climbed out of the car.

A long visit proved unnecessary. The elderly woman with a deeply lined face answered the door and then invited them into her living room. She was working on a huge jigsaw puzzle. She was very frail, while her disability made her appear even frailer. "You've come to see what polio looks like?" she said with little preamble. Rachel and Sarah exchanged a glance and nodded their heads.

The women threw back the crocheted afghan covering her legs. She pulled up her print housedress to above her knees. Her legs were bent and misshapen, thin as robin legs. "I can't lift them. I feel nothing in my feet. Poor circulation will eventually cause me to lose my legs at some point. I can't remember ever walking or running or playing as a normal child." Her voice was the only strong part of her body. "I've been confined to this chair my whole life. Now I need help getting in and out of bed, washing, and even eating. A physical therapist comes three times a week to exercise my arms, but they weaken just the same. I must try to keep whatever muscle I have from wasting away." She was almost as pale as skim milk. "My husband cooks my favorite foods, but lately even my appetite has abandoned me." She threw the afghan over her legs.

"We shall pray for you," said Sarah, visibly shaken.

"Thank you. I'm a praying woman myself." The woman opened her palms as though in supplication, her eyes deep-set and hollow. "But if you can prevent this from happening to others, then you should do so."

The woman seemed to affect Rachel deeply. She began to cry.

"No," the woman said kindly. "Don't cry for me. I'm in God's hands and there's no better place to be." She held out a hand to Rachel.

Rachel wiped her face, took the woman's hand, and hugged her gently around the neck. "We'll try our best."

Sarah murmured a prayer in *Deutsch* that needed no interpretation.

A few moments later Donna thanked the woman and then herded Rachel and Sarah from the room and out of the house. Rachel seemed reluctant to leave, but the woman had done her part. They had all seen firsthand what the disease could do.

No one spoke until they had climbed into the car and were almost back on the highway. Then Sarah said in a scratchy voice, "I'll help you, Donna. I'll do my best to convince the bishop." Her attitude had softened considerably.

"Thank you, Sarah. I would much appreciate that."

Rachel stared out the window, her chatter about horses and English teenagers gone.

Donna drove the short distance to the bishop's farm. "Does your bishop know we're coming today?"

"Yes. His wife said he's always home. But if he's not, we can sit and wait on the porch." Sarah kneaded her handkerchief into a ball.

Donna wondered if she should have left a note for Amber to brown the ground meat for tonight's chili. She pictured three women rocking on the porch until nightfall. But they waited no more than fifteen minutes after their arrival. A stooped, white-haired man emerged from the barn and limped toward the house.

As he approached, Donna thought she would have no problem convincing a simple farmer of the seriousness of the matter, easily enlisting his cooperation. As he struggled up the steps, she noticed that hay still clung to his pant legs and a ladybug was stuck to his long beard. It was easy to underestimate the unfashionable elderly.

"Good day, Sarah, Rachel," he said. "You are the social worker, Mrs. Cline? I'm James Mast. I hope you haven't been waiting long."

"Not at all. How do you do, Reverend Mast?"

"James will do. I've never set foot in a theological seminary." His smile turned his eyes into a web of wrinkles. "How can I help you?"

Donna opened her mouth but the squeaky screen door drew her attention. Mrs. Mast carried out a tray holding a pitcher of lemonade and four glasses. Four, not five—and then she disappeared back into the house. Bishop Mast poured with a shaky hand and distributed the glasses. After taking a hearty swallow, Donna concisely explained her work and the reason for her visit. Despite the brevity of her information, she left no *i*'s undotted and no *t*'s uncrossed.

James listened attentively, alternating between sipping his drink and stroking his long white beard. The ladybug flew off. When Donna concluded, he cleared his throat. "I have read a bit about the immunization program required by American public schools. True, it has almost eradicated several childhood diseases. And I have read that some of those diseases—whooping cough, measles, chicken pox—are beginning to make a comeback on college campuses."

"Exactly, sir. So if—"

He held up an index finger, silencing her. "I also have read the ingredients contained in some of those vaccines—aluminum, ammonium, formaldehyde, which are toxic chemicals—are being injected into young bodies. Did you know that at one time mercury could be found in vaccines?" He shook his head. "This is a complex question with convincing medical evidence on both sides. I spoke with a parent in this district who has nine children. The parents had the eldest five vaccinated according to the pediatrician's recommendation. The younger four were not and yet have never been sick, other than a minor cold. The older five always seem to be catching ear infections, tonsillitis, strep throat, and whatnot. The mother thinks those vaccines lowered her children's immune systems. But then again, if no one vaccinates, polio and other diseases will rebound. I am a simple farmer and a man of God. I cannot help you, Mrs. Cline. I won't order my district to pursue this when medical evidence seems split down the middle. I will leave this matter up to the parents and to God." He struggled to his feet. The meeting was over. "Would you ladies care to join my family for dinner? Don't worry, my *fraa* always cooks plenty." He patted a rounded stomach.

Sarah stood too. "No, Bishop Mast. We must tend to our own families."

Donna was speechless. Her facts and figures had abandoned her. She hadn't been prepared for someone who had read up on the topic. *Mercury in vaccines?* Mercury had been in many patent medicines, arsenic too. Often old-time drugs killed as many patients as they cured. "Thank you taking time for me, sir. If you have any questions, here is my phone number. I would be happy to discuss this further."

Intimidated by a gentle man with an eighth-grade education, she left her card on the table on her way down the steps.

❧

Jake stepped onto the porch with his third cup of coffee. He peered up at gray clouds with scattered patches of blue. The October wind cut through his flannel shirt, but at least the rain had stopped.

130   Mary Ellis

"Well, weatherman, do you think the rain has quit for the day?" Rachel called from underneath the overhang of the gift shop.

He hadn't noticed her, but as she approached the house, his chest tightened and his neck began to sweat. "I believe it's done. We should hit a balmy sixty degrees by noon."

Rachel skipped up the steps and shook like a puppy. Rain had dampened her hat brim and clung to her eyelashes, yet she still managed to look like a beauty queen—minus the heavy makeup. "You call sixty balmy? I call it barely tolerable." She pulled up the collar of her navy blue jacket. "I'm afraid I don't deserve my hourly pay this morning. My scheduled tour never showed up. The rain must have scared them off. I hope my afternoon group comes. I'll leave a note for your dad for when he does this week's payroll."

Jake leaned against the post. "You're on the time clock from when you arrive until the time you change back into your Amish clothes. That's the agreement you made with Jessie when she hired you." Briefly he feared she might quit or cut back on her hours. It was hard enough surviving from Saturday night until Wednesday morning without seeing her.

Rachel pursed her lips. "I can't accept pay for standing around and twiddling my thumbs. Goodness, I've already been nibbling from my lunch bag out of sheer boredom."

Jake consulted the sky once more. "It's down to a mist. Why don't you come along and help me? That way you'll earn your salary. Wait a moment until I get my jacket and Jessie's slicker off the hook. Keep in mind, I guarantee you'll get muddy."

"Count me in, no matter what the chore. I've been muddy before. Once I fell facedown in a spring pasture. I'd been helping my *daed* get his plow unstuck and suddenly the horse pulled it free." She grinned at the memory. "*Splat*, in between the rows."

"You were probably adorable even when covered in mud."

"Definitely not. Need I remind you what Plain folks fertilize with instead of chemicals? I ran straight for the house to take a shower. My father laughed for days about that."

Jake tried to form a mental picture of the King family—a family that was no more. "I can only promise cleaner mud than that spring field." He hurried into the house for extra gloves and their coats.

"What will we be doing?" she asked on their way to the equipment shed. "I should have found out before getting reoutfitted."

"We'll ride the quads into the hills to remove downed trees or branches that block the bridle trail. We'll check the fence lines too."

"I don't know how to drive a quad, but at least I know what they are now. I spotted them inside one of your barns."

He slid back the door. "Keeley's is an automatic." He pointed at the smallest of four. "You won't have to shift gears, only use the gas and brake pedals." He pointed out the controls one by one. "It's hard to topple them over, but you'll wear this just in case." He placed a helmet over her head and tightened the strap under her chin. Touching her face produced an electric sensation, the memory of which would linger for hours.

Rachel climbed astride without hesitation and turned the key. "If only my sisters could see me now. Amy and Nora would be shocked."

Jake gave Rachel a short lesson, and made her drive around the yard in circles, turning left and right and then braking to a stop.

"I think you're ready. I'll lead and you follow me. Honk your horn to get my attention."

She honked it twice for good measure and they were off. The sun shone brightly over the harvested fields, but standing water remained on their trail. They splashed through puddles with abandon, heedless of how muddy they became. For several hours they moved brush, sawed and stacked deadfall, and rode the fence line looking for breaks in the barrier to freedom.

Tired, yet energized at the same time, Jake raised a gloved hand and they rolled to a stop on an old logging road. "Let's take a break." He lifted off her helmet, receiving another jolt of current from touching her skin.

"I'm not sure I can walk." Rachel staggered over to a boulder and plopped down. "But that was fun. And look at the view of Twelve Elms from this high ground." She shielded her eyes to gaze over miles of scenery. "God certainly has blessed the Brady family."

"Why would you say that?" He plopped onto a fallen log a few feet away.

"Are you joking? Your family lives on this wonderful farm, surrounded by good crops, lush pastures, *and* Thoroughbred horses. You have your parents and siblings, plus a job you love. I would say those are all blessings."

"I would say all of that came from hard work—ours and our ancestors."

"Maybe so, but lots of people work hard their entire lives and don't come close to this." She gestured toward the land spanning before them.

"So you want to give God the credit? Now you sound like my parents. Dad is always thanking God left and right."

"Who else? Sickness, death, and financial problems can happen without warning, taking away everything we hold dear. Perhaps it's because of your father's gratitude that grace has been showered on Twelve Elms."

"I didn't think you were so religious."

She laughed. "I'm Amish, Jake. God is at the center of our lives, or at least He's supposed to be."

"Then why haven't you been baptized and joined the church yet?"

"I will, most likely. I need to work out some things first, but it's not because of a lack of faith." Most of her effervescence faded. "I believe in a just, loving God with my whole heart."

For some reason the statement irritated him. "A just, loving God would allow your parents to die in a house fire? Jessie told me about them. And this stable? Thanks to me, we're mortgaged up to our eyeballs. If this new trainer doesn't work miracles with Eager to Please, we can kiss this place goodbye."

"Only God can work miracles, not some horse trainer." She stood. "It sounds like you've gone out on a long limb. That's not God's doing; that's yours. Often people don't consult Him in prayer, but they still want to blame Him when things go wrong." She looked him in the eye. "I've known sorrow since my parents died. I'll never understand why they were called home so soon, but it's not my place to know. I'm to trust and obey. Aren't you a Christian like your parents, Jake?"

The question caught him off guard, a place he didn't like to be. "Sure, I'm Christian. I go to the Baptist church in Charm."

She replaced her helmet. "I'm just curious because you don't sound like one."

They locked gazes for several moments. He almost said something smart-alecky—words he would have regretted, but instead he hooked a thumb toward the quads. "I'd better get you back. You'll need to eat lunch and take a shower before your afternoon tour arrives."

"Goodness, I nearly forgot about them." She jumped on her vehicle, turned the key, and started down the trail.

Jake followed after her, a confused, disoriented feeling settling deep in his gut.

❦

When Rachel entered Sarah's kitchen late that Saturday afternoon, she was exhausted. She had given two back-to-back mounted tours that day with only a half hour in between. She'd looked for Jake but hadn't found him. A groom in the break room said Jake had driven to Lexington with his father. She had looked for him yesterday to no avail. All four scheduled tour groups had shown up with the perfect autumn weather. During her lunch break, Jake had been busy with therapy lessons for the blind children and was nowhere in sight at day's end. She had no idea if his dad had set a price for Calamity Jane or even if the horse was for sale. Now she had to wait three more days on pins and needles.

"*Guder nachmittag,*" she greeted, slumping into a chair at the kitchen table. She dropped her tote bag on the floor.

"You look like you could use this." Sarah placed a mug of coffee before her. "Plenty of milk and two sugars."

"*Danki.*" Rachel took a grateful sip. "I earned my pay today. Two long tours in the saddle. Do you need my help with supper?"

"Nope. It's already taken care of." Sarah sat down with her own mug.

"Let me guess what we're having...fried chicken?" Rachel angled her head toward the spattering skillet and the pieces already lined up on paper towels to drain.

"No, Miss Smarty, the chicken is for tomorrow to eat cold on the Sabbath. We're having ten-bean soup with ham and cornbread tonight."

"Yummy. I'll try to stay awake long enough to enjoy."

"Drink your coffee. You have a hayride and marshmallow roast this evening. Take your shower while I dish out your soup to cool."

Rachel shook her head. "Not tonight, I'm afraid. I'm too tired, Sarah. The porch swing sounds more my speed after my long day."

"You *must* show up. It's only across the street and over two farms. You can walk and then walk home when you're ready. After your rude behavior with Reuben, you don't want folks gossiping behind your back."

"You think they would? All I did was fall asleep. I didn't steal his wallet or his horse and buggy."

Sarah smirked. "They probably won't, but let's not take any chances. You're the new girl in the community. Maybe Reuben got his nose out of joint."

Rachel abstained from rolling her eyes. "I'd hate to have folks find out the truth—that I doze off during boring conversations. Perish the thought."

Sarah didn't laugh this time. "Please go, Rachel, even if you don't stay long. I think it's important."

Rachel almost asked how a hayride and marshmallow roast could possibly be crucial, but instead she downed the rest of her coffee. "I'll take a shower to perk up. I've always liked hayrides. If I fall asleep, at least hay bales are nice and soft."

Her cousin couldn't have looked happier. "I'll bring you in a second mug. Keep the water on the cool side."

During her walk to the farm, Rachel's spirits lifted. The shower, soup, and caffeine revitalized her. And she did enjoy Bonnie, Ruby, and the other girls. Between her job and chicken chores on Mondays, Tuesdays, and Thursdays, she had little time for a social life. She missed the friendly camaraderie of her sisters. Cousin Sarah was usually all business, but once Rachel spotted her pinching Isaac's backside when Sarah thought they were alone.

"Hi, Rachel! I'm so glad Sarah made you come." Bonnie ran down the driveway to meet her.

"I'm my own woman. I came because I wanted to." Rachel linked her arm though Bonnie's. "But I have nothing to contribute to the dessert table."

Bonnie clucked her tongue. "Shameful, but I'll keep your secret. There is usually too much food anyway. I would hate to go up a size before snagging a husband." She winked, patting her still-flat belly.

"You remind me so much of my *schwester*. Nora blurts out whatever comes to mind too."

Bonnie giggled. "We can't very well say what *doesn't* come to mind, can we? Look, they're boarding the wagon for the first hayride. Let's get in line."

"Where's Josh tonight?" Rachel whispered in her ear.

"He's on his way home from a wedding in Indiana, but he should show up later. I've missed him this past week." Bonnie made no effort to be discreet about whom she was courting.

"Things didn't turn out well with Reuben," whispered Rachel.

"So I heard. He is dull as a spoon. He didn't come tonight, maybe because *everyone* now knows how boring he really is." Bonnie stepped up into the wagon, dragging Rachel behind her.

"Sarah thought your district might gossip about my behavior."

"Puh-leaze. How backwater does she think we are? Many girls here have fought the yawn reflex with him, including me. No one will hold giving in to a natural impulse against you."

Bonnie had spoken into her ear, but Rachel felt guilty nonetheless. She truly hoped she hadn't hurt Reuben's feelings. "I fell asleep because I was overtired from work, not because of him."

"I stand corrected. Let's head to the back. I see two good seats." Bonnie pushed her down the aisle toward a spot on a bale.

Rachel squeezed next to a young man she didn't recognize from the previous social or from church. "*Mir leid*," she murmured. "My friend insisted on sitting in the back." She noticed then that Bonnie had sat next to Rosanna.

"Not a problem. If it gets cold, at least we'll be cozy." The man grinned and tipped his hat. "John Swartz. And you are?"

"Rachel King, new to the district from Lancaster."

"Ah, you're the one. I'm Amish too. I'm spending a couple months here to help my cousins with the harvest. Then we'll prepare the fields for winter."

Rachel blushed up to her hairline. She felt like a cow or hog at the livestock auction, awaiting the highest bidder. "Did Bonnie rig this up and force you to save this seat under penalty of death?" She spoke very softly.

"Nope. No death threats were necessary. I came to the hayride to see if the reports were true."

She wrinkled her nose in a pout. "What reports? The new girl in town should try one of those multihour energy drinks?"

John's lips curled up. "That's not the news I heard, but it sounds as though I missed something last week." He settled back against the hay, his heavy-lidded eyes closing in relaxation.

Rachel watched him a moment and then turned toward the scenery on her right. Deciduous trees blazed with final color. Leaves swirled through the air with every breeze. In the distance, hay had been rolled into long rows for winter feeding while corn stood sentinel-like, wrapped with twine. Farms on this road looked prosperous and tidy. After a few minutes she pivoted back to her silent bale partner. Curiosity had finally won the battle. "Okay, I must know. What was the *news* you heard?"

John hesitated and then straightened. "I heard that an outstandingly attractive woman had moved to Casey County and she lives directly across the street from me." He peeked at her from the corner of his eye.

Bonnie and Rosanna giggled on their bale. Rachel paid them no mind. "You're teasing, right?"

"I assure you I'm not. I had to see for myself." He leaned over as the wagon passed a wide-reaching tree. Limbs brushed his shoulder and dropped golden leaves over them both.

She crossed her arms, trying to ignore how close he was. Night had fallen, shrouding the world in secrecy. She held her breath until John scooted back to his position, the invasive branch cleared. "Look, there's Venus." Rachel pointed to a bright star, low in the eastern sky.

"So it is," he agreed. "Aren't you curious about my conclusion?" His breath next to her *kapp* tickled her ear.

"No, not really." Rachel folded her hands in her lap. Tree frogs struck up a ruckus from the dark woods.

"Not even a little?"

"For me to encourage you would be vain and prideful." Rachel sounded like a prim schoolmarm.

"*Ach,* I'll tell you anyway. I thought they were right." He sounded as though he'd won the classroom spelling bee.

Rachel was growing irritated. Why did he think she would be pleased with bold-faced flattery? "How has the harvest gone?" she asked, eager to change the subject. "Are you and your relatives almost finished?"

"*Jah*, we are. We'll start spreading composted manure next week. But I'm in no hurry to move home. My folks don't need me this time of year. I could stick around and get to know the pretty gal who lives across the road from my cousin Nate."

And so it went for the next interminable forty minutes. Rachel would talk or ask an agricultural question, and John would invariably change the topic back to her physical attributes. She was never more uncomfortable in her life. When the wagon pulled to a stop, she climbed over the side to escape. She practically ran toward the barn.

"Are you that hungry? I can't wait to hit the dessert table either." John clambered over the side after her.

Rachel grabbed a chocolate cupcake and a cup of cider before heading back into the cool night.

"You probably think I will ask to drive you home, but I live here." Laughing, he pointed at the ground.

She swallowed a bite of chocolate cake. "I thought nothing of the kind. I had planned to walk home alone…right now, in fact. I'm exhausted. *Gut nacht*, John."

"Don't be silly. I'll walk with you. There might be black bears prowling this time of year."

Nothing Rachel said dissuaded him. By the time she climbed the back steps, she would have *preferred* the company of a black bear. John Swartz all but followed her into the house before she was able to shut the door on him.

NINE

Through many dangers, toils and snares,
I have already come

Jake watched the sun break the horizon in the east from the kitchen window. He swallowed down another gulp of black coffee with a grimace. His third cup. All the caffeine wasn't helping his upset stomach, but after the restless night he'd spent, he needed a boost.

"You're up bright and early." His father stood in the doorway, wearing his usual faded jeans and flannel shirt, with the sleeves rolled to his elbows. "And I see you dressed for the occasion." His dad grabbed his favorite mug and headed to the coffeemaker.

Jake glanced down at his crew neck sweater, pressed jeans, and leather loafers. "It's not every day I turn the reins of Eager to Please over to a big-time horse trainer from Lexington."

"And you wanted to look the part of an owner rather than a groom or an exercise boy?" Ken pulled a box of cereal from the cupboard and a carton of cottage cheese from the fridge.

"Twelve Elms is the registered owner of Eager, not just me." Jake let the curtain drop in place and joined his father at the table.

"That may be true, son, but you're the one who had the idea to breed Man of His Word to Pretty in Pink. You practically hand raised that colt and have done well with him up until now." Ken dumped cornflakes into a bowl and passed the box across the table. "Win or lose, you should be proud of yourself, Jake. I want you to be the one this trainer works with. I'll stay in the background running the rest of Twelve Elms—the unexciting end. I have faith in you, son."

Jake swallowed down a tight knot. "Thanks for your vote of confidence, Dad."

"This Alan Hitchcock doesn't need to deal with too many bosses."

"His boss?" He snorted. "Hitchcock has probably forgotten more than I know. He'll run the show from today on. His expertise is what we're paying for."

"Just remember we're paying him, not the other way around. Make sure you agree with every decision regarding the colt. Don't let him run roughshod over you because you're young and green. Those savvy Lexington trainers can have inflated egos."

Jake studied his father's pale blue eyes. "You're worried about Hitchcock running us into the poorhouse?" His cereal remained untouched in the bowl.

Ken laughed with little mirth. "I'd be lying to deny it, but that's not the only reason. Some men won't take a twenty-three-year-old owner seriously. He might try to push you around, but you're ready for this day. You know more than you take credit for, so don't doubt yourself."

A reflection of headlights against the kitchen window drew Jake's attention. "He's here. We're about to find out where I stand in the world of horse racing." He and his father locked gazes. Then they rose to their feet and strolled out the door, casual-like—how Thoroughbred owners were supposed to act.

A tall, robust man of around forty straightened from a sleek BMW. "Alan Hitchcock," he said. "Which one of you gentlemen is Mr. Brady?"

"We both are. I'm Jake and this is my dad, Ken."

After the requisite handshakes, Hitchcock pivoted in place. "Nice spread you have here. How many acres—four, five hundred?"

"Twelve hundred, including the timbered acres in the hills."

"Good size for a small outfit. I don't recognize the name Brady in the racing business. You just buy this spread and plan to step it up a notch?" Hitchcock peered toward the barns and arena.

"No," said Jake. "This has been Brady land for four generations. I am the fourth Brady to breed horses in Charm." He shifted his weight but kept his focus steady. He chose not to mention that the previous generations bred mares primarily to drag plows through the clay or pull buggies similar to Rachel's mode of transportation.

"Is that right? I noticed your sign down by the road. Says you give wagon tours and riding lessons, plus put on rodeos and trail rides. Everything but birthday party pony rides for six-year-olds." Hitchcock softened his words with a good-natured smile.

Jake didn't flinch. "Yep, almost everything, but right now we have a colt named Eager to Please. And he's changed our long-range plans for the stable." He let his words hang in the air.

The trainer nodded. "So you said in your e-mail. I looked into his sire's bloodlines. Man of His Word has done all right for himself, but Pretty in Pink hasn't done much in this country other than as a minor pacing mare. I understand she has Irish blood in her veins."

"She does. Are you ready to see the colt now, Mr. Hitchcock?"

"I sure am, son. I didn't drive down from Lexington to buy an ice-cream cone at the Tastee Freez." He chuckled. "I'm not sure if

I missed downtown Charm or if I drove right through. It's rather charming if that was it—just like the name suggests."

Ken Brady offered his hand a second time. "Nice meeting you, Alan. My son handles the Eager to Please business, but I'm sure we'll meet in the office later."

"Nice meeting you, sir, but we need to clear up a few matters before I waste your time. The salary proposed in the e-mail will barely cover my expenses." He glanced again at the row of buildings and barns. "I'll probably have to rent an apartment in the area because I don't bunk with grooms and field hands." His tone put a disparaging cast on men who made their living in those vocations. "Based on what I expect to see in your yearling, I want a contract that includes a ten percent commission on future wins and any potential sale. As long as I get that, I'll move here to God's country and turn your pretty baby into a champion in the money." Hitchcock glanced at Keeley, who skipped up the driveway carrying the newspaper. Skinny Joe followed at her heels. "That is one ugly cat," he murmured.

Both Bradys ignored his comment.

"Sounds fair to me if it's okay with my son." Ken took a step back. "Now, if you'll excuse me." He walked away with a limp more pronounced than it had been that morning.

Sweat trickled down Jake's neck inside his collar. "I'm amenable to those terms. I'll have our lawyer draw up the contract if you agree to take the colt once you've seen him."

"Let's go. Tell me what you've done with him so far."

"I've had him on a lead and halter alone," Jake said on the way to the barn. "No bit in his mouth yet. I've been working him on a twenty-foot lunge rope in the arena."

"Good, good, plenty of time for a bit in his mouth. But we'll need to put a rider on him soon, somebody lightweight—not you. We must get him ready for the Florida races this winter for yearlings. He should train with other horses around so he doesn't develop any don't-come-near-me bad habits."

Jake tried to digest everything the trainer said, but his mind raced in a dozen directions at once. His queasy stomach from breakfast hadn't settled down one bit. Inside the barn, Jake walked to the colt's stall on legs that suddenly felt as though he wore thirty-pound ankle weights. What if Hitchcock laughed? What if he demanded reimbursement for his gasoline from Lexington for an utter waste of his precious time?

When the trainer unlatched the door and stepped inside the stall, he didn't say much at first. He approached Eager slowly, inspecting him from every angle. He ran a practiced hand down his flank, assessing the young horseflesh. The colt eyed him suspiciously a few moments and then returned to munching oats.

"He's too thin," declared Hitchcock, exiting the stall. He secured the latch behind him. "And I'll bet your feed doesn't contain near enough protein." The trainer went on to criticize the stall, the bedding, the barn's ventilation, the overhead sprinkler system—just about everything in their operation.

But not the colt. Other than thinness, he didn't have one negative thing to say about Eager to Please. And he conceded that too thin was superior to the alternative. The next half hour passed in a blur as Jake's head swam with Hitchcock's demands. Later, he found his father in the stable office with a fresh pot of coffee and two mugs, as though expecting him.

"Hitchcock gone?"

"Yeah, he went back to Lexington to pack."

"I thought he would take the job once he saw the colt."

"I wonder what he'll do when he finds out Charm has no apartments to rent?" Jake exhaled air he'd been holding far too long. When he met Ken's eye, they both smiled.

"Our bunkhouse will start looking better and better. Or he can rent a room at Miss Florence's B-and-B, if he doesn't mind heavy Victorian decor." They both laughed as they pictured the elderly widow's quaint inn, filled with doilies, bone china, and porcelain dolls up to the ornate plaster ceilings. "Maybe Alan will develop a taste for scones with clotted cream," said Ken.

"Or maybe he'll discover a soft spot for Miss Florence." Jake wiggled his eyebrows.

Ken covered his face with his hands. "Stop. I don't want to picture those two on her settee when I run into her at church."

Jake lowered himself to a chair, tired even though it wasn't yet noon. He debated how much to relay regarding Hitchcock's demands for improvements. He decided he would wait for now and enjoy a few hours of luxury. They had just hired a first-class trainer for a world-class horse.

❧

Ken shuffled into the kitchen the next morning after a scant three hours of sleep. That's all they added up to after subtracting the hours of tossing and turning, pillow punching, and pacing the living room floor so he wouldn't wake his hardworking wife. Exhausted, he had finally slumped onto the sofa, folded his hands, and closed his eyes to pray. At first he had no idea where to begin. He had so many worries, so many fears that he could have presented God with a shopping list of requests. So he started with simple thanks—for his loving wife, his healthy children, and the continued productiveness of Twelve Elms. After that the words wouldn't stop until he fell into a deep, dreamless sleep.

In the kitchen one of his chief reasons for gratitude stood at the stove. "Morning. You are a sight for sore eyes." He filled a mug with coffee.

His wife grinned over her shoulder. "Tuesdays aren't anyone's favorite days off. Most pharmacists want Friday through Monday.

But if I work weekends, it's more money in the family coffers." She expertly flipped a blueberry pancake.

"You're a fine woman, Taylor Brady. I'm glad you chose to spend your free day with us."

"Johnny Depp was busy. You were my second choice." She set a plate of pancakes and crisp bacon in front of him.

"Second choice is better than forty-third."

"By a long shot." Taylor carried over her mug and plate and bowed her head.

"Thank You, Lord, for this food we're about to eat." Ken shoved a whole slice of bacon into his mouth.

"A man of few words today?" Taylor ate with her usual moderation. "You look terrible, Ken. Didn't you sleep much?"

"A few hours, but I'm fine. This is delicious. I can't remember the last time you fried bacon." He devoured another piece.

"Man cannot live by granola, Greek yogurt, and oatmeal alone. Woman either. Just don't tell our doctor. What's troubling you?"

He shook his head. "You talk first. Tell me your agenda for today. I'm hoping you've planned something more interesting than housework."

"Peggy and Connie are coming over to help organize the annual benefit rodeo. They plan to bring lunch, so I just need to make the house presentable before they arrive."

"Did you get any commitments from the pros?"

"Yes. Once word spread that we're raising money for juvenile diabetes this year, I had several professional riders willing to come to Charm to put on a show. That disease has touched so many lives. Two riders promised to drag their friends too. Advance ticket sales have been brisk, much to our pleasant surprise."

"At thirty dollars a head?"

"Yep. With the rodeo and a full western buffet, I know we'll sell out. Kids are only ten bucks."

"What's on the menu?"

"You name it—pulled pork, barbecue beef and chicken, burgers, baked beans, coleslaw, corn on the cob, a variety of salads, corn bread, and tons of desserts. A couple people asked if there would be a beer tent, but I said no. Goodness, this is a charity for kids. Folks can stick to lemonade and iced tea for one afternoon."

"Whew, I hope Johnny Depp doesn't hear about the gourmet vittles. I won't stand a chance. You should have been a saleswoman."

"Don't find me any more jobs." Her brow lifted into a perfect arch.

"Who will cook all this food? Surely not the three of you."

"Bite your tongue. Connie commandeered local celebrity chefs from Somerset, Danville, Bowling Green, and here in Charm."

"*Celebrities?*" Ken fought back laughter.

"In their own restaurants they are. Regardless, these chefs are contributing their time and quite a bit of food. Peggy found a local ranch willing to donate beef and pork, and the Stolls have offered some chickens. The buffet is coming together. The girls and I will work out minor details today. By the way, Jake invited his blind riding students, free of charge."

"I hate to state the obvious, but these kids won't be able to see the performances."

"They can listen to the MC announcing events and share in the excitement. And you don't need vision to chow down on good barbecue. Now tell me what's troubling you, Ken. I could pack those bags under your eyes for a month-long trip."

"Would you have sweet-talked Johnny like this?" Ken wiped up the syrup with his last pancake. "Alan Hitchcock, our newest *employee*, started work the other day."

"The high-priced trainer from Lexington?"

"Yes, and he's got nothing but good things to say about the colt. He shares Jake's opinion that with the right program Eager to Please could be a serious contender."

"But?" She sipped coffee without taking her eyes off him.

"But the colt was the only thing Hitchcock liked. He demanded changes to his diet and a larger stall, and he practically fired two of our grooms. But they seem willing to adjust because jobs are hard to come by in Casey County."

"What's the problem?" she asked. "You knew he would make changes. His expertise is the reason we hired him."

"You're right, but Alan said he plans to take Eager to Please on a grand tour of racetracks as a juvenile. The colt needs to enter certain races as a two-year-old to be assured a slot in the Derby. These tracks are scattered all over the country. He intends to travel with an entourage of assistants, grooms, exercise boys, and a secretary, along with Jake. Hitchcock has a handpicked cadre for these positions—people he trusts to do things his way." Ken glanced up, but his wife's face remained expressionless. "Taylor, we're talking hotel bills, restaurant meals, fuel costs or airline flights, besides salaries for the next year and a half."

"And if we refuse to let him take this show on the road? Why can't he train our colt in Charm and schedule track time at the county fairgrounds?"

"According to Hitchcock, setting up mock races won't work. The horse needs to develop a competitive drive, and only well-matched horses will accomplish that. For now Alan will train him here, but he wants to take him to Florida this winter where they hold yearling races. Otherwise, he said Eager won't stand a chance."

Every drop of color drained from his wife's face. If she hadn't been seated she might have fainted. "This sounds like we took the lid off a box of snakes. Expenses keep spiraling out of control while the whole mess grows more complicated each day. Does this trainer realize we're not made of money?" Her voice sounded shrill, a rare occurrence for a normally serene woman.

"He does. We told him that more than once, but he doesn't care. He insists this is the only course of action."

Taylor reached for his hand. "What are you going to do, Ken?"

He gazed into her pretty brown eyes, eyes that had captured his attention and then his heart at the University of Kentucky. "I prayed about this last night for a long time, but when I woke this morning, I received no great intuition, no answer other than to stay the course we're on."

"How can we? Did some long-lost uncle die and leave you a million bucks?"

Sarcasm wasn't his wife's style. Ken peered at her. "Not that I know of, but I plan to take out that jumbo loan with the balloon payment. As Jake explained, we could refinance it at the end as long as our stable books show an increase in profits. Will you sign the contract with me? I can't...I won't...do it without your support."

Time suspended in their warm cozy kitchen. From the living room came the drone from the TV. Outside they heard the sound of a chainsaw as someone attacked the firewood pile. Luke, one of Jessie's house cats, rubbed against Ken's leg, purring like a lawnmower. Ken reached down to pet his soft fur while he waited for his wife's answer.

Taylor exhaled. "You know I'm nervous about carrying so much debt, but I refuse to argue against your plan without a concrete alternative. I'll sign the papers with you. I did pledge 'for richer or for poorer.' We just might be put to the test." She walked to the sink to wash breakfast dishes without her customary kiss atop his head or pat on his shoulder.

Ken would have to content himself that they were united in their decision...no matter what the outcome.

❧

Rachel passed out brochures to the Danville Garden Club with a bright smile. The ladies had made the trip to Twelve Elms their end-of-season celebration. They had been an enthusiastic group and were now heading to Bread of Life for lunch. "Come back and see us again," she called.

"Oh, we will," chimed several well-dressed women.

"Maybe we'll take the mounted tour next year," added a pretty redhead, to the great amusement of the others.

"It's available every Saturday nine months of the year. Be sure to sign up for our newsletter and check out our website. It's updated regularly by Jake Brady."

Jake. She thought about that *Englischer* more often than she pondered Reuben Mullet or John Swartz. Reuben had greeted her warmly last Sunday after church. Apparently, he'd forgiven her for falling asleep. He chatted amiably about news in the Mullet family and recent events around their dairy farm. After a good night's sleep, Rachel had no difficulty following the conversation and interjecting appropriate replies.

No difficulty…but also no interest.

Reuben was a nice-looking young man. He had many fine qualities, but he was as appealing to her as mud.

John's persistence last Saturday had continued until she closed the back door in his face. She'd said *gut nacht* not less than three times. He had chatted during the walk home and asked endless questions about her home, her hobbies, her job—everything other than plans for the rest of her life. She liked him, but he reminded her of the aggressive puppy in a litter—the one who barked and pranced on his back paws: *Pick me, pick me, pick me!*

After tying Buster and Bess to a round hay stanchion, Rachel filled their water trough with the hose. She had bonded with these draft horses during the past weeks as though they had spent years together. Thanks to a steady supply of apples, the Belgians responded to her commands with smooth efficiency.

"Rachel, can I talk to you for a minute?" Jake appeared suddenly over her right shoulder.

She almost jumped out of her leather boots. "Sure, I'm finished here." She turned off the faucet and dried her hands on a clean rag from her pocket.

"According to the schedule, you don't have another tour until late this afternoon." Sunlight shrank his pupils into small pin dots within a sea of blue.

"That's right. I planned to help the grooms or exercise boys until then. I love taking a few warm-up or cool-down laps around the track."

He laughed. "We never worry about you napping in the hayloft while on the clock. But if you'd like, I could use help with today's therapy ride."

"With the blind children? I would love to!"

Jake didn't hide his pleasure. "This is a special day for the kids. Only six are coming—the most proficient of the group. We're taking them on a trail ride to the lake. Each child will be assigned his or her own chaperone who will keep a lead rope on their horse and maintain constant supervision. But the children will hold the reins and control their mount with their thighs. We'll saddle the best-trained, gentlest horses Twelve Elms owns, but it's still quite a responsibility. Keeley, Mrs. Ingraham, and some parents will also be guides. Three dads had originally volunteered to come with us."

"But someone couldn't come?" Rachel sounded thrilled. She hoped the absent parent wasn't deathly ill or hadn't suffered an accident.

Jake stifled a cough. "That's right. One father was called out of town for business. The mom will pick the child up after work. Can I count on you?"

"Absolutely, Jake. I love trail rides. I'll saddle Calamity Jane and grab my lunch bag."

"No need. We're taking a pack mule to carry lunch and drinks for everyone." He began walking toward the barn. "And anticipating your response, I already had Jane saddled."

For some reason, Rachel blushed as though saddling a horse was somehow flirting with her. "In that case, I'm ready to ride."

When they reached the indoor arena, the two parents and Mrs. Ingraham were already tightening helmet straps, adjusting stirrups, and checking saddles and tack. "Which child will be assigned to me?" Rachel scanned the six enthusiastic young faces.

"Bethany Morris, so be prepared to have your ear talked off."

"I'm not worried. I have two of them." She hurried to the little girl, who stood next to the teacher. "Hi, Bethany. My name is Rachel." She touched the child's arm lightly. "We're riding together today."

Indeed, Bethany chattered like a magpie, but Rachel didn't mind. She was every bit as excited. Although the children couldn't see the bright fall foliage or the rolling harvested hills, they could smell the last crop of fresh-mown timothy hay, feel the warm sun on their skin, and hear the buzz of insects in their last-minute frenzy. Three stable workers had ridden along to tend the twelve horses while chaperones assisted their charges.

Jake raised a hand to halt the group beside a clear, deep pond. The smooth surface reflected the sun like a mirror, dazzling the eyes of the sighted. "We'll stop here for lunch," he called.

"Where are we?" asked Bethany.

"By a small lake with a gravel shoreline," said Rachel. "There's a long fishing dock and a grove of picnic tables in the shade."

"Tell me everything you see. Leave nothing out."

Rachel described the vista in every direction. Bethany asked questions about any description unfamiliar to her, while her expression grew more and more delighted.

"Rachel, Bethany, over here." Keeley hailed them to her table. Once everyone had sat down, Keeley explained the position of each person so the children knew who they were eating with. Mrs. Ingraham and Jake distributed sandwiches, chips, fruit, and drink boxes while the two moms cleaned every pair of hands with Wet Ones. While the children chattered a mile a minute, Rachel kept an ear on their stories and an eye on Jake.

He passed out lunch to the grooms, pointed out something on a farm map to the teacher, and checked on each child. He flitted between his guests like a bee, making sure everyone received the attention they needed.

Everyone but me, that is. A shameful wave of disappointment crawled under her skin. Hadn't he agreed to be her friend? So why was he acting so standoffish?

Mrs. Ingraham suddenly stood and clapped her hands, commanding everyone's attention. "Boys and girls," she called. "Is everyone finished eating?"

In unison the six trail riders responded affirmatively.

"Then I want you to hand your rubbish to your assistant and stand up facing west. Remember, you should feel the sun on your face in the afternoon. Then join hands with your tablemates and once you're ready, walk toward the sound of my voice."

Amazed, Rachel watched as the children located each other's hands, extracted themselves from the table, and headed toward her steady stream of dialogue.

"We have spread blankets in the shade," said Mrs. Ingraham. "You can either take a catnap to rest for the ride back to the ranch, or you can sit and listen to Miss Brady read a story."

"Care to take a walk, Miss King, to the fishing dock?" Jake appeared at her side. "We don't allow the guests there for obvious reasons. We have a fifteen-minute break during story time."

"Sure." Rachel scraped everyone's refuse into a trash bag and carried it to the pack mule for the trip home. "I'm having so much fun. Thanks for inviting me."

"Bethany likes you. I see your ear is hanging by a thread."

"Sarah can stitch it up tonight after supper." She kept pace with him on their way to the dock. "This is a lovely spot, Jake. Are we still on Brady land?"

"Yes. This is our backup water supply in periods of drought." Jake grasped her elbow as they walked onto the narrow pier. "How is meeting eligible bachelors going at the Amish socials? I've been curious."

After a slight hesitation, she smiled. "You sound just like my cousin. To tell you the truth, I'm off to a mediocre start. I've met two so far, but I don't think I'm…compatible…with either Reuben or John." She chose an English word used often by Keeley.

"Hmm, Reuben and John. Those are good, solid-sounding names. I'll bet they're smitten with you." He watched her from the corner of his eye.

"Maybe, maybe not, but I plan to keep things casual with everyone. After all, who knows how long I'll stay in Kentucky?"

"Makes sense to me. Just play the field. But while you're courting a variety of Amish fellows, why can't you go out with me? I'm not asking you to leave your faith or cut your hair or do something sneaky, but why can't we go out to dinner or to a church potluck together?" He focused on a pair of mallards that landed in the center of the pond.

For a while Rachel watched the ducks swim around in circles. "Why not, as long as we keep it casual," she said, shrugging her shoulders. "But let's get back to the rest of the group."

"Sounds good to me. The grooms are bringing up the horses."

Neither spoke on the walk back, yet Rachel felt as if something irrevocable had shifted beneath their feet. She knew there wasn't anything *casual* about courting in the Amish world. And yet for some reason she couldn't stop humming for the rest of the afternoon.

TEN

'Tis grace hath brought me safe thus far

Friday morning

"Donna, get in here!"

Donna clenched her eyes tightly shut and counted to ten. But seven was as far as she got before she slid back from the computer and stomped from her cubicle. She waited to release steam until she reached the confines of Phil Richards' office. "You do realize the Department of Health has an intercom system besides working telephones, don't you? There's no need to shout my name if there's some *urgent matter* you need help with." She glared down at him.

Phil peered up at her over his wire rims. "Why should I bother looking up extensions in the directory when I have a perfectly good set of lungs?" He was dead serious.

"Oh, I don't know…maybe to maintain a professional atmosphere in the office?"

He threw his pen down on the blotter, but grinned nevertheless.

"Is that how you were raised, Cline? Taught to sass your elders as well as your boss? I doubt it. I had the pleasure of meeting your mother. She was one fine lady."

Donna slouched onto one of his plastic chairs. "You are my elder by a scant eleven years, Phil. And although I readily acknowledge you're my boss, a woman who secretly hopes to get downsized doesn't fear job security."

He laughed and leaned back in his chair. "Huh, big talker! You and Pete have two smart girls to still put through college, so you can't afford to get fired for years."

"You're right as usual, Mr. Richards. What can I help you with, sir?" She batted her eyelashes.

"That's more like it." He reached for his coffee across a messy desk. "What are you working on now?"

She stared at him, all joking aside. "You're kidding, right? I'm going through the restaurant inspections to prepare my annual reports. I've yet to update the database with information supplied by every health care provider in Kentucky. And I need to conduct some unannounced visits to nursing homes and daycare facilities. I haven't taken a real lunch all week."

"I'll put a gold star next to your name. But in the meantime, we have a problem. We have three more positives for polio infections from those samples gathered so far, all Amish children. The lab copied the CDC on the e-mail alert. Soon Atlanta will be breathing down my neck. How are you coming with convincing the community they need to get vaccinated?"

"Not too good, I'm afraid." She did her best not to sound defensive. "I found only one family who allowed me to administer the shots. The family has five children, but one was too young to receive. Only a handful of kids have been inoculated in the Amish and Mennonite communities in the area after all our canvassing."

He frowned. "Did you explain you're a registered nurse, licensed in this state to administer medications?"

"Yes, but questions regarding my training and expertise weren't the issue." She spotted a large moth trapped against the window glass. She longed to walk around his desk to set it free, perhaps feeling a bit of kinship with a bug.

"Then what in blazes is? You've had weeks on this. Did you go to every house that doesn't send their kids to public schools?"

She trained her eyes on him to stay focused. "To the best of my knowledge, I did. Unless a family lives without mail delivery or isn't listed on tax maps, I found them all. Some have already gotten their kids shots and the others possess definite ideas on the subject. They haven't avoided vaccines because they never *heard* of them. They have their reasons."

"I'd love to know what their reasons are." His voice turned soft and controlled.

"A few think the shots could actually cause the disease."

"That's nonsense. That hasn't happened in this country in years since we stopped using the oral Sabins."

"Some believe the shots will lower a child's overall immune system, making them more susceptible to unrelated maladies."

"That's an unproven theory that refuses to die."

"I agree, but a few parents believe vaccines in general interfere with God's will. If that's their position, we can't force them."

"Whose side are you on?" His eyebrows drew together over the bridge of his nose.

"The State Board of Health's, of course, but I'm not licensed to carry a gun to hold to people's heads."

"I could make that happen if you like…a few lessons, a discreet shoulder holster. You could be like one of those lady cops on TV." He pantomimed a quick draw from beneath his armpit.

"Remember me? I'm one of those crazies who believes the Second Amendment needs to be retired to the history books."

"Loosen up, Cline. I was joking." He squinted down his nose at her. "Sounds to me like a few Amish parents did some hit-or-miss reading and convinced others of their so-called research. Aren't there any leaders in the community you could talk sense to?"

"That would be the district bishop. He is the church leader for the twenty-five or thirty families in his area. There are several in Casey County. I talked to one I found an inroad with and got nowhere."

"What do you have in mind in light of three more positives in Charm? You must have some insight into how their collective mind works."

Donna felt a surge of resentment from his word choice. *Collective mind?* These were Amish and Mennonite Christians, not a colony of aliens that beamed down from a yet-to-be-discovered planet. Mothers and fathers who wanted only what was best for their children. But because he was correct about her and Pete needing to put two daughters through college, Donna selected her words carefully. "There is no easily influenced collective mind, but I will try speaking to a bishop on the other side of the county, away from Charm. What affects one will affect all. Maybe a different bishop will be more medically progressive in his thinking and will be willing to exert some influence."

"Good idea. Get right on that. Finish up those reports you're in the middle of, put whatever else on the back burner, and give this top priority." He picked up a paper on his desk to peruse. "What are you still doing in my office, Mrs. Cline?" He was only half teasing.

"I plan to first do my own reading on the status of this disease along with current research on these vaccines. I don't want to enter any debates without full information about potential risks and side effects." She straightened from his uncomfortable plastic chair.

"Whatever it takes to get those Amish kids lining up for shots is fine with me. It's not only polio we're worried about. We need to protect the kids of Casey County and surrounding areas from mumps, chicken pox, measles, hepatitis B, and a whole variety of infectious viruses." Phil focused in earnest on his stack of reports.

Donna retreated sheeplike from the room. But what else could she do? Argue against something that as a medical professional she believed in? But she also was a firm believer in personal choice for American citizens. Too often government bureaucracies only presented medical evidence which supported their current position. Often years down the road more in-depth research revealed a different conclusion altogether. Sitting down in front of her monitor, Donna clicked on a popular search engine. A little more time behind her desk before she hit the field wouldn't hurt a thing.

❦

Rachel let the shower stream run down her back and shoulders far longer than necessary. She washed her hair, applied conditioner, and aimed the showerhead at her sore muscles. Today's mounted ride had been more tiring than others. And exhausted was the last thing she wanted to be. After drying her hair, she wrapped it in a bun and put on her prettiest dress in a deep shade of lavender.

Sarah did a double take when Rachel emerged from the bathroom. "I've not seen that one yet. You Pennsylvania gals are quite the fashion plates of the Plain world, *jah?*"

"*Nein,* not really. I just save this one for special occasions." She walked to the cutting board on the counter and began slicing tomatoes, cucumbers, and celery for the salad.

"What's the occasion? Did Bonnie or Ruby get word to you about the singing tonight? I hope Josh picks you up. The hosting family lives several miles away."

Rachel regretted her word choice regarding the dress as her mind spun with ideas. She carried the finished salad to the table and distributed plates, forks, and cups. "I'm not going to the singing."

"Then where are you headed in your *special* dress?"

Isaac shuffled into the room and sat down. "If your cousin thought it was your business, *fraa*, she would tell you." He winked at his wife and then bowed his head.

Sarah carried over the pot of beef stew and bowed hers for silent prayer. Then her eyes practically bored holes through Rachel's forehead.

Rachel ladled one small scoop of stew but took a full plate of greens. "It's no secret. And Sarah may ask anything she likes. Jake is picking me up in thirty minutes."

"You're scheduled to work on a Saturday night?" Sarah filled her bowl and Isaac's.

"It's not work. He's taking me to supper in Charm."

"Then why are you eating?" asked Isaac—the man who seldom spoke and never asked questions of her.

She flushed. "Because I'm starving, but I don't want to eat like a brood sow in front of him."

Isaac's confused expression remained while Sarah snorted, perhaps in response to the porcine analogy. "Are you saying this is a *date* with him?" No one could mistake her opinion of that possibility.

"It's not exactly a date. I told him I'm willing to see friends who are Amish, Mennonite *or* English because I don't intend to get serious with anyone."

Sarah swallowed a mouthful of salad. "I don't see the point of seeing *Englischers* socially. That's just wasting your time." She speared a cherry tomato. "Will you take English clothes to change into later?"

"No, I plan to wear this all night." Rachel was careful not to drip salad dressing on her outfit.

Isaac held up his bowl for a refill. "Because you don't see the point, *fraa*, aren't you glad you married me and don't need to concern yourself?" His right brow arched.

"Of course I am." Sarah remained silent from then on, but she glanced across the table at her young cousin surreptitiously.

Rachel finished as quickly as possible and washed her dishes. "I'll take my key in case you're already in bed."

"Why would we go to bed early?" Sarah placed a hand on her hip.

"Just in case. Sounds like he's here." Rachel grabbed her purse and sweater and sprang out the door at the first sound of a car.

Jake turned around and opened the passenger door. "You look awfully nice tonight," he said when she climbed in.

"Which is it—awful or nice? And where are we headed?" She buckled her seat belt on the second try.

"Definitely nice. It's a restaurant you might like called Bread of Life. I hope you're hungry. They have a delicious buffet or you can order off the menu. The owners are Mennonite. And they have a sundae bar for dessert."

"Good choice, not too far away. I've been there with my cousin." Rachel regretted eating half a supper, borne of pride and vanity.

"I won't keep you out late because you're probably going to church tomorrow."

She tried shifting under the restrictive belt but almost strangled herself. "Won't you attend your church? Or do you have services a different day?"

"I'll go if someone twists my arm." Jake passed a car at high speed.

"Why would that be necessary?"

He wet his lips with his tongue. "It shouldn't be, I suppose, but let's talk about something else. My dad and I discussed a price for Calamity Jane if you're still interested."

Rachel fought the seat belt to face him. "You bet I am! What price did you decide on?"

"She's a fine mare who gave us several nice colts, but now she's simply a gentle riding horse, not worth so much as in her younger years. We thought four hundred dollars would be fair."

"Don't be ridiculous, Jake. Jane is worth far more than that. I have money from the sale of my parents' farm, so charge me what you would anybody else."

Jake kept his focus on the road. "Her price is four hundred dollars. I suggest you accept the deal, Miss King, because Monday morning I'm posting an ad in the break room that Calamity Jane is for sale. Someone else will snap her up by noon."

Crossing her arms, Rachel took less than a moment to decide. "I'll take her. You'll have my check on Monday." He was being overly generous, but she couldn't take a chance of someone else buying *her* horse.

Jake's hand left the steering wheel long enough to shake. "You drove a hard bargain, Miss King."

"And I believe I've taken advantage of our friendship." Nevertheless, she couldn't sit still from her excitement.

Within ten minutes they pulled into a parking lot full of cars, a few buggies around back, and one bus. He opened her door and reached for her hand. "I'll put a sign on Jane's stall: Owner—Rachel King, Charm, Kentucky." Jake dropped her hand and formed a square with his fingers.

"Don't tell her yet. I want to be the one to break the news that I'm her *mamm.*"

He cocked his head to the side. "Now that you mention it, I see the family resemblance in the long legs and silky hair."

She flushed. "Because Jane is absolutely beautiful, I thank you for the compliment."

Inside the restaurant they browsed among the gifts until someone called the name Brady. The hostess led them to a table in the back. "What looks good to you?" he asked once she left.

"The buffet, what else?" Rachel closed the menu and tried not to stare at her dinner companion. She had painfully little experience with courting.

"The buffet for both of us," he said to their waitress. "With sweet tea."

"Help yourself, folks." The young woman had barely uttered the words when Rachel sprang to her feet, out of anxiety not hunger.

Neither took much time selecting food. Jake loaded his plate with fried chicken, mashed potatoes, green beans, and a huge serving of salad. Rachel bypassed the chicken, choosing ham and corn on the cob instead. Later, they opted to split a strawberry sundae for dessert, although she couldn't eat more than two bites.

When the sundae was nothing but melted cream in the bottom of the bowl, Jake set down his spoon. "Mark your calendar for four weeks from today—the second Saturday in November." He wiped his sticky hands on a napkin.

"What's going on?" Rachel took a sip of iced tea.

"It's the Twelve Elms annual rodeo to benefit juvenile diabetes. We've lined up professional riders who'll volunteer their talents. Then our students will put on a show, followed by a western barbecue during the late afternoon. In the evening, we auction off donated prizes and gift certificates to the highest bidder."

Rachel pressed a hand down on her stomach. "The barbecue will sound great the day of the rodeo. Right now, not so much. Will I have mounted tours that day?"

"No, we don't schedule rides during our fund-raiser. You could take the day off, but I would love it if you showed up. I invited the school for the blind as our nonpaying guests. You could sit with Bethany and explain what's happening in the arena."

"How much for a ticket?"

"Thirty bucks, except for Brady employees who work the show.

They get in for free." Jake leaned back in his chair. "That goes for everybody, so don't get antsy."

※

For the third time that night, Rachel caught a whiff of Jake's spicy aftershave. She loved the scent because it reminded her of baking day in *mamm*'s kitchen. "I wouldn't mind paying the fee because it's for a good cause. Count me in! I will be happy to be Bethany's eyes for the day. I can't think of a better way to spend a Saturday afternoon." Rachel licked the last of the strawberry jam from her spoon and placed it in the empty bowl. Then she blushed, feeling Jake's gaze on her.

"Thanks for agreeing to see me along with Reuben and John." His handsome face turned serious. "I haven't had this much fun in a long while."

"Think nothing of it. I've enjoyed your company as well."

As though her statement required proof, Rachel couldn't stop smiling, not at the table, not wandering the shop while he paid the bill, not even on the drive back to the Stolls'. But she knew she had better stop speaking the truth to Jake Brady or she would find herself beyond a point of no return with an *Englischer*.

※

Sunday morning

Jake turned over and buried his head beneath the goose down pillow, trying to return to his sweet dream about Rachel. In his dream, they were at some sort of a play or show. She had her arm affectionately looped around his waist with her head on his shoulder.

"*Jake.*"

Rachel called his name in her melodic voice, perhaps from across the room or better yet, from the kitchen of their first home together as newlyweds.

"Jake! Are you awake? I need to speak to you."

He bolted upright and shook off the last pleasant vestiges of his dream. It hadn't been the gentle voice of his beloved Rachel, but the exasperated tone of his mother.

"Give me a minute," he called, pulling on sweatpants. Jake opened the door a few inches.

His mom stood before him without makeup and with her hair damp from the shower. "Goodness, a freight train outside your window couldn't wake you."

"What time is it?" He scratched his stubbly chin.

"Almost seven thirty. Time to get up."

The dense fog slowly began to clear. "Wait a minute. It's Sunday, my only day to sleep in."

Taylor nudged the door wider with her knee. "I suppose that's one way of looking at it. It's also the Sabbath, and your family goes to the nine o'clock service."

"Thanks for the invite, Mom, but I'm bushed. This is my chance to catch up on beauty sleep." He tried closing the door, but her foot was quicker than his slow reactions that morning.

"When was the last time you joined us at church? You always liked attending Sunday school and VBS when you were a little boy."

Jake shook his head. "Mom, you've been working too many hours. I'm twenty-three years old, not seven."

"So you've outgrown your faith? You don't consider yourself Baptist or even a Christian anymore?"

"I didn't say that. I'm just exhausted. It's been a tough week. Maybe next Sunday." He started to close the door.

"That's not good enough, son." She pushed the door open and

walked into his room. "While you live under our roof, you'll follow our example. This family worships on Sunday mornings. When you get your own place, you can make your own rules." She crossed her arms.

"You must be joking. You're going to *make* me go to church? Force religion down my throat? I thought America was a free country."

"America might be, but this is still your dad's household. And we'd like you to set a better example for Virgil."

Jake scraped his face with his hands. *What has gotten into her?* She had never made a fuss about attending services. He went four or five times a year to keep them happy. When he met her gaze, she looked as determined as him. "Fine. I'll take a shower and meet you downstairs."

Taylor turned on her heel and marched out the door. No "thank-you" or "atta-boy" or anything.

But he saw no point making this into a big deal—it was an hour out of his week beside the drive time. No one would know what he thought about while the minister droned on about turning the other cheek or the narrow road to heaven. Jake had nothing against religion, but at his age he felt he had plenty of time to worry about making amends. Of course he believed in God, but as far as an up-close-and-personal relationship? He had no time for that. He was too busy working to sin anyway. He didn't drink more than an occasional beer, never swore since the time his grandmother washed his mouth with soap, and never set foot inside one of those girly dance clubs. The two bachelor parties he attended had been at a racetrack, where they had eaten spicy nachos and made two-dollar bets all evening. He would worry about heaven when he was an old man.

An hour later, dressed in chinos with a polo shirt, Jake arrived in the kitchen. It was the first time he had worn clothes other than jeans in months. "Good morning, everyone."

Virgil and Keeley's eyes bugged from their faces. "Who are you? And what have you done with our brother?"

"Very funny. Eat your Fruit Loops and be a good little girl." He pulled Keeley's ponytail.

"Breakfast?" asked his mom. "We're leaving in five minutes." She pushed a box of glazed doughnuts across the table.

"I think I'll choose the breakfast of champions." Jake poured Wheaties into a bowl, added milk, and then wolfed down his cereal. He took a donut to eat on the ride to Charm. "I'll drive separately. No sense cramming five people into one car."

Taylor handed him a travel mug filled with coffee. "In that case, Virgil can ride with you."

Jake looked at his younger brother with a pang of guilt. When was the last time they had thrown around a football or raced the quads, just the two of them? Whenever Virgil asked him, Jake was always too busy. "Good idea. I can find out which teams look good this fall." He ruffled a hand through Virgil's hair. "Nobody knows stats like my brother."

For twenty minutes, Virgil explained the prospects for every major NCAA football team. Before Jake knew it, he was following his dad's car into the parking lot of First Baptist Church of Charm. Old ladies wearing big hats along with young ones in pretty dresses milled around the steps, gossiping until the last minute.

Jake slipped into the pew on the end, cramming Virgil against Keeley. His father pressed himself against the wall to make room. The only alternative would be to take the empty seat in the row ahead. However, Becky Thompson resided there—a woman who talked boatloads any chance she got. Not fond of chitchat, Jake planned to let his thoughts drift to a blue-eyed Amish gal with the prettiest face in Kentucky. But after the Bible reading, two hymns, and a contemporary praise song, Reverend Bullock caught Jake's attention with his first sentence.

"Christians often think they need to obey the Commandments

and follow Scripture so they won't be judged harshly at their death, so they can one day find a place in the Promised Land. Some young folks think they have plenty of time to worry about that. After all, barring an accident, they're not going anywhere for a while."

Jake blinked. Had this preacher read his mind while still miles from the church? What sort of tricks did they teach at theological seminary?

"But if they think like that, they might miss the incredible gifts God has in store for His believers. In Ephesians, children are instructed to obey their parents because it's the right thing to do. Everyone knows that. But if you read further, it also promises life will go well for you and you will enjoy a long life on earth. Right here and now—no waiting for the next life. God promises us comfort, guidance, and joy if we only surrender our will. Put down your burdens and follow Him. We don't have to worry about what we'll eat or wear as long as we have faith. God has never let me down. Sometimes He tells us we must wait and be patient. Sometimes the answer is no because our plans aren't in keeping with His. But if you build a relationship with Him, you won't be disappointed." Reverend Bullock's flushed face began to perspire as he surveyed the congregation.

No one in the room doubted the man's sincerity...except maybe one. *Oh, yeah? Then why are there Christian homeless people? Why do sick folks still die even though a whole town full of believers prayed for healing? And why are there so many Christians in jail if we're all supposed to walk the straight and narrow?* Caustic thoughts and recriminations flitted through his head, yet Jake knew the minister believed every word he spoke. Where did faith like that come from? Jake leaned forward in the pew to focus on the sermon. While he listened, he grew irritated at times or at least defensive, but by the end something gnawed at him.

Give up control?
Surrender your destiny?

No matter how hard he worked and must continue to work if his dream with Eager to Please were to come true, Pastor Bullock said the future was out of his hands.

After the service, Jake followed his brother outside, only partially aware of Virgil's plans for the afternoon. Jake's head swam with things he didn't like, but the idea that continued to bother him came back to Rachel. Without stepping one foot inside an Amish church, without understanding much about the various Plain sects, Jake knew she believed every word the minister uttered...lock, stock, and barrel. And how would *that* bode for their future?

ELEVEN

And grace will lead me home

K en closed his eyes and rubbed the bridge of his nose for the third time that afternoon. He'd spread the November bills across his desk to see what he was dealing with. When they covered the surface two deep and he still had a stack in his hand, he opted for a different approach. Next, he separated bills into a pile for household expenses, one for their boarding and training operation, and a third for the training of Eager to Please. Alan Hitchcock had brought with him a tidal wave of financial demands. Between improvements to the barn; a new staff of grooms, exercise boys, and a part-time secretary; regular veterinary checkups; and an array of supplements and special feed, Eager to Please had become an expensive juvenile. At least Alan had agreed to move into the bunkhouse, saving them the added expense of his stay at Florence's bed-and-breakfast.

None of the new expenses had been unexpected, and it wasn't as if the Brady family didn't have sufficient funds to pay these obligations. Thanks to the jumbo loan Ken had taken out, their business account contained enough for at least six months, if not a year. It just felt wrong to pour this much money into a pipe dream. Sure, some men took these kinds of chances on a regular basis, but those people weren't descendants of Jeremiah Brady.

Inhaling a deep breath, Ken pulled the checkbook from his desk drawer and attacked the piles one at a time. Systematically he wrote checks, affixed stamps, and lowered their bank balance bit by bit. Two hours later, he focused on the Twelve Elms balance sheets. Due to Jake's diligence with their website, blog, Facebook, and whatever other marketing wizardry he set up, their business had grown threefold. Every stall had been leased, and they had a waiting list with another dozen names. Neither Jake, nor himself, nor their other trainers could handle additional classes. Even Rachel King and her wagon tours brought in more income than usual during the fall. Yet none of it made him feel proud or content or even hopeful for the future.

Keep your life free from the love of money, and be content with what you have. Ken's grandmother had stitched the words of Hebrews 13:5 into a sampler and hung it on the wall. Maybe that's why their expanded business failed to bring him joy. A man who constantly obsessed over money didn't have his focus where it should be. All he had ever wanted to be was a horse trainer…the everyday kind who helped people win blue ribbons at county fairs, raised kids' self-esteem and gave them a sense of responsibility by caring for an animal, and took folks on overnight journeys to discover the great outdoors. That had been all Jake wanted too until he was bitten by the fame-and-fortune bug. Now some days Ken barely saw his son. And when he did, the young man seemed to have become a stranger.

Ken left his office in search of a strong cup of coffee. He found the subject of his concern poring over a packet of papers at the kitchen table. "That must be something special to drag you out of the barn in the middle of the day."

Jake glanced up and smiled. "This could be good news, Dad. Keeley delivered this to me when she brought up the mail." He plucked out one sheet to peruse.

Ken poured coffee and sat across the table, noticing dark smudges beneath his son's eyes. "Tell me what gold mine you've discovered."

"The Kentucky Department of Development is offering grants to expand the therapeutic riding program in this state. They have concluded that the relationship developed between horse and rider can assist individuals to relate better to people as well. They will award grants of up to two hundred thousand to buy horses, build another barn, plus a lodge for a life skills camp. With this grant, Twelve Elms can train handicapped adults for future jobs such as grooms, exercise boys, and stable workers." He dropped the paper on the table.

Ken stared at his son. "Haven't we already bitten off all we can chew?"

"Not really. Hitchcock has taken over my work with Eager to Please. He's brought his own personnel, freeing up regular Twelve Elms employees. I know our client list has grown, but don't you understand? We can help more than just one school for blind children. There are plenty of kids and adults with physical and developmental disabilities who could benefit from therapeutic riding." Jake's face glowed with the energy of a new idea.

Ken hated to derail his enthusiasm with practical considerations. "Leave the papers on the table for me to read after supper. Right now, my brain is exhausted from too much time spent on the books. I'm going to saddle up for a ride into the hills. With as cold as it was this morning, who knows how long the trails will be ice-free?" He patted his son's shoulder on his way to the door.

Jake jumped up. "Hang on. I'll saddle up Pretty Boy and ride with you. Clearing my head sounds like a great idea."

Within half an hour father and son reached the highest point on Brady land. The sun had already begun its western descent as daylight hours grew shorter and shorter. They sat side by side gazing over pastures that soon would be muddy from rain or buried beneath a layer of snow. "I never get tired of this view," Ken said after a minute.

"I love late fall." Jake rotated both shoulders to relax. "When the harvest is finished, yet there's still time for trail rides."

"Plus we're less busy in November." Ken contemplated asking about Hitchcock's progress with the colt but squashed the idea. They spent enough hours talking business. "How goes it with Rachel? Your mother tells me you two are dating. Jessie thinks it's a smashing idea, according to her last e-mail."

Jake turned toward him in the saddle, squinting from the sun. "We are. This Saturday will be our second official date, even though we eat together whenever she works. We plan to attend Mom's fund-raiser and sit with our blind riding students. Along with Mrs. Ingraham, we'll make sure the kids understand everything that happens during the rodeo."

"That should be quite an event. Prince William's wedding to his bride, Kate, was no better orchestrated than your mother's affair. She and her friends have seen to every detail." Ken loosened his grip on the reins, letting his horse graze on sweet grass, normally forbidden on trail rides.

Surprisingly, Jake allowed Pretty Boy to do the same. "I really like Rachel. To quote Jessie-the-romantic, she might just be the one. At least, on my part."

Ken exhaled through his teeth. "Wow, I never saw that coming. Don't you think her being Amish might make long-range plans difficult?"

Jake shrugged but looked his father in the eye. "I don't know why it should. Amish people are Christians, the same as Baptists. What's the big deal?"

"The big deal is the Amish take their faith very seriously. It's the central driving force of their lives."

"Rachel can't take religion more seriously than you and Mom. You two pray about everything. Sometimes I think you seek divine guidance to decide which movie to see at the Somerset mall." His smile indicated he was being playful, not cynical.

Several responses sprang to Ken's mind.

But you don't take your faith seriously.

You seldom pray about anything.

When was the last time you sought divine guidance for even a monumental decision?

He chose not to voice any of them. He would only hurt his son's feelings and drive a wedge in their already fragile relationship. "I wish you the best of luck with that young woman. She seems very nice besides being hardworking and pretty as a picture, just like your mother when I met her at school."

"Speaking of Mom, shouldn't she be home from work by now? I hope she's started supper. I am starving." He pulled up his reins. "Let's go, Pretty Boy. I'm ready to tie on the feed bag too." Jake galloped down the trail, leaving his father in his dust.

But Ken appreciated a slower-paced ride back to the barn. That gave him time to contemplate his son. And this conundrum had nothing to do with finances for a change.

❧

Second Saturday of November

"I'll make a deal with you, sweet birds. If you let me cross your pen without attacking my shins, I'll scatter extra dried corn besides your regular feed." Rachel held her gathering baskets in one hand while placing the other on the gate.

Most of the chickens paid no attention as they went about normal business. But two or three hens studied her menacingly. It was as if they knew she was about to steal their eggs. Fortifying her courage, she opened the latch and entered their sanctum as though walking on proverbial eggshells.

Rachel had promised to collect eggs before she left for work because she had extra time that morning. Instead of driving Isaac's horse and buggy to work, Jake was picking her up in his truck. She had finished two barns already, delivering the eggs to Sarah for washing and sorting. But this pen, flock number three, always contained a few members who resented her intrusion. She walked gingerly among the birds, careful not to step on toes or talons or whatever they were called. As she passed two of the three troublemakers, Rachel made soothing clucking sounds, with an occasional "that's a nice birdie" thrown in for good measure. Reaching the barn, she rushed inside and slid the door closed. Hens with evil intent would have to climb the narrow ramps and enter through small openings in the wall. Those led directly to their nesting boxes. Rachel worked as quickly and quietly as possible, gathering today's efforts to fill her baskets.

Twenty minutes later, she exited the barn like a thief in the night, but she didn't get far. One fat, red-faced, ruffled-feathered hen blocked her path. Other curious chickens clustered nearby to see if there would be bloodshed. Holding out her baskets as though they were shields of protection, Rachel advanced. "Look here, Henny Penny, these eggs haven't been fertilized, so they couldn't grow into a baby chick anyway."

The hen marched toward her, pecking the ground with eager anticipation. Rachel ran for her life. Through the flock she hurried, shoving aside those directly in her path with her baskets. She didn't slow down until the latched gate was safely closed behind her.

"Why are you so out of breath?" asked Sarah in the sorting room. She peered at Rachel over her reading glasses.

"They came after me again in number three." Rachel began carefully unloading her eggs onto the conveyor belt.

"Did you get pecked or scratched?" Sarah glanced down at her ankles.

"I outran them this time."

"Are you sure this isn't all in your head?" Sarah appeared to be biting her cheek.

"I don't think so. I've made three enemies in that flock. If I had a say-so, those would be sent to market next. They would look good on somebody's dinner table up in Louisville."

"*Nein*, those are all young laying hens in number three. You'll just have to make your peace with them." Sarah focused on the quantity of eggs. "Thank you for your help."

"You're *welcum*. Now I'll change for work."

"Change? But you didn't get dirty. Why not just wash your hands?"

"I'll wear English clothes today, and because Jake is picking me up, I might as well put them on right now."

Sarah switched off the conveyor belt. "Why is your boss picking you up?" Her expression rivaled that of the beady-eyed red hen.

"Because today is the Brady charity rodeo. This year they're raising money for the Juvenile Diabetes Association. People pay thirty dollars a ticket but see several shows, including one by professional riders, and eat their fill from a barbecue buffet." She replaced her empty baskets on the shelf. "All the money collected goes to charity."

"What does this have to do with mounted horseback tours?" Sarah ignored the dozens of eggs waiting to be sorted and washed.

"Nothing. Twelve Elms doesn't schedule tours during this annual event." When she noticed Sarah's eyebrow arch, she quickly added, "But it's still a workday for employees. I will be helping Mr. Brady."

"The young one?" Sarah's resemblance to Rachel's adversary increased.

"*Jah.*"

"Help him do what, exactly?"

The atmosphere turned almost as ominous as Rachel stiffened her spine. "I will sit with him and his blind riding students. We will describe the various events in the arena for the visually impaired."

Sarah snorted, switched on the conveyor belt, and resumed sorting eggs.

Rachel knew her cousin had nothing against the blind, so she let the matter drop. "I'll see you after work." She strode quickly toward the house wearing a smile triggered by only one thing—spending the day with Jake.

When he pulled into the Stoll yard in his shiny red pickup, Rachel was waiting on the porch. She wore brand-new blue jeans and a long-sleeved, peach-colored sweater beneath her flannel-lined, quilted Twelve Elms jacket. She'd purchased the jeans and sweater at the Charm discount store while running errands with Jessie late one Saturday. Her freshly shampooed hair was tucked under her ball cap. No bun or ponytail on such a special occasion.

"Hi, Jake," she greeted, jogging down the walkway. Her pace rivaled that in the chicken pen.

He opened the passenger door with a gallant bow. "Your carriage awaits, my lady. It might not be as quaint as yours, but it's faster."

As he turned around next to the house, Rachel spotted Isaac and Sarah in the doorway. They stood shoulder to chest, not smiling. She felt a twinge of guilt, followed by a spike of irritation. Wasn't she a grown woman capable of making her own decisions?

"I know we just saw each other, but tell me your news since yesterday at four o'clock." Jake flipped back a lock of hair from his face.

Rachel relayed her egg collection drama and Sarah's assertion that she might be delusional. Then she detailed the contents of Amy's last letter, which had been waiting on her bed. "She thinks she might have news for me, but prefers to wait until her next doctor's appointment. Hmm, I wonder what *that* could mean?" She pressed her hand to her mouth and chuckled.

"Announcements from married couples usually mean one thing. I would start knitting baby blankets if I were you. And regarding the peculiarity of birds, I once had a crow stalk me every time I drove the tractor. He flew behind me squawking until I finished work. I never figured out if he liked me or hoped I would mire down in the mud."

"Crows are very intelligent birds. He was probably trying to figure out what you were doing." As usual, Rachel relaxed in Jake's company. He had a way of putting her at ease with his effortless conversation.

All too soon, however, they reached the overflow parking lot of Twelve Elms. Jake drove in on an access road and parked behind the house. Mrs. Ingraham and eight of her students were waiting for them under a large elm tree.

"Hi, Miss King. Thank you, Mr. Brady," she called. "We're so excited about today's rodeo."

Bethany waited to hear from which direction footsteps approached. Then she charged toward them at full speed, hands extended. The other girls followed on her heels. "Rachel, Jake! Will either of you be barrel racing or calf lassoing? How about riding the jumper course?"

Rachel was soon enveloped in a group hug by three little girls. "Not me. I get to spend the day with you!"

Jake received almost as enthusiastic a welcome from the boys. "No riding for me either. Rachel and I have the day off. Our only assignment is to see that you have a great time."

"That shouldn't be too difficult." Mrs. Ingraham pulled two knotted ropes from her bag. "We're already enjoying ourselves. And I can smell the barbecue cooking." She pressed the rope into each girl's hand. "The girls will hold Miss King's rope while the boys will stick with Jake. I'll bring up the rear to make sure we're all together." While she organized the children, Mrs. Ingraham asked Jake, "Don't you have to work this event?"

"My mother and her friends insisted on using volunteer staff, so the family gets to enjoy the rodeo. But I'm sure my dad will find something to do. He doesn't know how to relax." Jake made sure each boy had a firm hold on the rope.

"Before we enter the arena, we'll stand in line for popcorn, cotton candy, or candy apples," said Mrs. Ingraham. "But remember, only one treat per person. You don't want to spoil your appetite for the buffet later."

Jake gave each child their own ticket to hand to the collector. As they passed into the show barn, a volunteer clown from a nearby church gave them free balloons that advertised their private school. Seats had been reserved for them in the first row so they could avoid climbing the bleachers. Rachel didn't know what to look at first.

"Step right up and take your seats, ladies and gentlemen." A voice resonated over the loud speaker. "Our first show is about to begin—the Twelve Elms hunter-jumper class. You're in for a treat."

Jake leaned over toward Rachel. "I recognize that voice! It's my dad. He must be helping the professional announcer." The boys were sitting on his right, flanked by the teacher.

Rachel was on his left with the girls. "This probably isn't work for him. It sounds like he's having fun."

While the children ate their treats, the loudspeaker announced each contestant. Rachel did her best to explain the pattern of fences for the jumper course and the riders' maneuvers to her girls.

Sighted or not, the children loved the show, clapping loudly for each performer. Afterward they stayed in their seats while workers set up for the professional rodeo. The kids chattered away while the fences were removed and barrels carried into the arena.

Jake decided to narrate the rodeo events to both the girls and boys because he was more knowledgeable than either Rachel or Mrs. Ingraham. With the boys on both sides of him and the girls sitting at his feet, he explained barrel racing, calf roping, team roping, and bareback riding in succession.

"Will there be bull riding?" asked a freckled-faced little boy.

"No, my mom doesn't like it or bronc riding either. She thinks both are too dangerous for man and beasts alike."

The kids clapped enthusiastically during the nonstop action, wild with enthusiasm. But Rachel found herself watching Jake more than the contestants.

"Who's ready to chow down?" he asked after the final event. The chorus of replies nearly damaged their eardrums.

Rachel glanced at him during their supper of barbecue beef, corn, coleslaw, and pulled pork. He patiently wiped chins, poured lemonade, and cleaned up spills while never tiring of their endless questions. Even Mrs. Ingraham remarked what an unusually patient young man he was.

He's unusual in just about all respects. The more time she spent with him, the fonder she became. That realization frightened her as much as it pleased her.

"May I have dessert, Rachel?" asked Bethany. "I've finished my supper." She tilted her clean plate in Rachel's direction.

"Oh, course. Who else wants chocolate cake or cherry pie?" Rachel scrambled to her feet and then hurried to the dessert table with two requests for pie and two for cake.

"I hope you're not eating all those yourself, Miss King." Jake appeared over her shoulder. She hadn't seen him leave the table.

"No, but I might sneak back later once my dinner settles, as long as no one is looking." She grinned up into his handsome face.

"You and I can have dessert later, but Mrs. Ingraham said they're leaving after this."

Rachel blanched at the news, secretly wanting the evening to go on forever. "But why?" she asked. "There's still the parade of show horses and dressage later. And what about winners of the silent auction gift baskets?"

"She said dressage would be too hard to explain to blind students, and none of her kids bought raffle tickets. Anyway, most of them are tired. She said that makes them accident-prone. Let's finish picking out desserts. My boys all want chocolate cake."

Rachel couldn't hide her disappointment on the way back to the table. She distributed her pie and cake with forced gaiety.

"But I'll sit with you during the parade," he said, over the children's heads. "And you can ask me any question you like." He winked while no one else was looking.

"Sounds like a plan." Without thinking, she winked in return. *Oh, goodness, what in the world am I doing?* But that was one question she didn't dare answer.

᪐

Jake and Rachel walked an overexcited group of kids to their bus in the parking lot. None were ready to leave, but Mrs. Ingraham insisted they had taken advantage of Brady hospitality long enough. Truth was, as much as he enjoyed his students, Jake was eager for some time alone with Rachel.

"Where to now?" she asked when the bus turned onto the highway. Both of them waved until they could no longer see the children.

"Anything you like. You pick."

"Let's watch that fancy-schmantsy dressage. Those horses and riders all look like snobs." She lifted her chin high and wiggled her nose in the air.

"Don't let Jessie hear you say that. She trained most of those dressage students."

"I'll behave, don't worry. Then I want to watch the fund-raising in the show barn. I have my eye on basket number twenty-seven. I bid thirty dollars and I'm hoping to win."

"Thirty bucks?" Jake took her arm as they walked back to the arena through the crowd. "Must be something special in that one."

"You're not kidding. It's loaded with bubble bath, shower gel, body lotion, candles, tins of flavored teabags—tons of great stuff."

"All sounds rather smelly to me."

"Yes, but a gal shouldn't smell like horses all the time. I want to smell like peaches and raspberries and the ocean on my days off. Look, there's Keeley." Rachel pointed at his sister. "Is she *juggling*?" Rachel took a step toward a cluster of people.

"She is." Jake grabbed hold of her arm. "People throw money into her hat for charity. How about if we spend the rest of the evening as just the two of us? Haven't you had enough company for one day?"

She looked a tad apprehensive but nodded. "Sure, let's head into the arena. I would hate to miss any of the high-class horses in action."

After dressage they wandered into the show barn, where his mother had created a wonderland. White linen covered every round table and padded chair, while strings of tiny lights twinkled overhead. Bowls of flowers and mixed nuts waited on each table. Even Jake was amazed by the transformation. "It looks like a wedding reception in here," he said. "Let's take that one over there." He guided Rachel to a small table for four.

"Not like any Amish wedding. Is *this* where they'll announce the winners of the baskets?" She peered around as though in a trance.

"Yep, the final event. Look, now my dad's wearing a tux." Jake waved at a well-dressed waiter. Ken Brady and the celebrity chefs circulated around the room with long-stemmed glasses of pink lemonade.

"I have never had so much fun in my life," she said, lifting two glasses from his dad's tray. "Are these for free?" Rachel selected a Brazil nut from the bowl once Ken had moved on to other guests.

"They are. Mom treats the silent auction bidders very well."

Rachel shrugged out of her jacket and hung it on the back of her chair. "This room is too fancy for baseball caps." She pulled off the hat, allowing her hair to fall down her back and shoulders. It cascaded like a waterfall of wheat-colored silk.

Jake was transfixed by her beautiful mane of hair, especially since he'd never seen it not in a braid or ponytail.

She noticed his stare and blushed. "I shouldn't have done that. I got carried away."

"Why not? I promise not to ogle the next time."

"There won't be a next time. An Amish woman never wears her hair down in public. It's to be shown only to her husband. I'm ashamed of myself." She quickly coiled it up and jammed it under the cap—messy, but fairly concealed. "There, that's better."

"Why? I'm not criticizing, only curious."

"It's written in the Bible that a woman's crowning glory should not be displayed." Rachel selected an almond from the bowl.

"Do you always take everything in the Bible literally?"

"Well, yes. It's the Word of God."

"It was written more than two thousand years ago."

"What difference does that make to Christians?"

For that, Jake had no immediate reply. He fished through the mixed nuts looking for another Brazil nut.

"You're a Christian, right? Don't Baptists take God's Word seriously?"

"I'm sure they do. Don't judge Baptists by my example. It's just that I'm young and still need to make my mark in the world. It easier to be devout when a person's old and living on a fat pension check."

Rachel gazed at him with an expression of confusion. "Being a Christian never gets easy. It's not supposed to. What do you mean 'make your mark in the world?'"

"I have to establish Twelve Elms as a world-class training facility. If not in the world, at least in the state of Kentucky. And I need to make a living to support a future family someday."

Her bewilderment didn't ebb. "Can't you earn a living and follow the Lord's path?"

"Generally speaking, yes. I can be nice to folks, give to charity, and try not to get jealous when a buddy buys a new truck. I never kill folks and I don't steal, unless you count the cookie jar on the kitchen counter." He looked up, hoping to see her smile.

But Rachel remained stoic. "Why do you say 'generally speaking'? Nobody can live a faultless life, Jake. By human nature we're doomed to sin and fall far short of the glory of God, but that doesn't mean we shouldn't take the Bible literally and try our best."

Jake glanced around the room. Everyone else was laughing and enjoying the event, while they were locked in theological debate. "In the Gospels, Jesus told His disciples they must give up their jobs, homes, families—leave everything and follow Him. How does that relate to the twenty-first century? My father is devout, but his family is glad he never abandoned us to follow the life of a monk, praying from sunup to sundown."

Rachel was silent for a moment. "You and I might not be called to be missionaries, but God can still be central in our lives. We can still pray about all matters." She reached for his hand.

Her touch washed away his discomfort. "True enough." He squeezed her fingers in return. "Mom is at the podium. She's about to announce the winners for each basket and gift certificate."

Rachel dug a slip of paper from her purse. She had written the number twenty-seven with red marker. "Wish me luck."

"I have a good feeling about this." Jake accepted two more glasses of lemonade and settled back in his padded chair. One by one, the highest bid was announced for each donation. When Taylor Brady called out a name, the winner marched forward to claim their prize with face aglow.

"Oh, dear. These baskets are fetching large sums. Somebody probably passed my thirty-dollar bid five minutes after I placed it."

He forced himself not to grin throughout the first twenty-six donations. Finally, his mom held up the special basket. "Folks, number twenty-seven contains enough goodies to make any woman feel like the Queen of Casey County."

The friendly crowd of benefactors laughed. "And the winning silent bid is…three hundred fifty dollars!"

Rachel groaned. "Not even close. You can tell I've never been to one of these before." She slumped onto her elbows.

"And the winning bidder is…Jake Brady. My son! Goodness, I never thought him the type for this stuff. Come on up, Jake."

Acquaintances in the crowd slapped his back as he strode to the podium to collect his prize. Rachel was sitting wide eyed as an owl when he returned. "This is for you." He set the basket in front of her.

"Have you lost your mind?" she whispered. "*Three hundred fifty dollars?*"

"The bidding had already reached three hundred by the time I got to the table. That's what it cost to win."

"But you could buy that stuff at the mall for a fraction of that."

"This is a charity fund-raiser for the Juvenile Diabetes Association," he said, close to her ear.

"Oh, yeah, I forgot." She fingered the ribbon on the basket. "Thank you, Jake. This is the most generous thing anyone has ever done for me."

But for the rest of the evening, until he walked her to the Stoll back door, she refused to look him in the eye. It was as though the basket was a giant shame to her, similar to the brief interval without her baseball cap.

TWELVE

The Lord has promised good to me

The November horse sale was a highlight in an equestrian's year. With a major contender for the Kentucky Derby in eighteen months, Jake had been anticipating this sale for weeks.

"About ready to go, son?" his father called up from the foot of the stairs.

"Be right down." Jake tightened the knot on his tie before slipping on the cashmere pullover. The sweater had been a Christmas gift from his grandmother. He'd never had an occasion to wear it until now, but he wanted to look like a serious owner, not your average horseman with a few fillies to sell. He had polished his leather loafers until they shone and pressed his chino slacks.

I wish Rachel were coming with us.

That particular errant thought ran through his mind on a regular basis. What interest would an Amish girl have at a horse auction? There would be registered Saddlebreds, Thoroughbreds, and quarter horses. Standardbred buggy and draft horses were usually sold at local county auctions. Yet he wanted her by his side no matter what the occasion. Jake entered the kitchen to a raucous chorus of whoops and wolf whistles.

Keeley looked up from her bowl of cereal. "Who are you?"

Jake ignored her and headed straight for the box of donuts.

"Don't pay any attention to them. You look nice, son." His mother buzzed his cheek with a kiss.

"Had I known what you planned to wear, I never would have returned that tuxedo." His dad chuckled in a similar fashion to his twelve-year-old sister.

"Don't be silly, Ken. That's a brand-new flannel shirt. You look nice too." Taylor bestowed a kiss on her husband's cheek as well.

Jake devoured his first donut and carried his second out the door. "I'll check to see how Bob's coming along with loading the trailer." He stepped onto the porch. Fog hung low over the fields for as far as the eye could see. The sun was a mere amber glow on the horizon behind the thick haze. Rain threatened, but patches of blue to the south promised clearing later.

"Just about ready to go," said Bob Sullivan, the barn manager and a longtime Twelve Elms employee. "Two colts and four fillies—more yearlings than we've sold in several years."

"We're putting our faith behind the colt we're keeping." Jake reached between the rails to scratch the muzzle of a lovely brindle-colored horse. Keeley wanted to keep this filly so much, but Jake insisted on the sale. "We don't need any more riding horses, squirt," he had told her. "Besides, you have a fine mount." Now with the filly's huge round eyes fixed on him, he regretted his decision. "Don't worry, little missy. Somebody nice is bound to buy you."

Keeley's favorite shook her silky mane in disagreement. Their eyes locked between the bars of the trailer as Jake ate the rest of his donut. "Hey, Bob. I changed my mind. Take this brindle back to her stall. She's not for sale." He scratched the horse's nose once more. "Perhaps we'll earn enough on the others that her price won't be missed."

Bob released the ties and led the horse down the ramp. "Keeley will be overjoyed." He offered a gap-toothed smile.

"Let's go, son." Ken latched the trailer door and double-checked the hitch and electrical connections to the taillights. "We have to get these horses unloaded into the sale barn and registered with the director. Then you and I need to check into the hotel and find some supper." He inserted himself behind the steering wheel.

Jake waited for Bob to climb into the backseat before he slipped into the front passenger side. No matter how many years they attended this horse sale, his father always enumerated the exact same sequence of events. But Jake said nothing. With a two-hour drive to Lexington, there was no sense starting out on the wrong foot.

That afternoon the registration process went smoothly, as he figured it would. Jake scratched the brindle filly from the sale roster and then verified the pedigree and particulars for each horse they planned to auction. Bob stabled the horses and left to spend the evening with longtime Lexington cronies. The Brady father and son checked into their hotel and then headed to their favorite steakhouse for dinner, where they dined every year. Three times horsemen interrupted their meal with questions about Eager to Please. Everyone had heard the tales about their colt. And no, he was not for sale.

Jake fell asleep that night with visions of moneybags dancing through his head like sugarplums at Christmas. The attention Eager to Please garnered didn't drop off during breakfast the next morning. Several old-timers stopped at their table in the hotel dining room to shake Ken's hand.

"I brought my checkbook if you want to put Eager to Please on the auction block," said one man, slapping Ken on the back.

"I didn't know you had a million bucks lying around, Frank." Ken grinned with pleasure.

"A million dollars. What did you pour in your orange juice this morning?" His friend picked up the glass and sniffed. Both men laughed good-naturedly.

"Wait until after the Florida yearling races, Mr. Holt. That price is bound to go up," Jake added in a far more serious tone.

"Anything is possible in this industry." After another hearty backslap, Mr. Holt returned to his breakfast table.

"Bob brought me a copy of today's sale program while you were in the shower—hot off the presses." Levity faded from Ken's face.

"Good morning, gentlemen. Ready to order?" asked a sweet-faced waitress.

"I haven't looked at the menu yet," said Ken, "but I guess I'll have what I get every year."

"Why mess with a winner?" She punctuated her question with a wink.

"Two eggs over easy, rye toast, two buckwheat cakes, country ham, and keep the coffee coming." Ken handed her the menu and flexed his knuckles.

"I'll have the blueberry pancakes and coffee. Thanks." Once the woman left, Jake added, "You're mighty brave when Mom's not around."

"She does keep me on a short dietary leash, but there's something we need to discuss before we're interrupted by more Eager to Please admirers." Ken tapped the closed program with his finger.

"What's that?" Jake took a gulp of juice.

"You seem to have omitted an important detail when listing the particulars for that coal-black colt."

He kept his gaze steady. "At the registration table I read from my notes prepared at home."

"There's no mention about the difficult delivery. You didn't say that the dam died giving birth to that colt." Ken watched him over his coffee mug.

"Why on earth would I reveal that? You don't write a short story about every horse for sale. You just list their physical description and give complete details of the bloodline."

His father set his jaw. "There's a line for other significant information. Buyers have a right to know that the horse might have suffered oxygen depletion until we were able to get him out. That could affect his neurological development and temperament down the road."

Jake glanced around to make sure they weren't being overheard. "Please, Dad, keep your voice down. No way would any other seller list that fact."

Ken stared at him. "Then those other sellers would be unethical."

Jake sighed. "If I would have listed possible oxygen deprivation at birth, the price would drop significantly. We need these yearlings to fetch decent prices this year, especially since I gave in and let Keeley keep the brindle filly."

"The price they bring should reflect the potential of the horse these people are buying—nothing more and nothing less." His dad sounded like a mystical sage sitting high in the Himalayas, dispensing wisdom.

Jake's mouth dried out as his irritation grew. "We have no idea if the colt was adversely affected during birth. Some horses and people survive oxygen loss with no lasting effects. The vet thoroughly examined that horse and pronounced him sound." He leaned across the table. "People would think us foolish to list that detail."

Ken's face darkened. "Those who would think our integrity foolish must possess none themselves."

Jake gritted his teeth. They were two bulls squaring off in the pasture. "Rich folks can afford to take that kind of high road. *We* can implement the high road once we put Twelve Elms on the right track."

"I can't believe I'm hearing you right. This isn't how your mother and I raised you—"

"Here you go, boys. Breakfast is served." Their friendly waitress set down two steaming plates of food. "More coffee?"

"Yes, ma'am." Father and son spoke simultaneously.

"Why don't we eat and think this over carefully." Ken picked up his fork and knife.

Jake stared at his pancakes dripping with melted butter and maple syrup with a waning appetite. His dad had a point. And they were *family* besides business partners. He forced himself to eat half the stack before continuing their discussion. "I know you raised me to have a strong code of morals. And I should be grateful, but in this business how will we survive following the Good Book letter for letter?" He set down his napkin. "We don't have a choice."

"There's always a choice, son. God's way...or the other."

For a full minute in the busy hotel restaurant, time stopped like in one of those silly romantic comedies when two people in a crowd reach some impasse.

Ken sipped coffee, wincing from the hot temperature. "I would like you to talk to the director. Tell him some details were inadvertently omitted."

Jake slouched in his chair. "You realize that since the program has been printed, any additions, deletions, or changes must be announced before the auction starts. Instead of a one-line memo in a program filled with trivia, now they'll broadcast the information over the loudspeaker, giving the detail far more importance than it deserves."

Ken shrugged with nonchalance. "That's on you, son. But I'll feel better knowing the colt will bring exactly what he's worth. And so should you. Now, let's eat up and get to the sale. I want a good seat."

And so should you...

No doubt he should, but at the moment that wasn't the case.

They finished breakfast, checked out of the hotel, and drove to the auction site. Little was said on the way other than comments on the weather or Lexington's heavy traffic.

Bob greeted them with his customary cheeriness. The man always stayed overnight with a cousin, sparing Twelve Elms the expense of his hotel room. "I've given all five sale horses a final brushing. They look good, don't they? There's been talk around the barns about Eager," he said. "Grooms gossip like old women at a quilting bee."

"So I've noticed," said Jake. "Excuse me, Bob. I need to stop at the registration counter before we sit down."

"Didn't you get the program I left at the front desk for you?"

"Yeah, thanks, but I forgot something about one of the horses. Save me a seat in the arena." Jake strode off to discourage more questions. Let his dad tell the manager about his bad decision.

Although he possessed little ability for fortune-telling, his prophecy about the black colt had been correct. The horse brought half the selling price he should have. All told, the annual auction disappointed Jake in more ways than one. Every business required a concise plan of action, yet he wasn't remotely on the same page with his father.

෴

During the next few days after the rodeo, Rachel lived the normal life of an Amish woman. She attended church services on Sunday with Isaac and Sarah, arriving and departing in their horse and buggy. On Monday, she and Sarah washed clothes and ironed shirts and dresses. On Tuesday they cleaned house from top to bottom, and then they baked bread and desserts for the rest of the week in addition to their regular farm chores. They got along fairly well because Sarah made few comments and asked only one question regarding Saturday. Her comments amounted to: "I suppose you're not hungry after all the gourmet food at the fancy shindig," and "I hope young Mr. Brady isn't getting any big ideas about you."

Her sole question consisted of: "Where did all of these scented beauty products come from?" Picking up the basket, Sarah turned it left and right to study.

Rachel pulled off the ribbon and cellophane. "I'll unload it in the bathroom linen closet. There's enough to share, so take whatever you like." She explained the silent auction at the fund-raiser and the bidding process, neglecting to mention the final price paid by Jake. Charity or not, that would have branded him as reckless in Sarah's eyes forevermore.

Her placid life changed abruptly on Wednesday. When she came in from work, Rachel found a letter from home on the kitchen table...opened.

"*Grossmammi* has a few things to say to you," said Sarah. The delicious smell of chicken soup filled the room as she stirred the pot. "I suspected she would."

"You've already read my letter?" Surprised, Rachel picked up the two sheets with her grandmother's fine, neat script. Sarah had never invaded her privacy before.

"It was addressed to both of us, so of course I did." Sarah dropped more vegetables into the soup.

Sure enough, two names were written on the face-up envelope: Mrs. Sarah Stoll and Miss Rachel King. Rachel carried the letter into the living room to read, where a warm fire burned in the pot-bellied stove. A strange sensation of dread lifted the hairs on her neck as though she'd been caught shirking chores as a child.

Dear Rachel,

I pray this letter finds you in good health. Your grossdawdi, Beth, and I are well and happy to have the harvest behind us. I will let your schwester fill you in on the Lancaster news

*since Beth hears more gossip than me. And because I have a
more important bone to pick with you.*

Rachel slumped onto a chair close to the fire. The heat felt good
in the cooler-than-average weather.

*Your cousin says you wear English clothes at your new
job. I don't understand why you don't work for Sarah and
Isaac—those who put a roof over your head and food on
your plate. Sarah told me their chicken farm keeps growing. Isaac must build another new barn before next spring.
And if you must work with horses, can't you find a Mennonite horse farm? Too much time spent with Englischers only
leads to too much worldliness. You know what happened to
Amy's brother-in-law. His job on the English logging crew
led nowhere but to his downfall. Do not wander foolishly
from the path of righteousness.*

Come home. We miss you.
Grossmammi

Rachel buried her face in her hands as a wave of sorrow washed
over her. She visualized her mother and grandmother rolling out
pie dough at the kitchen table. She and her sisters had always been
in charge of the fruit fillings. They would eat more blueberries,
cherries, or apples than ended up baked in any pie.

But *grossmammi* was wrong to blame *Englischers* for Elam Detweiler's fall from grace. Amy's brother-in-law had been smoking,
drinking beer, and sneaking out at night long before he worked on
the logging crew. No one knew where Elam had gone after he left
Paradise, Missouri. Nora had been his last tie to the Amish lifestyle.
When she married Lewis, nothing remained to keep him in town.

Rachel folded the letter and jammed it into her apron pocket.
She would wait for a cooler head before writing back. Was she like
Elam? Absolutely not. He was rebellious, contrary, and opinionated

besides being fascinated with *Englischers*. She merely wanted to ride Thoroughbreds. That did not put her on the road to ruin.

At least Sarah hadn't told their grandmother she was courting Amish and English alike. *Grossmammi* probably would board the next Greyhound bus headed west. She smiled, picturing the white-haired matriarch marching up Sarah's driveway with her satchel in one hand and shaking her index finger. How she loved that woman. Sarah probably didn't want to panic loved ones back home until Rachel refused to come to her senses, but one of her two Amish beaus had already dropped from the competition. Last Sunday after church, Becky told her that John Swartz had returned home. That left only Reuben Mullet who had shown any real interest in her. And she spent too little time at Plain social events to meet new people.

Lately she preferred walking the forest paths in the evening or staring out her bedroom window while thinking about a tall, blond-haired man with brown eyes and a tender heart. So maybe, deep under her skin, she wasn't that different from Elam Detweiler after all.

❦

Friday morning Rachel crossed swords with her cousin for the second time that week when she arrived in the kitchen wearing English clothes.

"Why are you dressed like that?" asked Sarah.

Isaac peered up over his newspaper and frowned. "Do you want me to hitch up the rig?"

"No, *danki*. Not today." She smiled at him before turning her focus to Sarah. "Jake is picking me up because after work I'm going with him on an errand." Rachel hurried to pour a mug of mental fortification. "So I might as well wear English clothes."

"What kind of errand?" Isaac's bacon started to spatter in the pan.

"He's picking up four cats from the vet that have been spayed or neutered and given their shots. These were strays that found their way to Twelve Elms. We're taking them to a no-kill shelter near Somerset. Once they're fixed, they have no trouble finding homes. The Bradys already have three cats."

Sarah shook her head. "Don't bring any here. Chickens don't like cats."

"I promise I won't." She gulped her coffee and created a sandwich with scrambled eggs in between two slices of toast.

"Will you be home for supper after dropping off the cats?" Sarah lifted the bacon from the pan with tongs.

"No. When we're done Jake wants to try a new all-you-can-eat pizza buffet. Ten different kinds each day."

"Pizza is pizza. It all tastes the same." Sarah thumped the plate of bacon on the table. "This sounds very much like a date."

Swallowing her mouthful of sandwich, Rachel dabbed her lips. "That's because I suppose it is. I told you I planned to court both Amish and English and not get serious with anybody."

"Can I have a refill on my coffee, *fraa*, if you're not too busy butting your nose in Rachel's life?" Isaac's question curtailed discussion at the Stoll breakfast table.

When Jake picked her up fifteen minutes later, Rachel practically ran to his truck. All too soon they arrived at Twelve Elms, where work pulled them in different directions. But she didn't mind. The November weather was mild. Flocks of migrating birds drifted overhead in large patterns, and she would spend the day with Bess and Buster on the tour wagon. What could be finer? *Spending the entire evening with Jake.* And she had that to look forward to all day.

Promptly at four o'clock, he walked into the stable office. She and Keeley had been cleaning and organizing after their last tour. "Ready to go?" he asked. His hair was still damp from a shower.

"Give me five minutes." Grabbing her tote bag, she headed into the ladies' room. With her heart pounding in her chest, Rachel washed her face and hands, changed shirts, retied her ponytail, and rubbed on peach hand cream. After a spritz of raspberry body mist, she studied herself in the mirror. She looked...English. That had never been her goal, yet it had crept up on her like fog. For a moment she felt guilty. But the moment passed when she saw Jake at the foot of the office steps.

"You look nice and smell good too," he said.

"Gosh, Jake," called Keeley through the open window. "You need to watch some romantic movies or take lessons or *something*. You are so lame."

He blushed to a shade of bright red. "I should have waited to say anything until we were alone. Keeley is like a tick that crawls up your pant leg and burrows under the skin. You scratch and scratch, but you can't rid yourself of her."

Rachel took his hand. "Don't worry. We have one of those in the King family too. Her name is Beth."

"So saying you smell nice isn't the stupidest compliment you ever received?" He tightened his hold on her hand, his embarrassment gone.

"Not by a long shot. The Kings are famous for left-handed compliments. When I was learning to cook, my father loved to say, 'This doesn't taste nearly as bad as the last time you made it.' Once my *mamm* told me, 'Thank goodness your sore throat is gone. Now you can sing like a regular frog instead of a dying one.'"

Jake drew her close, slipping his arm around her waist. "The Bradys and the Kings have more in common than anyone would have guessed."

Rachel should have batted away his bold gesture. Such displays of affection were forbidden in the Plain culture, even among engaged couples. But she didn't. Another line had been crossed between them, and that worried her far less than it should.

At the vet's office, Dr. Bobbie Kirby greeted Jake like an old friend instead of a client. "Your four new adoptees are ready to go, Jake. Fit as fiddles with all their shots. They're very friendly too. Don't worry about bringing the carriers back soon. Just use them for your next delivery. There will always be more stray cats in Casey County."

"Thanks, Doc. What do I owe you?" He extracted his checkbook from a back pocket.

The vet placed a statement on the counter. "I wish vet bills were at least tax deductible. You sure pay enough during a calendar year." While Jake wrote out the check, Dr. Kirby studied Rachel, who stood by the door trying to keep a low profile. "Who are you?" she asked. "Jake's new girlfriend?"

Before she could reply, he answered, "I wish, but no, we work together and are just good friends."

"If I can offer a biased opinion, this guy has a heart of solid gold. Too bad I'm not twenty years younger." The vet smiled brightly at Rachel.

He rolled his eyes. "Besides the fact you're already married to Dr. Mike." Jake tore out the check and picked up two of the pet carriers. "Thanks, Doc. See you next time."

Rachel nodded at the woman, who kept staring at her. "Nice meeting you." She hurried out the door with the other carriers, a bit discombobulated. *I wish?* Her earlier frisson of guilt returned, yet she'd had many chances to discourage him and had taken none.

At the no-kill shelter, Jake requested that she stay in the car. "If you come inside, you'll want to take just about every cat home. That's how we ended up with Luke and Leia—Jessie helped me that day. I refuse to bring Keeley here."

"Keeley considers Skinny Joe to be hers, not yours. So she ended up with a cat after all." She and Jake locked gazes before he jumped out to take the carriers inside the shelter. During his two trips, Rachel had time to ponder the vet's assessment: *This guy has a heart of solid gold.* That was only one of the things she liked about him. He wasn't just nice to kids and stray animals. He made her feel very special instead of exactly what she was—a run-of-the-mill Amish girl with no particular skills or abilities.

During supper that night, they feasted on buffalo chicken, veggie delight, and pineapple ham pizza. They drank endless iced teas and then took a long walk to the town square to burn off the extra calories and their nervous energy. Rachel never asked about the time or worried how late it was getting to be. She never considered Sarah's potential pique should this date surpass her preconceived notion. And when Jake leaned over to kiss her by the fountain, she didn't even *think* about trying to stop him.

THIRTEEN

His Word my hope secures

Saturday

Rachel lay in bed for a long time waiting for sleep to come. As much as she'd enjoyed Jake's kiss, it didn't bode well for her resolution to keep things casual with the men she dated. Friends, even good friends, didn't kiss each other on the lips. Yet she and Jake had kissed, not once but twice. The second smooch occurred on the Stoll porch when he walked her to the back door. Once again, she hadn't tried to discourage him. She simply closed her eyes and puckered up. Rachel half expected Sarah and Isaac to have been waiting in the kitchen, tapping their toes and pointing at the clock on the wall, but the room had been dark with a sole light burning at the foot of the steps.

This morning Rachel found an empty kitchen when she crept downstairs bundled in her bathrobe, carrying her Amish dress, apron, and *kapp*. She breathed a sigh of relief, but before she drank her first cup of coffee, Sarah swept open the door.

"Ah, I see you will be Amish today," she said, setting her basket of eggs on the counter.

Rachel picked up the eggs to wash. "I am Amish every day, Sarah. My heart stays Plain no matter what clothes I wear."

"Hearing you say that does my heart good. *Grossmammi* expects me to keep an eye on you despite the fact you're gone three days a week." Sarah wrapped her arms around Rachel's waist in a brief but affectionate hug. "How about oatmeal and fruit? We've eaten enough eggs this week. It's cold today. Hot oats will stick to our ribs."

"Sounds *gut*. I'll slice the fruit before I shower."

A little while later, when Rachel emerged from a steamy bathroom, the scent of cinnamon, sugar, and nutmeg wafted from Sarah's stove to fill the room. Throughout breakfast with Sarah and Isaac, she waited for one or the other to question her about last night.

I noticed you didn't get home until eleven sixteen and twenty seconds.

We saw you kiss your boss and have already mailed letters to our grandmother and all of your sisters.

Nothing spoke louder than a guilty conscience, *rumschpringe* or not. Testing the water before joining the Amish church usually didn't include dating *Englischers*.

Isaac finished his breakfast and straightened from the table. "Eat hearty, Rachel. Take your time. I'll hitch up the rig." He donned his hat and closed the door behind him.

"Did you enjoy the pizza last night?" Sarah asked as she poured herself another cup of coffee.

"Yes. Whoever would have guessed pineapple on pizza tasted good?"

"That sounds awful. Are you coming home after work or seeing Mr. Brady? There's a singing tonight."

"I'm coming home. And you may call Mr. Brady 'Jake' so I don't think you mean his *daed*."

"One's the same to me." Sarah took a deep swallow of coffee.

Rachel squeezed Sarah's shoulders before leaving. "I'll see you at supper. If there's any Hawaiian pizza left from the one we brought home, I'll bring you a piece." All the way to work she thought about Sarah. She hoped her behavior with Jake wouldn't get her cousin in trouble with *grossmammi*. She had been thinking solely of herself lately instead of others.

Jake met her on the driveway of Twelve Elms before she had a chance to park her buggy. He jumped up to ride the rest of the way with her. "Good morning, Miss King. I trust you slept well."

As much as she hated lies, she couldn't admit to staying awake and thinking about their walk in the town square. "I always sleep well when the weather cools down, Mr. Brady. Only hot, sticky nights keep me tossing and turning." She parked the buggy under the barn's overhang. "Have you seen the schedule? I wonder how many I'll have for today's mounted tour."

"None. That's why I wanted to talk to you. This time of year, especially the closer we get to Christmas, tour bookings really drop off. You'll be lucky to get half a dozen during the entire winter." He deftly unhitched her horse and led him into the paddock.

"Uh-oh. This sounds as though I'm being laid off." She grabbed her lunch and tote bag from the seat. "Is this my last day?"

Jake focused his honey-brown eyes on her. "Not by a long shot. I would fire Keeley or Virgil before I'd get rid of you."

Despite temperatures being only in the fifties, her face grew very warm. "Are you transferring me to the gift shop? Because if so, I won't change into my jeans and riding boots."

"Nope. Not the gift shop. Consider this a promotion. When there are no scheduled tours, I want you to work as an exercise girl. At first you'll mainly ride our boarding clients so they don't get fat."

Jake pulled open the office door for her. "Eventually you will be assisting the trainers too."

She paused in the doorway, wanting to be alone with Jake for a few minutes more. "Are you serious? Nothing would please me more. As fond as I am of Bess and Buster, I would love riding horses around the arena or on the track. I could still take Bess apples at lunchtime."

"I'm completely serious. When there are no tours, report to Larry for your assignment. You'll also work with my dad and me. Larry has another exercise girl, Cara, who will teach you the ropes."

"No one will mind me joining the training team?" She hoped she didn't sound as insecure as she felt.

"Of course not. The other employees like you, Rachel. And you receive a lot of positive feedback from the tourists." Jake took her hand. "Let's talk inside. We're letting the heat out. Keeley is still in the house, so we'll have privacy."

She entered the warm office and settled into a chair by the window. "What kind of feedback? I've never passed out a single comment card since I took over from Jessie."

"People who booked tours over the Internet receive a follow-up e-mail that asks how they liked it. You haven't received a bad report yet."

Rachel ducked her head. "Speaking of Keeley, what will she do on Saturdays when there are no tours?"

"What she does best—sleep late, watch TV all day in her pajamas, and munch on chips." Jake took hold of one of her *kapp* strings and twirled it around his finger.

She yanked it back and tucked it behind her ear. "Keeley has no friends?"

"None with cars. Mom always works on Saturdays. Once in a while when Jessie is home, they go to the movies or shopping at the mall." This time he reached for her other ribbon.

"Stop that," she scolded with little conviction. "You're not

Skinny Joe after a piece of yarn." Scrambling to her feet, Rachel picked up her bag. "Now that I'm officially an exercise girl, I'll change into riding clothes." She paused in the doorway and looked back. Jake had already switched on the computer. "Do you suppose I might ride Eager to Please someday?"

His face softened. "The unofficial employee-of-the-month wants to mount a raging beast?"

"I would love to." She waited, afraid to exhale.

"He's not here, Rachel. But when he returns, I don't see why not. Of course, we'll need approval from Alan Hitchcock. He's in charge of Eager's training."

Rachel hefted her bag to her shoulder. "Where is Eager?"

"In Florida for the winter months. They run yearling races to prepare for the two-year-old stakes races in May. He'll be back by spring."

"I didn't get a chance to say goodbye." Her exuberance over the promotion ebbed.

Jake's eyes grew round. "The Hitchcock entourage left a week ago on your day off. I didn't realize you'd grown attached."

"I would sneak in sometimes after work to scratch his ears. He loved it."

"Sorry, darlin'. I'll tell you what. When the colt comes home, I'll assign you to Eager's team. You're light enough to ride him around the track."

"Thanks, Jake. I won't eat another slice of pie or third piece of fried chicken again."

He leaned back in his chair. "You're perfect just the way you are. Anyway, you'll burn off any extra calories working the boarders. You won't be riding in a wagon pulled by slow, fat Bess all day long."

"*Fat?* Wait until I tell her. You had better start checking over your shoulder, Jake Brady." Rachel stalked off, feigning indignation on behalf of a huge draft horse. It was the only thing she could do to not think about the touch of his fingers on her cheek, or his casually spoken endearment. *You're perfect just the way you are.* Was this a proper way to talk to an Amish woman?

❧

As lovely as Jake's Saturday morning had been, the day went downhill from there. After introducing Rachel to the trainer she would report to, he'd left her in Larry's capable hands. Dad thought Rachel should take orders from someone other than him so there would be no complaints of favoritism around the employee lounge. Jake thought it a good idea too. No way could he work with her constantly. The temptation to hold her hand or sneak a quick kiss would be too great. Earlier, two dangling *kapp* ribbons had proven irresistible.

Rachel's happiness over her promotion to exercise girl kept his spirits up during an onerous morning of dozens of e-mails. By the time Jake left the office with a stiff back and a crick in his neck, the only thing on his mind was seeing Rachel at lunch. Maybe his mom had left a pot of soup in the kitchen they could carry to the porch for some privacy. Eating with your jacket on was preferable to Keeley's surveillance of his romantic abilities. Her frequent comments regarding his shortfalls did nothing for his confidence. Or maybe Sarah had packed Rachel's lunch, in which case there would be enough for two. If the trail wasn't too muddy, he would suggest a picnic at the mill.

But his father curtailed his plans with a mandatory meeting to discuss Hitchcock's progress with Eager to Please. Ken was worried about the escalating expenses. And he was especially curious as to why Jake remained in Kentucky instead of accompanying the horse to Florida as planned. What could he say? *I'm afraid my girlfriend will marry somebody else while I'm gone?* No. Jake wanted to communicate his plan to continue to get new clients. When they returned from the diner in town, Jake spotted Rachel in the arena exercising one of their boarded Saddlebreds. That one glimpse would have to suffice until after work.

At four o'clock he lurked under a bare elm she would have to pass. "May I walk you to your carriage, my princess?" He pushed off from the tree trunk as she approached, already wearing her Plain attire.

"I do feel like a princess on the back of those expensive horses. One is more handsome than the next. I took apples to Calamity Jane, Bess, and Buster to make sure their feelings weren't hurt. What if they saw me from their stall windows?" Rachel fell in step at his side, close but not touching.

"Did you tell Bess about my unkind remark?" He shortened his stride to lengthen the duration of their walk.

"I decided against it. After all, why should one human opinion lower her self-esteem? Beauty is in the eye of the beholder."

"You're absolutely correct." Jake jammed his hands down in his pockets. With only a few minutes together, he didn't want to discuss draft horses, even if Bess was the world's prettiest. "What are your plans for tonight? If you'd like, we could see a movie in Somerset. Keeley will know what's playing at the mall."

When she turned her face to him, the sun sparkled in her blue eyes, while a lock of blond hair peeked from the side of her *kapp*. She looked heartbreakingly beautiful. "Thanks for the invite, but two dates within two days wouldn't be very casual." Her dimples deepened with her smile. "Tonight I'll attend an Amish singing if I'm not too tired when I get home."

"Would you like me to take you and pick you up when it's finished?" He spoke without thinking.

"No, I'll drive myself. If it's too far, one of my friends has a car and could pick me up." She entered the paddock for Isaac's gelding. After a gentle stroke down his black mane, she led the horse to her buggy.

Jake followed at her heels, similar to Skinny Joe but with one more eye. He was no less devoted. "Do you huddle around a campfire while someone strums a guitar?" He held the bridle while she attached the harness.

"No guitars or other instruments, and if there's a bonfire to roast marshmallows, it would be after the singing. We sit at long tables—girls on one side, boys on the other—inside someone's barn or outbuilding. The Amish use the *Ausbund* for hymns. Here the Mennonites sing old-fashioned hymns in German but contemporary songs in English. It's more like church than a campfire sing-along, but we socialize afterward."

"Do people of all ages show up?" He offered his hand as she climbed aboard.

Rachel hesitated before accepting, always surprised by gallant gestures. "No, singings are for young people of courting age or close to it. Once an engaged couple ties the knot, they no longer come to singings."

"I'm starting to catch on." He handed her the reins.

"We're both learning new things, no?" She released the brake. "Thank you for helping with my horse, Jake. I'll see you Wednesday."

With his chance about to slip away, he caught hold of the harness. "There are two questions I've been meaning to ask, Rachel. Would you like to work on Thursdays? It's not mandatory, but if Sarah can spare you, the stable needs extra help. I know Mondays and Tuesdays are busy at home."

Rachel pulled a quilt over her knees. "I'd love to work Thursdays, maybe every other week until spring or until they send me back to Pennsylvania. I'll check with Sarah and Isaac." She laughed with that magical sound.

Jake felt his palms begin to sweat. Even in jest, he hated the idea of Rachel going home. *This* was home—Twelve Elms Stables of Charm, Kentucky. "We'll take any day the Stolls can spare you."

"What was your other question?" She shielded her eyes with one hand.

"I wondered if you would like to go to church with me tomorrow. I'm curious as to what your service is like, so I thought you might like to see what goes on in a Baptist church."

For half a minute Rachel stared at him. Apparently, his question had caught her off guard. Jake forced himself to wait, not filling the air with pointless chatter. His patience was rewarded.

"Sure, why not? I *am* curious. What should I wear? I own no English clothes other than my work duds."

"Wear an Amish dress, of course. Just expect to turn a few heads, and someone might ask a question or two."

"Not to worry. Plain folks are used to stares and nosy questions. What time should I expect you?" She shook the reins against the gelding's flank. Her buggy started to roll.

"I'll pick you up at eight."

"Perfect. I'll be ready," she called without turning around. Rachel was already headed back to her own world.

Jake thought about jogging along to the highway but restrained his juvenile impulse. At least he would see her tomorrow. And that was about as long as he could wait.

❧

Sunday morning

When Jake casually mentioned that Rachel would be joining them for services, his family reacted as though he announced his imminent move to the south of France. Questions flew through the kitchen, which he either ignored or answered with a flat "no." Only Jessie, home from college for the holidays, showed little surprise. When the fervor died down, he asked his sister, "Don't you have anything to add?"

"Only that I saw this coming long ago." Jessie graced him with a toothy smile. "Don't worry. I'll run interference to keep Keeley and Virgil at arm's length. I would hate for Rachel to see the real Bradys in action too soon." Jake thanked her with a nod and headed out the door, feeling his mom's eyes boring into his back.

At the chicken farm Rachel was waiting on the porch, despite a cool drizzle under a dismal gray sky. When she climbed into his truck she lifted her palm in warning. "Don't even ask how Sarah and Isaac reacted to my accompanying you this morning. Let's talk about this lovely weather or the upcoming Bengals game...anything but the Stoll breakfast conversation."

"My family couldn't believe it either. I'll give you my news first, and then you can tell me about last night." Jake looked in both directions before pulling onto the highway. "The no-kill shelter called yesterday. Three of the cats have already been adopted, and someone is interested in the fourth one."

Rachel clapped her hands. "That is great news! Much better than mine, I'm afraid. The singing went fine, but afterward Reuben Mullet occupied all my time talking about his dairy herd. I don't know how I can meet the rest of the district if he monopolizes every minute."

Jake tried to act sympathetic while inside he celebrated hapless Reuben shooting himself in the foot. *One competitor out of the running.*

Too soon they arrived at the First Baptist Church of Charm. Rachel sprang out of the vehicle. "I noticed this church's steeple when I arrived in town. Now I get to see the inside too." She clasped his hand as they hurried up the steps, not waiting for the call-to-worship bell or the rest of his family. Selecting a pew near the front, Rachel spent the time studying each new arrival to the sanctuary. During the service they shared a hymnal, bowed their heads in prayer, and listened intently to Reverend Bullock's sermon. When they finally filed out into the cold rain, Rachel's face was glowing.

"That was great! What an inspiring message. And to think I once asked if you were Christian. What a goose I was." She skipped down the stone path, dodging puddles of standing water along the way.

Jake tried to keep up with her, feeling like a phony. She pegged him as genuinely spiritual, but wasn't he just a poser, going through the motions?

❧

Donna arrived at work dreading the meeting with her boss. She had avoided him for as long as possible, communicating through text messages and e-mails, and was conveniently out in the field whenever she knew he would be in the office. But Phil Richards refused to be put off any longer. When she walked into his office at nine o'clock, she was armed with a twenty-ounce cup of coffee and a stack of archived news printouts for ammunition.

"There you are, Cline!" he barked from behind his desk. "I started to think you skipped town with some Latin dance instructor and have been fudging your paperwork to keep the paychecks coming."

"That might not be a bad plan, except I have two left feet." She took the chair across from him.

Phil did not laugh. He didn't even smile. "What's going on with the Amish? Where are your numbers for new inoculations?"

"I'm here to update you." She forced a smile. "The state techs and I finished our door-to-door canvass of the Amish and Mennonite homes in the county. Some agreed to have their families checked for the virus, but many refused to submit samples for the test."

"I already know that much. That's how we found the four new cases. How many vaccines did you administer?"

"Less than half a dozen."

"That's not good enough. What's wrong with these people?" His face scrunched into an unappealing frown.

"There's nothing wrong with them, Phil. If you will calm down, I'll try to explain their logic."

He appeared surprised at her response, but he clamped his mouth shut and settled back in his chair. "You have the floor, Mrs. Cline."

"Most felt the collection of stool samples to be embarrassingly invasive of their privacy, even after I explained about the new cases of polio. They asked if any of the children had become paralyzed and I had to say no."

"Why are you giving them reasons not to immunize?"

"I'm not, but I researched this to the best of my abilities. These children don't have the wild polio virus that can paralyze. The last case of wild polio in the US was in 1979, and three of the four children in Charm are asymptomatic, like ninety-five percent of all infections. Even in the sick little girl, no one would have discovered polio if she hadn't been hospitalized from other conditions."

"What about the five percent who do catch polio?" Phil leaned across his desk. "You wouldn't want one of your kids to be one of them."

"True, but the virus so closely resembles the flu that most parents don't realize what they have. The children recover completely within a week and will have lifetime immunity. Less than one percent of cases result in paralysis, and even many of those recover eventually. More American children drown each year taking baths, but the CDC hasn't banned bathtubs."

Phil narrowed his eyes. "I hope you haven't been spouting your *research* to the county residents."

"No, I haven't, not unless someone asks a direct question. But with people leery about potential toxins in vaccines, how could I just ram this down their throats?"

"Maybe because it's *your job*."

Donna sucked in a deep breath. "For the record, Phil, I had my kids immunized and have never regretted the decision. But there are two sides to this issue."

He squinted as though focusing on small print without his glasses. "But you only work for one side."

"One Mennonite woman asked me how the first child contracted the virus. I said I didn't know but I would look into it."

"Well, as the hospital researchers and pediatricians don't even know, what did you come up with, Sherlock Holmes?"

"We'll never know for sure, but tests show the child's virus was almost identical to the oral polio vaccine given throughout the world, but not in the US since 2000. Based on how the virus mutates, it's been circulating for two years. Yet the little girl never left the country." She crossed her arms.

"I read all this, Donna. Get to your point." Phil picked up a folder from the stack.

"The child had been shuffled between four hospitals while trying to figure out what's wrong with her. That's where she caught it—in the hospital. Maybe a foreign health care worker didn't receive enough vaccine to trigger immunity and passed the virus to her. Now this little girl is a carrier. Why should the Amish, who choose to separate from the world, trust our system? And with the girl's compromised immunity, her polio might very well become paralytic."

Phil scraped his face with his hands. "You're making a lot of assumptions, Cline. And even if the child caught it in the hospital, what does it matter? Folks travel, including the Amish. Nobody can remain separate in the world anymore. You'll never know if that person sitting next to you in the bus station is a carrier or not. People who don't know they're infected can spread it for two months. If twenty-five people got sick, twenty thousand more could have the virus if they haven't been immunized. Our job is prevention, period."

She sighed heavily. "I can't argue with that."

"Then go back there and give them the worst-case scenario. You need to explain that this can turn into a powder keg down the road. I want every family tested so we know exactly where we stand. Go to their leaders. No disease is eradicated as long as Americans travel overseas."

She rose slowly to her feet. "I'll call on the bishop again."

"Donna, your job is to protect the health and well-being of county residents, and testing won't endanger kids or step on anybody's toes."

"I understand, Phil." She tried to keep her frustration out of her response.

"I want a full report in two weeks detailing your success rate. If you don't like your job, you could look into cake decorating or telemarketing."

He was only half joking. But what did she expect?

That afternoon she stopped on her way home from work to talk to her pastor. Although her church didn't use a small, wooden enclosure to divulge sins and shameful behavior like the Roman Catholics, nevertheless, Donna needed to purge a guilty conscience. She had allowed her desire to respect Amish autonomy to cloud her judgment as a nurse and medical professional. So she sat knee-to-knee with her minister, pouring out the crux of her inadequacies.

When she finished, he placed his hand atop hers. "It sounds as though you've had a change of heart since beginning this project."

"My boss made some valid points, but I want to do what's right. This just isn't as black and white as I'd like it to be."

"Few things in life are, Donna. You've been using Internet research and medical statistics to deal with this. Maybe it's time to consult the Lord. Then listen to what's in your heart instead of only what's in your head. God will help if you seek direction." He patted her hand as though she were a child.

When she left his office she felt disappointed. Send the matter up in prayer? Wasn't that always a clergyman's answer? Did he really think that worked with everything? *But why not give it a try?* She'd already talked the subject into a circle.

Maybe it was time to try another approach.

FOURTEEN

He will my shield and portion be,
As long as life endures

Wash day had its own cadence and rhythm. Rachel and Sarah would fix a large pot of soup to cook all day that would be ready for supper. The women coordinated tasks to have laundry and linens washed and dried by noontime. After their lunch of sandwiches and canned pickled vegetables, Sarah would bundle up and head to the barns to gather eggs, unable to stay away from her beloved birds for long. While Isaac tended other endless chicken chores, Sarah spent hours washing and sorting eggs by size and color.

Rachel gratefully stayed indoors—a good place to be in cold weather—and appreciated three hours to herself. While ironing dresses and Isaac's shirts, she thought about yesterday and her future in general. It was easy to let things happen, to drift along through life-changing events with only minor consideration. But those minor changes eventually added up to a new identity for Rachel King.

Plugging in the electric iron, she thought about how even one household appliance impacted her life. Sarah's Mennonite district permitted electricity from the grid for both homes and businesses. Although they still farmed with Belgians and drove horse and buggy rigs, electricity provided convenience and leisure Rachel hadn't known in Lancaster County. With so many electric lights, families stayed up longer in the evening. Candlelight or kerosene lamps turned low caused eyelids to droop soon after sunset. Although the King family used a propane refrigerator, stove, and washing machine, they hung laundry on outdoor clotheslines in fair weather and on ropes strung across porches in foul. They used no vacuum cleaner, toaster, or food processor. They heated the house with three wood-burning stoves—one in the kitchen, another in the living room, and a third in her parents' bedroom. They used a small potbelly only with a newborn at home, or on days with single-digit temperatures. Vents cut in the downstairs ceiling allowed heat to rise into the upstairs bedrooms, but she and her sisters had often slept wearing socks under heavy quilts.

Was Rachel becoming spoiled? No doubt about it. Life would take some readjustment when she returned to Lancaster. But it wasn't easier chores that worried her this chilly December afternoon. She and Jake had taken another step toward the irrevocable chasm separating their two worlds. One step closer to the point of no return every Amish youth was warned about.

She had loved the Baptist church service down to the last detail—voices raised in songs of praise, folks giving testimonials about how the Lord had worked in their lives, even the minister's sermon. His message had convicted her of self-absorption and inspired her to try harder during the upcoming week. Who could ask for more? Not that she found Amish preaching lacking in any way, but standing by Jake's side had felt...right. Rachel gave her Sunday dress a few more swipes with the iron and hung it on a hanger. That was the long and short of it—Jake Brady. She never would have attended an English church if not for him.

When she returned home, Sarah and Isaac had studied her carefully, as though she might have grown an extra appendage. "What was so special about the Charm church?" Sarah had asked.

"Louder music."

"Did people inquire about your clothes?"

"*Nein.* I drew a bit of attention, but everybody just smiled or nodded at me."

"Did they have a big potluck afterward?" Sarah's curiosity escalated.

"Not today, but Jake said they sometimes have church picnics in the summer. Everyone brings food to share to the pavilion behind the church."

"Jake." The tone of Sarah's one-word reply changed the mood of their conversation. "Jake Brady had no business asking you to join his family as though you were his girlfriend." She stomped off to check on her brooding hens, ending further discussion about Sunday afternoon.

Rachel didn't mention she'd accompanied the Brady clan to a sit-down restaurant near the interstate. Half the Baptist congregation had been there or arrived during the meal. Everyone had waved or called cheery greetings. She also didn't speak of the stroll huddled under a huge umbrella, enjoying the last autumn foliage in downtown Charm. Their kiss, shared beneath a glorious red oak, would also remain a secret. Rachel would savor the tender memory well into old age while bouncing *kinskinner* on her knee.

Just like it was easy to become spoiled by the electrical appliances in Sarah's home, Rachel could effortlessly slip into Jake's world. She already felt too comfortable with him and too much part of the Brady family. It would be easy to stop at the discount store on her day off for a few English dresses or skirts to wear to Jake's church services. Or maybe buy a few pretty sweaters and certainly an extra pair of jeans for future trips to Somerset or to Bread of Life.

Before she knew it, she would be running around without her *kapp*, while the Plain dresses lovingly sewn by her late mother gathered dust in the closet, relics of her former life. *Mamm.* What would she say about Rachel's behavior since she had found a job at Twelve Elms Stables? *What wouldn't she say?* "Is this how your *daed* and I raised our four *dochders* to behave?" That had been Edna King's exclamation whenever working the garden turned into a hose-drenching free-for-all or the basket of weeds ended up on Beth's head.

Indeed not, but Rachel felt trapped like the hapless moth in a sticky spider web. The more she fought her circumstances, the more ensnared she became. She adored working with horses at Twelve Elms. But if she wasn't careful, she would fall in love with Jake. He was so handsome, so kindhearted, so attentive…and so wrong for her. Deep inside Rachel hadn't changed. She loved being Amish. If she left her faith, she would have to leave behind her beloved sisters and close the door on a world that had nurtured and protected her. She would shame the memory of her parents and break *grossmammi*'s heart.

She had assured Sarah that she could peek at the English world without wishing to join it, but she'd better not keep peeking at Jake or she would never find a suitable mate among her Plain brethren. It wasn't his handsome face or fast truck or fancy horse farm that was hard to resist. It was how he made her feel about herself. And falling in love with him would be a major mistake.

"I said, could you help me take down and fold the sheets?" Sarah's question finally registered. "What has you so distracted?"

"Of course I'll help." Rachel shook away her fog. "Is it all right if I drive to Becky's tomorrow after we clean house? I've not spent nearly enough time with my new friends here."

"It's fine with me. People will stop inviting you to things if you don't show some interest." Sarah smoothed out her wrinkled apron on their way out to the porch.

"I would really like to know if Josh has any brothers. I need to expand my horizons, even in a small town like Charm."

Sarah slapped her on the back, hard enough to cause Rachel to stumble. "That's a great idea! Finally, I might have some good news to report to our *grossmammi*."

❧

Second Wednesday in December

Jake reached for a ream of paper to fill the printer and spilled his cup of coffee. Only his quick reflexes prevented liquid from flowing onto the computer keyboard. He muttered a rude word under his breath and then pulled off his sweatshirt to blot the mess.

"You're no longer fond of the Kentucky Wildcats?" His father stood in the doorway, running a hand along the back of his neck.

Jake realized the sweatshirt supported his favorite college basketball team and his parents' alma mater. "The Wildcats are fine and dandy, but coffee into the keyboard would be disastrous. I can always wash this." He wiped the desktop one last time before balling up his shirt.

"Rachel just called."

Jake immediately stopped fussing with the spilled coffee and gave his dad his undivided attention. "What did she say?"

"That she isn't feeling well and won't be in to work today." Ken jammed both hands into his back pockets.

"Is it serious? What's wrong with her? Is there something I can do?"

His father grinned. "I'm sure it's not life threatening. She probably caught one of the bugs making the rounds."

Jake swallowed down his next stupid question but not his anxiety. He didn't wish to appear like a nervous Nellie. "The last time we talked, she didn't mention she was coming down with anything."

"That's how rude viruses tend to be—showing up without any warning. It's probably just a cold, son, not the bubonic plague." Ken's guffaws could be heard halfway to the kitchen.

Shaking off his dad's inane remark, Jake returned to his computer screen. With Rachel out for the day, he had little incentive to finish paperwork and head to the arena. There would be no lunchtime rides up to the pond or shared mugs of cocoa in the outdoor bleachers. He had to endure a full day without seeing her.

Jake checked his e-mail account for yesterday's report on Eager to Please's progress. Alan Hitchcock might be expensive, but the man was thorough. Almost daily he furnished the times and distances for each training sprint, plus measurements and weight changes every week. After poring over the figures, Jake began reducing his inbox one e-mail at a time. He'd nearly cut the clutter in half when his cell phone jangled. The fight song for the U of K jarred him from the screen's hypnotic spell. "Jake Brady," he said into the mouthpiece. He glanced at the unknown number displayed while advancing to the next e-mail.

"Hello, Mr. Brady? This is Alfred Terry of the Terry Point Investment Consortium. I hope I'm not interrupting anything. Alan Hitchcock gave me your cell number." The voice on the other end sounded middle aged and well heeled, as though the man were wearing a thousand-dollar suit.

"Not at all. What can I do for you, Mr. Terry?" Jake leaned back in his chair away from the desk.

"It's what I can do for you." He allowed a few moments to pass to pique Jake's interest. No doubt a technique the man learned from some motivational speaker. "I head up a consortium of investors who sometimes take chances on long shots, mostly in futures and commodity trading. I'm down here in Tampa with my wife, escaping from the Midwest wind and snow. We've been coming to Florida for years." Terry punctuated his comment with a pleasant chuckle.

Jake glanced at his watch. "How can I help?" No doubt the man wanted to rent the arena for a night-at-the-races charity fundraiser. His wife was probably too shy to call on her own. Hitchcock should have provided the stable office number, not Jake's personal cell phone.

"Truth is, I love the ponies. My buddies and I make a trip to Arlington Park outside Chicago our monthly outing. And I never miss the yearling races because they are so close to our condo. I've had my eye on that horse of yours." A second pause in the conversation yielded the desired response.

Jake stopped rolling his eyes and straightened in his chair. "Are you talking about Eager to Please?"

"I certainly am. That is one fast colt, Mr. Brady. I've not seen that much spirit in so young a Thoroughbred since I began following the racing industry."

Jake's heart swelled like a proud parent at a football game or ballet recital. "I appreciate your taking the time to call me, Mr. Terry. It's hard for me to get excited up here in Kentucky with only a pile of stats to rely on."

Mr. Terry cleared his throat. "Glad to help, but I'm not calling as a member of Eager's fan club, although I'd be happy to join if you have one. When I watched your horse run three days in a row, I called a few investors and asked them to hop a plane. With as cold as it's been already up north, they readily agreed to a few days in the sun."

Jake wished he would spit out whatever he was trying to say, but impatience usually got a man nowhere. "It's been cool and rainy in Kentucky too," he murmured.

"My investment team has been here a few days and like what they see. Or at least they want to believe what I'm telling them. We don't usually invest in unproven racehorses, even those with impressive training times like Eager's. Too much can happen to a spindly-legged colt when we're this far from the stakes races."

Jake frowned in confusion, even though no one could see his expression. "Why would a group of investors be interested in my yearling? Do they plan to place a large bet on the Derby at a Vegas sports book?"

"No, no. We're not gamblers. We're interested in owning Eager to Please. We would take the chance on him making it to the big races."

Pain radiated across Jake's shoulders into his neck from tension. "Alan Hitchcock gave you the wrong impression, Mr. Terry. My horse isn't for sale. We bred and raised him from one of our mares. We hope to take him all the way as a three-year-old."

"You ought to be mighty proud, young man, but my consortium is prepared to offer Twelve Elms three million dollars. That's an excellent price for an unproven juvenile, certainly a good return on your stud fees and training expenses."

An uncomfortable queasiness churned Jake's belly. He glanced around to make sure no one had entered the stable office unseen and was awaiting his response. But he was alone, and this time it was Mr. Terry on the receiving end of a pregnant pause. "Thanks for your vote of confidence and I'm flattered by the offer, but I will reiterate our position. Eager to Please in not for sale."

"I understand, but keep my cell number in case you change your mind. Three million dollars can buy plenty of dreams for a young man like you. If that colt breaks his leg or twists a gut, you'll end up with nothing but an expensive pet and a bucketful of bills to pay."

Jake said goodbye and hung up as quickly as possible. He knew he shouldn't have made a snap decision without consulting his parents. After all, Twelve Elms owned the horse, not just him. A wise man would have crunched the numbers, consulted business advisers, and then taken a vote among the interested parties. But Jake Brady wasn't a wise man. He *loved* that colt like a pampered lapdog. Would a childless couple approach a large family pushing a stroller with a newborn? *Because you haven't grown too attached yet to that infant, how about selling him to us at the going rate?*

Jake looked through the rest of the e-mails with little enthusiasm. A new boarder request, contract extensions for trainers, and inquiries about spring reservations failed to hold his interest. He had done something he shouldn't have, but he couldn't call Mr. Terry back. Instead he left the office as though stung by a bee.

"Hey, Jake, how about lunch?" asked Keeley. She and Jessie were dunking toasted cheese sandwiches into tomato soup in the kitchen.

"No, thanks. Not hungry. I think I'll skip lunch and saddle up Pretty Boy." He fled the house before one or the other asked to tag along.

A ride up into the hills might mitigate his guilt and convince him he made the right decision. But no matter how hard he rode or what tranquil vistas he observed, peace refused to come to Jake Brady. He was an arrogant young man, full of himself and full of grandiose aspirations. He couldn't face his parents or his siblings without talking to Rachel, or at least seeing her lovely face.

Thank goodness she was home sick today. He could drive to the Stolls' farm as a concerned employer, curious as to how she was feeling. But first he would stop at Flower Mart on Charm's town square for a get-well bouquet. He probably wouldn't tell her about the phone call. How could he talk about Mr. Terry's offer without revealing his true nature—a selfish man who placed himself far above others, even the family he loved?

❧

Rachel closed the door behind Jake and tightened her grip on her shawl. Although fully dressed, she couldn't get warm enough, despite a roaring fire in the woodstove.

"That was an odd visit." Sarah's comment had been directed at the sewing in her lap. She'd stayed in the kitchen after supper with Isaac, who had spread seed catalogs across one end of the table.

"Not so odd." Rachel wiped her reddened nose for the fiftieth time that day. "The Bradys have been worried about me since I left a message on their answering machine. I said I was sick, but I should have clarified it's only a cold."

"*Harrumph.* You owe them no explanations. If a person is sick, they're sick." Sarah pulled the fabric close to her nose and squinted at a row of stitches.

Annoyed, Rachel chewed her lip. "*Jah,* but the Bradys are more than my employer. They're my friends." She carried the bouquet— a gift from Jake—to the sink.

"I gathered that much by two dozen long-stemmed roses." Sarah glared over her reading glasses. "You would think some famous *Englischer* had died with all those expensive flowers."

Refusing to take the bait, Rachel clipped the stems shorter and hunted for the largest vase in the cupboard.

"I've worked in the English world, but nobody dropped by with roses when I caught the sniffles." Sarah punctuated her statement with a cluck of her tongue.

Rachel glanced at Isaac, hoping for his usual intervention. Huddled over the catalogs, he was ignoring both of them. "Well, maybe *you* weren't employee-of-the-month." She attempted a humorous tone but failed. She sounded snappish and mean spirited.

Sarah set down her needlework. "I went to work and did my job. That's really all anybody should expect."

Dabbing at her nose with a sodden tissue, Rachel pivoted

on her heel. "That's all Twelve Elms does expect. I'm dating Jake because I like him, not because it's part of my job description."

"You're *dating* him? I thought you were seeing both Amish and English men as *friends?*" Sarah pursed her lips in an unattractive thin line.

"Enough, *fraa!*" thundered Isaac. "Leave the girl alone." He did not glance up from his catalogs, but his shoulders went uncommonly stiff.

"Sorry, cousin." Sarah turned meek as a lamb.

"No, I'm the one who should be apologizing. I'm out of sorts from this head cold."

Sarah sprang up and pressed her palm to Rachel's forehead. "You're running a fever. I'll finish arranging the flowers and then bring you a cup of tea. You jump into bed and cover up with an extra quilt."

Rachel did as instructed without argument. Climbing the stairs on heavy legs, she entered her cool bedroom only half as distressed by their argument as usual. Despite her head and body aches, and even though her throat felt scratchy and her nose dripped like a faucet, Jake's visit had lifted her spirits better than any herbal tonic. He didn't seem to notice her bulbous nose, or how her eyes watered or that she was wrapped in the world's shabbiest shawl. Jake had smiled, told her that Twelve Elms wasn't the same without her, and then handed her the armful of flowers. Then he greeted sullen Sarah and stoic Isaac, wished her a speedy recovery, and headed for his truck.

No one had ever given her a florist shop bouquet before, not to mention two dozen long-stem roses.

And no one ever jumped in their car...or buggy...just to see if she was feeling better.

That night Rachel fell asleep thinking about a man who made her feel cherished. She knew the ache in her heart had nothing to do with a virus or the cool temperature in the bedroom. She was in love. Tomorrow, or as soon as she was no longer sicker than a dog, she must talk to someone about what to do. Not Sarah or Isaac, not one of her sisters, and surely not her grandmother, despite how much those people loved her. Rachel needed an objective outsider. *Ah-choo*. With another shiver, she burrowed deep under the covers and fell asleep. But as fate would have it, cowboys riding sleek Thoroughbreds peppered her dreams all night, while black crows huddled along telephone lines, cackling and cawing with distress.

❧

Rachel's virus lasted two more days with chills, body aches, sneezing, coughing, and sheer misery. Sarah behaved like a dutiful nursemaid, bathing her brow with damp cloths, feeding her bowls of chicken broth, and bringing her endless cups of tea with honey and lemon. Her own *mamm* couldn't have been more devoted. Even Isaac, twirling his hat between his fingers, stuck his head inside her door several times to ask if he should fetch the doctor.

But by the third day she was up and around, eager to leave her bedroom. The only part of her body still achy was her back from too much time in bed. Sarah refused to allow her to help with chores that day, but at least Rachel could walk the farm to stretch her legs and inhale fresh, clean air. She didn't ask if Jake had called or made a return visit. Best to let that sleeping dog lie until she was fully recovered. After all, she didn't know what to say to him anyway.

Saturday morning she left another message on the Twelve Elms answering machine that she wouldn't be at work again. She chose a time when no one would be in the office to take the call. Then she bundled up in her warmest cloak and heavy bonnet, hitched up Isaac's rig, and left the farm before Jake heard her message. She imagined him peeling up the Stoll driveway, bearing more flowers, offering a ride to the hospital, or demanding an explanation. But no shiny pickup crossed her path on her way to the bishop's house. And for that she whispered a prayer of gratitude.

Rachel knocked once timidly on the side door. When she heard no stirring within, she rapped harder on the wood panel.

"Hold your horses," called a female voice. "This is as fast as my legs will go." When the door swung wide, Mrs. Mast stood scowling. Then her expression changed to one of confusion. "Rachel? Sarah's cousin from Lancaster?"

"Yes, ma'am," she replied, adopting the polite, English term to address an older woman. The Amish seldom stood on such formality.

"You came by yourself?" She peered around to see if others might be hiding behind porch posts.

"*Jah*, I've come to talk to the bishop. If you don't mind," she added.

Mrs. Mast blinked. "Of course I don't mind. That's James's job. You'll find him in the barn sharpening his cutting blades for next year. Talk all you want, but I would slip those muck boots over your shoes. It's been muddy around the barn from all the rain lately." She pointed to a knee-high pair of boots, nodded, and then closed the door.

Rachel pulled on boots that would have fit Paul Bunyan, had he been seeking spiritual advice, and then she trudged to the barn.

Bishop Mast's face revealed surprise to see her in his workshop. "What can I do for you, Rachel?" he asked, setting down his files. "I didn't see you at preaching this past Sunday. Was there something in my sermon you didn't understand the week before last?"

"*Nein*. I have more general questions than that." She yanked off her scratchy outer bonnet, leaving her *kapp* in place. "About the Amish faith and the Mennonites and the Baptists."

He narrowed his gaze. "I'm only qualified to explain one of those—the middle one." A ghost of a smile tugged at his mouth.

"I had better explain before I ask my questions." She glanced around the neat but dusty shop, tired from the drive over.

"Sit there." The bishop pointed at the sole stool at his workbench before lowering himself on an upturned feed bucket.

Rachel settled herself comfortably, smoothed her skirt, and then blurted out, "I went to an English church last Sunday—the Baptist one in the center of Charm. I liked their service. No offense," she added, blushing.

"None taken." Bishop Mast splayed his hands on his knees.

"I was invited by the family I work with, by the young man in particular. Jake Brady. He's my boss, but it wasn't part of my job."

"I wouldn't think it would be. Sarah told me you give farm tours." James stroked his pure white beard, which reached to his belly.

"I'm also helping to exercise horses until the number of tours picks up." Rachel studied the sawdust and filings on the floor.

"Although lots of things were different in the service, lots of things were the same." She forced herself to look at him.

"I guess you should ask your questions, young lady."

Rachel nodded. "Is Baptist a different religion than Amish or Mennonite?"

He thought for a moment. "Technically, no. All three are sects of Christianity. We worship the same God and His Son, Jesus. The fundamentals are the same."

"Then why are folks shunned who leave the Amish church back home?"

"There is more to being Amish or Mennonite than simply worshipping the Lord in a church, no matter which denomination. It is a lifestyle committed to old ways, committed to the path of salvation. This life on earth will determine whether or not we one day take our place in Paradise, as promised in Scripture. Although the life you lived in Lancaster County looks more difficult than the English lifestyle to the unknowledgeable, it is easier to stay on a righteous path. The Plain sects remove themselves from the world to eliminate many temptations and the constant bombardment of sinful influences."

Rachel shrugged her shoulders. "You're saying it's *easier* to be Amish than to be English?"

"It's not easy for any Christian to find salvation, but yes, I feel it's harder for those in the modern world to stay focused on God and Scripture."

She thought about that, trying to absorb what she heard. "A Christian's heart should belong to God no matter where they worship."

"That is true, but there's more going on in *your* heart than a theoretical discussion of sects. You need to talk to your family and friends, and then spend time in prayer. You seek an answer from me I can't give. Decide who you are, Rachel King, and the correct path will be revealed to you." His aged, weathered face softened with the kindness of her *grossdawdi*.

"*Danki*, Bishop Mast. I will do what you say."

"And I shall lift you up in prayer many times over the next few days."

"You had better make that *weeks*, Bishop. I've never been quick with anything."

FIFTEEN

When we've been there ten thousand years

Rachel drove back from Bishop Mast's not in the best of spirits. Her head ached, but it had nothing to do with lingering symptoms from her cold. What had she been thinking? That she could fall in love with Jake, switch over to his Baptist church, and yet everything else would remain the same? She was one foolish woman. Blessedly, Isaac met the buggy when she pulled up to the barn.

"Let me unhitch and tend to the horse. Go inside and warm up by the fire." He grabbed the bridle so the gelding didn't drag the buggy straight to his barn stall, where a full bucket of oats waited. "What errand was so all-fired important that you had to leave so soon after being ill? You were practically on your deathbed two days ago. You're still pale as a ghost." The man stared at her, not joking in the least.

Steadying herself with one hand, Rachel gingerly climbed down. "Have you ever seen a ghost, Isaac Stoll?" She smiled up into his weather-lined face.

"*Jah*. A couple of months ago I saw a white plastic one hanging from the ceiling at Kmart. Looked just like you." He returned the grin.

"*Danki* for taking care of the horse. I would like to warm up. It was a long drive back from Bishop Mast's house."

Isaac's eyes rounded. "You drove all the way to the bishop's? Why didn't you take Sarah with you? She could have driven the buggy."

Rachel thought about her reply. "Because I had a personal matter to discuss with him." She picked up her purse from the seat.

"And you didn't want your cousin interrupting every other sentence?" He smirked rather than smiled. "I guess you Lancaster gals are no dummies." Isaac chuckled all the way to the barn.

She opened the kitchen door to a blast of warm air and the sweet scent of cinnamon. The room was empty, but three apple pies, fresh from the oven, lined the counter. After hanging up her cloak and bonnet, Rachel went to the sink to wash, letting the hot water cascade over her hands longer than necessary.

"There you are." Sarah bustled into the kitchen. "Isaac just about swatted my backside for letting you leave on such a cold day like this. I told my *ehemann* that imprisoning women was frowned on in the state of Kentucky." Sarah filled the kettle at the sink and set it on a burner to heat. Then she noticed Rachel's blanched face. "What's wrong? Are you feeling poorly again?" She pressed her fingers to her cousin's brow.

Maybe it was due to Sarah's tender ministrations, coming on the heels of the bishop's patient counsel, but Rachel burst into tears.

"Goodness, should I send Isaac for the doctor or maybe call nine-one-one?" Sarah wrung her hands in her apron. "Can I help you to your room to lie down?"

"Neither, but I would love a cup of coffee if there's any left from lunch." Tears coursed down her cheeks. "And maybe a slice of pie might help too, if those aren't already spoken for." Slumping onto a chair, she caught Sarah's skeptical expression.

"So you're not still sick, but you are crying. I take it things didn't go well at Bishop Mast's?"

Rachel buried her face in her hands. "You could say that."

Sarah placed two mugs of coffee on the table before sitting down with the pie, two plates, two forks, and a knife. "Did he bawl you out for going to an English church when we have a perfectly fine Mennonite one in Charm?"

"*Nein.* He was very kind and patient with me." Rachel words sounded muffled from beneath her hands.

"Then I suppose you didn't tell him what you've been doing—dating an *Englischer.* And not just any *Englischer,* but your boss of all things. That's the stuff they make into bad television shows." Wrinkling her nose, Sarah attacked the pie with her sharp blade.

Rachel peered up, dabbing her face with a paper napkin. "No, I told him the truth. I asked him questions about the Baptist faith and how it differs from the Amish and Mennonite."

"And what he said made you cry?" She slid large slices onto plates. "I told you not to monkey around tempting the Lord's disfavor." Sarah handed Rachel one of the mugs.

"Actually, he explained there's not that much difference between the Christian sects in theology."

Sarah tilted her head to one side. "Then why are you sobbing as though the world were about to end?"

"Because my world is about to. The big difference comes with the Amish lifestyle compared to the English. The bishop made me realize I can't just turn Baptist. I would have to leave behind everything and everyone I know and love." A floodgate of tears opened anew.

"You don't want to stop being Amish?"

"I don't. That's why I'm miserable. I'm in love with Jake Brady, and I don't want to be." Rachel cut off a piece of pie with her fork, but it tasted dry and flavorless on her tongue. She swallowed it down with a gulp of coffee.

Sarah could have said "I told you so," or "See what happens when you don't take *grossmammi's* advice?" But she didn't. Instead, her eyes grew moist and shiny. "Eat more pie. That usually helps when I'm upset with life." She sipped her coffee with a face filled with pity.

Rachel tried another bite, noticing this time the crust tasted far less dry. "I didn't want to fall in love with him, Sarah. It just happened."

"That's why you shouldn't date *Englischers*. Stuff like that happens when a person's young."

Rachel scraped the remaining apples from the crust. "You talk as though you're fifty years old."

"I'm old enough to know that broken hearts heal with time. You would be shocked at how fast too." Sarah pushed the pie pan across the table. "What are you going to do—quit your job? That's what I would recommend." She began to devour her slice.

"No, I love my job. I don't want to leave Twelve Elms."

"You can't live in two worlds forever, Rachel. Sooner or later you will have to choose. Why prolong your misery? Look at you—shedding tears all over my fresh-baked apple pie."

Rachel waited until they had both finished eating before answering. "I'll never have a job like this again. I love working with horses." Emotion began to clog her throat as her limbs grew weary. "But I will certainly break up with Jake. He's not my boss anymore since I was promoted to exercise girl. With any luck, once I make it clear we can't be friends he and I will rarely cross paths." She lifted her eyes to meet her cousin's gaze.

Sarah sighed. "It's not luck you need, but the providence of the Lord. He is the only one who can help you heal."

"Truly, Sarah, I'll be fine at the stable. But if I'm uncomfortable, then I'll quit." A large tear dripped from her chin.

"I trust your judgment. If you're feeling okay, why not come to church with Isaac and me tomorrow? Maybe we'll go visiting in the afternoon, somewhere where there are young men who are your own kind. Right now, go upstairs and take a nap. You look terrible. I don't need help fixing dinner. I can cook chicken and dumplings in my sleep." She sprang up, the girl-time drawing to a close.

"You and Isaac are silver-tongued flatterers. He told me I looked like a ghost." Rachel set her plate and mug in the sink.

"Isaac said that? Used the word 'ghost'? There's no such thing." Sarah dug in the cupboard for her big pot.

"There was a plastic one hanging from the ceiling in Kmart. Apparently she and I are dead ringers." Rachel patted Sarah's shoulder on her way out of the kitchen. "*Danki* for cutting up the pie early."

"What are cousins for?" Sarah cast her one last solemn look.

Up in her room, Rachel slipped off her apron and shoes and then crawled beneath the quilt with her dress on. She closed her eyes, but despite her fatigue, sleep refused to come. The enormity of what she'd just admitted to Sarah, along with what lay ahead, welled up inside her. She would have to look Jake in the eye and say they had no future together. His being English made all the difference in the world. Christians might all be the same under the skin, but being Plain was a lifetime of choices. Choices that kept them separate from others. How ashamed she felt to have encouraged his attentions…ashamed and selfish.

All the sweet apple pie in the world couldn't take that bitter taste away.

૭౨

The last person Donna expected to hear from on a rainy Tuesday morning was an Amish tour guide.

"Hello, Donna? This is Rachel King."

She leaned back from her daunting stack of case files and focused out her steamy window, not seeing anything. "How are you, Rachel?"

"I'm fine now, but I had a bad cold recently. Thank goodness, it wasn't polio, *jah*? While I was sick in bed I thought about you. How is your project coming along to vaccinate folks?"

Donna thought about what to say and opted for complete honesty. "Not that well, I'm afraid. Folks heard that the sick little girl might have caught the virus from a health care worker and they don't wish to cooperate."

"Is that how she got sick?"

"We don't know. We'll probably never know for sure, but it's possible. I've done more research on the topic and realized that regardless of where the child contracted it, this situation is very serious. Plain folks cannot afford to ignore polio or other communicable diseases any longer."

"Dear me, I'd hoped for better news. I told my grandmother about meeting you and about the four positive tests for polio here in Charm. She still remembers when state authorities came to Pennsylvania and set up clinics all over town. About a third of the folks got the shots, including my granny."

"Your grandmother lives in Lancaster?"

"Yes, ma'am. I am visiting a cousin who lives here."

Donna's head swam with ideas. "I need another audience with the Mennonite bishop. Do you think you or Sarah could arrange this again? He and I need to discuss this, and I'd love to have you there too."

There was the briefest of hesitations. "Sure. Why don't you come talk to Sarah and me today. I will be going back to work tomorrow."

Donna consulted her day planner of staff meetings and routine appointments with lab techs and then shut the book. "When would you like me to come?"

"How about now? Sarah and I are cleaning house. Any excuse that takes us away from that would be fine with us." The young woman giggled.

Checking her watch, Donna scrambled to her feet. "I can be at the Stolls' in thirty minutes or less."

"We'll be ready with a pot of coffee. If you're lucky, maybe one of the pumpkin pies will be ready to eat."

"I'm plenty lucky just to have met you, Rachel, with or without pumpkin pie."

When Donna pulled up at the chicken farm's back door, the two women walked onto the porch, dressed in heavy wool with full bonnets. The offer of refreshments appeared to have been rescinded. "Good afternoon," she called, opening the car door. But before Donna could step out, they hustled down the steps and climbed inside her sedan—Sarah into the backseat again, with Rachel up front. "Does this mean we're calling on Bishop Mast today?"

"I thought you said you needed to talk to him," Sarah said, slamming the car door twice as hard as necessary.

"I do, but I assumed it must be arranged in advance—"

"It's Tuesday. Where would a farmer be in December? I called his *fraa*. She said he's home. I said we would come, so let's get going. I don't like leaving my chickens alone for too long."

Rachel pivoted on the seat just enough to reveal her smile. "Even better than pumpkin pie and coffee, *jah*?"

"Definitely, *jah*. Thank you, Sarah. Off we go."

When they arrived at the small, modest farm, the bishop's wife met them at the door. "It's too cold for the porch today. Go sit in the living room, although there won't be much of a fire until the evening. I'll holler out to James in the barn." Mrs. Mast pointed down the hallway with a thin finger. "Don't bother hanging up your coats. You probably won't be staying that long."

Sarah led the way, while Rachel and Donna exchanged an

amused look. Once they were seated in the austere front room, they had only minutes to wait.

Bishop Mast entered the room with a stiff gait. "Mrs. Cline, Sarah," he greeted. "Good to see you again so soon, Rachel." He patted the young woman's shoulder on his way to the rocking chair. He waited to address Donna until he had lowered himself to the cushioned seat. "I suppose you bring me news about the sick little girl. Is she any better?"

Visions of the medical review board swam through Donna's head. She could lose her job for divulging protected medical information to the public, yet the child's mother assured her she wanted no one to contract this virus from her daughter or anyone else. "The child is quarantined in an undisclosed medical facility, where she receives treatment for her immune deficiency disorder. She hasn't yet developed paralytic polio."

"Thanks be to the Lord," said the bishop. The three women echoed his sentiments.

"But due to her weakened resistance, her body hasn't been able to shed the virus either, which is usually what happens by now. It's hidden in her bloodstream, but it can be spread to others."

"For how long?"

"It can hide for years, unless doctors can strengthen her body's immune system to fight off the virus. No one will be allowed in contact with her who hasn't been vaccinated."

Sarah shifted on her chair. "Did her family get the shots?"

"They have." Donna glanced at Sarah and then back at the bishop.

"Some people think she caught it in the hospital from a doctor or nurse." The bishop's tone was as smooth as warm milk. "Unfortunately, many will be even more reluctant to trust English hospitals."

"She very well could have caught it from a health care worker, or from another child in the hospital, but in the end, it doesn't matter for those of the Plain faith. You cannot separate yourselves from the world—not in this day and age."

"How can you say it doesn't matter?" He stopped rocking.

"Because an infected person could have the virus incubating for decades, all the while spreading it to those who are unprotected. If a person's immunity becomes weakened, he or she could develop polio. The Amish and Mennonite travel throughout the US and Canada. They come in contact with other travelers in bus and train stations or in restaurants. It doesn't have to be in a hospital. Because no one stays in one place anymore, the only way to be safe is to get the vaccine."

"Have there been recent outbreaks?"

"In the last ten years, outbreaks have occurred in Africa, India, the Dominican Republic, and Haiti. Who knows how many people in those countries are carriers and don't know it?"

The bishop paled. "Several Mennonite districts sent construction workers to Haiti to assist rebuilding after the earthquake. Things still aren't right in that country. We must remember them in prayer."

"That's true, but we should do more than pray. We must make sure Casey County citizens are safe and stay that way."

The elderly man stared out the window. "I will order every family in my district to be tested, and I'll ask the other area bishops to do the same. But I cannot order members to get shots. That must be their choice."

"I'm grateful for whatever help you give me. I'll leave flyers to pass out that explain how and when samples will be collected."

"I could write to my bishop in Pennsylvania," said Rachel. All heads turned in her direction. "He's as old as *grossmammi,* so he would remember when people came to Lancaster County to vaccinate for polio. Most children received the shots, but that was a long time ago. They have *kinner* of their own, even *kinskinner,* by now. My grandmother said she doesn't remember anybody getting sick from the vaccines."

"Do you think your bishop would be willing to travel here and talk to Kentucky folks?" Donna held her breath.

"I can ask. I'll call tonight and ask him to call me from a payphone."

"If he does, our grandmother will probably come too." Sarah winked at Rachel. "She's been itching for a chance to talk to you."

Rachel blushed a shade of bright pink.

"Call as soon as possible," said Bishop Mast. "We'll hold a district meeting as soon as he and your *grossmammi* arrive." He turned his focus back to her. "Thank you, Mrs. Cline, for your diligence. If it be God's will, a crisis can still be avoided." He rose shakily to his feet. "Let's go have some cookies. My *fraa* whipped up a batch of chocolate chip the minute Sarah asked to stop by today. She only *acts* like she doesn't like company." His smile couldn't be more genuine.

ॐ

Jessie climbed stiffly out of her friend's tiny two-seater, eager to stretch her legs and her back. The drive home from their Lexington campus took only a couple of hours, but she felt worn out. Sherry had spent nearly the entire ride talking about her soon-to-be ex-boyfriend. She loved him. She loved him not.

All Sherry needed were daisy petals to pluck to help make her decision. Twelve Elms Stable had never looked so inviting as when they pulled up the lane, despite an overcast sky and a thick mist hanging in the air. "Thanks for the lift," Jessie said. "Not having wheels on campus has its downside. I appreciate your letting me borrow yours this past year." Jessie walked around to the back of the sports car.

"It has its disadvantages too. My mom is threatening to charge me for my share of the insurance premium. Like I'm not broke enough already." Sherry popped open the trunk with her key fob.

"I can't believe all our stuff fit in here." Jessie peered at the assortment of boxes and bags. "I've never seen so much dirty laundry. Didn't you ever use a washing machine all semester?"

"Why take the time when a mall is so close by? My dad said, 'Buy what you need while at school.'" She lifted out one of Jessie's two suitcases.

"It must be nice to have a rich father, even if he spends most of his life away on business. Where's he now—Hong Kong or Dubai?"

"Geneva." Sherry's smile faltered. "I suppose it's not so bad now that I'm no longer a kid, but I envied you with a dad always at home. Remember the time he measured the length of your skirts with a tape measure?"

"How could I forget? '*No daughter of mine leaves the house with less than eighteen inches of fabric.*'" Jessie emulated her father's voice. "He made me return everything I bought to the store. There's sweetly old fashioned and then there's downright prehistoric."

Both girls laughed as Jessie dragged the heavier of the two suitcases out of the trunk. "Have a great Christmas vacation, Sherry. And remember what I told you. If your mom goes skiing or anyplace else over the holidays, don't sit home playing video games and texting your ex. Come spend Christmas with the Bradys. We're just as ridiculous as that sitcom family in reruns."

Sherry hugged Jessie fiercely. "Thanks, I might take you up on the offer whether Linda Sue takes off with her boyfriend or not. You have that irresistible sugarplum brother living under your roof."

Jessie shook her head, amused whenever Sherry referred to her mother by her first name. "If you mean Jake, he still lives here, but I'm not so sure about the sugarplum part. Your memory appears to be flawed."

Her friend climbed into her car and turned it around in a narrow arc. "My memory is just fine. Women cannot appreciate a good man if they are biologically connected. Keep your cell fully charged and turned on." With a wave of her manicured hand, Sherry drove off toward the suburbs of Georgetown—another hour away.

Jessie dragged in her luggage, feeling a tad guilty about Sherry's crush on her brother. Should she have mentioned that Jake was over the moon in love? And with an Amish girl, no less. Seeing them together in church when she came home for the weekend erased any doubt in her mind. And she was fairly certain Rachel felt the same way about him. But considering the circumstances, Jessie had kept silent about Jake's intentions. How could it possibly work out? Would Rachel give up her bonnets and capes forever and then drive off to Florida to honeymoon at Disney World? Or would Jake turn in his belts for suspenders, his Reds baseball cap for a black wide-brim hat, and his pickup for a well-mannered Standardbred buggy horse?

Jessie shook off the idea like a dog after a bath. "Is anybody home?" she hollered once she was inside the kitchen. "Virgil, Keeley, Mom?" Utter silence reigned throughout the house. Here was the major difference between her family and their fictional namesake—on the show somebody was always home to greet wayward travelers.

She trudged to the laundry room with her suitcases, pulled out her toiletry bag and hairdryer, and left everything else on the floor. Tomorrow she would tackle that beast after a good night's sleep in her own bed, but for now she headed straight to their home office to update her Facebook status. She had to let the world know the Princess had left her realm in Lexington and would now rule over underpopulated, slow-moving-as-a-limping-tortoise Charm, Kentucky. Tired of her small-screened tablet, she would stay in touch with her loyal subjects on Dad's large computer monitor.

When barely midway through commenting on her friends' postings, Jessie spied Jake's battered briefcase open on the floor.

The guy had bought it at the secondhand store, thinking it gave him a sophisticated, cosmopolitan air. Unfortunately, instead he looked like an entry-level lawyer living on a budget while trying to pay off student loans.

A corner of one book caught her eye. Jessie bent to pull out the thin volume. *Plain Answers About the Amish Life* by Mindy Starns Clark. Reaching deeper into the bag, Jessie extracted *Living Without Electricity* by Stephen Scott and *Amish Life* by John A. Hostetler. The latter featured a sweet-faced little girl in a pink pinafore and black apron, coloring in a workbook with a red crayon. Jessie didn't know whether to laugh or cry. Her heart swelled with emotion as she realized that her brother was truly serious about Rachel. "Oh, Jake, how will this turn out?" she whispered to the rosy-cheeked child. Abandoning her Facebook profile, Jessie left the office in search of her love-struck sibling.

She found him in an unused corner of the family barn, which was home to Buster and Bess, Pretty Boy, Keeley's new brindle mare, and her usual riding mount, along with Virgil's, Dad's, and other horses they had acquired but were too sentimental to part with. Jake, however, was not handling anything equine. Instead, he cuddled one-eyed Skinny Joe in the crook of his elbow, petting the animal with long, tender strokes. Joe purred with the lung capacity of a much larger feline.

"What's going on, big brother?" Jessie crept closer and spoke softly, not wishing to startle either of them.

"You home for a while?" he asked, scratching Joe beneath his whiskery chin.

"I am. Three weeks. Can you tolerate me that long?" She reached out to wrap Joe's skinny tail around one finger.

"I'll try. Maybe I'll take up Zen meditation to calm my nerves." Jake's dimples deepened with his grin.

Jessie studied the pitiful cat. "No matter how much this poor thing eats, he stays scrawny and his fur remains sparse."

"That's why I'm worried about him out here. The vet said nothing's wrong with him, just bad genetics." Jake placed the cat into a wooden box lined with soft wool horse blankets. He had folded them high all around to practically create a cave for Joe. A water dish and a brimming food bowl sat on a ledge just below his new home.

"What's the extension cord for?" Jessie pointed at the coiled reel.

"I picked up a sunlamp at the hardware store, the kind dairy farmers use to keep water troughs from freezing during the winter." He lifted a blue plastic sack from the floor. "The barn isn't heated like the arena, and I don't want Joe's water bowl icing over. The poor guy's not allowed in the house like Luke and Leia." He dropped his chin.

"Dad had to draw the line somewhere, or Keeley would bring every stray cat indoors."

"Well, I don't want poor Joe shivering this winter with his pathetic fur coat." Jake scratched the cat's nose while Joe arched his neck in his warm new haven.

Jessie felt a lump rise into her throat. "You're a softy, Jake Brady. No doubt about it."

"Keep quiet about that, okay? I don't want my reputation as a bad boy to suffer."

"*Bad boy?*" She laughed hard enough to scare Joe deeper into his box.

Jake calmed the cat with a cooing sound. "Don't worry, Skinny. This loud woman will soon be gone. The refrigerator with free food beckons."

Jessie nudged her brother with her hip. "I found your stack of Amish books in the office. Reading up on Rachel's culture, huh?"

"Yep," he said, stringing the extension cord along the back wall with hooks. "I don't want to keep asking dumb questions forever."

"So if I look under your mattress, will I find sweet Amish

romances instead of girlie magazines?" She giggled in spite of herself.

He scowled at her and then concentrated on installing Joe's winter heat source. "What's under my mattress is none of your business. Is there a point to this conversation, little sister? Or were you just anxious to bug somebody now that you're home?"

Jessie tugged on his jacket sleeve. "I'm worried about you, Jake. It seems like you've really fallen for Rachel." She dropped her voice to a whisper.

"What's there to worry about? I'm a big boy." He pulled the heat lamp from the box and clamped it to the back wall above the cat's new quarters.

"That you'll get your heart broken."

His eyes flashed with anger. "Why is that, Jessie? Because you think Rachel couldn't *possibly* fall for me?"

"No, but I can't see you trading your fancy wheels in for a horse and buggy. And the relationship won't work if *somebody* doesn't change. Will she be willing to give up being Amish?"

Jake ignored her for a long while, maybe hoping she would go away.

When he remained silent, she continued in a faltering tone. "Okay, I'll butt out. But just for the record, I hope things work out for you. You're both really nice people."

He angled another glare in her direction. "Time will tell. I can only hope and pray for the best. Now leave me and Skinny Joe to our work."

Rachel has him praying? Jessie exited the cold, damp barn as quickly as possible. She wouldn't want Jake noticing how unlikely she believed his dream to be.

SIXTEEN

Bright shining as the sun

Wednesday

S it," Sarah demanded when Rachel walked into the room. "You will eat a hearty breakfast before leaving this morning, and I'm not taking no for an answer. This is your first day back to work after being sick. You will need all your strength today."

Rachel filled their mugs with hot coffee and slumped into a chair. "I'll give you no argument. My appetite has returned with a vengeance."

Sarah carried over a pan of scrambled eggs, a platter of sausage patties, a plate of buttered toast, and a casserole dish of baked apples. "You must be on top of your game with what lies ahead."

Rachel slanted her cousin a frown. "I suppose you're not referring to exercising fancy show horses in cold, wet weather."

"Nope, because I don't have the slightest idea as to what that entails." Sarah carried jars of strawberry preserves and blueberry jam to the table. "Because you've decided to break up with your boss, it makes no sense to drag your feet. Just swallow the bitter pill and get it over with. Then you can make a fresh start—a new beginning."

"Any additional clichés you wish to add to your sage advice, *fraa*?" asked Isaac, sauntering in from the laundry room. "Or have you run plumb out?" He hung his hat and chore coat on a peg before washing his hands at the sink.

"I didn't hear you come in, *ehemann*," said Sarah with a slight hitch in her voice.

"That much is apparent. I sneaked in to see if you were abiding with my request to butt out." He fought back a smile. "But I see you are not." He shook his head, sighing.

Sarah poured him a cup of coffee and set it on the table. "Rachel arrived at the decision to stop courting the *Englischer* by herself. I had nothing to do with it. I'm merely bolstering her determination with a good meal."

"She's right, Isaac. This is my choice. Please don't be cross with your wife."

He sat across from them. "You *sure* you're fully recovered? You're not still suffering hallucinations or bouts of confusion?"

"Isaac Stoll! By the way you talk a person might think you have a low opinion of your devoted *fraa*."

"Then that person would be wrong. You are the joy of my life— the very reason I get up every day and labor long hours in the chicken barns." He winked while holding out his plate.

Lovely color bloomed across Sarah's cheeks. "That's more like it." She delivered a large scoop of eggs and then spread a thick layer of preserves across his toast.

Rachel looked from one to the other. Would she ever meet the right match—a man who was as well suited to her as Isaac was to Sarah?

Not likely, if recent Amish social events were any indication. She forced herself to eat a scoop of eggs, a sausage patty, and one slice of toast to appease her cousin. "*Danki* for breakfast, Sarah. I will tell the Bradys I won't work Thursdays anymore."

"*Gut!*" Sarah reached for a second serving of apples.

"I want to help more around here."

"*Gut.* Three days a week should be plenty with those *Englischers*." Rachel swallowed the cold dregs of her coffee. "It'll be enough because I want to avoid Jake."

"Out of sight, out of mind. That's what I always say."

Isaac set down his fork and knife with a clatter. "I'll harness your horse, Rachel, before Sarah rubs any more salt into your wounds." He brushed a kiss across Sarah's *kapp* on his way to the door. "As you seem to need something productive to do, *frau*, please keep my breakfast warm while I'm gone."

Rachel shrugged into her bonnet and cape and stuck the lunch she'd packed last night into her tote bag. "What's for supper tonight—need I ask? Which feathered friend will meet her earthly demise?"

"None of my babies, Miss Smarty-Pants. We're having meatloaf, mashed potatoes, and carrots, so hurry home." Sarah's expression turned poignantly sweet.

All the way to Twelve Elms, Rachel tried to rehearse what she would say. But each canned speech sounded lamer than the last. When she parked in her usual spot and turned her horse into the small paddock, blessedly no one came running from the house bearing armfuls of flowers or expensive baskets of sweet-smelling toiletries. She didn't know whether to cry or rejoice. However, her reprieve lasted only until she exited the ladies' room outside the office, dressed in her riding attire.

Jake waited in the doorway of the employee break room. In lieu of a bouquet or gifts, he offered an ear to ear grin. "I sure am glad to see you." His bulk effectively blocked her path to the lockers. "If you hadn't showed up to work, I planned to drive out to the Stolls whether Sarah chased me around with her broom or not. And this time I would bring the doctor instead of a bunch of roses."

"I didn't think English doctors still made house calls." They stood uncomfortably close. "Excuse me, Jake. I must put my Amish clothes in my locker." She tried to squeeze past, but their hips and shoulders brushed, sending jolts of electricity...and annoyance...up her spine.

He moved over half a foot. "Sure thing, and no, doctors usually don't. But if I bribe him with free riding lessons for his offspring for life, you would be surprised what country docs will do." He followed on her heels, looming above while she stowed her bag in the locker. "I couldn't stand working another day without seeing your pretty face at lunch or in the arena."

Rachel stuffed her ponytail inside her Twelve Elms cap. "Bribing a medical professional would be a stupid thing to do. I'm glad you didn't try it." She turned abruptly to face him. "Please let me pass, Jake. I'm already late for work."

"You don't have to worry about getting fired." He stepped back, but only a foot. "Promise you'll eat lunch with me. I packed salami sandwiches with dill pickles—the kind you like—ripe red pears from our trees, and I filled a thermos with sweet tea."

"No, I can't." Rachel marched toward the office door.

He caught her arm with a firm grip. "Okay, how about after work? You can exercise Calamity Jane while I ride Pretty Boy up to the pond. It's not supposed to rain this afternoon, and my horse needs some exercise."

"I don't think so." Pulling away, she bolted down the steps toward the barns.

"Rachel, what's wrong with you?" Jake jogged after her, catching up with little effort. "Are you sore I showed up at the Stolls'? Or sore because I only stopped by once?" He grabbed her jacket near the elbow.

Please, Lord, grant me patience and the correct words. She turned and placed both hands on his chest. "While I was sick in bed I had time to think—"

"About what?" he interrupted, immediately agitated.

"About you and me...and where this relationship is headed."

"Rachel, it's not been long enough to tell if—"

"Stop and let me talk!" She stomped her foot. *So much for the gift of patience.*

"Whew, sorry." Jake halted on the path, his head rearing back.

Rachel stopped too and closed the distance between them. "It's been long enough—long enough to know we're kidding ourselves. You seem to possess the idea I'll eventually turn English. That you will tempt me with your sweet talk and expensive presents and fancy horse farm." She flourished her hand at the elm trees that lined the drive—bare, yet still magnificent. "You might be able to bribe the local doctor, but not me."

Every bit of blood drained from his face. "I wasn't trying to bribe you. I thought you liked me as much as I liked you. Apparently, I was mistaken." If a draft horse had kicked Jake in the gut, he couldn't have appeared more dumbfounded.

It would be so easy to reassure him and salve his wounded feelings. *I do like you, Jake, every bit as much.* So easy, but so pointless. "We're not children anymore. Who I *like* has little importance. I'm Amish, Jake, and I intend to marry somebody Amish. That's what is expected of me, and that's what I plan to do. I'm wasting your time and you're wasting mine." She hadn't intended to sound so abrupt, so heartless, but the situation had careened out of control.

Shutting his eyes, Jake dropped his chin and then scuffed his heel in the dirt once or twice. When he looked up, his mouth had thinned to a harsh line. "I get it, Rachel. You've probably been telling me this for a while, but I'm too thick-skulled to listen." He exhaled through his teeth. "I won't pester you anymore. You're a good employee, Miss King. Don't feel like you need to quit your job. Now if you'll excuse me, I need to check today's training schedule."

He walked away before she had a chance to soften the blow. It felt very much to Rachel as though that balky horse just connected with its second victim.

&

Jake made it until noon before he had to get away from the stable. Every chore presented another reminder of her. Bess and Buster, with flowers in their braided manes, were munching apples from their newest exercise girl. When he looked for Pretty Boy to check his hooves, someone had moved the horse next to Calamity Jane's stall. While eating her hay, Calamity Jane watched him with one mocking brown eye. *If you were a different man, a better person, she never would have dropped you like a hot kettle lid.* Even Keeley couldn't resist inquiring where Rachel had gone, as though it was his responsibility to keep track of women who didn't love him. When he grabbed his lunch from the break room refrigerator, the sight of a meal large enough for two tipped him over the edge.

Jake tossed the paper sack into the trash and hurried from the room. He didn't need anybody asking questions that were none of their business, such as "How are things going with the Amish girl?" He spun his tires through driveway gravel as he left Twelve Elms. A cloud of dust followed in his wake until he reached the paved lane used by tourists. Once on the county road he drove fast, and then he drove even faster after he turned onto the state highway. With no place to go and plenty of time to get there, he decided to put some distance between himself and Charm.

What did men do on television when their lives were falling apart? They went out and got drunk. But that wasn't possible in

Casey County. His parents had chosen this part of Kentucky specifically because it was dry. No alcohol meant no temptations for impressionable teenagers, no blurry-eyed farmhands after tying one on the night before, and no wondering whether or not to serve wine at dinner parties or beer at cookouts for their imbibing friends.

But a dry county made life difficult when a man needed a drink for *medicinal* purposes, and Jake faced one of those times now. He drove mindlessly north, listening to the radio set on a country station. The music from Nashville about men down on their luck with low wages or no jobs and cheating wives salved his wounded soul. Only the low fuel signal broke through his self-absorbed trance. It was a sound he hated after once ignoring the chime for too long and then having to walk for miles. Gas stations were few and far between in rural areas. He spotted a sign which promised a town in four miles and was prepared to stop there.

A few minutes later, Jake pulled into the BP station on fumes and in a sour mood. The fill-up cost him seventy dollars, but a blinking neon beer sign indicated he'd reached the nearest "wet" county. Jake parked on the main street and entered the dim interior of a tavern that hadn't been updated since Nixon was president. The linoleum floor was an indistinguishable color, while the smell of old fryer grease and unwashed bodies hung in the air. He loved the place. Slipping onto a worn red stool, he swiveled around to read wall signs that advertised beers he'd never heard of.

"What'll it be, cowboy?" A voice spoke from behind—a voice hoarse from smoking, he thought.

Jake pulled off his ball cap, stuffed it into his back pocket, and smiled at the thirty-something blonde. "I'll have a beer."

"Draught or bottle?" Her smile revealed unusually white teeth.

"Draught, a tall one."

"We have our nine regular handles this month, plus two

seasonals." She placed a laminated card before him that listed the beers and wines, along with photos of rainbow-hued blender drinks. "We have five kinds of frozen margaritas too."

Jake stared at a blob of dried catsup on the card rather than the beer choices. "Why don't you choose one for me, darlin'. I don't want to make any more decisions today." He returned the best smile he could.

"You got it, but the name is Kim. Only my better half is allowed to call me darling."

Color rose up his neck. "Beg your pardon, ma'am," he murmured, ashamed.

Moments later, she set a giant frosty mug on a cocktail napkin in front of him. "You're forgiven. This one is my husband's favorite. If you don't like it, it's on the house."

"Thanks." Jake took a long pull of the dark amber liquid and almost gagged. But with Kim watching his reaction, he swallowed it down and wiped his mouth on his flannel sleeve. "It's good," he lied. "Nice and cold." At least, that part was true.

"Glad you like it. I myself prefer light beers—colored water, as my husband calls them. You want to see our lunch menu? We have great daily specials."

"No, thanks. I'm here to drink." He gulped down another mouthful. Surprisingly, this swallow didn't taste anywhere near as foul as the first.

When she wandered away to serve other customers, Jake caught his reflection in the mirror above an array of liquor bottles. He looked like an old young man. That's what he got for being a nice guy, for playing by the rules. Didn't women prefer the wild bad boy type? The love 'em and leave 'em kind who moved on long before vows or commitments could be spoken? Lifting the mug, he drained the contents down to the foamy bottom.

What was America's passion for beer all about? The stuff tasted like yeast, barley, and hops, fermented and then strained to get the chunks out. Why would anybody want to brew and then bottle a beverage made from grains not much different than horse feed? Nevertheless, when his cheerful bartender returned, he ordered a second mug of the odorous stuff.

"What would a man drink if he was celebrating or seriously drowning his sorrows?" he asked when she refilled his glass.

She stared at him. "This is Kentucky, home of real Kentucky bourbon." She pointed to a group of bottles along the top shelf, each one sporting a famous name he was vaguely familiar with. "If price was no object, a man would order a shot or two of this stuff." Kim selected a bottle and set it before him. "Aged in oak barrels for five, seven, or eight years, until the master says it's ready. Whiskey doesn't get any smoother than this. You could shoot it down or sip it slow from a snifter." Miming both actions, she placed the two styles of glassware on the bar.

Jake reached for the shot glass. "Pour me one, Miss Kim, and leave the bottle."

Hesitating, she leaned over so other patrons wouldn't hear her comment. "Cowboys might have said that in olden days, but that's strictly for TV shows now. Our best bourbon sold at bar prices would cost you a fortune."

Jake reached for his wallet and drew out his credit card. "I only look like a poor, down-on-his-luck loser. Actually, I'm a rich horse breeder." He laced his words with so much sarcasm they fooled no one.

Kim's face filled with pity as she cracked the seal on the expensive spirits. "I'll just charge you by the drink, not the full bottle. Maybe you won't even like this stuff." She poured the shot glass to the rim and headed to the kitchen pass-through window. A bell had signaled the arrival of several stacked cheeseburgers with mounds of French fries.

Jake stared at the expensive golden liquid without tasting it. Teetotalers like his mother called it the devil's brew, a weak man's courage, and plenty of other disparagements. He focused on the shot glass as though waiting for some mystical sign.

"Looks like you have something on your mind, son, and are hoping that whiskey holds the answers." Ken slipped onto the next bar stool as though entering a bar were an everyday occurrence.

"Dad. What are you doing here?" Jake's tone conveyed more shock than anger.

"I could ask you the same question. I recognized your truck out front and thought I would keep you company. Then I'll drive you home once your sorrows are sufficiently drowned." Ken slicked a hand through his graying brown hair.

Jake snorted. "How do you plan to drive two trucks home?" He lifted the stein for another sip, but ignored the bourbon.

"God looks out for drunks, or so I've heard. He gave me the idea to come to Rabbit Creek today to drop off the diesel generator that needs repair. Jack Daws rode along with me. I already sent Jack back to Charm with my truck. So I'm here till you're ready to go home."

Kim wandered over after delivering food to the pool players. "Hi, there. What'll it be? Care to see our menu?"

His father tipped his hat. "Ma'am, I'd love a bowl of the chili listed on your signboard, along with a cup of coffee if you have any."

"Coming right up. I just brewed a fresh pot. How about you?" she asked Jake. "Ready for some lunch?"

"No, ma'am. Not hungry."

After Kim jotted down the order, poured Ken's coffee, and strolled away, Jake pivoted on his stool. "I'm not drunk," he snapped. "This is only my second beer."

"Maybe not yet, but I see a bottle of 120 proof sitting in front of you and a glass already poured. It won't take long now." He studied his son as though he were a fascinating insect.

Jake lifted the shot, sniffed, and set it back down. "I'm still debating about trying this." He focused on a wall calendar, positioned on the previous month. "I came in because Rachel broke up with me." He blurted out the words with little emotion. "I started driving and ended up in Rabbit Creek, out of gas. After filling my tank, the neon beer sign in the window beckoned to me." His palms opened, his fingers clawing toward his chest.

"As signs have done for many brokenhearted young men and a few old ones too." Surprisingly, his father's tone held no censure. "From what I heard, alcohol usually doesn't help, but I won't stand in your way if you're bound and determined."

Jake took another gulp of beer and pushed away the mug. "Don't tell the bartender," he whispered, "but I really hate the stuff."

Ken laughed as though he hadn't a care in the world. "I understand it's an acquired taste." He wrapped his hands around his coffee cup. "Keeley overheard your conversation with Rachel. She tore into the house all upset."

"Oh, great." Jake rolled his eyes. "Now the whole stable will know what a loser I am."

"Your sister isn't like that. She's really mad at Rachel and not about to spread rumors. She vowed never to speak to her again and plans on communicating with her solely with sign language during their tours."

"Without any deaf friends, Keeley has been itching for a reason to practice her sign language skills."

Kim delivered a steaming bowl of chili topped with cheese and a basket of warm bread. The smell whetted Jake's appetite. "May I have a bowl of that too, along with a Coke?"

"You got it, darlin'," she teased. "Nobody can resist our chili for long."

While his father ate, Jake stared at his reflection in the mirror. "What am I going to do, Dad? I really love that woman. I can't bear seeing her every day right now, but I don't want to mess up her new position at work."

Setting down his spoon, Ken cocked his head to one side. "Your problem is you're too pale."

"What?"

"You're practically as white as a sheet. You need some sunshine. A trip to Florida ought to do the trick. You could check on the colt's progress firsthand. Make sure that Hitchcock isn't ordering steak every night for supper on our dime. Some time away from Twelve Elms will do you good."

"What about my chores?" Jake leaned back as Kim delivered his chili and Coke.

"I'm not retired yet. And we have plenty of hired help to fill in while you're gone."

Jake began to devour his lunch, almost scalding his tongue in the process. When he scraped the bottom of the bowl, he finished his soft drink in three gulps. "When can I leave?"

"How about tomorrow? Pack your bags tonight after supper. Set the GPS and cruise control, and you'll be among palm trees before you know it."

"Let me pay our tab and then let's get out of here." Jake pushed away his beer. "Miss Kim," he called. "Charge me for that bottle since you had to crack the seal." He set his credit card next to the empty bowl.

She walked over and patted his hand. "Bourbon ain't like milk, my friend. It won't go bad. I'm charging you for the coffee, beer, and the chili. But your drink and the Coke are on me. No arguments."

Jake left enough cash to cover a healthy tip and walked out of the Rabbit Creek Tavern with his father. The aged 120-proof bourbon remained untouched in his glass. He would have to take Kim's word that Kentucky made the finest spirits in the world.

❧

Rachel punched out at the time clock Friday afternoon with a grateful sigh. She had managed to work the rest of Wednesday and all day today without running into Jake. The head trainer kept her busy from the moment she arrived. She barely had time to wash up and wolf down her peanut butter sandwich lunch before her new boss barked another order. Not that she was complaining. Better to stay busy than to sit around pining for Jake.

It was what had to be. She knew it was the only sensible option.

Yet she felt as though she'd slammed the door on her heart's desire.

Punching Sarah's number into her cell phone, Rachel waited patiently for her cousin to pick up.

"Stoll's Free-to-Roam Chicken Farm."

"It's Rachel. I can leave early because of some schedule changes. I'll be home soon. Why don't you let me fix dinner tonight? It's high time I earn my keep."

"You earned it yesterday helping me clean the laying boxes. And you only got pecked twice."

Her cousin's laughter brightened Rachel's mood as she hurried toward her buggy. "My arch nemesis walked the other way when she saw me coming. I will mark the occasion on my calendar."

"If I let you cook, what will you make? My *ehemann* won't just eat anything. He's very picky."

Rachel snorted. "Isaac is the most laid-back husband in the world. I'm pretty sure he'll eat spaghetti and meatballs, buttered green beans, and cabbage salad." Her menu came to mind at that moment.

"Spaghetti?" she asked. "I suppose that will be all right as long as the sauce isn't too spicy. Should I start the meatballs?"

"*Nein.* It's my turn to cook. You go soak in the tub with a mug of sweet ginger tea, and maybe read one of those craft magazines you love."

"Like a lady of leisure?" The rest of Sarah's comments were muffled by laughter. "Okay, I'll give it a try."

But the irrepressible Sarah didn't relax at the end of her workday. When Rachel entered the kitchen less than an hour later, the table had been set, plump meatballs sat draining on paper towels, and green beans simmered on low heat. A large pot of water roiled away on a back burner. "Sarah Stoll, what have you done? I wanted to make dinner tonight."

"Then get busy, missy. The spaghetti still needs to be dropped into that pot and the jar of sauce heated. Plus you need to add dressing to the cabbage I chopped. I'm going out to the barn to see what Isaac is doing." Sarah tugged her apron over her head and slipped out the door.

Rachel's dinner was ready in less than ten minutes. Isaac even finished work thirty minutes early, allowing the three of them to eat immediately. Rachel suspected Sarah was responsible for their early supper hour.

Once Sarah wiped up the last dab of sauce with a bread crust, she looked Rachel in the eye and announced, "Because we are done eating, I think you should head over to the Yosts'. They're having a marshmallow roast tonight. You need to get out and socialize." Sarah laced her fingers together and cracked her knuckles.

Rachel considered inventing a myriad of excuses why not to attend, but if the gleam in Sarah's eye was an indicator, tonight was some sort of test. *Am I broken up with Jake Brady and serious about courting Amish men?* "Sure, I'll go. The Yosts don't live too far."

"*Gut.* And as you cooked our delicious supper, I'll clean the kitchen."

"Sarah, I only—"

"Don't fuss with me. I've had enough leisure time for one day. Now go get ready, and wear your rose-colored dress. That horrid brown one makes you appear anemic."

Isaac glanced up from his apple cobbler. "I advise you do as your cousin suggests, Rachel. Sarah has been planning this all day and can handle any barrier you throw up."

She rose to her feet. "Well, I haven't managed my life very well, so I'm open to suggestions. *Danki*, Sarah."

"Don't thank me. Just meet somebody nice so you'll settle down here and not run back to Lancaster."

Unfortunately, the dating pool of eligible men had shrunk instead of expanding in Casey County, according to one of her friends. Bonnie explained within five minutes of her arrival that all of the Old Order Amish had moved from the area.

"Where did they go?" Rachel stood far back from the huge bonfire. Roaring blazes still made her nervous since the horrible night she'd lost her parents back in Mount Joy.

"The entire district pitched in to buy five thousand acres in Tennessee. Five thousand acres, can you imagine? It's supposed to be fertile farmland too."

Rachel could not imagine it. That much land would cost tens of millions of dollars in Lancaster County—far beyond the reach of any Plain community. "What about the Old Order Mennonites?"

"Staying put, far as I know." Her friend stood on tiptoes scanning the crowd for her beloved Josh. They had announced their engagement recently and were planning a January wedding during the slow-paced time of year. "Let's move closer to the fire. It's dying down. Soon they'll bring out the marshmallows." Bonnie dragged Rachel to a row of lawn chairs. The moment they sat down, Bonnie jumped to her feet. "There's Josh! I'll see you later, Rach." She flew off as though her feet had wings.

"Hello, Miss King. You've come out of hiding at last." Reuben settled into Bonnie's vacated chair the moment her friend left. "I feared I would never see you again. My sister heard from Sarah that you'd been under the weather recently. Leah had been buying eggs at the time. *Gut* to see you're feeling better. Sarah said you might quit your job at the horse farm soon. Things too hectic for you there? Say, we may need help with making cheese this winter. I'll check with my *mamm* and *daed*."

Rachel stared as Reuben inhaled a deep gulp of air. All that had been uttered without the slightest break or hesitation. She didn't know which comment to respond to first. "I'm fully recovered, *danki*, but your sister heard incorrectly—I won't be quitting my job at Twelve Elms in the near future. So please don't speak to your parents on my behalf." She smiled politely. The thought of working around fermenting dairy products made her queasy, even though she only smelled burning logs and branches. Wood smoke had once been a pleasant scent to her. Now it left her light headed and disoriented.

"Right then, but let me know if that changes anytime this winter. My *mamm* and sisters all would like to know you better." Reuben scooted his webbed chair closer. "Did I mention we're thinking about adding a herd of dairy goats to our Holsteins and Jerseys? There's growing demand for both natural goat milk and goat milk cheese. And some ethnic groups in Louisville love to eat their meat. Can you figure how they serve it?"

Rachel hadn't expected to be drawn into a conversation quite so soon. "Maybe in stews or soups?" she stammered. "Or panfried with onions and peppers, like fajitas?"

Reuben's mouth dropped open. "Goat-meat burritos? I can't imagine any fast-food joints springing up soon, but anything is possible in the English world."

No, some things aren't remotely possible, she thought glumly. "Tell me about your Jersey herd. Those are the ones with the big ears, right? Their calves are so cute."

"If Sarah and Isaac didn't have every barn devoted to poultry, I'd give you a calf next spring as a pet," he said with sincerity.

Rachel smiled, taking in every detail of Reuben Mullet in a span of twenty seconds. He was a handsome man with thick, sandy-blond hair, blue eyes, and straight teeth. He was a hard worker who cared about his dairy cows, his family, and her, if she would only allow him. But she wasn't assessing bloodlines in racehorses to determine which would make a better sire. She was human, and despite his highly flattering devotion after a long absence, she couldn't generate one ounce of romantic interest in him. She would never marry him any more than she could Jake Brady, but for completely different reasons.

That night Reuben drove her home in his enclosed buggy while two of his sisters rode in the backseat. When they parked at the Stolls' walkway, he jumped down, sprinted to her side, and offered his hand.

Like a true gentleman.

When he walked her to the back door, Reuben ducked his head, blushed bright pink, and asked, "May I kiss you good night, Rachel?"

Despite her decision not to see him again, she couldn't bear to tell him her true feelings. So she nodded yes and closed her eyes. He gave her a quick kiss on the lips and fled back to his buggy.

Like a well-mannered Amish fellow.

Rachel entered the kitchen and wiped her mouth with her sleeve.

Like the true snake in the grass I am.

SEVENTEEN

We've no less days to sing God's praise

For the next three weeks, Rachel had had little trouble avoiding Mennonite social events. During the Christmas season folks spent more time with their extended families rather than the district as a whole. Plenty of aunts, uncles, and cousins visited the Stolls, many staying for several days. Rachel busied herself cooking, cleaning, and keeping up with laundry to allow Sarah and Isaac more time with their guests. Baking a steady stream of cakes, pies, and Christmas cookies prevented Rachel from wallowing in her misery. But no matter how many people visited, Sarah never neglected her beloved chickens. They ate before anyone else.

Life was different at work for Rachel too. The head trainer cut her back to Wednesdays and Fridays. An unusually cold, rainy spell kept the expensive show horses confined to the indoor arena. Owners didn't want their prized animals getting wet and muddy. Because trainers and exercise personnel were getting in each other's way, hours were reduced until March.

Rachel offered no argument. Jake was gone and wouldn't return until spring. After not seeing him for several days, she finally learned the story from one of the grooms. He'd left town the day after their breakup. By the time he returned to Charm, she would probably be back in Pennsylvania, thus ending the most enjoyable period of her life on a bitter note.

Once the holidays passed, back-to-back ice and snowstorms canceled Sunday services two weeks in a row. Slippery roads created dangerous conditions for people and horses. Rachel and the Stolls spent Sabbath mornings in silent prayer and Bible study. During the afternoons, Rachel wrote long, chatty letters to her three sisters but avoided the topics most on her mind. She couldn't bring herself to talk about Jake or the shameful way she'd led on Reuben.

Her weather-imposed exile came to an abrupt end on the following Sunday morning. Sarah woke her with an impatient shake. "Get up, sleepyhead. The roads are clear and the forecast calls for dry and sunny weather. We might hit forty degrees today. We leave for church in half an hour."

Rachel swung her legs over the side of the bed and nodded. "I'll be ready." The sooner she faced the Reuben conundrum, the better. Waiting would only make him despise her more once he learned the truth. When they arrived at church, she spotted no familiar blond head on the men's side of the room. Now that she'd come this far, Rachel hoped he was at the service so she could swallow her bitter pill. Afterward she walked with Sarah and Isaac to their buggy.

"Rachel? Could I have a moment please?" Someone called out her name.

She turned and saw Reuben's mother coming toward her. "*Guder mariye*, Mrs. Mullet."

"*Guder mariye*, but please call me Constance."

"I was looking for Reuben earlier. Didn't he come with you today?"

"No. He was in a buggy accident almost two weeks ago. He's been released from the Charm Hospital and transferred to a rehab facility in Somerset."

Sarah patted Rachel's back. "I'll wait in the buggy to give you two some privacy."

Rachel swayed on her feet, feeling a little dizzy. "What?" All this time she thought only of herself while poor Reuben had been injured. "How is he?"

"Getting better each day. It'll be a long while before he walks without crutches, but at least the doctors believe he will walk. His *daed* wouldn't let me tell you over the phone, and with our weather lately, I couldn't come to church until today."

Rachel pressed a hand to her throat. "How did it happen?" A light rain began to fall, which she barely took note of.

Constance Mullet raised her umbrella to shelter them both. "We're not completely certain. Reuben said he was waiting at a stop sign. It was night and the intersection had no street lights. The other road had the right-of-way with a yellow flasher but no stop sign. Highway patrol doesn't know if he didn't see the oncoming truck or if his horse got spooked and bolted across the road. Reuben doesn't remember." Constance lifted her gaze to meet Rachel's.

"Mercy me," she murmured. "Did he suffer a head injury too?"

"Just a concussion. He can recall the rest of his life except for the accident. Thank the Lord."

"Yes, thank Him for His mercy." Rachel's shoulder muscles relaxed.

"He sure remembers you just fine," Constance continued. "You're all that boy talks about whenever we visit. How pretty you are, how sweet tempered. It's Rachel this and Rachel that." Constance fluttered her blond eyelashes.

Rachel's relief proved short lived. "Will he make a full recovery?"

"He'll probably walk with a limp, but he will be fine." Constance pulled out her cell phone to check the time. "We're driving to Somerset to see him around one. Do you want us to pick you up? I know he would love to see you."

Rachel's mind sorted and processed the details at lightning speed. "*Danki,* but if you don't mind I'll make the trip another time. May I have the address of the facility?"

"You'd probably like a few moments alone without his *mamm, daed,* and four *schwestern, jah?*" Constance Mullet chuckled good-naturedly. "Seeing that you two haven't announced your engagement, I shouldn't permit it. But considering Reuben has a roommate and the staff is constantly going in and out, I suppose it would be okay." She dug in her purse for a business card. "Here is the address, phone number, and visiting hours. It's about an hour by car."

"I appreciate your coming here, Constance. Tell Reuben I will see him soon."

❧

Just how soon no one could have predicted. Crammed into the front seat of a pickup with Ruby and her cousin, Josh, Rachel waited until the Mullet family left the rehab facility. She had bribed her companions with buffet dinners at Bread of Life besides offering to pay for the gas.

"There they go, heading toward their hired car and driver," announced Ruby. "You want us to come in with you?"

"No. I won't be long."

"Good luck. Be brave." Ruby, privy to what Rachel planned to do, hugged her tightly.

Rachel jumped out and strode to Room 204 as fast as she could. She carried no flowers, no get well card, no box of chocolates. She brought only the grim announcement that whatever Reuben had planned for their future wasn't going to happen. Her news would certainly send the man into despair.

Reuben struggled to sit up when she entered the room. "Rachel! What a sight for sore eyes you are. You just missed my folks and sisters by five minutes."

Closing the privacy curtain, she pulled up a chair and delivered her overdue confession within sixty seconds of arrival, not wanting this mean-spirited sham to continue another moment.

He listened attentively as she explained she could never see him as anything more than a friend, and then she effusively apologized for not being forthright sooner. She begged for his forgiveness and continued friendship.

He neither fainted, gnashed his teeth, nor tried to hang himself with the traction equipment. In fact, he took the gut-wrenching news with complete composure. "Ah, don't fret about it. I pretty much figured that out, but I thought I'd see how far you would go with this." Chuckling merrily, he reached for the TV control. "Did you know this place has cable? One station runs old Westerns all day long. Want to watch *Gunsmoke* for a while?"

Rachel was the one who needed a moment of composure. "I would, except that Ruby and Josh are waiting to drive me home. I'd better go."

"Ruby Miller?" His eyes rounded. "She was my next choice for courting if you ever dumped me. Do you think you could put in a good word for me?"

Rachel assured him she would and then shook hands with Casey County's happiest dairy farmer. Everything discussed in conversation on the ride back to Charm put Reuben in a good light, setting the stage for a bit of matchmaking down the road. Actually, the more she thought about it, the more she thought Reuben and Ruby would be perfect together.

"Home, sweet home," said Josh as they turned up the chicken

farm driveway. "Looks like the popular Stolls are getting more company, even this late in the day."

Rachel leaned forward to see past Ruby to the new arrivals—one tall, gaunt, very old man, one plump, white-haired old woman, and one tiny blond girl in a ghastly brown dress. "As I live and breathe…" she murmured. The bishop, *grossmammi*, and Beth stood out in the drizzle talking to Sarah and Isaac as though it were a midsummer afternoon. "Thanks for the ride," she squeaked, her voice suddenly gone. Jumping out of the truck, moisture filled her eyes as Rachel ran toward three of her favorite people on God's green earth. By the time she reached her family, tears streamed down her face—tears of joy.

※

Donna tried not to think too much about what lay ahead of her that morning. Her husband and her two daughters had finally stopped asking questions during breakfast and while they all dressed. She had no answers, only plenty of questions of her own. She had invited Pete, Amber, and Kristen to accompany her today for moral support. Now she wasn't so sure that had been a good idea. When a woman could potentially make a total fool of herself and be run out of town on the proverbial rail, did she really want an audience? But having three more friendly faces in the Old Order Mennonite Church would bring the total to five, counting Rachel King and Sarah Stoll.

Donna had also invited Phil to attend so that he might see what she was up against. But he'd politely declined, citing a previous commitment. Sleeping until noon under a layer of warm blankets didn't constitute a *previous commitment* in her opinion, but forcing a person to attend church seldom worked.

Isaac Stoll would be there too, but whose side he would be on remained to be seen. The Lancaster bishop and Rachel's grandmother had recently arrived from Pennsylvania and were also unknown variables at this point. They could either help make her case for vaccines or seal her fate in Charm's Amish and Mennonite communities. Either way, as Pete turned their SUV into the parking area—filled almost entirely with buggies—Donna knew the showdown between the Kentucky State Department of Health and the Plain believers of Casey County had arrived.

Rachel and Sarah were waiting on the front stoop as Donna and her family approached. Kristen and Amber glanced around, wide eyed with fascination, but at least they were smiling. Anything different from the same old, same old was fine with them. Pete, true to form, greeted the occasion with his usual confidence. He loved to say, "If it ain't the end of the world, there's nothing to worry about. And if it is the end of the world, but you know the Lord, you have nothing to worry about."

Donna agreed with him in theory, but she possessed far less peace of mind. "Good morning, Rachel, Sarah," she said as they climbed the steps. "You know Amber and Kristen, and this is my husband, Pete."

"Hi," greeted Rachel. "Good to see you again." She grinned at the two teenagers. "And this is my grandmother, Edna King, and my hometown bishop, Abraham Esh." As though they were the next contestants on a television game show, two elderly Amish people appeared in the doorway on cue.

"I was just staying out of the wind until you got here," said Edna. "How do?" The woman shook Donna's hand as though it were a pump handle, demonstrating far more strength than most women her age.

"I'm fine, thank you. This is Pete Cline." Donna pointed at her better half. Pete nodded and then stretched out his dry, chapped fingers.

"How do?" repeated the grandmother, giving Pete's arm a good workout too.

"Good morning. A blessed Lord's Day to you all." The black-clad preacher spoke in a gracious tone. "Let's go inside. The service is about to start. Mr. Cline, I'll show you where to sit. You ladies and young women should follow Sarah."

Within minutes, Sarah, Rachel, Edna, and Donna were seated in the front row on the left. Pete sat equally ringside between the Lancaster bishop and Isaac Stoll.

"Preaching first, and then you and Abraham will get your chance to talk." Sarah provided the only advance explanation Donna would receive.

James Mast, Sarah's bishop, conducted a lovely Christian service that probably would have been more recognizable in English. Prayers were silent, but the bishop gave specific requests of what to pray for. Hymns were sung out of key without musical accompaniment, and all Scripture was read in German, but Donna sensed the presence of God in the room.

Bishop Mast delivered the first sermon in *Deutsch,* and then a younger minister delivered the second message in English. Kristen and Amber, who had been seated with Mennonite teenaged girls, appeared mesmerized by the proceedings, even though they could only comprehend around half of the service. Once it was ended, the bishop cleared his throat to regain the congregation's attention. "Today we welcome guests into our midst. The *Englischers* are Donna Cline, a nurse and social worker for the State Department of Health, along with her husband and daughters: Pete, Kristen, and Amber."

Murmurs of welcome filled the room, the loudest coming from the youthful corner.

"Visiting from Lancaster County is Sarah Stoll's *grossmammi,* along with her cousin, Beth King, who is also Rachel King's *schwester.* Edna King brought her bishop, Abraham Esh, who wishes to address our district. First we will hear from Mrs. Cline." Bishop Mast took his seat on the right-hand side.

Donna heard indistinguishable whispers as she walked to the front of the room. She chose to get right to the point—Plain people deserved plain speeches. "Thank you, Bishop Mast, for allowing me to address your district. As you know a total of four polio infections have been discovered here in Charm. I wish to thank everyone for their cooperation with our sample testing. Blessedly, no new cases have turned up, and none of the four children have developed paralytic polio as of yet." She paused so that her words could be absorbed. "Unfortunately, the little girl remains hospital-ized and her infection might develop into a paralytic form down the road. I obtained her parents' consent to disclose this information." Scanning the congregation, most watched her without any expression whatsoever. "I have listened to your concerns these past weeks and then did my own research. We'll probably never know for certain how the little girl contracted a virus that hasn't been in the United States for years. Somebody who had been out of the country, perhaps even a doctor or nurse, might have exposed her."

Murmurs rose throughout the room, many of them agitated.

"Although I'm not Plain, I can imagine what you're thinking—that this is what we get for associating with *Englischers* and for trusting modern medical facilities. And I can't disagree with that initial reaction." Several formerly benign faces turned astonished. "Unfortunately, the Plain communities of America can no longer remain completely separate from the world. Too many people travel to foreign lands, including humanitarian workers to Haiti, Africa, and India. We, both English and Mennonite, go to help our fellow man in need as Scripture dictates, and to spread the Good News about our Lord. Even if no one from Charm travels abroad, foreigners come to Kentucky on vacation or to work or to relocate. They could bring with them a virus that might not make them sick but could easily infect a community such as this.

"You no longer have the luxury of keeping your children safe by keeping them removed. They will interact with strangers in restaurants, libraries, and bus stations throughout their lives, in addition to the English medical system should they need stitches or an X-ray. Vaccines are the only way to protect their health. Mrs. King remembers when the Pennsylvania Board of Health came to Lancaster County back in nineteen seventy-nine after a polio outbreak in the Netherlands, which had already spread to Canada. About one-third of the residents were inoculated back then, most of them children. Health care workers set up clinics in more than one hundred districts in barns and outbuildings. Bishop Esh has traveled from Mount Joy at Rachel King's request to answer questions you might have about the procedure. He also remembers the board of health's visit clearly and doesn't recall a single parent regretting their decision due to side effects or some adverse reaction."

Pausing again as chatter increased, she let the congregation talk a minute and then raised her hand for silence. "In the end, the decision is yours—each mother's and father's. Some English parents refuse shots for their kids for their own reasons. No one will try to force you into something you feel strongly against, but after you listen to Bishop Esh, if you decide to get your family immunized, there are papers on the back table. They explain where to go, how to prepare, and what you can expect, and have my personal cell phone number and address as well. Take a paper home and give the matter some thought and prayer, as I have done. Thank you for listening. God bless you on this lovely winter morning."

Edna King and Bishop Esh walked to the front as Donna sat down, relieved and proud of herself. She had done her best. Even Rachel's and Sarah's *grossmammi* had a few words to say on the subject. This, as with all matters, was now in God's hands. Glancing over the men's side of the room, she spotted her husband trying subtly for her attention.

"Well done," he mouthed. And if she hadn't been sitting among those taught to control their emotions, she probably would have started to cry.

꩜

Florida

Jake gazed over an empty racetrack just as the sun broke the horizon to the east. Within the hour trainers and exercise boys, jockeys and owners, local and national news media, Thoroughbred devotees and sports enthusiasts would fill the track and grandstands, ready for another busy day in the winter racing circuit. The weather was warm and sunny, with a refreshing breeze from the west. His hotel was clean, comfortable, and reasonably priced. He'd enjoyed a breakfast of fake eggs, English muffins, fresh mixed fruit, and strong coffee, all complimentary. There had been plenty of warm water for his shower because he didn't have to share the hot water tank with five other family members.

Alan Hitchcock had greeted him graciously, surprised yet pleased he'd come down for the rest of training. The man had talked nonstop during dinner last night about Eager to Please's latest times and distances. Alan told him about the procession of jockeys being considered to find the right match between professional rider and highly spirited colt. Hitchcock took Jake to a fine steakhouse, insisting the meal was his treat and wouldn't appear on any expense account receipt. The restaurant served delicious Black Angus steaks covered with sautéed mushrooms and onions with a dollop of blue cheese sauce—just the way Jake liked it. His potato had been twice baked and served with cheddar cheese and sour cream. A Caesar salad opened the feast, while chocolate cake with hot fudge sauce had brought the memorable meal to a close.

Then there had been the reunion with his beloved horse. Eager to Please tossed his mane several times, nickered, and clearly not only remembered Jake but was happy to see him. The horse had filled out during the weeks he'd been in the land of flat tracks, warm days, and plenty of bugs. His sprint times were impressive and improving each day.

Yet despite the gourmet food, comfortable digs, and excellent reports from his hired trainer and staff, Jake was not a happy man. Part of his melancholy had to do with Rachel. He replayed each of their encounters in his mind over and over to see if he'd been offensive or had somehow sabotaged his chances for a future with her. Nothing came to mind. But seeing her pretty face whenever he closed his eyes, hearing her musical laughter ringing in his ears, and recalling the sweet scent of ripe peaches that clung to her accounted for only part of his misery.

Far more serious matters were on Jake's mind that day than his nonexistent love life, despite how overwhelming their breakup had seemed back in Charm. Arriving in Florida brought him face-to-face with the enormity of what he had done. Filled with bluster and lofty dreams of grandeur for his colt, he'd turned down a very generous purchase offer on an unproven juvenile. While sitting in his home office in Kentucky, anything and everything seemed possible. But here powerful men with deep pockets surrounded him, those who bought racehorses the way he bought T-shirts at the mall. One bad decision, one unlucky accident might not break these men's bank accounts or change their lifestyles. Not so in the case of the Brady family. God forbid, but if Eager to Please broke a leg or something else happened that ended his racing career, Jake's family could easily lose the farm and everything else Ken and Taylor had worked for their entire lives. Why had his folks agreed with his idea? Because they loved him, pure and simple. His mom and dad encouraged each of their children to work hard and to follow their dreams. And how had Jake repaid their trust and devotion? By making a crucial decision—one that affected all Bradys—by himself.

Guilt and shame washed over him, turning his stomach queasy. For a few moments, he feared he might become physically ill, throwing up the egg-substitute omelet just as exercise boys rode their Thoroughbreds onto the track for some easy warm-up laps. Steadying himself on a fence post, he sucked in several deep breaths to calm his nerves.

Who was Jake Brady amid all this old and new money? According to Hitchcock, these men ordered two-hundred-dollar bottles of wine, purchased five-thousand-dollar suits, and had homes in several states and, occasionally, even other countries. Alan had entertained him during last night's dinner with tales of flashy owners throwing elaborate parties for trainers, jockeys, and the news media in hopes of wooing away winning personnel from current contracts or garnering favorable advance reviews in the racing papers. The way Hitchcock described the behind-the-scene activities, it sounded like a cross between *Lifestyles of the Rich and Famous* and the TV soap opera *Dallas*.

He was Jake Brady, proud graduate of Charm High School and the Casey County Community College, who owned only one suit from the men's outlet store and wouldn't know the difference between oysters and calamari if his life depended on it. And his lack of sophistication had never bothered him one iota until he showed up down here. Jamming his hands down into his pockets, Jake headed back to the barns to spend some alone time with Eager. When he arrived, the grooms were already feeding his colt and changing the water bucket. With pride he picked up a brush to groom the magnificent horse as he'd done so many mornings in the past.

"I thought I'd find you here early." Hitchcock appeared in the stall doorway. "Chomping at the bit to see what your boy can do?" The trainer looked casual but refined in his striped pullover sweater, pressed jeans, and polished boots.

"Yes, sir, I am." Jake voiced the words with little emotion.

"Jose, take our boy out and get him warmed up. He's finished with breakfast. This is Eager's owner. Mr. Brady didn't come to Florida to watch him chew oats."

Actually, that's exactly what Mr. Brady came for this morning. But

Jake stepped back as the young man nodded respectfully and led away the horse. *Mr. Brady*. Funny—he didn't feel like an owner or even an owner's son. He felt like a fraud, a poser who was grasping at things he didn't even understand.

"Did you hear the news about Treacherous Blue Waters?" asked Hitchcock.

"No, who's that?" Jake leaned a shoulder against a smooth polished wall.

"He won the Breeder's Cup five-furlong race at Santa Anita two months ago."

"What happened to him?" he asked, dreading the answer.

"Suffered a stress fracture of the ilium—that's a bone in his pelvis. Luckily, he should heal with sufficient rest. It doesn't look as though he'll need surgery, but the horse will be out of commission for a long while." Hitchcock held the stall door open for him.

Jake had to breathe through his mouth to quell his nausea, which had returned with a vengeance. "You know what, Alan? Something I ate at the hotel isn't sitting well on my stomach. I need to take a walk and get some fresh air. I'll catch up with you later to watch some timed sprints."

Hitchcock chuckled merrily. "You got it. No matter how many times these stalls get cleaned, a horse barn always smells exactly like a horse barn. Check in at the track infirmary for some antacids if you don't feel better soon."

Jake strode away as fast as his legs could carry him—away from the stalls and lunging area, the owners' clubs and jockey lounges. He marched past the row of pari-mutuel windows that on race days would have long lines of gamblers. He passed the restaurants and snack bars, uncertain of exactly where he was going. Then a small metal sign caught his eye: Trackside Chapel. Jake pictured one of those small rooms inside hospitals with a few pews or rows of chairs and a tiny altar, a place where patients or family members could come to terms with a grim diagnosis. This chapel was inside a mobile trailer so it could be easily moved to other locations around the country. He ducked his head under the doorway, expecting to be alone inside.

"Come on in," boomed a voice.

Glancing up, Jake spotted a burly guy, covered in tattoos, sitting in the front row. "I didn't know anybody was already in here."

"I'm a volunteer who staffs the chapel two days a week. The name's Ed Bonner. I found Jesus in prison while serving time for assault with a deadly weapon. The guy survived or I'd still be in the slammer, fearing for my life each and every day. Now I'm more worried about my soul." Bonner's laughter revealed several missing teeth. "Where'd you learn about Jesus?"

Jake blinked like an owl, undone by the man's forthright approach. *Nothing like not beating around the bush.* "I don't know. My parents took us to church when we were babies, then Sunday school, VBS, the whole nine yards. I guess I've always known Him."

The parolee nodded toward an empty chair. "My folks never set foot inside a church. Lucky you, to have had Jesus during the tough times."

Anger snaked up Jake's back. How could this guy assume he knew his life story after two minutes? "You think so? I might have heard of Him, but I can't say I spent much time with the guy. I'm a fraud, a Sunday-morning Christian who talks the talk but hasn't walked the walk a single day in his life." He spat out the words as though they were vinegar.

The chapel's host was unmoved. "Join the club, my friend. It ain't easy, is it? Sit down. I'm willing to listen and offer a little advice if you're willing to give me some in return. This is a two-way street here." His tone soothed, and his smile was genuine.

Jake stared at the man, fixing his gaze on a scar that ran from his hairline to the bridge of his nose. "Why not? If you think you could possibly benefit by anything I have to say, I'm in." He slumped into the opposite chair.

And for the first time all day, his nausea had vanished.

EIGHTEEN

Than when we'd first begun

Wednesday

Rachel left for work with mixed emotions. On the one hand, she regretted leaving her little sister, who so desperately wanted to spend every waking moment with her. She'd had to close the bathroom door in Beth's face twice, insisting that some activities demanded solitude. Beth was lonely back in Pennsylvania with all her sisters living elsewhere. She'd cried when Rachel refused to allow her to tag along to Twelve Elms.

On the other hand, Rachel was relieved to leave *grossmammi* for a few hours. As much as she loved her grandmother, the woman had watched her like a hawk since arriving, as though she waited for some telltale sign Rachel was planning to jump the fence. Between the two of them, Rachel had as much privacy as one of Sarah's hens trying to lay an egg.

Grossmammi needn't worry about Rachel leaving the Amish faith. The only person for whom she might have considered the idea was now living hundreds of miles away in another state. He hadn't called or written any letters, not that she could blame him. She'd made her feelings painfully clear last month and hadn't seen him since. To please Sarah, she returned to Mennonite socials and made every attempt to meet new people. Too bad all of the other Amish had moved to Tennessee. She tried to muster feelings for Reuben beyond friendship to no avail. Much to her surprise and relief, he hadn't been devastated by her confession. In fact, he and Ruby were practically a courting couple now that she had revealed Reuben's admission to her friend. Life was strange. Ruby hadn't been the least bit dismayed she was Reuben's second choice. Apparently, she was a far more practical woman than Rachel and not waiting to hear romantic bells and whistles.

Slipping her packed lunch inside her bag, along with her hidden English clothing, Rachel stepped from the warm kitchen into frigid air. Her breath turned into a fog of condensation under an overcast gray sky. As usual, dear Isaac had already hitched up the buggy by the time she reached the barn. He had even placed a lap robe close to the barn's potbelly stove to warm.

"Drive carefully," he said, handing it to her.

Rachel climbed up and spread the cozy cover over her legs. "I'll get there and back safely, God willing. No long workdays during the winter, but it'll still be dark by the time I return tonight. I'm sure I'll be ready for supper and a cozy fire by then."

"Your *grossmammi* and Sarah are waging a battle of wills over who'll cook the meal, and it's escalating." Isaac glanced toward the house to make sure Rachel hadn't been followed. "Sarah told Edna that at her age she ought to rest in the rocking chair. Edna replied that, left to your own devices, granddaughter, you would cook chicken three meals a day, seven days a week, all year long." Isaac buried his face in his hands, undone by a fit of laughter. "Who knows what we'll find on the supper table tonight."

"I'll hurry home. I wouldn't want to miss any King family fireworks. But I advise you to steer clear if those two start to fuss."

He lifted his gaze, his eyes watery. "If I've learned nothing else, cousin, it's never get in between two angry stray cats...or women." He slapped the gelding's rump and headed to the house, still chuckling.

Rachel drove the three miles to Twelve Elms, trying to keep warm while sorting out her emotions. Without warning, tears began to stream down her face. But unlike Isaac, her tears weren't from uncontrollable laughter but from abject sorrow. How could she work there after how she treated Jake—the only man she ever loved and probably ever would?

I still love him. Despite her brave attempts to put him out of mind, to ignore the cherished way he made her feel, she couldn't stop thinking about him. What difference did it make if she was Amish and he Baptist? As long as they were both Christians, it shouldn't matter. But it certainly mattered to *grossmammi* and Bishop Esh. Although she wouldn't be shunned if she turned English because she hadn't taken the kneeling vow, she might as well be. She would become an outsider, an acquaintance allowed to participate in Amish life only in peripheral ways. But she would have the love of Jake Brady. And now that she'd spurned him, his devotion grew ever more precious in her memory.

Once Rachel arrived at the stable, she had no time to pine over broken relationships. The head trainer started giving orders the moment she exited the ladies' room dressed in jeans and her heaviest sweatshirt. She stayed busy for hours, working horses in the lunge ring, the indoor arena, and even on the lower hills. Pretty Boy needed exercise, according to her boss, so he selected Rachel to take him up the wet, sloppy trails. With Jake gone, she seemed to have fallen out of favor with the other employees, but that didn't bother her. No one's opinion could be lower than her own.

Finally Larry looked at his watch. "Why don't you take your lunch now? When you come back, I'll probably have you help the grooms muck out the stalls in the show barn. We have potential clients coming this week to check out our facilities. I want everything looking top-notch."

"Sure," she replied. And truly she didn't care that she would spend the afternoon shoveling smelly wood shavings into wheelbarrows and then rolling them to the composting dumpster. Nothing could sour her already foul mood. After washing up and retrieving her lunch from her locker, she strolled into the break room. Unfortunately, the all-male inhabitants made her rethink her choice. On impulse, Rachel headed to the back door of the Brady residence. Jessie was home for the week due to an appointment for wisdom teeth extraction. Rachel hoped she could spend a few minutes with Jake's older sister.

Jessie answered the door on her first knock. "Hi, Rach, what's up? Looking for Keeley?" The right side of her face looked mildly swollen.

"No, it's you I came to see. Do you think we could eat lunch together?" Rachel imbued her words with as much optimism as possible.

"Sure, come on in. I can't chew much, so I'm having an exciting bowl of chicken noodle soup. What do you have in your bag?" She slipped into a chair and gestured to another one for her guest. In front of her was a bowl of soup, and beside was a thick textbook, a highlighter at the ready.

Rachel pulled out her sandwich. "Chicken salad on whole wheat with lettuce and tomato. Do you want half? I have an apple and chips too."

"Sounds good, but you go ahead. I'd better be careful for at least another day. Anyway, I've loved this soup since I was four years old." Scooping a spoonful, Jessie smacked her lips with the requisite *Mmm, mmm, good.* "What's on your mind, other than watching me eat with one side of my mouth?"

Rachel chewed a bite of sandwich and then swallowed. "I know I shouldn't be asking this, but do you know how long Jake plans on being away? Someone mentioned that he went to Florida to oversee the training of Eager to Please. It's just that he hasn't called me or written any letters or sent a message. Not that I expected him to after what I said to him." When she sputtered out of air, she reached for her carton of milk.

Jessie's eyes nearly bugged from her head. "Golly, I've never heard you talk so much at one given time. What gives? My brother said you two broke up. That's part of the reason why he headed south."

"Desperate times call for desperate measures," Rachel murmured, heartened by Jessie's admission. She dropped the rest of her sandwich onto the waxed paper. "Jessie, I might have made the biggest mistake of my life."

"Do you mean by becoming an exercise girl? Or does this have something to do with Jake?" Jessie's spoon paused midway to her mouth.

"It has everything to do with Jake," she wailed, bursting into tears." Suddenly the tension of the previous week, compounded by lack of sleep due to Beth's chatter, conspired to bring Rachel to the breaking point. "I love him. I tried not to but it sneaked up on me."

"That will happen." Jessie caught sight of Rachel's wounded expression. "Sorry, I'm not making light of the situation, but personally I'm overjoyed."

"How can another woman's misery make you happy?" Rachel dabbed her face with a napkin.

"Trust me, I'm not glad you're miserable, only that you're in love with my brother. Because, rest assured, he's still in love with you."

"Even after the wretched way I treated him?"

"Yep. People are funny like that. They'll forgive someone they love almost anything."

Rachel stared out the window. The light rain was rapidly changing to snow. Roads would become slick by quitting time. "What should I do? I'm open to advice."

Jessie's face sobered. "I need to ask you something first. What happened to the two Plain guys you were dating? Jake told me about them."

"One of them went home without bothering to say goodbye. The other was in a buggy accident, but I told him the truth when I visited him in the hospital—that he was just a friend and would never be anything more. He's now courting one of my girlfriends with my blessing." She attempted a smile. "So there are no other men."

"Are you sure about this, Rachel? You're sure you're in love with my brother?"

"Without a shadow of a doubt." She answered in a weak but decisive voice. "But what can I do now? I've burned my bridges."

Jessie jumped up and enveloped her in a warm hug. "Bridges can be rebuilt. Keep the faith, sister. Where's there's life, there's hope."

❧

Jessie watched their newest exercise girl head back toward the barns with a heart nearly bursting. She had heard the blow-by-blow account of what had been going on from her little sister via e-mail. Describing the situation with Rachel and Jake, Keeley alternated between anger and sadness every fifteen minutes. No matter how many times Mom or Dad ordered Keeley to stay out of it, the girl just couldn't help herself. She was very fond of Rachel and absolutely adored her big brother. She'd grown up watching so many Disney happily-ever-after fairy tales that she believed romance always worked out in the end.

Jessie, older and a tad wiser, knew that sometimes that wasn't the case. What was wrong with Jake that his women of choice never returned the same level of affection? Was he too kind? Did nice guys finish last like the country songs professed? She truly hoped not, because once she finished college, she wanted to meet her own Prince Charming and settle down. In the meantime, she had a little long-distance matchmaking to do. Closing her economics textbook, Jessie quickly washed her soup bowl and retreated to their home office with her cell phone. Keeley was still at school, but her father could wander into the kitchen looking for a snack or cup of coffee to reheat.

Once the door was closed behind her, Jessie punched in Jake's cell number from memory.

"Jake Brady."

"It's me, Jake. Jessie. I'm home for a few days. How's it going?"

"Fine. Is something wrong?" Alarm crept into his voice.

"No. Absolutely nothing. In fact, you might find what I have to say particularly interesting."

His unease didn't abate. "Why aren't you at school? Did you get expelled?"

"Of course not. I had two wisdom teeth extracted, if you must know, but I brought my assignments for the week home. Now, will you shut up and stop asking dumb questions? This is important." Jessie waited a couple of moments. Then fearing he'd hung up or their call had been disconnected, she asked. "Jake, are you still there?"

"You told me to shut up. Why don't you come to the point, little sister? I have things to do down here."

"Okay, fine. I just ate lunch with Rachel King. Remember

her—cute Amish gal with long blond hair and gorgeous blue eyes?" Unfortunately, Jessie resorted to their usual banter when dealing with her elder sibling.

"I think so. Wasn't she the one who told me to get lost, that she could never imagine a future with me? That Rachel King? Of course, she's only joined the growing list of women who find Jake Brady unacceptable as a boyfriend." His scornful words covered a world of hurt.

Jessie stopped joking around. "Rachel came looking for me today, up to the house. I didn't initiate this. She said she was miserable and had made the biggest mistake of her life. Those were her exact words, Jake. Then she started crying. We both know there's not a manipulative bone in her body, so this is for real." Jessie paused, waiting for what she anticipated would be a joyous reaction. She received instead total silence on the other end.

Finally, he spoke. "What happened to the two guys she was also dating?" Ice could have crystallized on his words.

"One of them skipped town to a new job without bothering to say goodbye. She said she didn't much care. The other had some kind of accident, but when Rachel went to see him in the hospital, she set him straight. They are just friends and nothing more. He's already going out with one of her friends. What do you think about that, big brother?" Considering the time he took to reply, apparently not much.

"There are plenty of Amish fish in the sea, even in Kentucky."

"Will you listen to me, please?" Jessie's tone bordered on outrage. "Rachel regrets whatever she said to you and wants to get back together. She *loves* you. I think you should come home as soon as possible."

Jake's tone also changed to one less angry, more sorrowful. "I appreciate the call, Jessie, and what you're trying to do. As sisters go, I could have done worse than you. But I'm afraid it's not as simple as just come home and all will be well."

Jessie rubbed the bridge of her nose. A headache was building between her eyes. "Look, Jake, people mess up. This was a big decision she had to make—a lot is at stake for her. Are you saying you're not man enough or Christian enough to forgive her?" Annoyance ratcheted up from his typical male stubbornness.

"It's not that I can't forgive Rachel. I just can't leave Florida right now."

She scratched her nose, trying to figure him out without picking an argument. "Aren't we paying Alan Hitchcock a barrel of money? I thought he took down a secretary, grooms, and exercise staff with him. If the guy didn't need you before, I'm sure he can manage without you until Eager comes home in the spring. Tell him there's a family emergency back in Kentucky. If you had seen Rachel's face, you would know that's no lie." Jessie giggled, hoping humor would break through his protective shell.

For several long moments she listened to her brother breathe into the mouthpiece. At first she thought he was planning an ego-saving solution. When she realized he was crying, her blood chilled in her veins. "What's going on, Jake? What aren't you telling me?" she whispered.

"I did something really stupid regarding Eager to Please, something I should have told Mom and Dad about right away. But I was too greedy and too full of myself. I've messed up, and now I'm afraid to tell our parents. I've ruined our lives."

Jessie swallowed hard. "Well, you know Dad's motto about worrying—"

"Please don't make jokes, Jess. This is really serious."

"Then come home. Leave Florida tonight or no later than tomorrow morning. You can sit down for a heart-to-heart with Dad and Mom and get this off your chest. Then once you're back you can straighten things out with Rachel. It's what she has been praying for." Jessie waited but heard only silence on the other end. "Say something, Jake. You're scaring me."

In a strangled voice he moaned, "I'm so ashamed of myself."

Inexplicably, Jessie started to cry too. "So come home." She was practically shouting into the cell phone. "We are your family. We love you. There's nothing you could ever do to change that."

"I will, Jessie, in a few days. There's a guy down here who's been talking to me. It's been helping a lot. We've been straightening each other out. Please don't worry about me. Sorry I dumped this on you."

Her anxiety soared to new heights. "Who is this guy? You're talking to some stranger at a racetrack, and you think he can help more than your family?"

"It's okay. I met him in the trackside mobile chapel. He's a sort of a counselor for Christians, and for those who call themselves that but act very differently."

"Okay, that's good, I suppose. But what about Rachel? What should I tell her?"

It took him a few moments to answer. "For right now, nothing. I promise to come home soon. I just don't know when. Trust me, after what I've done she wouldn't want a man like me even if I turned Amish tomorrow. I need to figure out how to fix this before I face our parents."

Jessie exhaled a long, pent-up breath. "Fine, but I'll tell you the same thing I told her. There are no burned bridges that can't be rebuilt." Her voice cracked as tears streamed down her face.

"Thanks, Jessie. I don't know if I ever mentioned this before, but I love you." Jake's end of the line went dead.

She stood sobbing, terrified of something she didn't understand. Finally, she wiped her face and marched back to the kitchen. The lacy snowflakes of an hour ago had increased to the first real snowfall of the season. Pulling on her boots and shrugging into her coat, Jessie headed to the arena in search of Rachel. She would say nothing about her conversation with Jake, but she would insist that Rachel head for home right now. The last thing this family needed was a horse and buggy on slippery roads.

❧

Jake clicked his cell phone shut, and for a long time he simply stared out the hotel room window. A steady rain beat against the glass, matching his dismal mood. His sister's compassion and willingness to love him unconditionally only further underscored his shortcomings. Yet at the same time, Jessie had also given him a glimmer of hope. Rachel still loved him. She regretted breaking up and wanted to get back together. If only he could fix the mess he'd created with this horse.

He no longer wanted to be the proud owner of a Kentucky Derby winner.

He no longer wanted to be a member of horse racing's elite inner circle, throwing money around wherever necessary to put on a good show.

He only wanted to be Jake Brady, son of Ken and Taylor, boyfriend of Rachel King, just an average-joe trainer of average-joe horses. But was he ready to go back to Casey County and face the music for his lies and duplicity? He had little choice. But first he needed to talk to a friend—call a lifeline, as they say on TV.

Jake drove back to the racetrack, parked in the guest lot, and hiked to the trackside chapel. Ed Bonner would be able to give him advice. He'd already straightened out a boatload of misconceptions Jake had about being a Christian. But when Jake entered the chapel-on-wheels, he was greeted by a scribbled note, not a two-hundred-pound, shaved-head former felon with a heart of gold. *Be back later, called away on an emergency. Ed.* Without any other place to go, Jake lowered himself onto a folding chair. First, he studied things hanging on the wall: framed scenes from the

Bible, including Jesus in the Garden of Gethsemane and Moses parting the Red Sea; several standard prayer plaques, including the Serenity Prayer used by Alcoholics Anonymous; and various hand-lettered signs instructing visitors not to eat or drink here or conduct any business that wasn't the Lord's. He had a difficult time picturing someone pulling out an Avon catalog or advertising flyers for their farrier service, but one could never predict human behavior.

With his perusal of the surroundings complete, Jake bowed his head in prayer. He prayed for forgiveness for an ongoing pattern of selfishness and arrogance. Once he finally exhausted that minefield, he prayed for a way out of this mess for his family's sake. He might deserve to live under the freeway overpass in a cardboard box, but his family did not. Tears started anew as they did each time he revisited his shame.

Suddenly, the jangle of his phone nearly knocked him off his chair. "Jake Brady," he said with a voice dry and raspy.

"Hello, Mr. Brady? This is Alfred Terry. Do you remember me? We talked a few weeks ago."

Jake's mind whirred, landing on the possible connection. *No, it couldn't be.* He squeezed his eyes shut, barely able to breathe. "I think so," he stammered, sounding much like an adolescent.

"I represent the Terry Point Investment Consortium that's interested in Eager to Please. A few snowbird members have been attending the juvenile races and continue to be impressed with your colt. That horse keeps improving, almost on a daily basis." He paused to give Jake a chance to speak.

He could barely string three words together. "We've been lucky so far."

"Yes, you have. When the consortium got together today for lunch, your horse's name came up. We're prepared to up our original offer by twenty percent, hoping you'll change your mind about selling him. I know you've had your heart set on seeing your name as owner on the Derby program someday, but what if we list you as breeder—Eager to Please, bred by Jake Brady, Twelve Elms Stables. Will that and the increased bid sweeten the pot sufficiently?"

Jake opened his eyes and focused on a picture hanging on the wall. Jumping up from his chair and screaming, "That would be awesome!" wouldn't be acceptable behavior in a house of the Lord, so he rose shakily to his feet and began pacing the room. This time his delayed response wasn't a sales maneuver but an attempt to regain composure. "Yes, Mr. Terry, I believe you have a deal. But I must clarify something—Twelve Elms owns Eager to Please, not just me. My parents also must sign off on the bill of sale, but I foresee no resistance to your offer. I can have our Kentucky attorney start drawing up the paperwork if you like."

"Yes, I would, the sooner the better. I'm authorized to speak for the consortium. Will Tuesday of next week be enough time for your lawyer to prepare documents? I can fly up with my attorney and sign that afternoon if it would be convenient for your family."

"I'll speak to my parents tonight, sir, but I'm fairly certain Tuesday will work out with their schedules. I'll get back to you tomorrow if there's a problem."

"Splendid! I'll start making arrangements to move Eager to Please to our facilities, pending Tuesday's executed contract. Say, do you think your trainer, Mr. Hitchcock, might be interested in working for us to continue his program with Eager? Whatever he's doing seems to be effective. Of course, we would expect him to renegotiate his contract. And I don't wish to overstep any boundary if you wish to keep Mr. Hitchcock for another horse in your stable."

Jake cleared his throat, hoping to sound professional and less like a man at the end of the plank on a pirate ship. "I can't speak for Mr. Hitchcock, but I will pass along your interest in his services. At this point, we own no other colts with Eager's potential."

"Great news! Let me get the wheels turning on my end, Mr.

Brady, and pass the good news on to my partners. You've made me a very happy man."

Alfred Terry hung up without hearing Jake's reply, which was just as well. The only words that came to mind were *Thank You, Lord.* When Ed returned from his errand twenty minutes later, Jake's head was bowed, his eyes still wet with his tears.

"Hey, what's wrong, man? What happened?" Ed put a meaty hand on his shoulder.

Scrambling to his feet, Jake embraced his friend in a bear hug. "You go first. Tell me about your emergency. Is there something I can do to help?"

"Everything is fine. My ma called all upset because her cat climbed high up a tree and refused to come down. She didn't want to bother the fire department. By the time I got there with an extension ladder, the cat had come down all by itself. Crisis averted." Ed sat down and stretched out his muscular legs. "What's up with you?"

"Remember how I told you I got my family in over their heads because I wanted to become a big shot?" Jake slicked a hand through his hair.

Ed's mouth pulled into a grin. "Well, you had a few better reasons than that, but go on."

"That man who earlier offered to buy our horse just called back. He's still interested and even upped the price."

"What will you do? Hold out for the highest bidder?" Ed scratched his stubbly chin, smirking.

"I'm selling him as fast as our lawyer can draw up the papers. I can't wait to crawl out from under this pressure. But first I'm going home to tell my parents everything. They need to know what a jerk I turned into."

"Nah. You just went through a temporary period of jerkiness. It happens to the best of us, but you seem to be recovering."

"I used to think only the corrupt ever get ahead in this world, especially in the horse-racing business. Whether or not that's true, I don't want to live that way. At the time I asked God for help, He sent Alfred Terry back to me."

"The Lord listens to prayer, Jake, but He usually doesn't answer quite so soon. Don't go getting spoiled, man. You can't expect immediacy every time."

Jake shrugged. "I can't promise I won't goof up again. Is there any chance of moving this mobile trailer to Charm, Kentucky?"

Ed laughed. "There are churches all over the world. Pick one. But I'm staying down here where it's warm. You need to keep lines of communication open with *the Man* wherever you are." He pointed toward the ceiling and then extended his hand. "If you do that, you'll be fine."

Jake shook with more energy than necessary. "Thanks, Ed. I owe you."

"Don't mention it. The next time I need a good talking-to, the roads that brought you south can take me north just as easily." His expression softened. "What about that horse of yours? Can you bear to part with him after raising him from the moment he stood up on spindly legs?"

Jake pondered that for a moment. "I'll miss him, that's for sure. But Alfred Terry has a better chance of taking him all the way than Twelve Elms Stable. Deep pockets make a huge difference in the racing world. Wherever Eager to Please goes and whatever happens, a bit of him will always be mine, right here where it counts." He thumped his chest with his fist. "No bill of sale in the world will ever change that."

NINETEEN

Amazing grace! How sweet the sound
That saved a wretch like me

Kentucky

Once back in familiar territory, Jake went the long way around to reach Twelve Elms Stables. He wanted to drive through downtown Charm, all eight blocks of it. As though he'd been gone for a period of years rather than a month, he gazed at the historic town hall with its restored clock tower, the police station, county courthouse, furniture store, pizza shop, and the Tastee Freez, shuttered for the season. He admired the soaring steeples of three churches, one of them his—First Baptist. Like a tourist on a bus trip, he craned his neck with new appreciation.

A person never knows what he has until it's gone. He'd almost lost everything he held dear trading his future on a long shot. Tired and stiff from fourteen hours on the road with only short caffeine and restroom breaks, Jake drove up his driveway with a surge of adrenaline. An energy drink couldn't match the jolt he received when the two-hundred-year-old house loomed into view.

It was late on a Saturday night. Rachel would have gone home to the Stolls by now. Jessie would be back on campus or out on a date. Keeley and Virgil should be in bed, but Keeley was probably reading or updating Facebook under her covers. And his parents? Mom either had to work or was preparing for tomorrow's adult Sunday school class. Dad, no doubt, had fallen asleep in his recliner watching college basketball. No matter how intense the action, Dad drifted off as soon as he put his feet up in a warm room. Jake sighed happily. It felt good to be home with the comfortable routines and people he loved.

Parking behind the house, Jake spotted his father exiting the family barn. Ken walked with his head down, as though deep in thought. "Everything okay with the horses?" Jake asked, stepping away from his truck.

Ken nearly jumped out of his work boots. "Good grief, Jake, don't sneak up on a man like that. You almost gave me a heart attack!" He pressed a palm against his chest.

"Sorry, Pops." Jake ducked his head. "I thought you heard me coming. I'm not exactly the quiet type."

Ken's arm slipped around his son's shoulder. "I've had a lot on my mind. Welcome home, son. It's good to see you."

They embraced like typical men—brief and awkward, but a lump rose up Jake's throat just the same. "It's great to be back, Dad."

Ken cocked his head to one side. "Jessie said you were upset about something but didn't say what. Are you ready to talk now?" Concern deepened his crow's-feet into creases.

"Sure, but let's go inside and warm up first. Jessie doesn't know my woes. That's why she couldn't spill the beans." Jake retrieved his suitcase from his truck, along with empty fast-food wrappers and coffee cups, and followed his father up the steps. "Where is everybody?" he asked. The house was unnaturally dark and silent. Not even the TV droned in the living room.

"Your mom is working the late shift. She'll be home within the hour. Jessie took Keeley back to campus for a sleepover—some kind of a little sister thing. Keeley wore out her shoes shadowing Jessie this past week. Now she's dead set on attending U of K too."

"Hasn't she figured out Jessie will have graduated by the time she gets there?"

"I don't think so, so don't point that out. We'll let the idea ride for a while. It's helping to improve her grades." Ken pulled two soft drinks from the refrigerator and handed one to Jake, but he only switched on the light above the stove. Maybe he thought a dim atmosphere would make their heart-to-heart less intimidating. Both men sat down at the table.

After a long swallow of Coke, Jake summarized the last month in five or six sentences. Then he set down his drink and looked his father in the eye. "Early in December I got an offer for Eager to Please from a rich group of investors. I should have told you and Mom, but I didn't. I messed up—a realization I only arrived at recently." He forced himself not to break eye contact.

"Someone offered to buy the colt? For how much?"

"A lot. Enough money to pay back everything we've borrowed with interest, along with the current bills and training expenses, and maybe have enough left over for you and Mom to take a second honeymoon."

Ken balled his hands into fists. "Why would you keep that from us? We certainly had a right to know, didn't we?"

His father didn't curse or pound on the table. He didn't even raise his voice above a normal conversational tone, but his son could tell he was profoundly disappointed. Jake tasted the burn of acid in his throat but wouldn't allow himself to cry. He was a man, not a child who had done wrong and was desperately seeking his parents' forgiveness. Instead, he enumerated the stark truth—every conclusion he had reached while on the telephone with his sister and while sitting in the trackside chapel. He told his father what kind of person he had been and how he desperately wanted to change.

Ken allowed him to talk without interrupting. "I'm glad you've come home. The fact you're troubled by this means you're headed in the right direction. What do you plan to do now, son? How can your mother and I help?"

Exhaling slowly, Jake folded his hands in front of him. "I want to be a man like you, Dad—a man who thinks before acting and isn't ashamed to bow his head in prayer. I found a friend in Florida who started me talking to God, but I'm worried about slipping back into my old ways."

His dad smiled. It was small and fleeting, but it was a smile nonetheless. "Tell me what happened in Florida. Who is this new friend?"

Jake summarized as best he could, detailing the afternoon he found the trailer empty and surrendered himself in frustration and utter despair. "God answered my prayer. My phone rang right then and there in the chapel. The head of the consortium called while I sat there crying. He repeated his bid to buy Eager to Please. He even increased the offer. He said our colt kept running better and better, and that his investors still wanted a chance to take him the distance."

Ken's eyes grew round as dinner plates. "He called *again* wanting to buy? What did you say this time?"

"Because Mr. Terry was offering an additional twenty percent, I said yes." He raised his hand before his father could interrupt him. "I know once again I made a decision without consulting you and Mom, but the only reason I did so was because I was afraid to let the fish slip off my hook. I told him Twelve Elms was the colt's owner and you and Mom had to sign off on the paperwork. I really didn't want to go solo this time." He ended his confession with a lighter heart.

Ken rubbed the back of his neck, his relief evident on his face. "Thank you for that, Jake. It seems you really have seen the error of your ways."

If Jake wasn't mistaken, Ken's fingers were trembling. "I have," he said as he grasped his dad's hand. "I want to try life your way— by the book, or rather by *the* Book. I'm glad we sold the horse. He didn't seem to be a very good influence on me."

Ken's wry expression returned. "You sound like a lead-foot who blames a speeding ticket on his fast car."

"Nah, it's not Eager's fault I developed a big head. All he ever wanted was to eat buckets of oats, munch down the alfalfa, and run like the wind. I will miss that colt, but on Derby day the Bradys can still make popcorn, mix up some lemonade, and watch our boy run for the roses. Mr. Terry said he'll list me on any future programs as the breeder. I hope that won't be too egotistical."

"We'll allow you an occasional human weakness. I still possess a few of my own." Ken tipped up the can and drained his soda. "What are your intentions?"

"Let's see, tomorrow I'll go to church with y'all. Then I hope to tuck into Mom's good home cooking. And I need to swing by Rachel's too. According to Jessie, she's had a change of heart."

"*Y'all*? My, my, one month in the Deep South and listen to how you talk." They shared a good laugh as his father turned to the window. "I hear your mom's car in the yard. I'll walk out to see if she brought me home a surprise." He fixed Jake with a pale blue stare. "Welcome back, son. And I don't just mean to Kentucky."

"Thanks, Dad," he murmured, unable to say more. He closed his eyes and for a few minutes enjoyed total silence in the Brady house—a rarity these days. Tomorrow would be soon enough to reveal the price offered by Mr. Terry's investors.

One near heart attack per night for his father was enough.

❧

Rachel put on her black dress, white apron, and white prayer *kapp*. Beth had already been peppering her with questions about her plans for the day, so she opted for the complete truth. "I won't be going to the Mennonite Church with you, *grossmammi,* and the Stolls today." Rachel continued to brush her long hair before coiling it up into a tight bun.

Beth stopped dressing to stare at her. "But you're all ready to go. Do you suddenly feel sick?" She pressed the back of her hand to Rachel's forehead the way their *mamm* used to do.

"*Nein*, I feel fine."

"But it's the Sabbath. What else can you do instead?" Her sister looked confused.

"I intend to worship on the Lord's Day, just not in the Mennonite Church. I'm going to my friend's church, and he's Baptist."

Beth plopped down on the bed. "Is he your boyfriend?"

"*Jah*, I suppose he is...or at least he will be."

"What will *grossmammi* say?" Her voice lowered to a whisper.

Rachel took pity on her younger sister and sat down next to her. "She is not going to like it, that's for certain. But I'm a grown woman, and I must make my own decisions."

Beth glanced at the closed door. "Are you jumping the fence? That's what she's been worried about. I heard her talking to Aunt Irene about it when they didn't know I was listening."

"It's not nice to eavesdrop, but as far as turning English, I honestly don't know. I might at some time in the future. A lot depends on whether or not Jake is willing to forgive me."

Beth covered her face with her hands and began to cry. "Why? Don't you like being Amish anymore?"

Rachel drew Beth's head down to her shoulder, enfolding her in an embrace. "I love being Amish. In my soul I will always be Plain, but I also love Jake Brady with my whole heart. I can't bear the thought of not spending my future with him."

Beth gazed up with the saddest eyes Rachel had ever seen. "Does he love you? Because if so, why doesn't he turn Amish?"

"I believe he does love me, but it's much easier for me to change than it would be for him. I can't imagine how he could take over the family stable if he became Amish."

"And his business is more important than Jesus?"

"Of course not, and I won't ever leave the Christian faith either. I will pray and worship and try to follow a righteous path for the rest of my life. But it could be as a Baptist instead of a member of an Old Order Amish district."

Beth frowned, attempting to make sense of everything. But at least she stopped crying. "Have you told Nora and Amy yet?"

"No, but I will write to our sisters soon."

"Amy, and especially John, will have something to say about this." A hint of a smile came and went.

"I'm sure they will, but I need to do what's right for me." Rachel brushed a kiss across Beth's brow. "I must go now, but we'll talk more about this later. Please don't worry." She hurried down the stairs and out the door, grabbing her coat and purse along the way. She was grateful the kitchen was empty. That was not the case inside the horse barn, however. Isaac was filling water troughs with the hose.

"*Guder mariye*," she greeted in *Deutsch*. "Could you please hitch the small buggy with Sarah's mare? I'm driving to services alone today."

"Going to a different church, I take it?" he asked.

"I am, if you're willing to loan me a horse and buggy."

"I wasn't placed on earth to tell you what you can and cannot do, Rachel. That's your cousin's job." He gestured with his chin over her shoulder.

She turned and came face-to-face with Sarah.

"Are you attending Jake's church? You dashed out the door as though chased by a pack of wild dogs."

"*Jah,* if I may borrow your rig."

"It's not my *rig* I'm concerned about. Did you inform our grandmother of your plans?" Sarah sounded remarkably composed.

"Not yet, but I plan to talk to her. Right now I must leave or I'll miss the entire service."

"Climb up then. I brought you a warm covering." Sarah handed her a blanket she'd been holding behind her back.

"Thank you, Sarah. I will always be grateful for everything you and Isaac have done for me."

"Just don't skid off the highway. You have to face *grossmammi* later." When Rachel covered her legs and picked up the reins, Sarah slapped the mare on the rump.

"I'll be careful," she called. The roads turned out to be wet but clear of ice. Rachel arrived in downtown Charm during the opening hymn at First Baptist. Slipping in quietly, she found a seat in the last row. Once again her Plain attire drew a few curious glances and several smiles. Closing her eyes, Rachel relaxed against the pew and allowed the uplifting music, fervent prayers, and passionate sermon to wash over her like a summer shower. Then she sent up a few personal prayers of her own. After Reverend Bullock delivered the parting benediction, Rachel remained where she was. The congregation filed past her into the lobby, nodding and smiling. As she scanned the crowd, her gaze suddenly locked with Keeley's.

"Rachel, what are you doing here?" The twelve-year-old's face brightened as though bathed in sunshine.

With Jake stopping at the end of her pew, Rachel had no chance to answer her fair-weather tour partner. "Hi, Jake. Welcome home. I had hoped and prayed you might be here this morning."

"How did you even know I'd returned from Florida?" He stood ramrod straight while his parents stepped around him, dragging Keeley with them. They both smiled warmly at her but left to give her privacy with their son.

Rachel shrugged, growing less confident by the moment. "I didn't, so I prayed for that too."

Jake glanced around the church but didn't sit down until everyone left the sanctuary. "Is this a good spot to talk or would you rather go someplace else?"

"This is fine. We'll both be forced to tell the whole truth and nothing but." She attempted to smile, but it didn't generate in him her sought-after response.

"What do the Baptists owe this special occasion to?"

"I treated you poorly, Jake. I was rude and nervous and fearful of the unknown. And I'm sorry I wasn't honest."

"Apology accepted. You might not have won a diplomacy award, but you were plenty honest. I've been barking up the wrong tree for a long time." He sounded cool and in complete control.

She shook her head so hard her *kapp* strings swung like pendulums. "That's not true. I wasn't honest with myself." She heard the hitch in her voice, but there was no turning back now. "I love you. I felt something special the moment we met." She focused on the simple altar with a silver cross, open Bible, and a vase of white roses atop a lace cloth. "But your being English scared the socks off me."

He pivoted slightly on the hard pew, drawing her eyes back to him. "Nothing has changed, Rachel. I'm still an *Englischer.*"

"You're wrong. *I* have changed. If my parents' death on a warm summer night taught me nothing else, I learned that life is short. So if you can forgive me, I would love to see if we can make a future together." She held her breath as she looked down at her clasped hands.

His face softened as he lifted her chin with one finger, causing her to meet his gaze. "I forgave you right away. People do that when they are in love. I left town to give you some space."

She struggled to catch her breath. "When I came to work and found you gone, I felt ripped in half. I couldn't keep my mind on my chores. I tried dating other men, but nothing changed the fact that I'm in love with you, Jake Brady. And if I need to turn English for us to be together, then I will. Your God is the same as mine. Jesus came to show us the path to heaven through love and forgiveness. I don't believe it matters if we call ourselves Amish or Baptist or whatever."

Jake wrapped his arm around her shoulders and held her close for a moment. He released a huge sigh. "What do you say we get out of here? I'm dying to kiss you, and I simply can't do that in church."

As they stepped out hand in hand into the brilliant sunshine, butterflies took flight in her stomach. "Walk me to where I left my horse and buggy," she said. When they reached the bare sycamore tree, she turned up her face in full expectation of a kiss. But after a long moment, she opened her eyes.

Jake was leaning against the buggy wheel with his arms crossed over his chest. "I did some stupid things regarding Eager to Please that could have been disastrous for my family. Fortunately, God took pity on me and sent a miracle of sorts. I'll tell you the whole story when we're not standing out in the cold."

"I've also made mistakes and done things I'm not proud of. I'm in no position to judge you or anyone else." Rachel took a step closer.

"In that case I'd like that kiss if you don't mind."

She glanced over her shoulder. Apparently no Baptists lurked behind trees, spying on mischief makers, so Rachel closed her eyes to receive the sweetest, most tender kiss of her life. "Yes, that's what I remembered," she murmured. "The kiss I'd been unable to forget."

"And all this time I thought you hung around the stable because of our pretty horses." His grin looked boyish and handsome.

"That changed the first time I mucked out an entire row of stalls."

He chuckled and then his expression sobered. "Where do we go from here, Miss King?"

"First, I'm going home for an honest chat with my grandmother. She won't like me jumping the fence one bit, but her love for her granddaughters has a habit of rising to the surface like cream. On the other hand, Sarah might sic her attack hens on me...or blame herself. I wish to avoid either situation."

"Should I follow you in my truck and come inside when you break the news?"

"You're welcome to follow me home, but then you should head back to Twelve Elms. This is something I must do alone. If all goes well, you and I will have the rest of our lives together."

❧

"Are we going to buy eggs while we're there?" Amber asked.

"Definitely, two or three dozen." Donna kept focused on the road to watch for deer or darting raccoons. "Everyone knows that the Stolls' eggs are the best in Kentucky." She grinned, remembering Sarah's droll reply after hearing praise. *"Whether it's the truth—and it probably is—or not, we Plain folk don't set ourselves above anyone else."*

"I told my friends at school about Sarah and Rachel," said Amber. "Some of their moms have started buying chickens and eggs from them. They agree that the taste is worth the extra trip."

From the backseat, Kristen asked, "Can we buy some chickens from Sarah too?"

Donna peered at her younger daughter in the rearview mirror. "Yes, if Isaac has any ready for the freezer. I've had a hankering for Southern fried chicken with baked beans and a skillet of greens for weeks."

"Fattening, Mom, fattening," said Amber, always the teenager. "I'll have mine grilled with the skin removed."

Kristen leaned forward and put her small hand on Donna's shoulder. "Not a chicken to cook. I want live chickens for pets. Dad could build a little house for them and fence in part of the yard. Each morning I could feed them dried corn and after school gather up eggs."

Her young face glowed with so much enthusiasm Donna hated to break her bubble. "Why don't you check with your father on this one? If you mention pet chickens, I have a feeling a dog from the pound will start to sound better and better." Kristen grinned and leaned back, content for the rest of the ride.

Donna used the quiet that reigned in the car to appreciate perfect February weather. For the first time in days the clouds had cleared, revealing a blue sky that took her breath away. Bits of frost remained in shaded areas, but they would burn off by noon. Rolling fields, moist and brown, waited patiently for spring, when they would be tilled and planted in the endless cycle of death and rebirth. Donna had experienced her own miniature rebirth lately. She had been strengthened and renewed during her weeks of working with the Mennonites and Amish. Their simple faith had regenerated her own. She was even getting along better with her crusty boss—nothing short of a miracle.

She drove up the Stolls' lane trying her best to dodge the puddles. Nobody Plain wasted good money on driveway gravel until they got stuck once or twice. When she parked near the house, her daughters scrambled out, but Donna paused a moment to compose her thoughts. How should she express gratitude to these two women, strangers from a culture that purposefully separated themselves from the modern world? They had gone out of their way to help with a job they didn't fully understand or agree with.

While she still sat behind the wheel, Rachel exited a chicken barn carrying a basket of brown eggs. Kristen and Amber ran to join her, their long hair flying behind them in the breeze. Donna enjoyed the postcard scene of youthful beauty gathered to giggle and chat on a sunny winter morning. Then something odd niggled at the back of her mind. Rachel looked different. Donna leaned forward, gaping at the young woman like a tourist viewing Amish people for the first time. Her overall appearance of modest, solid-colored clothing was familiar, but Rachel wore no Amish dress with cape or black apron. She had on a long denim skirt and an oversized chocolate brown turtleneck with her work boots. And her hair! A thick blond braid hung down her back to her waist. Although her face was devoid of makeup, she wasn't wearing either her full black bonnet or even her white prayer *kapp*.

Donna jumped from the car and hurried to join the group with almost as much pep as her girls. "Hi, Rachel. Happy Saturday morning to you."

"Hi, Donna. Same to you."

"I couldn't help notice that you look practically English. What happened, if I might ask?"

Kristen's mouth dropped open while Amber moaned, "Mom, not very subtle. We were trying to find a polite way to ask Rachel and you just blurt out the question."

Rachel threw her head back, laughing. "It's okay. Not beating about the bush is the Amish way. We're rubbing off on each other." Surprisingly, she embraced Donna with a hug. "You go first. Tell me your news on the project and then I'll share mine."

"The State Department of Health's program has been deemed a success," Donna said. "We tested almost everyone in the Plain community and vaccinated nearly eighty percent of the children. Eighty percent! That's better than Pennsylvania's compliance rate and far better than what we hoped for."

"This means Mom gets a gold star by her name," said Kristen.

"This means she won't get fired," corrected Amber.

Rachel looked from one to the other and then at Donna. "Both results sound useful to me. Congratulations."

"I came here today to thank you and Sarah, and, of course,

Grandma King and Bishops Mast and Esh. I couldn't have come close to compliance if not for your help."

"Sarah's in the house. She'll be glad to see you. But *grossmammi* and the bishop have gone back to Lancaster." The corners of her mouth pulled down. "My grandmother isn't too happy with me."

"Does this have anything to do with your new clothes?" asked Donna. Amber and Kristen blinked, waiting in anticipation.

"It has everything to do with them. Jessie Brady took me shopping at the mall in Somerset for new outfits. What do you think?" She shyly pivoted in place.

"Great, but you would look pretty in a feed sack," said Amber. "Are you turning English?"

Rachel flushed to a shade of warm peach. "I don't like saying the words, but I probably am…one small step at a time. I'm dating Jake Brady, and he's already proposed—twice."

Kristen clapped her hands as though at the circus, while Donna and her older daughter murmured more reserved expressions of congratulations.

"I love him, but we're not getting married just yet. He wants me to have an adjustment period."

"It's a big decision to change how you've been raised."

"True. That's why we'll wait to get hitched."

"But you're pretty sure Jake is the one." Amber placed her hand over her heart.

"Oh, yeah, that much I know. My grandmother talked my ear off, but I can't go back to Lancaster with her. As much as I love her and Beth, this feels like home now. Because I haven't been baptized yet, at least I won't be shunned, but things won't remain the same either."

"You haven't been baptized yet?" Kristen's shock was apparent.

"No, we wait until late teens or early twenties, once a person knows they want to stay Amish."

"Will you be baptized in Jake's church?" asked Amber.

Rachel smiled. "I haven't thought that far ahead, but I suppose I will."

"Where will you live until your wedding?" Donna asked her second nosy question on the heels of each of her daughters'.

"I didn't know what would happen with my cousin. Sarah wanted me to go back to Lancaster so she could wash her hands of me." Rachel winked, impishly. "But when she realized that wasn't going to happen, she appointed herself my big sister and started calling the shots. 'This will be a proper courtship, whether you're jumping the fence or not,'" mimicked Rachel in Sarah's tone of voice. "I'm only allowed to work at Twelve Elms two days a week, and I have an eleven o'clock curfew while living here. And she goes shopping with Jessie and me for English clothes to make sure they are modest."

"Wow, she sounds just like a mom," said Kristen, grinning at Donna.

"Just like. Then Sarah insisted that Jake and I get counseling from both Bishop Mast and Reverend Bullock."

Donna squeezed Rachel's arm. "That's because she loves you."

Rachel linked her arm through Donna's. "And I love her. Let's go inside to warm up. Sarah will be relieved to hear the polio crisis has been averted." Amber slipped her arm around Rachel's waist, while Kristen took Donna's hand. The four women crossed the wet grass and climbed the steps. Once they reached the porch, Donna spotted the kitchen curtain fall back into place. *Mother Hen has been watching her favorite chick's outdoor goings-on.*

Then the door suddenly swept open. "Donna Cline! I thought you would never come up to the house," said Sarah. "Let's have coffee and cut this pie I baked. It's growing staler by the minute."

As Donna and her girls were ushered into the warm, comfortable kitchen of the Stolls, under her ribs her heart began to swell. Orphaned Rachel King was once again in capable hands.

TWENTY

I once was lost, but now am found;
Was blind, but now I see

March

Rachel waited until the first of March before penning her overdue letters to Amy in Maine and Nora in Missouri. She spent the first page describing her job and how much she enjoyed working with horses. She filled the second page with chatty news about Sarah and Isaac and their ever-expanding chicken farm. Smoothly she transitioned into her relationship with Jake Brady, and although they saw each other little at work, they went out every Thursday and Saturday night, besides attending Baptist church services together—a schedule devised and approved by Sarah.

Her pulse quickened when she detailed how they had fallen in love while teaching blind children to ride, raising money for juvenile diabetes research, and ferrying stray cats back and forth to a low-priced vet for spaying and neutering. Because both of her sisters had hearts of gold, they would be pleased by all three activities.

Once Rachel reached the third sheet of her missive, she knew her update would not be as well received. How could she tell her elder sister, Amy, a member of an ultraconservative district in Harmony, Maine, that she was jumping the fence?

And how would free-spirited, independent thinker Nora react to her leaving the Amish faith after what she experienced with Elam Detweiler? Nora's first love had left the Plain lifestyle when she chose a quiet, unassuming shopkeeper over him. Nora and Lewis were happily settled in the aptly named town of Paradise, Missouri. Nora had chosen the simple life over Elam's offer of reckless excitement, and now that she was married and with her first baby on the way, she knew she had made the right choice.

Would either woman understand her desire to marry an *Englischer*, or would they dissolve into tears as Beth had done? Poor Beth. She had written no less than six letters trying to change Rachel's mind. A few had contained subtle manipulations by guilt over their dead parents or for their grandparents' broken spirits. A couple letters used logic and reason to convince her that Amish was a more practical way to live. And Beth's final plea had been a dire, doom-and-gloom forecast of Rachel's descent into a godless existence, ending with the eventual loss of her eternal soul. Rachel imagined either her grandmother or Aunt Irene standing over Beth's shoulder during the writing of that letter. She sent up a silent prayer and forged ahead. To the best of her abilities she explained to Amy and Nora that she might have fallen in love, but she would stay Christian until she drew her last breath. In closing, she invited both sisters to their late fall wedding—a good time to get away for people in agriculture, whether Amish or English. She could only hope her *schwestern* would still accept her after hearing her decision.

July

The hot sun beat down on Rachel's back and shoulders, raising beads of moisture just below her hatband. Her T-shirt stuck to her back, while her blue jeans felt like sauna body wraps with the humidity. Sarah wouldn't permit her to wear long, baggy shorts like Keeley—her partner on the tour wagon, but it didn't matter. She was doing a job she adored with the two most docile draft horses on the planet. "Get up there, Bess," she called, shaking the reins. "A mani-pedi awaits you in the barn." The bells attached to the leather straps sent up a musical progression of notes. After explaining to tourists a dozen times that only reindeer on sleighs wore bells to work, she and Keeley finally gave in. They purchased strings of one-inch bells at the craft shop and painstakingly sewed them to Bess and Buster's harnesses on their day off.

"What about your boy horse?" asked an adorable five-year-old. Sitting in her mother's lap, the little girl had asked plenty of questions for someone so young.

Rachel grinned at the tiny tourist. "A big strapping horse like our Buster with painted toenails? Goodness, no. We reward him for a job well done with Granny Smith apples. Those are his favorites."

"Mine too!" she said. Her large brown eyes shone with delight.

"At the end of the tour you can feed Buster an apple if it's okay with your mommy," said Rachel. The child's expression rivaled that of a lottery winner. After everyone petted and fed the plump draft horses or bought souvenirs and ice-cream cones, Rachel passed out the brochures detailing the services at Twelve Elms.

Unexpectedly, the apple-lover broke free from her mother's grip and ran toward Rachel. "I wish I could live here with you and Miss Bess," she wailed, wrapping her arms around Rachel's leg. "I want a horse so much!"

She patted the child's head. "Maybe someday you will have one."

"I won't. We live in an apartment in Lexington." As she cried, her mother slashed a finger across her throat and shook her head vigorously. "We can't have a dog or cat or even a goldfish." The child's sobs increased.

Rachel picked up on the woman's body language. "It's just as well. All horses do is eat and then eat some more. You should see the mess we must clean up from all that eating. This way you can visit Bess and Buster without any stinky chores to do."

The child wasn't buying it. She clung tighter to Rachel's leg. Gently Rachel pried off her hands and kneeled down to speak eye to eye. "Don't cry, little one. Someday you might move to where you can have a horse. No one knows what the future holds. In the meantime, you can read books about them and color pictures, and a tall horse will keep watch as you sleep. We have some special presents for you since yours were the best questions ever asked at Twelve Elms." She rose to her full height. "Can you spare a few more minutes?" Rachel addressed the woman. "I would like you and your daughter to come to the gift shop with me."

That afternoon, little Nancy took home several coloring books, two collections of horse stories, an oversized T-shirt displaying various equine breeds, and a four-foot-tall stuffed Appaloosa with bold white and tan spots. Rachel paid for everything. The young mother relaxed now that the tears had ceased, and the child went home fortified with dreams for the future.

Rachel knew all about dreams and how they sometimes did come true.

"There you are!" Jessie walked toward her with the zeal of a schoolteacher on playground duty. "I have been looking for you since the last tour ended." She reached Rachel's side, breathless.

"Your search is over. Here I am." She flourished a hand from her head down to her toes.

Grabbing her by the sleeve, Jessie dragged Rachel to the house.

"We need to get your wedding plans underway, missy. It's already July. Your wedding is *this* November, not next. That's only four short months away."

Rachel allowed Jessie to pull her up the steps and through the back door into the kitchen. Glossy magazines, menus, colorful brochures, and catalogs covered the surface of the oak table. "Which months are the long months?" she teased.

"You sit there." Jessie pointed at a chair. "And your wedding planner will sit here." She plopped down at the head of the table by a yellow legal pad and a row of sharpened pencils.

"Wedding planner? Who's that? And why would I need one?" Rachel reached for a cookie off the plate in the center.

"It's me, you goose. Every bride-to-be of the twenty-first century uses a wedding planner. I shall be yours."

Rachel bit the inside of her cheek. "Jessie, the marriage will be at the First Baptist Church of Charm, the reception here in the indoor arena, and the meal will be cooked by some of your mom's celebrity chefs. They have already volunteered. I believe everything's planned." She smiled, unable to contain her mirth, and reached for a second oatmeal raisin crisp.

"What about your wedding dress? Or do you plan to wear your Levis and riding boots?" Jessie tapped her tablet with a pencil point.

"No. I thought I would sew my dress." Rachel dabbed crumbs from her lips.

Her future sister-in-law's face fell. "Don't you need my help?" Jessie couldn't have sounded more pitiful.

"Dear me, of course I do." Rachel picked up a brochure. "What have you got here? Let's take a look at these wedding cakes."

The cake featured on the cover was a veritable garden of flowers, arbors, and hedgerows made of spun sugar. A tiny bride and groom stood hand in hand under a lacy plastic archway. The creation couldn't be fancier unless a real babbling brook flowed across the surface from a hidden water pump. As much as Amish folks loved their sweets, they would be aghast at such an extravaganza. "So... are these wedding cakes for sale?"

"Relax. I know you probably want to bake your own, but the guest list will probably top two hundred and may approach three if your kin come from Lancaster County. So I suggest a compromise. Mom's best friend loves to bake. She wants to make your cake as a gift to you and Jake. All you need to do is pick out a general idea from these photos and tell her your favorite flavor. What do you say?"

"What a generous gift. I like spice cake and Jake loves chocolate. Could we do a layer of each?" Rachel's excitement began to build as she thumbed through the cake brochure.

"Certainly you can. You're the bride. Here among the English, that's a very big deal. You can have anything you want for your wedding and even boss people around to do your bidding." Jessie grinned, perhaps anticipating this attention for herself one day.

The idea of barking orders didn't appeal much to Rachel. Weddings within the Plain culture were certainly special occasions, complete with a buffet meal, practical gifts, flowers, a cake, and one attendant each for bride and groom. But marriages rated no higher than any other life passage—birth, graduation, baptism, joining the church, birth of each child, and finally, death. But not wishing to hurt Jessie's feelings, she looked at the pictures and chose the simplest of wedding cakes. No babbling brooks or fountains spouting pink lemonade.

That afternoon Rachel and her maid of honor, serving in a dual capacity as wedding planner, selected the floral arrangements for church and reception and the menu for the meal—roast rosemary chicken, prime rib, new potatoes au gratin, green beans with mushrooms, fruit ambrosia, Caesar salad, and corn bread rather than dinner rolls. Rachel insisted Jake join them for the menu planning. The corn bread had been his suggestion. Jessie rolled her eyes twice at his insistence of something so down-home at a formal affair, but he said he loved it. When Rachel objected to the term "formal," Jessie readily approved Jake's choice of bread.

"Okay, we're making progress." Jessie placed a large check mark next to the third item on her list. "Now let's talk dresses, both for you and your attendants. How many bridesmaids will there be?"

Jake raised his hands in surrender. "Okay, here's where I make my he-man exit." He kissed Rachel's cheek and scrambled from his chair. "All I need is the final number so I know how many buddies to ask besides Virgil."

"You're abandoning me to your sister?" asked Rachel, only half joking.

"Where's your cell phone? Keep it close by. Remember your first wagon tour when you had the walkie-talkie next to you?" He ruffled his fingers through her hair, which fell freely down her back today. "Just press my speed dial number, and I'll come running from wherever I am, night or day."

Jessie arched a well-plucked eyebrow. "There will be *no* panic situations for our bride with me as wedding planner. Be off with you. You're only the mildly consequential groom. We still have a lot to cover—invitations, the photographer, music both during the service and the reception, and of course the bridal shower, to be thrown by me and Keeley."

Jake bent low to Rachel's ear. "If she tries to plan our honeymoon or suggests she tag along as tour guide, don't waste time with the phone. Just run for the door and don't look back." His whisper was loud enough for his sister to hear.

"Go now," she warned. "Before there's bloodshed."

Once the door had closed behind him, Jessie focused on her legal pad. "Regarding your attendants, do you think either of your married sisters want to be matrons of honor or maybe both? What about Beth? Will she serve with Keeley as a junior bridesmaid? Between Bonnie, Ruby, Rosanna, and Mary—which of your friends will you invite to stand up with you?" Instead of looking exhausted after all the planning already, Jessie's blue eyes sparkled with anticipation.

Rachel had heard the English expression three-ring circus many times, but it never made much sense until that moment. "I heard from my sisters. Amy and John will not attend, although I will always be welcome in their home in Maine, along with my husband. Due to her pregnancy, Nora and Lewis most likely will not attend, either. And I probably won't know until shortly before the wedding regarding Beth. As far as my Mennonite friends? They will be invited guests. I don't need more attendants if I have you and Keeley and maybe one sister."

Jessie's mouth formed the letter *O*. "But with a wedding as large as this, it's customary to have—"

Rachel held up her hand. "Stop, please. I know you mean well, Jess, but I'm not even officially English. This needs to be toned down, especially if some of my relatives might show up. Let's think of it as a hybrid Amish-and-English wedding." She placed her hand atop her future sister-in-law's and squeezed.

In the end, the orchestra playing show tunes was ruled out along with the soprano soloist in church. Rachel opted for a harpist during the nuptials, and a pianist playing classical music during the meal. And no dancing. On the topic of wedding photography, Rachel again refused to give in to Jessie's demands. The giant album with companion DVD to play on the television was ruled out. She'd been raised to believe photos were graven images and therefore forbidden. To respect Jake and his family, she agreed to a limited number of pictures that included her, but the photographer couldn't take pictures of any Amish or Mennonite guests.

Rachel decided that Jessie and Keeley could buy English brides-maid gowns of their choosing. However, should Beth wish to participate, she would wear her Sunday black dress, even though she hadn't been baptized yet. No further discussion was necessary.

Suddenly her cell phone signaled an incoming text. Rachel read the words with a sigh of relief. Jake's message was short and to the point: *Get away from my sister while you still can. Meet me behind the family barn. Make sure you're not followed.*

Smiling, Rachel snapped her phone shut. "Something has come up, Jess. I'm afraid we must end our planning session. Thanks for all your hard work on our behalf."

Jessie swept her brochures and catalogs into a large pile. "Well, we've made headway, at least. With me in charge, this will be the best wedding Casey County has ever seen. Wait until you hear my plans for your hair." She winked playfully.

With that Rachel bolted for the door and didn't slow down until well beyond view of the house. Breathless, she found Jake leaning against an ancient elm, chewing on a long blade of hay. Because a straw hat shielded his face from the sun, he looked like an Amish lad instead of a part owner of a Thoroughbred farm. "I believe I shook off my tail." She inhaled deep gulps of air.

Wrapping his muscular arms around her, Jake kissed the top of her head. "Just say the word and we'll elope to Nashville. We could see the sites, listen to some good country gospel music at the Grand Old Opry, and save ourselves the fuss."

"And break your sister's heart? Think again, Mr. Groom. If Jessie hadn't hired me for tours, you and I never would have met. Let her do this for us. She's really enjoying herself."

"I'll put up with anything other than karaoke at the reception to make you my bride." His string of kisses from temple to jaw finally found her lips.

Rachel kissed him back with more passion than proper for

Amish courting couples. "What's this?" she asked, drawing away a little. She pulled a letter from his shirt pocket.

"That's the news I couldn't wait to share with you. I'd been hoping to find something to occupy my time now that Eager to Please has moved to Mr. Terry's stable." Jake extracted a single sheet from the envelope.

"You don't wish to breed any more horses?"

"For clients, yes, but I don't want to breed any more Brady mares. I seem to turn into a monster with delusions of fame and fortune."

"You never stopped being Jake Brady." Rachel wrapped an arm around his waist and hugged him.

"Thanks, but this will give me an outlet that shouldn't corrupt my fragile soul." He tapped her nose with the paper.

"Spill the beans already." She plucked the sheet to read.

"I won a grant from the Kentucky Department of Development. Twelve Elms can now expand the therapeutic riding program to serve other disabilities besides the blind. We can provide private lessons, overnight rides, summer camp, and job training for equestrian careers. Dad and I will put up two hundred thousand and the state will match the amount to build additional barns, a specially equipped lodge, and add miniature horses. We'll even have a heated lounge so parents and other guests can relax and watch the arena activities while staying warm and dry."

"Congratulations! I'm so proud of you. Isn't this better than winning the Kentucky Derby?" Because she needed to get back to the Stolls' before Sarah sent out her feathered posse, they strolled hand in hand in the direction of his truck.

"Yes, but who knows? In ten months we might enjoy that too, at least in our hearts. Maybe this is similar to giving up a baby for adoption. You might not have been able to meet the child's needs, but you pray they excel wherever they go in life."

"Could be, but you'd better take me home, Jake Brady. If I'm late from work, Sarah might not let me go out with you tomorrow."

"What have you got in mind for our date, Miss King?" He opened the door to his pickup like a gentleman.

"Let's head to the mall. Jessie insists we serve mango punch at the reception and something called tiramisu. I couldn't say yay or nay since I haven't a clue what they taste like. We'll check every restaurant in the food court until we find one that serves them." She stepped up into the cab and pulled down her long skirt modestly.

"I can't think of a better way to spend an evening. After all, you should feel like Queen-for-a day as the bride-to-be."

"Please," she begged. "Eager isn't the only one who can turn a humble person into a monster. Given any encouragement, your sister could easily turn me into Frankenstein with the blink of an eye."

❧

November

Rachel heard the knock at the back door somewhere in the far recesses of her mind. She had too many other details swirling around the gray abyss to process an everyday occurrence such as a knocking sound. Things had gotten out of hand due to her tireless wedding planner. Rachel had assumed those of that profession were supposed to make life easier for the bride and groom. Instead, she felt pulled in a dozen directions at once due to Jessie's wedding etiquette guide. Jake offered to sneak into his sister's room while she slept, steal the book, and burn it on the brush pile in the middle of the night. He would leave the window open and then cite news reports of an area cat burglar absconding with the oddest of items. Even if Jessie figured out the culprits, the source of their frustration would already be ashes.

Right now Rachel sat at her desk writing and addressing a stack
of thank-you notes for the harpist, pianist, minister, church organ-
ist, each of the celebrity chefs, florist, photographer, and their wedding cake creator. Jessie explained that if she finished these now,
she wouldn't have to do them after she got home from their honeymoon in Nashville. Rachel sighed as she finished one of the cards.
In the world she had grown up in, a sincere *danki* to those providing a gift or service was all that was required.

These handwritten cards followed on the heels of more than
sixty thank-you notes for her shower gifts. Although Rachel appreciated each generous present, did anyone truly need an electric
iced tea maker? A clear glass pitcher of water and tea bags sitting
in a sunny window worked just as well. And who had thought
up a bread machine? Her *mamm* and *grossmammi* would fall off
their kitchen stools laughing. However, now that she lived in a
home connected to the electric power grid, she adored the micro-
wave, automatic coffeemaker with timer, and her new crockpot.
She could throw in chunks of round steak and chopped vegetables, go to work, and then come home to beef stew...or in Sarah's
case, chicken stew. Soon she and Jake would move into their own
bungalow on the grounds of Twelve Elms. Each day she marveled
at the progress of the construction of their first home.

Her cousin stuck her head inside Rachel's bedroom, interrupting her daydreams. "Could you run downstairs to see who's
pounding on the door? I've been on the third floor cleaning out
the attic. My knees are acting up today."

"Certainly. I didn't know you were above me instead of below."
Rachel sprang from her chair and down the steps.

"It's probably another delivery man bringing more stuff you
don't need. I can't understand why folks are buying both shower
and wedding presents. One or the other should be enough.
The Queen of England probably never had this fanfare for her

marriage." Sarah's comments trailed Rachel throughout the house, her voice rising in volume to accommodate the distance.

Rachel might have responded, but when she yanked open the door after another knock, the sight rendered her speechless. A small green-eyed Amish girl stood clutching a battered suitcase in both hands. Peering out from an enormous black bonnet, she was practically swallowed up by the dark, heavy material.

"Don't you recognize me, *schwester*? It's only been five months."

"Beth!" Rachel pulled her younger sister into an embrace, almost crushing her slim frame. "Of course I do. I just gave up hope that any of my family would attend the wedding."

Beth squirmed after a few moments. "You can hug me later. I want to get out of these traveling clothes." She dropped her bag on the floor and began peeling off layers.

"Are you alone?" Rachel checked the driveway before shutting out the cold wind.

"*Jah*. *Grossmammi* had planned to come with Aunt Irene... but something came up." Beth plopped down into a chair. "Do you have anything to eat and drink? I would love a sandwich and glass of cider."

"Your wish is my command." Rachel hurried to the refrigerator. "I can't believe she let you travel by yourself."

"I'm fifteen, not ten, and I'm officially on *rumschpringe*. But like I said, *grossmammi* wanted to come even though the bishop advised against it. 'That's my baby out there in Kentucky. Somebody needs to make sure she will be taken care of and hasn't fallen in with a rough sort.' That's what she told Bishop Esh. After hearing that, he changed his mind." Beth picked up the glass of cider as soon as Rachel set it down. Half the contents disappeared in a hurry. "*Gut, danki*."

"What came up with *grossmammi* that she wasn't able to come after the bishop gave his permission?" Rachel finished making a ham-and-Swiss sandwich, added a handful of chips to the plate, and then sat down next to her sibling.

"Must we discuss our grandmother now? I just arrived five minutes ago." Beth's eyes squinted into a beady glare.

"Yes, we must. You're frightening me." A shiver of anxiety ran up Rachel's back.

Biting into the sandwich, Beth chewed before speaking. "All right then. *Grossmammi* has cancer but it's treatable. Amy and John and their baby are on their way to Lancaster to make sure she gets those treatments. Nora and Lewis had planned to surprise you at the wedding, but her doctor said no. She's too far along to make the trip and must stay put. You know..."

"Yes, I am aware of her condition." Rachel chuckled at Beth's shyness.

"Nora will send the quilt her district is helping to make once it's done."

Rachel tried to hold back an unexpected wave of tears. She took a moment to gather herself, and then she said, "Jake and I will visit Missouri after Nora's you-know-who arrives, and we'll schedule a trip to Pennsylvania as soon as possible."

Beth didn't answer until she devoured the sandwich. "That would be a *gut* idea. Say, do you think Sarah would mind if I have another one? I'm still hungry."

"I don't mind at all." Sarah swept into the room carrying a huge bag of discards for the church rummage sale. "But I don't know why Rachel feeds you deli ham when there's a bowl of fresh chicken salad with pecans and grapes. *Welcum,* cousin." Sarah brushed a kiss across Beth's *kapp*.

"I would love some chicken salad!" Beth exclaimed. "*Danki*."

"Didn't our grandmother give you money for the journey?" asked Sarah over her shoulder at the sink. "You're practically starving."

"*Jah*, she did, but I saved it to buy Rachel a wedding present." Beth lifted her pale green eyes to meet Rachel's blue gaze.

Sarah snorted. "Good luck finding something that the Princess Bride of Charm doesn't already have." She stuck a spoon into the bowl of salad and placed it on the table.

Rachel looked from one to the other and burst into a torrent of tears. "I'm so glad you came. Your being here is my best gift so far."

Beth giggled. "Stop your blubbering, then. You never used to be a crybaby. What have these *Englischers* done to you?" She spread chicken salad thickly on two slices of homemade bread as though her mouth were as large as an ox's. "I came to make sure this Jake Brady is good enough for a King sister. If he doesn't treat you properly, I'll be back." She winked over the top of her two-fisted sandwich.

Rachel wiped her eyes. "He's good to me. Don't worry about that, but I wanted you here so much."

"Do I get to be in your wedding? I sewed a new Sunday dress." Beth took a huge bite.

"Absolutely. I saved you a spot." Rachel tried unsuccessfully to control her emotions.

"While I eat, bring me out the dress you made. Have you finished it yet?"

Rachel did as instructed, but when she slipped the plastic covering from the expensive wedding gown, Beth's sandwich slipped from her fingers onto her plate. "You sewed *that* with all those little pearls and pin tucks and fancy ruffles?" Beth stared as though at a two-headed hippopotamus.

"It's called *ruching*," Rachel said, pointing at the delicate gathers of fabric. "But no, I bought this gown at a bridal store. Between my chores here, my job at Twelve Elms, and helping Jake organize his new therapeutic riding program, I ran out of time to sew."

"See what has happened to your *schwester*?" asked Sarah. "She's fully English now, even taking driving lessons as though it would be safe on Casey County roads with *her* behind the wheel of a car."

Beth looked from Sarah to the extravagant wedding dress and then back at Rachel. "It's okay, cousin. She might be wearing funny clothes, but I'm sure she still sings out of tune, can't see more than two feet in the dark, and couldn't thread a needle in less than five minutes if her life depended on it." Beth's young face crinkled with amusement. "She's still my big sister...and I love her. This Jake Brady person is about to become the luckiest man on earth."

RECIPES

&

READER'S GUIDE

Chicken Paprikas
(Chicken and Dumplings)

1 onion, chopped
4 tablespoons shortening
1 tablespoon paprika
¼ teaspoon black pepper
1 tablespoon salt
4- to 5-lb. chicken, disjointed
1½ cups water
1 cup sour cream
1 cup sweet cream, if desired
Flour to thicken, if desired

Brown the onion in the shortening, add the seasonings and chicken, and then brown the chicken for 10 minutes. Add the water and then cover and let simmer slowly until tender, about 45 minutes.

Remove the chicken and add the sour cream to the drippings in the pan and mix well. (For more gravy, add a cup of sweet cream to the sour cream. If desired, add flour to thicken.)

Add the dumplings (recipe on page 338), and then arrange the chicken on top. Heat through and serve.

Dumplings

3 eggs, beaten
3 cups flour
1 tablespoon salt
½ cup water

Mix all of the ingredients together and beat with a spoon. Drop the batter by teaspoonful into boiling salted water. Cook approximately 10 minutes, drain, and rinse with cold water. (Note: dumplings float when they are almost done. Drain well and add to paprikas.)

Chicken Paprikas may be served over noodles instead of dumplings.

Author's Note: This is a Hungarian recipe, not Amish, from my mother, which she got from her mother, but I think Sarah Stoll would have liked it! I also love this recipe with boneless, skinless chicken breasts, not readily available in my grandmother's day.

Chess Pie

Aunt Peg Hersman Triplett
(Recipe provided by Linda Hersman Hitchcock, Kentucky resident)

½ cup (1 stick) butter

1½ cups sugar

2 tablespoons cornmeal

3 eggs

1 tablespoon white vinegar

1 teaspoon vanilla

1 9-inch unbaked pastry shell, homemade or favorite store-bought

Melt the butter and then stir in the sugar and cornmeal. Add the eggs one at a time, beating well, and then add the vinegar and vanilla. Pour into the pie shell. Bake at 350 for 40 to 45 minutes until set and lightly brown on top.

Author's Note: Linda told me this pie is a Kentucky favorite. Many versions of Chess Pie exist, some with cream or milk, and some with flour in place of cornmeal. Still others add lemon in place of vanilla and eliminate the vinegar. Some even add chocolate, although Linda feels her Aunt Peg's recipe is the best. This recipe came from her mother (Linda's grandmother), who died in 1933. The origins for Chess Pie are murky, but it has been suggested the recipe originated in England and was then brought to the Virginia Colony and Kentucky, where it became popular. Chess Pie is usually served at room temperature and doesn't need embellishment, although whipped cream is nice. It can be stored at room temperature and was probably held in a pie safe in previous eras. Chess Pie is made with ingredients readily available on a farm, quickly assembled, and easily doubled or tripled for a large family. Enjoy!

Kentucky Corn Bread

Nannie Lizzie (Neely) Bray from eastern Wayne County, Kentucky

2 tablespoons lard
2 heaping cups cornmeal
1 heaping cup self-rising flour
Salt
1 pint buttermilk

Preheat oven to 400 degrees. Use a tablespoon and put two scoops of lard in a 10-inch iron skillet and place in the oven while it is preheating. (Mom always used lard, but I have found that shortening works fine and is easier on my heart and mind.)

Meanwhile, Mom used her cupped right hand as a measuring cup. In a mixing pot or bowl, put 2 heaping cups of cornmeal mix, 1 heaping cup of self-rising flour, one generous pinch of salt, and mix with the right hand. (She never used a spoon to mix.) Get the buttermilk ready on the counter.

Remove the iron skillet from the oven. Make sure all of the lard is melted. Roll the lard around the skillet and halfway up the sides. Pour the extra in the cornmeal and flour mixture. Make sure that ¼ inch of oil remains in the skillet. Put the skillet back in the oven to get really, really hot.

Mix the cornbread mixture up by adding some buttermilk. Stir with the right hand and add buttermilk until it is a thick mixture, but can still be poured with a little help from the hand.

Take the skillet out (the lard might be smoking a little, but you can see the swirls from the heat). Pour in the cornbread mixture (it should sizzle when it hits the oil), scraping the bowl, and then put the skillet back in hot oven. Bake for about 20 minutes or until the bread is firm to the touch in the middle.

This makes for a crunchy crust on the sides and bottom. If there are any leftovers, they will not be the crust and they will not be thrown out. Leftovers can be used for the famous Kentucky cereal, AKA corn bread and milk.

Author's Note: This comes from Donna Taylor, who was taught by her mother, Nannie Bray, a lifelong Kentucky resident. It is a *procedure,* not a recipe, for cornbread. As unbelievable as it may seem, she never used a measuring cup and her bread was always the same. But her mother *never* used a recipe, *never* owned a cookbook, and *never* had an official measuring cup or spoon. But nevertheless, everyone loved her cornbread.

DISCUSSION QUESTIONS

❧

1. In what ways would it be difficult for someone Amish to hold down a job in the English world?

2. How might raising a contender for the Kentucky Derby conflict with a Christian's ethical code?

3. Why do many Amish and some Mennonites reject the idea of vaccinations?

4. Why does Rachel prefer working at Twelve Elms instead of for her cousin Sarah?

5. What challenges does nurse/social worker Donna Cline face with her new assignment?

6. Both Jake and Rachel are attracted to lifestyles different than their own. What does Jake aspire for that puts him at odds with his parents?

7. Why does the Amish bishop originally refuse to help Donna, and what makes him change his mind later on?

8. What are some of the factors contributing to Rachel's decision to date Jake?

9. How does Jake's view of the role of religion in his life change over the course of the story? What precipitates the changes?

10. Jake and his dad butt heads on more than just the financial drain of Eager to Please. Why else is Ken displeased with his son's behavior?

11. Rachel's faith becomes more of a stumbling block to their relationship than her being Plain. What attempts does Jake make to find common ground?

12. Sarah must tread carefully with her cousin. What influence does she have on Rachel's future?

13. Jake's poor decision almost changes his family's future forever. In what ways does his character grow from one rash act?

14. Donna is conflicted by several aspects of her job. How does her faith help in fulfilling her obligations?

15. There is no decision in life without consequences. In what ways will Rachel's life change if she follows her heart?

ABOUT THE AUTHOR

❧

Mary Ellis grew up close to the eastern Ohio Amish Community, Geauga County, where her parents often took her to farmers' markets and woodworking fairs. She and her husband now live in Medina County, close to the largest population of Amish families, where she does her research…and enjoys the simple way of life.

❧

Mary loves to hear from her readers at maryeellis@yahoo.com

or

www.maryellis.net

A Tragedy…a Refusal…a Shunning
Will Their Young Love Survive?

Amy King—young, engaged, and Amish—faces life-altering challenges when she suddenly loses both of her parents in a house fire. Her fiancé, John Detweiler, persuades her to leave Lancaster County and make a new beginning with him in Harmony, Maine, where he has relatives who can help them.

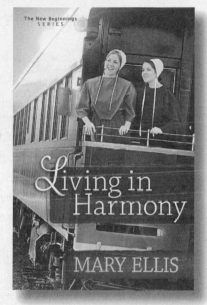

John's brother Thomas and sister-in-law, Sally, readily open their home to the newcomers. Wise beyond his years, Thomas, a minister in the district, refuses to marry Amy and John upon their arrival, suggesting instead a period of adjustment. While trying to assimilate in the ultraconservative district, Amy discovers an aunt who was shunned. Amy wants to reconnect with her, but John worries that the woman's tarnished reputation will reflect badly on his beloved bride-to-be.

Can John and Amy find a way to overcome problems in their relationship and live happily in Harmony before making a lifetime commitment to each other?

A New Home…
A New Friend…
A Catastrophe…
Does she have a future to hope for?

Nora King is a woman in love. When Elam Detweiler leaves the ultraconservative Amish district of Harmony, Maine, and moves to Paradise, Missouri, Nora boldly follows soon after. But is she in love with the man or the independence and freethinking he represents? Though she soon finds work she enjoys and a new best friend in Paradise, Nora can't decide whether she wants to capture Elam's *Englisch*-leaning heart or commit finally to her Amish faith.

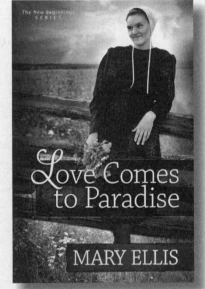

And then, unexpectedly, Lewis Miller comes from Harmony to offer Nora what every woman hopes for—a lifetime of unconditional love. As Lewis attempts to claim her affections, Elam's interest piques. Suddenly, Nora is irresistible to him. Wooed by two such different men, will Nora come to her senses before Elam's thoughtless choices ruin her reputation beyond all repair? Will Lewis's pursuit survive the challenge?

☙

Love Comes to Paradise is about fresh starts…and how faith in God and His perfect plans provide peace and joy in a turbulent and ever-changing world.